BEAUTIFUL LIES

EMERY ROSE

For my sister, Kathleen. I'm so damn lucky to have you in my life. You're the real MVP.

PLAYLIST

"Unsteady" - X Ambassadors
"I Can't Go On Without You" - Kaleo
"Colors" - Halsey
"Us" - James Bay
"83 Days" - Wafia
"Scars" - James Bay
"Rocket Man" - Elton John
"Exit Wounds" - The Script
"Pretty When You Cry" - Lana Del Rey
"Bitter Sweet Symphony" - The Verve

PROLOGUE

I wrapped the blanket around my shoulders and climbed the ladder to the top bunk. "Watch me fly, Kill. I'm Captain Courageous."

Killian snorted as he pulled on his pajama top. "You're Captain Stupid."

"Is it a bird? Is it a plane?" I said. "No. It's Connor the Wonder Boy." I leaped from the top bunk and for about a second, I really felt like I could fly. Then the ground rushed up to meet me and I landed with a loud thud. All the air got knocked out of my lungs. I rolled onto my side and curled into a ball. "I can't breathe," I wheezed.

"You're an idiot," Killian said, cracking up.

"Them's fightin' words," I said, lunging at him. He dodged out of the way and I crashed into the dresser, making him laugh even harder. For some reason, I laughed with him. We were cracking up so hard, tears sprang to my eyes. We stopped laughing when we heard the heavy footsteps in the hallway.

"Get in the closet," Killian said.

"No." I crossed my arms and widened my stance, like I'd seen Killian do.

He grabbed me by the shoulders and shoved me into the closet.

"Stay in there and don't come out until I say so," he warned before he shut the door, leaving me in the darkness, in a space where I couldn't breathe for real. My stomach churned as I heard the bedroom door opening.

"You're supposed to be in bed. What the hell's going on up here?" Seamus asked, slurring his words. He'd been drinking Jack Daniels tonight. Maybe he'd just leave and that would be the end of it. I folded my hands in prayer and silently prayed, my lips moving but no sound coming out of my mouth. "Where's your brother?"

"Asleep."

He wouldn't bother checking. He never did. Our dad didn't really give a shit about me. He'd said so more times than I could count. He called me a sorry excuse for a son and all kinds of other things, none of them good.

"I'm going to bed now," Killian said. "Go back to your TV and whiskey."

Killian. Keep your big mouth shut.

"You think you can tell me what to do, boy?"

I heard the sound of bones crunching followed by a grunt from Killian. I covered my ears with my hands, trying to block out the sound of Seamus' punches. Killian's grunts. He wouldn't cry. He wouldn't scream. He wouldn't run. He would just stand there and take it until Seamus was done treating him like a human punching bag.

I'm sorry, Killian. I'm sorry. I'm sorry. I'm sorry.

"That's the best you could do?" Killian asked, and then he was laughing. Like an idiot. Why did he have to poke the bear?

I heard Seamus' fist hit Killian's body and the sound of Killian crashing to the ground. The floor underneath me vibrated from the impact.

"You're moving into your own room this weekend. You're too old to share a room. You hear me, boy?"

Killian didn't answer.

He probably couldn't. I wanted to burst out of the closet and fly at Seamus, pummel him with my fists. Make him bleed. Make him feel the pain. But my puny fists would bounce right off him. He wouldn't feel a thing.

Someday, I would take the punches for Killian. I'd be *his* superhero.

And someday, I'd make sure Seamus paid for everything he did to us.

I heard the door close behind Seamus and counted to ten before I opened the closet door. Killian was doubled over, an arm wrapped around his ribs. I crouched next to him and put my hand on his back.

Killian lifted his head, his eyes meeting mine for a split second, long enough for me to see his busted lip and the bruise already forming beneath his right eye. He swept his tongue over his lip, catching the blood before it dripped onto the moss green carpet.

"You should have told him it was my fault," I said.

"It makes no difference."

Killian was right. It didn't matter if we were good or bad. On nights like this, the end result was always the same. "I'll be right back."

"Wait a little longer," he said, wincing as he got to his feet, weaving a little. I grabbed his arm to steady him and helped him over to the bottom bunk.

Then I tiptoed to our bedroom door, put my ear against it and listened. Downstairs, I could hear the TV, an announcer's voice talking about the bad things going on in the world. I eased the door open and checked the hallway. It was safe. *Safe.* I almost laughed out loud at that thought. But I wouldn't.

I knew how to be quiet, so quiet, as I crept down the hallway, avoiding the squeaky floorboards that might give me away. It had been months since Seamus had done this, but the routine was the same.

I ran a washcloth under the water, gathered my supplies from the bathroom cabinet and returned to the bedroom, closing the door behind me.

I cleaned up Killian's face as best as I could while he lay on the bottom bunk with his eyes closed. "Can you sit up?" I asked.

"Just leave it."

"The tape makes it better. You said so last time."

He sighed and got into a sitting position, his jaw clenched to fight the pain and keep from crying out. I helped him out of his pajama top then wrapped his ribs with the surgical tape. Firm but gentle so I didn't hurt him any more than he already was. I tried to patch up all the cracks. Hold his broken body together. Like always, Killian didn't even flinch.

When I finished, he lay down on the bottom bunk and I returned the supplies to the bathroom, rinsing the blood from the washcloth before I tossed it in the hamper. Sometimes I thought I should hang the bloody washcloth in Seamus' room so he could see it first thing in the morning when he woke up, not drunk anymore. But that would be like waving a red flag at a bull.

I climbed into the top bunk and stared at the glow-in-the-dark stars I'd stuck on the ceiling a few months ago. Mrs. Garcia, our babysitter, gave them to me for my seventh birthday. I'd pointed them out to her in a shop one time and she'd remembered. When I'd first stuck them on the ceiling, I'd been disappointed that you couldn't even see them. Turned out that stars needed darkness to shine.

"We need to tell someone," I said.

"Who you gonna tell?"

I'd been over this in my head about a million times. My thoughts kept me up at night. I had too many of them racing through my head. Sometimes I couldn't slow them down.

"Mrs. Garcia," I said.

She was always nice to us, but she didn't speak very good English and I doubted she understood half the stuff I said to her. I'd been known to pour out my heart to that woman and was always telling her stories, but all she did was smile and nod. She loved all the pictures I drew for her though and always called them *mas bonita* which sounded like a good thing. She gave us hugs and sometimes I wished I could just stay wrapped up in those hugs forever. Killian always broke free and said he was too old for hugs, but not me.

4

"Maybe I need to learn Spanish, so she'll understand what I'm saying. Or I could draw her a picture, maybe. Or how about we tell Father Mc—"

"We're not telling anyone," Killian said.

"But maybe they can help us. Get us out of here."

"Nobody will believe us."

"They might. We can at least try."

"Let's say someone believed it, you know what would happen to us?"

Killian was only three and a half years older than me, but sometimes he acted like he was an adult and I was the stupid kid. "What?"

"Foster care."

"That's okay. I'll do whatever it takes to help you," I said, even though I wasn't too sure what foster care was. But the word *care* gave me hope. "It's gotta be better than this."

"It's not," Killian said as if he knew exactly what foster care was like. That was Killian though. He knew a lot of things that most kids didn't so maybe he did know. "Do you wanna be separated?"

"We're brothers. They'll keep us together."

"Just promise me you'll keep your mouth shut, okay? Keep it between us. Nobody needs to know what goes on in our house."

I hated this. I hated the secrets and lies. I hated hiding in the closet like a big fat baby. I hated that there was nothing I could do to help Killian. I rubbed my chest, trying to ease the ache, but it never seemed to go away these days. Sometimes I felt like there were big cracks inside me. Like I broke a little more every time Killian took a punch.

"Promise me," he said again.

I stared at the stars, wishing I could be anywhere but here. There must be something better out there. But if it meant being separated from Killian, I'd keep my mouth shut. I wasn't a snitch or a tattletale. Not even my friends knew about any of this. "Promise."

I heard him exhale as if he'd been holding his breath, waiting

5

for me to agree. He had to know I would. I was always on his side and he was always on mine. It was us against the world.

"Tell me about our mom," I said a little while later. I'd been thinking about her a lot lately, wondering if she was okay and where she was. If she had enough food and money. "When do you think she'll come back to get us?"

"Never. She's not coming back."

"But you said..." I let my words drift off. "Those were just stories then? Like fairy tales? Did you make it all up?"

Killian didn't answer.

"Was she really beautiful?" I asked, clenching my fists. "Was she really nice? Did she love us? Did she tuck us in at night?"

"You ask too many questions."

"Just tell me the truth. Did she read us bedtime stories? Did she really do all those things, or did you make it all up?" I asked, my voice rising.

"Keep your voice down."

"Answer my questions," I said, through gritted teeth. I dug the heels of my hands into my eye sockets to stop the tears. Seamus' voice played on a loop in my head.

Boys don't cry. Stop being a fucking pussy.

"I don't know...that's how I remember it," Killian said so quietly I had to strain to hear him.

"Someday I'm gonna find her and we'll live with her."

"Yeah, okay, you do that."

I will, I thought. I'll do that for you. For *us*. "You keep this room, Kill. I want you to have the stars."

He grunted, but he didn't fight me on it. That was how I knew he wanted the stars but would never admit it.

CONNOR

I *am peaceful. I am strong. My past does not define me.*

I repeated my mantra as the needles pierced my skin, digging into scar tissue, and hitting every nerve ending.

A soft knock came on the door and it opened to reveal Eden, her green eyes shining with tears her smile couldn't hide.

Shit. I put those tears in her eyes. "Hey, Connor... Jared."

Jared lifted the tattoo needle from my chest and leaned back on his stool, wiping the sweat off his forehead with the back of his arm. He'd been working on me since ten this morning before the shop even opened. Hours to go yet but it was taking its toll on both of us.

"Hey gorgeous," Jared said, giving her a big smile.

"You guys mind if I hang out?" She'd already dragged a stool inside the private room in the back of the shop, so she wasn't waiting for an answer, but we told her it was cool. She perched on her seat, her tiny shorts showing off her long, tanned legs, an iced coffee clutched in her left hand. The rock on her finger, an emerald surrounded by diamonds that Killian gave her three months ago, sparkled in the light coming through the back window.

Eden took my hand in hers and gave it a squeeze. "I thought

we should be together today. At least for a little while." Her gaze dipped to my chest. It was the first time she'd seen me bare-chested in a year. A visual reminder of the night four men came seeking retribution.

"Connor," she whispered. "Does it hurt?"

Like a motherfucker. "No more than usual." It was a lie, and she probably knew it. So did Jared. Tattooing over scars was one of his specialties. He'd wanted me to wait eighteen months to two years, ideally, but I couldn't wait any longer than I have. I wanted the scars covered. Today.

"You good?" Jared asked me.

"Yeah."

Jared studied my face for a few seconds before he got back to work.

"It's beautiful," Eden said.

Eden saw beauty in the ugliness, but I guess she was referring to my design—a colorful Japanese dragon. I'd been chasing that dragon for years, but now the artwork would cover up the carved letters on my chest. SNITCH. Of all the things I'd been called in my life, I never expected to be that person.

"Tell me a happy story," I said. Eden was a magician, and I was hoping she'd conjure one up out of thin air.

"Once upon a time, there was a boy," she started. "A beautiful boy with dark hair and cerulean eyes. Let's call him..." She tapped her chin and narrowed her eyes, pretending to think. "Connor Vincent. The boy grew up battling demons and when he got older, he became a dragon slayer. He's brave and fierce and courageous."

"I think you're mixing up the brothers in this fairy tale."

"Oh, well, his brother is all those things, too, but you're the hero in this story."

I was nobody's hero. "Does this story have a happy ending?" I asked.

"Of course. But first, the hero needs to win back his lady love."

My lady love... my first love, my first everything, had kicked me to the curb. She'd waited until I'd physically recovered, three weeks after my father's funeral, a month after the night that had nearly cost me my life, and Eden and Killian's lives. Ava told me I made her cry too much. Made her feel too much of everything—the good... but mostly the bad and the ugly.

"It's too much, Connor. I can't handle it anymore. You need to set me free."

I couldn't blame her. It was self-preservation on her part. But it was killing me that she'd moved on with someone new. "She still with Zeke?" I asked as if I didn't already know. *Go on, pour a little salt on my wounds.*

Eden chewed on her lower lip. "Yeah."

Zeke was a silver-spoon Ivy league graduate. Ava couldn't have found anyone more different than me. But then, I guess that was the whole point.

"You should ask her on a date," Eden said, taking a sip of her coffee.

A date. Like that would solve our problems. "You're saying I should court Ava who is currently screwing your buddy Zeke?" Not to mention Ava wouldn't even speak to me, let alone accept a date with me.

Eden tucked a lock of blonde hair behind her ear. "They're more like friends with benefits if you ask me."

Benefits I wasn't currently getting. Not for lack of offers. But the look on Eden's face when she stared at my chest... yeah, I couldn't go there.

Hello, hand, we really need to stop meeting like this.

"Does he make her happy?" I asked, not sure why I was continuing down this torturous path.

"What they have is easy," she said, choosing her words carefully. "Zeke is fun, and he's cool to hang out with, but he isn't the great love of her life. He's a flicker, not a flame."

Ever the optimist. "Yeah, well, she's been burned by the same flame too many times. Now my girl is too scared to play with fire."

Eden smiled triumphantly. "You called her your girl."

She'd always be my girl. It didn't matter who she was with or how long we were separated by time or distance, Ava would always be mine. I knew in my heart that nobody could ever love her the

9

way I do. It simply wasn't possible. Unfortunately, I'd fucked up too many times and that was what it always came back to. Our history was long, with moments of pure bliss, but the bad outweighed the good for her, and there was no way to wipe the slate clean and start fresh.

Fucking hell. Love hurt.

My chest tightened, and I took deep breaths, trying to fight through the pain. Not only the tattooing but the daily struggle of life as a recovering addict. It's a journey of one baby step at a time and I was attempting to scale fucking Everest.

"Time for a break," Jared said, wiping the blood off my chest. Removing his latex gloves, he let himself out and closed the door behind him, leaving me alone with Eden. I sat up on the table, wishing I could cover my chest so she wouldn't have to look at it.

"I guess that wasn't such a happy story, after all," Eden said.

I mustered a smile for her. I needed a cigarette, but she stayed a little longer, chatting about happier things. Namely, a mural she'd been commissioned to paint in a boutique on Bedford Avenue.

"You'll be able to give up the day job soon," I said.

"That's what Killian keeps saying. But I love working at the bar." She slid out her phone and checked the time. "Sorry. I need to get to work."

I stood, and she stared at my chest for a few seconds before she lifted her gaze to my face. "I'd hug you but... probably not a great idea."

My eyes locked with her green ones. "You okay?"

She nodded and exhaled a breath. "Yeah, I'm good. Killian and I went to the cemetery this morning."

I rubbed the back of my neck, knotted with tension. I haven't been to the cemetery since the day we put my father in the ground, and I had no intention of ever visiting his grave. His funeral had been a circus—thousands of police officers had lined the route we'd traveled to the church in Bay Ridge. A sea of blue paying their respects to a man who had hidden his dirty little secrets underneath his badge. Seamus Vincent had been one of NYPD's finest. What a sick joke.

"I'm surprised Killian went," I said.

"Killian is full of surprises these days," she said. "He talks and everything."

We shared a laugh over that one. Prying open Killian had never been an easy task, but Eden did it. She cracked him wide open, then she gathered up all the broken pieces and helped him glue them back together.

When Eden left, I exited through the back door and leaned against the brick wall next to my Harley to smoke a cigarette.

"That shit's gonna kill you," Jared said, joining me in the fenced-in vacant lot with weeds pushing up through the cracks. It always amazed me that weeds had such a strong survival instinct and managed to thrive in the most unlikely places. "Give me one."

I shook a cigarette out of the pack and handed it to him, along with the lighter. "Thought you quit."

"I did."

I eyed him as he took his first drag. It's the best one when the nicotine hits your bloodstream and gives you a rush. He closed his eyes and exhaled. "Damn. Why is all the bad shit so good?"

I took another drag of my cigarette and tipped my head back, not bothering to answer. The clouds looked like brushstrokes painted on a hurt-your-eyes blue sky, a day so like last year it was almost eerie.

"I'm thinking about opening another shop," Jared said.

"Where?"

"California."

What. The. Fuck.

"Winter's coming. I hate the cold. I'm thinking San Diego. All-year-round perfect temperature."

It was the end of September, and on a day like this, winter seemed like a long way off. The air smelled like hot tar and garbage, an odor intensified by the heat. "When's this happening?"

"As soon as you can get me the money."

I tossed my cigarette on the ground and crushed it under the sole of my motorcycle boot, thinking about Jared's words. Killian and I had inherited money from our old man. Seamus never spent a penny he didn't need to, and after thirty-plus years on the force, with a chief's salary for the last five years of it, and a mortgage-free house in Bay Ridge, we'd ended up splitting a shitload of money. A hell of a lot more than I'd expected him to have or ever give us. Blood money, I called it. Killian used his money to fund programs for at-risk youth. Mine was still sitting in an account untouched. When I offered my share of the money to Killian, he refused to accept it. I wrote him a check for the money I owed him, but he never cashed that either. But, then, we weren't on speaking terms at the time.

"You want me to buy you out?" I asked.

"Yep."

"What happens if I don't?"

Jared rubbed a hand over his blond buzzcut, his eyes narrowed as he took another drag and exhaled. "I'll sell it to someone else."

He'd been talking about leaving Brooklyn for years, but that's all it had ever been. Talk. This time, it was more than just talk. He was ready to get out. "What about the building? You looking to sell that, too?"

The tattoo parlor was on the first floor and Jared lived in the apartment above it. His grandfather bought the building fifty years ago, back when real estate was cheap in Williamsburg before the hipsters had invaded and prices skyrocketed.

"I'll keep the building. You can move into my apartment and pay rent."

He was offering me first shot at something I'd always wanted. I scrubbed my hand over the stubble on my jaw. Was I ready to run my own shop? Sink money into a business that tied me to this neighborhood? Even though I was done running, the thought of putting down roots put me on edge. But what scared the shit out of me was that I might fail. Failure was not an option. I'd burnt too many bridges already, and I'd spent the better part of a year trying to rebuild them, not always successfully either.

"Lee and Gavin aren't interested?" I asked, referring to the other tattoo artists.

"Nah, they don't wanna run a shop," Jared said, tossing his

cigarette. "Think about it. You've got a week until I start considering other offers."

I followed him inside, ignoring Claudia's heated gaze as she came out of the restroom, her tits practically falling out of her low-cut black top. She licked her lips and fluttered her eyelashes, sending a message that was loud and clear. Claudia was hot, with long dark hair and curves in all the right places, but she didn't do it for me.

"Someone's been spending a lot of time in the gym," she said.

I turned my back to her before she got a close-up view of my chest. Claudia was our receptionist and piercer, and had offered, on more than one occasion, to suck my dick. I had to hand it to her for being direct, but I never took her up on it, and I never would.

I closed the door, effectively shutting her out.

"Mind if I watch?" she asked from the other side of the door. I shook my head, but it wasn't necessary. Jared knew I didn't want an audience. Eden had been an exception.

"I need you on the desk," Jared said.

She huffed out a breath and I heard her heels clicking across the black-and-white tiled floor.

"You going there?" Jared asked, dipping the needle into cyan ink.

"Nope."

No more words were exchanged while Jared worked on my tattoo which gave me time to think about his offer. Part of me was saying that I wasn't ready for this kind of responsibility. The other part of me was saying that it was time to step up to the plate and prove myself.

I stared at the pressed-tin tiles on the ceiling and let my thoughts drift to the girl with lavender hair and silvery gray eyes. Ava Christensen had been the best thing in my life, but I ruined us.

I PARKED my Harley on the sidewalk in front of Defiance MMA & Fitness and locked it up. The gym closed fifteen minutes ago so I was hoping to catch Killian on his way out. I pushed through the front door of the converted warehouse, surprised it wasn't locked yet. Killian was in the cage with Nico, a kid he was training, and I stood back to watch them grapple.

In my early teens, I'd spent hours watching Killian's training sessions at a gym in Bay Ridge. While he'd trained, I'd drawn, and created a comic book that my old man had found hidden under my mattress. Turning Seamus Vincent into the evil villain of my graphic comic hadn't been one of my brighter ideas. He'd burned my sketchbook and punched me so hard my ears were ringing for a week. Killian hadn't been home that night. If he had been, he would have intervened. I was thirteen at the time, and a sick, twisted part of me took pride in the fact that I'd taken that punch to the head.

I watched as Killian got Nico into a chokehold he couldn't free himself from. "Tap the mat, Nico," Killian said. Reluctantly, Nico tapped his hand on the mat and Killian released him. They got to their feet and faced each other.

"Tapping out isn't the same as losing," Killian said. "You did good today."

Nico nodded, but I could tell by the look on his face that he wasn't convinced.

"Nico," Killian said, willing Nico to listen and believe his words. "You did good."

"Yeah, man. Thanks," Nico mumbled. He climbed out of the cage and we exchanged a greeting before he headed to the locker room.

"I'm closing up now," Killian said.

"I'm not here to work out. You got a minute?"

"Help me clean the mats," he said, shooting a look at my motorcycle boots. Killian's always been a stickler for rules, attempting to give structure to a world of chaos. Wearing shoes on the mats was forbidden. "And I'll give you more than a minute."

I kicked off my boots and lined them up against the wall under the black and red gym logo. Killian returned from the supply closet with brooms and Swiffer mops and we got to work, sweeping the jigsaw mats.

Nico came out of the locker room in jeans and a T-shirt, his gym bag slung over his shoulder, and followed the path around the mats, careful not to step on them in his street shoes. "You need help cleaning?" he asked.

Killian shook his head. "Get some rest. Drink plenty of water. And if you need me for *anything*, you call me."

Nico nodded, and I wondered if he knew how lucky he was to have Killian in his corner. I was tempted to take Nico aside and caution him not to squander the faith Killian had in him. But maybe this kid was smarter than me. "Thanks," Nico said.

Killian walked him to the door and clapped Nico on the shoulder, saying something in a low voice I didn't catch. A pep talk, or words of advice, maybe. Killian had taken Nico under his wing nine months ago when he opened this gym and I got the feeling Nico wanted to follow in Killian's footsteps. Once upon a time, Killian had been a UFC champion. When his opponent, Johnny Ramirez, died of his injuries two years ago, Killian walked away from his MMA career. It had been an accident, but Killian's guilt ran deep, and he vowed never to step foot in the Octagon again. Instead, he coached guys like Nico.

After Nico left, Killian joined me on the mats.

"How's Nico doing?" I asked, knowing he came from a similar fucked-up background as we did.

"His piece of shit stepdad put his mom in the hospital."

"Fuck."

"She won't leave him. She's too scared of being on her own," Killian said.

It was easy to judge someone from the outside looking in, and a lot of people thought it was easy to just up and leave. Why stay with an abusive partner? Why not report an abusive parent? But it wasn't always that simple. "And Nico feels it's his duty to protect her," I guessed.

"Yeah." We worked in silence for a while, mopping the mats with disinfectant.

"Heard you got a new tattoo," Killian said.

"Yeah. Eden stopped by to offer moral support."

At the mention of her name, his lips curved into a smile that came more easily now than it used to.

"Jared's looking to sell his shop," I said, introducing my reason for stopping by. "He's giving me first dibs."

"You ready for that?" I heard the doubt in his voice that told me he didn't think I was.

"It's time I take some responsibility."

"Running your own business is a full-time job. You can't take off whenever you want. You can't just turn up, do the tattooing, and leave when your shift ends. It's a hell of a lot of—"

"I know that," I said through gritted teeth. I took deep breaths through my nose, trying to calm myself. *I am peaceful. I am strong. My past does not define me.* "How about a little support? Like, 'hey Connor, good job. You're a kickass tattoo artist. I believe in you.'"

He clenched his jaw, and we completed the chore in stony silence. Maybe Killian was full of surprises when it came to Eden, but with me, the struggle was real. I had nobody to blame but myself. In the past, he'd given me more chances to make things right than I'd ever deserved. But now that I was doing all the right things, it was too little, too late.

In a parting shot as we left the gym, he said, "If you're serious about this, you should talk to Zeke."

"What a great fucking idea. I'll ask my ex-girlfriend's new boyfriend for help."

"Do you know how to put together a business plan? Because I sure as hell didn't."

"I'll figure it out." I straddled my Harley and his hand gripped my bicep to stop me from putting on my helmet and leaving.

"I want to believe in you," he said.

He released my arm, and I stared down the street at the warehouses that lined the block, their corrugated metal doors shut for the night. A tricked-out black Caddy cruised past, rap music blasting from the open windows, the sound fading into the night air as it turned down the next block. "But you can't do it."

Killian rubbed his jaw and squinted into the distance. "I'm trying. That's the best I can give you right now." He turned on his heel and strode away, beeping the locks of his SUV.

That's the best I can give you right now.

At this point, I'd need to perform three miracles and get canonized for sainthood before he put his faith in me.

My phone vibrated in my pocket, and I slid it out, checking the screen. Tate. "How did today go?" he asked, skipping the greeting. I checked over my shoulder. Killian was already pulling away from the curb, burning rubber to get home to Eden.

I gave Tate a recap of my day without bullshitting him. He was like my priest and I was the sinner sitting in the confessional box. Tate was a good sponsor, and he'd talked me down from the ledge more than once over the past year. When shit got too much to handle, I called him instead of trying to score.

He listened, without interrupting, and when I finished, I waited for his words of wisdom or encouragement or whatever was on today's menu. Chicken soup for the soul, and all that shit.

"Sounds like you made a lot of progress," he said.

"Which part of what I told you was progress?" I asked, rubbing my hand over my chest. The tattoo was starting to itch like hell, and I could still feel the ridges of the scars under my fingertips, but you couldn't see them anymore. Progress.

"Have you tried to score today?"

"No."

"Was your first thought ... I need to get high to make it through this day?"

"Not my first thought." But it was always there, that little voice in the back of my head telling me it knew a sure-fire way to take me away from it all, make me forget the world. It promised me euphoria, and sweet relief, however fleeting.

"There you go," Tate said. "Progress."

I chuckled. "Yeah. I'm in a great place."

"A hell of a lot better than last year. Just take it one step at a time. Keep doing the work, and the big shit will sort itself out."

"Right."

After a beat, he said, "Keeping shit like that inside eats away at a person. He deserves the truth."

Tate hadn't brought this up in months, and I'd been grateful for it, but I guess he felt that it deserved a mention on the one-year anniversary.

"That's all I'm gonna say about that. Call if you need me."

"Thanks."

I cut the call and pocketed my phone. Maybe Killian had a right to know, but the truth was ugly. How could divulging it help?

Would Killian believe that I withheld the truth to protect him? I warred with myself daily. I didn't know what Ronan Shaughnessy was fully capable of. He'd been the puppeteer pulling all the strings, and he'd made me dance for him. If I told Killian, I doubted that he'd just let it go. That wasn't his style. He'd storm the castle, trying to play the white knight, but he'd fail just like I had. She didn't want to be rescued. She'd chosen her second family over her first and left me and Killian behind without a backward glance. I envisioned Keira Shaughnessy, the sister Killian knew nothing about, the sister who had no clue we were related. Attempting to get close to her had been my downfall.

There was no easy way out. But then, had there ever been?

I lit a cigarette and took a drag, wishing all the bad shit didn't taste so damn good. I briefly entertained the idea of calling Claudia and taking her up on her offer. Or hitting up a bar, ordering a club soda and lime, and finding the first hot girl willing to have sex. It wouldn't be that difficult, and maybe that sounded cocky, but girls were attracted to my physical appearance. Pretty on the outside, something entirely different on the inside.

Ava once called me an onion.

"You make people cry. And you have so many different layers ... you never know what the next one will reveal."

An onion. Jesus Christ.

2

AVA

"Zeke, honey, would you like more cake?" my mom called through the screen door.

"No thank you."

"How about more of the baked ziti and meatballs? Or the wedding soup? You loved that." My mom comes from a big Italian family, and in her world, food is love. She wouldn't rest until she stuffed Zeke like a Christmas turkey.

"I loved it all," he said, flashing her a big white smile. Zeke looked like he stepped out of a Ralph Lauren ad, with his blond hair and sun-kissed skin. Not only was he easy on the eyes, he wasn't an asshole. "But I can't eat another thing."

"I'll pack a doggy bag for later."

"I won't say no to that," he said with an easy smile.

"Suck up," I teased. Zeke winked at me. He knew how to play the game, a whole lot better than I did. Zeke was raised in Greenwich in a sprawling house with a swimming pool and tennis courts. Yet here he was in the backyard of my parents' rowhouse, talking to my grandparents, aunts, and uncles who all talked over each other, my sister Lana, and her husband Joe, and winning them over. He could charm the birds out of the tree, and within five minutes of walking in the door, he'd charmed my entire family. Two hours later and he was still doing it.

"Help me in the kitchen," my mom said, summoning me. I knew what was coming and sighed as I crossed the backyard and yanked open the screen door.

"I like that boy," she said, donning yellow rubber gloves to protect her manicure. She plunged the dirty dishes into the soapy water. Scrubbed, rinsed, and handed me a plate to dry and stow in the cabinet.

"When are you guys going to get a dishwasher?" I asked, aiming for a diversion.

"I offered to buy her one," my dad said from his spot at the kitchen table. He flipped the page of his newspaper, which he preferred to hanging out with my mom's family. Or anyone. Unlike my mom who loved to surround herself with people, my dad liked peace and quiet.

I inherited his cool Nordic looks—white-blonde hair and pale skin—but personality-wise, I was a mix of both parents. I'd taken a quiz once that told me I was an extroverted introvert. Conflicted, like me.

"If I wanted a dishwasher, I'd buy it myself," my mom said, handing me another plate. "I like washing dishes. It gives me a chance to look out the window."

"And spy on the neighbors," I joked, earning a chuckle from my dad.

My mom flapped her hand at me, dousing me with soapy dish-water, her gaze still focused on the window where Zeke was front and center talking to Lana. She looked impeccable, as always, with chestnut-brown hair cut in long layers and expertly applied makeup that didn't detract from her classic beauty. We looked nothing alike, had very little in common, and we weren't that close. She lived on Long Island and we only got together for holidays, and then it was polite chit-chat, at best.

Lana always wore heels, no matter the occasion, and shopped at Nordstrom, which guaranteed that her tasteful designer outfits won my mom's approval. I shopped at vintage stores and flea markets, which never won me any points. My current ensemble was a vintage Ramones T-shirt, shredded jean cut-offs, and black combat boots. Maybe I should have made more of an effort to please my mom. At least my T-shirt covered my tattoo, something guaranteed to put a frown on her face every time she saw it.

When I was eighteen, Connor inked soaring bluebirds on my right bicep. A year later, I had barbed wire inked around the bluebirds. When Connor found out about it, he stormed into the lounge of my residence hall at St. John's University mid-study session. He threw me over his shoulder, kicking and screaming, and sequestered me in my room, demanding an explanation.

"You're the barbed wire, Connor. I want out."

"You're mine. We belong together."

"Make a choice. Me or drugs. I refuse to stand by and watch you kill yourself."

"I'm not going to die, baby. I've got it under control."

As usual, we ended up naked, and he fucked me until I forgot my own name, let alone the reason for my concern.

"Is it serious with you and Zeke?" my mom asked.

I shrugged. "No. We're just hanging out."

"You don't bring a boy to your father's birthday lunch if you're just 'hanging out.' He's so handsome," she said in a dreamy voice that made her sound like a teenager with her first crush. "With such good manners. And he's so easy to talk to. He's a keeper. Don't let that one go."

My mom didn't say the words, but she didn't need to—Zeke was everything that Connor wasn't. Money and status were important to her, and even though we'd never had either one, she still aspired to it. But I didn't love Zeke, and he didn't love me. Whatever we were doing, it had probably reached its expiration date. Bringing him over today had been a mistake.

"I have a feeling he'll move on to bigger and better things. With his education, he could be working on Wall Street or heading up one of his dad's companies in no time."

"Zeke likes running the bar with Louis. Before that, he was a bartender, Mom. He doesn't have huge ambitions."

"One day, he will. Mark my words. That boy is going places."

I sighed. Of course, Zeke would get the benefit of the doubt. My mom had probably Googled his family already and knew their net worth.

"Honey, why don't you come into the salon and let me do your hair?" my mom said, removing her gloves. She tucked my lavender hair behind my ears and peered at my face, frowning at my signature black eyeliner—thick and winged. "Such a beautiful face. You don't need all that black eyeliner. Let me fix your hair. I bet Zeke would love—"

"Mom. No. Just ... no. We need to go to work."

I brushed past her, trying not to notice how her face fell in disappointment. It always seemed to end this way with us. "Hey, Zeke. We should go."

I hugged everyone goodbye, and Zeke and I got out of there as quickly as possible. Which wasn't quick enough. My mom held us up in the kitchen, taking her sweet time to pack up leftovers for Zeke.

I climbed into Zeke's Jeep Wrangler and collapsed against the seat, drained. "I'm sorry I subjected you to my family."

"No worries. They're cool. Food was good. It was worth the trip."

"You know that you're too good to be true, right?"

He smiled. "Funny. That's what I always thought about you."

Proving yet again that he was just too perfect. And full of shit.

ZEKE and I were laughing as we walked into Trinity Bar. The laughter died on my lips when I saw Connor sitting on a barstool, his folded arms resting on the zinc bar top as he talked to Louis. Just like it always did, my pulse raced at the sight of him. He looked over at the door, his electric-blue eyes searing me with their intensity. And I needed to remind myself how to breathe. How to stand on my own two feet after he'd just pulled the ground out from under me.

How could one person create such a strong reaction in me? Why couldn't I ever be free of him?

I still remembered the boy who was all elbows and knees, his dark hair falling into his eyes. He wasn't that boy anymore. At twenty-four, his broad shoulders and six-pack abs threatened to burst the seams of his white T-shirt. His dark hair was cropped short, his face chiseled and harder-looking than it used to be.

But he was still the most beautiful boy I'd ever laid eyes on. And he still made my heart ache.

In the past eleven months, I'd only seen him once. I knew his schedule, knew where he'd be at any given time of the day, and I went out of my way to avoid him.

Sitting in Trinity Bar on a Saturday afternoon was not part of his daily routine.

"What are you doing here?" I hated how cold my voice sounded. I hated how the heat and the light in his eyes faded. Most of all, I hated that I still cared about his feelings when he obviously didn't give a damn about mine.

His gaze swung to Zeke, dismissing me. "Do you have a few minutes?"

"Sure," Zeke said, pulling up a stool next to Connor like this was perfectly normal, even though they'd never been friends.

I breezed past them, dying to know what Connor could possibly want from Zeke, but I forced myself to keep walking, my boots tapping across the hardwood floor. As I passed the open doors leading to the courtyard, I glanced outside. It was almost October but felt more like a summer's day. Hipsters crowded the picnic tables, talking and laughing over the music, the air scented with roasted pork from Jimmy's Taco Truck, and the lavender and mint I planted.

When I reached the safety of the office, I sank into the black leather swivel chair and took a few deep breaths, trying to pull myself together. Plenty to keep me busy here. Working at Trinity Bar was the perfect job for me. I made my own hours, excelled at social media, which I used to promote the bar, and loved the orga-nizational aspect of the job. I wore many hats—doing the paperwork, accounting, booking the entertainment, running promotions, tending to my little garden in the courtyard—so I never suffered from boredom. If I wanted to socialize, I could. If I wanted to hole up in the office, that was cool, too. Yep, my life was hunky dory.

A little while later, I was reminding all my virtual friends to come out and see tonight's indie rock band when Zeke entered the office.

"Hey," I said, trying to sound casual. I spun my chair around to face him. "So, what was that about? Was it personal? I mean ... about us?"

Zeke shook his head and pulled me out of the swivel chair and into his arms. He kissed me, and I kissed him back. He was a good kisser, but his kisses didn't turn me into a bowl of Jell-O. I still had my wits about me, and I considered that one of the perks of this arrangement. Zeke released me, and I looked over at the doorway, feeling his presence even though he hadn't made a sound. For such a big guy—six feet, three inches of solid muscle—Connor moved like a ninja, a skill he'd perfected to survive his childhood.

Connor's eyes narrowed, his jaw working to contain his emotions, but I saw what he tried to hide. Jealousy. Hurt. Sadness. Anger. They flashed across his face before he locked it down and clenched his jaw, the muscle in his cheek jumping as we stared each other down.

You screwed up, asshole. It didn't have to be like this, I told him with my eyes.

Zeke took my spot in the chair I'd vacated and laced his fingers behind his head, cool as you like. I shot him a look. He shrugged nonchalantly like it couldn't be helped. Zeke had kissed me on purpose, knowing that Connor would see it. "I'll stop by on Monday before the shop opens. Does noon work for you?" Zeke asked Connor.

"Forget it," Connor gritted out. "Bad fucking idea."

Zeke flashed me a smile as Connor strode away.

"What was that?" I hissed, planting my hands on my hips. It

wasn't like Zeke to be cruel, but he had to know that throwing it in Connor's face would hurt him.

Zeke grabbed my stress ball, a smiling Buddha face, that I kept on the shelf with my color-coded binders, propped his feet on the desk, and tossed the ball from hand to hand. "Ava, you're gorgeous. You're smart. You're sexy. And you're totally cool. But I'm not the guy for you because you're still in love with someone else."

"I'm not ... Connor and I ... whatever we had ... it's ancient history," I spluttered. "We're over."

"Keep telling yourself that." Zeke delivered the words with a smile, but I still felt the sting. He tilted his head. "Why are you with me?"

Zeke was changing up the game. This wasn't what we did. We hung out, had fun, shared a good laugh, and had sex. We didn't bare our souls or push each other for answers to tough questions. Our deal started out like this: *How about we hook up exclusively?* In other words, we'd only have sex with each other, and when one of us was ready to move on, we'd call it quits. No harm, no foul. Perfect plan.

"Because it's easy," I said, deciding to be honest. "You don't come with a lot of baggage." I leaned against the edge of the desk and crossed my arms. "Why are you with me?"

"You needed a diversion. I'm good for that. But I'm starting to think I want more. Something real, you know? Like Eden and Killian have. Like you and Connor had ... *have*."

I didn't bother reminding him that Connor and I were over and that we had been for almost five years. *Five years* and I was still holding on to ... what? The ghost of a memory.

"You're looking for a real relationship?" I asked, surprised. Zeke had always been a player and maintained that he liked it that way.

He laughed. "Nah. I'm just messing with you. I'm not ready to settle for one person anytime soon. But this isn't about me. It's about you. I don't pretend to know Connor ... those Vincent brothers don't make it easy."

Zeke was right. Nothing had ever been easy with them, but their lives had never been easy either.

"But you know what I think?" I shook my head, curious to hear his thoughts. "When they fall in love, they fall hard, and it's for life."

"Love isn't always enough."

"Maybe not." He shrugged. "But that's for you to decide. All this oversharing is exhausting. Zeke's office hours are officially over."

"And I guess we are, too."

"We can still be friends." He flashed me a smile.

I groaned. "That's such a line. But somehow you make it work."

"What can I say? It's a gift."

"Thanks for everything. I don't regret a single minute of it."

"This is starting to sound like an after-school special."

"We're pathetic," I said, and then we were laughing and hugging.

I wished that things could be different. Loving Zeke would be so damn easy. But it wasn't meant to be.

Maybe you couldn't choose the person you fell in love with. Over the years, I'd tried so many times to steel my heart against Connor, but he always came in like a wrecking ball. He knocked down all the walls, destroyed the foundation, and left me with the rubble. Our brand of love would never make an after-school special. It was ugly and gritty and soul-destroying. Connor and I... there had been so many obstacles in our way.

But for a while, our love had been beautiful, and it had been everything.

How could you hate someone and love them at the same time?

3

AVA

TEN YEARS AGO

My empty stomach churned as I made my way down the crowded school hallway, the dingy beige walls closing in on me. I swallowed down the fear and popped another piece of gum in my mouth. No matter what I did, I couldn't rid my mouth of the bad taste. My mom had believed me when I told her I had a stomach bug. I couldn't keep food down. I barely left my room all day Friday. The same went for Saturday and Sunday. Now it was Monday. Time to face my personal hell. I pulled my beanie lower, hiding my shorn hair that I'd hacked off this morning, my white-blonde locks falling to the tiled bathroom floor. When my mom had seen what I'd done, she'd been rendered speechless. Not an easy feat but I'd managed to do it.

"You'll do anything for attention," Lana had hissed.

My footsteps faltered as I got closer to my locker. Would he be there? With that smirk on his face? His voice taunting me. My vision blurred, and the hallway tilted. I took a few deep breaths until the world righted itself again and shoved the memories down deep inside where they couldn't resurface.

In the sea of bodies, one stood out. Killian Vincent was hard to miss. At eighteen, he looked more like a man than a boy. It wasn't just that he was built like a young god or his height which was at least a foot taller than me, he could intimidate lesser mortals with just one look. Apparently, he had a notoriously bad temper and was always getting into street fights. Or so I'd heard from my sister Lana and her friends who were seniors, like him.

Yet Killian had been my savior.

My gaze swung to the guy on his right. Connor. A freshman like me. His dark hair messy and a little too long, his blue eyes so blue they didn't look real. Connor was the pretty one, I'd always thought, with finer features and long eyelashes that girls would envy. Something that probably would have horrified him if I'd said it aloud. Which I wouldn't. We'd never spoken.

But watching the Vincent brothers in church every Sunday had been one of my favorite pastimes. Thanks to my mom who got all the gossip at the salon and liked to pass it on over family dinners, I knew their mother had run off ten years ago, leaving Seamus alone to raise the boys. My mom always shook her head and sighed, calling the man a saint, but I'd never trusted Seamus Vincent's steely blue eyes and hard face. Sometimes Killian would be sporting a black eye, or a split lip and Connor would get dragged to his feet by the scruff of his neck when he failed to stand on cue during Mass. But Seamus Vincent was a pillar of the community, and nobody ever questioned his parenting skills.

As I got closer, I realized they must be waiting for me. Why else would they be standing in front of my locker?

"Hey Ava," Connor said. "I'm Killian's brother, Connor."

I nodded, no words of greeting coming out of my mouth.

"You good?" Killian asked.

I nodded again. His gaze swept over my face, trying to decide if I was lying. I could see that he knew I was, but he crossed his arms over his wide chest and nodded once. He wasn't going to call me out on it. My gaze swung to Connor. His lips tugged into a soft smile. It was too sweet, and I didn't know how to handle it, so I studied the intricate blue and black designs on his left forearm that he must have inked with Sharpies. Birds? Did they continue past his elbow where his blue plaid shirt was cuffed?

"If Jake Masters comes anywhere near you again..." Killian said,

28

drawing my attention to him. "If he even looks at you or breathes in your direction, you let me know and I'll take care of it. Understand?"

I nodded, which seemed to be the only thing I was capable of. Killian raised his brows at Connor and a look passed between them that seemed to communicate more than words could. Then he turned on his heel and strode away. It was only after he was gone that I realized I'd never thanked him for coming to my rescue. I busied myself with hanging my coat in the locker and packing my books for today's classes. Shouldering my backpack, I slammed my locker shut and spun the dial on the padlock. Connor was still there, leaning against the locker next to mine. His eyes were trained on my face, but I got the feeling he was taking it all in. The oversized hoodie, baggy sweatpants stuffed into my Ugg boots, the dark circles under my eyes.

He wasn't just looking at me, he was looking straight through me. *He sees me*, I thought.

"I get it," he said, his voice low.

"Get what?" I asked, staring at the black leather cord around his neck, a glint of silver disappearing inside the collar of his gray T-shirt.

"Trying to make yourself invisible," he said.

I swallowed hard, not sure what to do with his words, my gaze still focused on the pendant I couldn't see.

"St. Jude." I lifted my eyes to his, my brow furrowed. Connor pulled out the silver medallion, a saint's medal. "The patron saint of lost causes," he said, tucking it back inside his collar.

He reached out his hand, his fingers brushing my shoulder. I flinched from his touch and took a step back, tightening my grip on the strap of my backpack.

"I was just going to carry your bag," he said quietly like he was speaking to a wild animal he needed to approach with caution.

"I've got it," I said as the first bell rang, cutting through the voices around us. I ducked my head and started walking to my first period.

"Do you still dance?" he asked, falling into step with me.

I side-eyed him. The top of my head only reached his shoulder. He'd shot up over the summer. Tall and lanky, like he hadn't quite grown into his body yet. "How do you know I dance?"

His lips tugged into a smile, a dimple appearing in his right cheek. I knew he only had one and I liked that it was unique, not part of a matching set. "The dance studio is next to the gym Killian trains at. I used to watch you sometimes through the window." He ran his tongue over his lower lip, his eyes narrowed on me as if he was trying to gauge my reaction to that confession. His honesty surprised me. It also surprised me that the thought of him watching me didn't creep me out. "Sounds messed up. But it wasn't like that. Promise."

"What was it like?" I asked.

"You want the truth?" he asked as we stopped outside my classroom door.

I wasn't sure what I wanted. "You're going to be late for class."

He shrugged one shoulder. "Looks that way," he said, making no move to leave even as the late bell rang, signaling that we needed to be in our classrooms.

My eyes darted to my classroom door, wishing I didn't have to enter. I wanted to be impulsive. I wanted to take Connor's hand and ask him to run away with me. To keep running until we put this place far behind us. Instead, I put on my brave face and asked him to give me something else. "Okay. Give me the truth."

He reached into the back pocket of his faded jeans, coming out with a folded-up piece of paper. He pressed it into my hand and I looked down at it. When I lifted my head, he was gone. I watched him sauntering down the hallway like he was in no hurry to get anywhere. Before he turned the corner, he spun around and walked backward, his eyes never leaving my face. Even from a distance, his eyes were mesmerizing, and I took an involuntary step forward as if to close the distance between us. He raised his arm in the air before he disappeared from my sight.

"Are you planning to join us, Miss Christensen?" Mr. Salazar asked, his brows arched as he stood in the doorway, his hand on the doorknob.

I nodded.

"No hats inside the school," he reminded me as I slipped into the classroom. Funny how the school enforced some of their silly policies, yet they let others slide. Reluctantly, I removed my hat as I slid into my seat in the third row, next to my ex-best friend, Holly Chambers. Stupid alphabet, I thought, as I felt her judgment. She continued staring at me as I dug out my notebook, pen, and textbook from my backpack.

"Nice haircut," she said, punctuating it with a snicker.

My gaze snapped to her face. She wrinkled her nose as if she'd just smelled something bad. I gave her the middle finger and took some satisfaction when her dark eyes widened, and her jaw dropped. "What is wrong with you?" she asked, pulling a face. "Oh my God, you're so weird. I don't even know who you are anymore."

I pushed the memories of sleepovers, giggling over cute boy crushes, sharing a tray of brownies while we watched movies, out of my head. Holly had ousted me from our little circle of friends at the beginning of this year. It had been subtle at first. I'd ask her if she wanted to hang out and she'd tell me she was busy with family stuff. Every weekend she had a different excuse. Turned out she was still hanging out with our other friends, meeting up to go shopping or to the movies, having weekend sleepovers I wasn't invited to. I'd gotten to hear about it at the lunch table. One time I'd overheard a conversation where they were trashing me.

"I hear she gives good head. Who knew that perfect little Ava would turn into such a slut?"

"She always acted like she was so much better than us."

Welcome to high school. It was a miracle anyone got out alive.

Ava Christensen, the perfect little princess, was gone. This was the new me. My skin was thicker. I would not be a victim. I was a warrior. I squared my shoulders, repeating the words in my head. If I said them often enough, I would start to believe it. I wouldn't allow a douchebag like Jake Masters to destroy me. He'd taken enough, I wouldn't give him that power.

Mr. Salazar's voice droned on and on about the Cold War. Everything he said came straight from the textbook. No point in taking notes. I looked down at the folded piece of paper I'd set on my notebook then tucked it into my textbook for later. I got the feeling it was something special and opening it now, with Holly sneaking glances at me, would ruin it.

Connor was waiting outside my classroom when I exited, leaning against the wall as if he'd been there for a while. He pushed off from the wall, his gaze settling on my hair. I ran my fingers through the choppy layers.

"What are you doing here?" I asked. "How did you get here?"

"My magic carpet. You need a lift to your next class?"

I laughed, earning a smile from him.

"Hey Connor," Holly said, flashing him a big smile.

He jerked his chin in her direction. "How's it going?"

"Great," she said brightly. "I'm Ava's friend, Holly? We have fourth period English together?"

Friend. Right. I brushed past them and weaved my way through the kids in the hallway. Knowing Holly, she'd tell Connor everything I'd confided in her, back in junior high when we told each other all about our secret crushes.

"You need to point him out to me," she'd said. "If he's as cute as you say..."

"I never see him at school." It hadn't been a lie. I'd catch glimpses of him sometimes in the hallway, but they were fleeting.

She'd pouted. "Well, then we have to make it our mission to find him. Or you need to invite me to church sometime."

"You're Jewish," I reminded her, secretly thrilled about keeping Connor to myself, although I didn't know why.

After that, I'd stopped talking about Connor and Holly had stopped asking about him. I didn't even realize she had a class with him this year.

"Are you trying to get rid of me?" a voice next to me asked, and I caught the teasing tone.

I glanced at Connor. "I just need to get to class. So, you and Holly—" I stopped myself.

"I guess we have a class together." He shrugged one shoulder. "And I'm guessing you're not really friends."

"We used to be. We don't have a lot in common anymore."

"It happens."

"You can't walk me to all my classes, you know."

"Who says?"

"Why are you doing this?" I asked. "Did Killian..." I took a shaky breath. Killian couldn't have known what happened. He'd only caught the part where Jake had tossed me in the dumpster. After Killian had helped me out of the dumpster, I'd run away and hadn't looked back, although I'd heard the sound of Killian's fist slamming into Jake's face. I'd heard Jake's grunts and his words, "You're a fucking maniac. Get your hands—" Killian must have shut him up with another punch.

"Did you look at the paper I gave you?" Connor asked.

"Not yet. I was...saving it for later. This is me," I said, stepping aside to let kids get past.

Connor ran a hand through his dark hair and squinted at the classroom door. "I gotta run. Art class is the only one worth going to. When do you have lunch?"

"Fifth period."

"Same."

"Really? I never saw you at lunch." My eyes widened after I realized what I'd said. He gave me a lopsided grin, a mischievous gleam in his blue eyes. "I mean, not that I ever looked..."

"I usually hang out in the art room. Mr. Santos is cool with it. But I'm kind of flattered that you noticed. Meet you outside the cafeteria."

"You don't have to..."

But he was already gone, and I knew my words were wasted even if he'd hung around to listen to them. He'd be there, waiting for me. Leaning against the wall, his earbuds in his ears, the music blasting, his hand tapping out the beat on his thigh. He'd ignore his guy friends when they gave him shit for hanging out with the weird girl. If they hassled him about it, he'd tell them to fuck off. Connor, I would come to learn, didn't march to the beat of anyone's drum. He set his own rhythm. He was a law unto himself, a free spirit trapped in his own private hell.

Later that night, alone in my room, the hip-hop music in my ears drowning out the voices in my head, I unfolded the thick piece of paper and smoothed my palm over the creases. Unshed tears clogged my throat as I studied the drawing. It was the first of many Connor Vincent masterpieces I'd collected over the years. But this one...would always hold a special place in my heart. Blue-birds soared over the rooftops of Bay Ridge, their color vibrant against the gray, cloudy sky and the washed-out world below.

With a few strokes of a pencil and markers, he'd captured the feeling I got when I was dancing. Freedom. Joy. Flight.

You have magic in your hands, Connor Vincent. How had he seen so much from outside the window of my dance studio? My bedroom door swung open and my mom stood in the doorway. She still hadn't grasped the concept of knocking before entering even though I'd asked her to a million times. I folded the sketch and tucked it back in the textbook, safe from her prying eyes before I pulled out my earbuds.

She lowered herself onto the edge of my bed and let out a heavy sigh as she inspected my hair. "Let me at least tidy it up," she said, resignation in her voice. "I can't let you walk around like that. What would people think?"

"Why do you care what people think?"

"I own a hair salon. This is no time to argue with me, missy. Let's go. In the bathroom."

I followed her into the bathroom where a stool was already set up in front of the mirror. She spritzed my hair with water from a spray bottle and ran the comb through it, her heavy sighs letting me know exactly how she felt. I stared at myself in the mirror. All my life I'd been told by my mom and her friends, from strangers on the street that I was beautiful. Like a porcelain doll with bee-stung lips and gray eyes almost too big for my face. The jagged cut of my hair accentuated my cheekbones, made me look edgier. More like a badass. I liked it.

"Why would you do this?" she asked. "You have such beautiful hair. Girls would kill for this color and it's so nice and thick." I met her brown eyes in the mirror.

I'd tried to tell my mom about Jake back in September. "Oh honey, you're a beautiful girl. Boys do silly things when they have a crush on a girl. Just be nice to him," she'd said.

"That's the price you pay for flaunting it in his face and playing games with him," Lana had said when I'd attempted to confide in her. There had been a time when we'd been close, but that felt like a long time ago.

"I'm not playing any game," I'd insisted, not sure why I was still talking to her. I'd slammed out of her room and our already strained relationship deteriorated further. It had been the dance classes that drove the wedge between us. I'd shown a natural talent, according to Miss Iverson, our instructor and Lana hadn't. For me, dancing had come as easily as breathing. I felt the music in my soul, in every cell of my body.

"Why did you cut your hair, Ava?" my mom asked again, a scowl on her face as her scissors flew through my hair, attempting to make it look nice.

I wanted to tell her, but I knew I never would. I'd never tell anyone. My hand went to my cheekbone, surprised the bruise hadn't been permanent. Surprised that nobody could see the damage. I could still feel the sting, the heat in my cheeks, the gravel digging into the knees of my jeans as I knelt in front of that douchebag on the cold concrete. He'd yanked me to my feet by my hair and tears stung my eyes, but I refused to let him see me cry. I wouldn't give him that satisfaction. My mom was talking, but I wasn't listening to her words.

My thoughts drifted to those bluebirds, to the boy with mesmerizing blue eyes who wore a medal of St. Jude around his neck. "So those dance classes you take...what kind of music is it?" he'd asked over lunch.

"It depends. I take modern dance, jazz, and hip-hop."

"Cool. So you wanna be a dancer?"

I shook my head. "No. I mean, I just like to dance. My mom's always talking about Juilliard, but it's not my dream. I don't want dancing to turn into a competition."

"I get it."

"You do?"

"Yup. You dance for yourself because it makes you happy. You don't wanna be judged."

"Exactly."

We'd talked all the way through lunch, about everything and nothing, and it had been fun. I hadn't laughed or smiled that much in months. Not only that. Talking to him had been so easy and he had the ability to make me feel like I was the only person in the cafeteria. Like everything I said mattered to him.

"What do you think?" my mom asked, dragging me back to the present.

I looked in the mirror at my chin-length bob and mustered a smile for her. "It looks good."

"Don't you dare take the scissors to your hair again. You're still my beautiful girl," she said, her face softening. She planted a kiss on top of my head, her eyes meeting mine in the mirror. "I love you, honey."

"Love you too." I wished she'd find a different adjective for me than beautiful.

"Why don't you invite Holly for a sleepover this weekend?" she asked, her voice overly bright. "You girls always have so much fun together."

"Yeah, sure," I said, knowing it would never happen but she smiled, pleased with my answer.

4

CONNOR

I had a routine, something that had been lacking in my life before, but I strictly adhered to it now. At seven a.m. on Monday morning, my phone alarm chimed. I hauled my ass out of bed, dressed in jeans and a T-shirt, and ate fresh fruit, Greek yogurt, and granola. After guzzling a bottle of water, I refilled it from the tap and grabbed my backpack, already packed with my gym clothes.

You'd never know I was a millionaire. My one-bedroom apartment in Greenpoint looked like a college dorm room. My mattress and box spring sat on the floor in my bedroom, next to a crate that acted as a bedside table. In the living room, a worn plaid sofa sat across from a flat-screen TV flanked by battered wood bookcases heaving with well-loved books. A sound system, speakers, and crates stuffed with sketchbooks and art supplies, rounded out the décor. Despite the shabbiness of my apartment, everything was neat, tidy, and clean. I should take pride in that, applaud myself for turning a new leaf.

Rising early and keeping my life organized were two of those baby steps I'd taken. Yeah, I was going places, I thought, as I headed out the door, and strode two blocks to the motorcycle garage where I parked my Harley. I put over three hundred miles on my bike yesterday. I rode up to the Hawk's Nest Highway and got my adrenaline rush from shooting through the curves and taking the crazy hairpin turns. The winding road hugs the rock face, and the views of the mountains, river, and valleys gave me a natural high. Always a good thing.

At 7:55, Tate and I entered the church basement for our weekly NA meeting. Tate was in his mid-forties but looked older, with a craggy face and graying brown hair he wore long and pulled back in an elastic. Lean and wiry, he was a good five inches shorter than me, but he was tough as they came. Back in the day, he was in a motorcycle club and served time for armed robbery. His heroin addiction had started in prison. With seven years of sobriety under his belt, I was the first person he'd ever sponsored, and he was the only sponsor I'd never tried to bullshit.

We walked past the table laden with donuts and a vat of coffee and took our seats on folding metal chairs.

"Christ, it's hot in here," Tate grumbled like he did every week. Even at this early hour, the air was suffocating and smelled like mildew. The fans in the corners of the windowless room sounded like helicopter propellers but did jack shit to cool it down.

I sat back in my chair and tapped out the beat of the song playing in my head—Bob Marley's "Redemption Song"—on my thigh. My theme song for today's meeting. *You said it, Bob, mental slavery is a bitch. Emancipate yourself, brother.*

During the meeting, Tate used a toothpick to clean the motor oil and grime out from under his fingernails. He was a mechanic and owned a garage, and the grease gathered in the cracks of his hands that never looked clean. As we sat in the stifling heat of the church basement, I half-listened to people's addiction stories. I rarely shared my own story at the meetings. I was tired of rehashing the events and personal issues that had led me to this point in my life. These meetings were more of an accountability thing for me, an hour and a half in my weekly schedule that reminded me I was like everyone else gathered in this room.

My name is Connor, and I'm an addict. I admitted that I was powerless over my addiction, and my life had become unmanageable.

38

Fun times.

I hadn't done drugs in eighteen months. Technically, I'd been clean for that long. But a year ago, my doctor prescribed opioids after the operation to repair my broken jaw with titanium plates and screws. Why he'd given opioids to an addict was anyone's guess. Ava doled out the Vicodin as per the instructions on the bottle. She kept the pills locked in a drawer at Trinity Bar and counted them every single time to make sure I hadn't broken in and stolen them. That was what we'd been reduced to. She'd become my keeper, the trust so fractured that she needed to count fucking pills to make sure I didn't relapse. She couldn't even look at me without crying. And I couldn't look at her without remembering all the shit I'd put her through over the years.

Sobriety was a bitch. It forced you to take a moral inventory and look at everything more clearly.

I tried to focus on the meeting, but my thoughts wandered to the memory of Ava kissing Zeke. Son of a bitch. He'd wanted me to see that he'd staked his claim. Why had I gone into the bar Zeke co-owned, the bar where Ava worked, asking for his help? Fucking masochist. Ava and Zeke had come in the door laughing like they didn't have a care in the world. Which they didn't. Without me, Ava's life was better. Easier. Happier. The minute she saw me, she'd stopped laughing. When was the last time I made her happy?

I pictured us at eighteen, the summer Killian and I had moved to Park Slope. We'd rented a brownstone apartment across from Prospect Park, nicer than any place we'd ever lived before. Ava was lying on my bed, naked, her long white-blonde hair falling around her shoulders. Her creamy skin and that tiny, perfect body on full display. She propped her head on her hand and licked her cherry-red lips, her gray eyes heavy-lidded with a desire that matched my own. Muse's "Hysteria" blasted from my speakers, and the early-evening sunlight filtered through the open windows, making her porcelain skin glow.

Ice on fire, that was Ava.

"You can't sit around half-naked and expect me not to be tempted," she said. "I want you now."

I want you all the time. "Not done yet, Ava Blue," I said as I sketched her naked body, the curve of her hip, her flat stomach, round breasts with rose-tinted nipples that begged to be worshiped by my mouth, my tongue, my teeth.

She pouted, but I caught the wicked gleam in her eye before her eyelids closed and she slid her hand between her legs. "Guess I'll have to take care of myself then."

I tossed my sketchbook on the floor and stalked over to the bed.

"Oh, you want to join me now?" she asked as I pushed down my shorts.

I crawled up the bed, and she spread her legs for me, knowing I'd take care of her first. We'd learned everything together—how to play each other's bodies, how to prolong the pleasure until we were blinded by our need.

When I was buried deep inside Ava, her body wrapped around mine, I didn't think about the Oxy hidden in my closet. Or how I'd get more pills when my supply ran low. Ava didn't know about it. Neither did Killian. Not yet. I was still in denial, telling myself I wasn't an addict, and I could quit anytime. It was a slippery slope and I lost my grip on it a year later when I smoked heroin for the first time. It didn't take long before I was hooked and started shooting up. My relationship with Ava ended, and we'd never been able to get back what was lost.

Ava was my true love, but heroin had been my mistress. Tempting, forbidden, and demanding. More. More. More.

But that day, when we were eighteen, the possibility of what we could be seemed infinite.

"I see the way girls look at you. Are you ever tempted?" she asked me later, her head resting on my chest, her leg slung across my waist.

"Never," I said, running my hand up her calf. "You're the only girl for me."

"I want to be your forever girl."

"You're my everything girl."

"When I graduate from college, we'll get our own place. Just you and me."

"We can go anywhere. Where do you want to live?"

"California. Or anywhere. It doesn't matter." She placed her hand over my heart. "Your heart is racing."

"Because of you." It was the truth, but it was also a lie. Oxy made my heart race, too.

"Good answer."

"Do I win a prize?" I teased.

"You already did. I'm the prize." Her fingers tap-danced across my chest to the beat of the music. "I'll miss you when I'm gone."

"You're only going to Queens, babe, not the other side of the country."

"I know. But still. Dorm life, ugh."

Her parents wanted her to live in the dorms at St. John's University to get the full college experience. If it had been up to her mother, Ava would have been sent to another country, as far away from me as possible but my girl knew her own mind so Queens it was. "We'll spend our weekends together and I'll visit you so often you'll get sick of me."

"I'll never get sick of you," she said. "Not even when we're old and gray."

In that moment, we were whole, and we were perfect.

When the meeting ended, Tate and I escaped the heat of the church basement and exited through the side door into the outside air that was ten degrees cooler. We stood by our parked Harleys, taking deep breaths of fresh air. Or as fresh as it got in Brooklyn.

"You get anything out of that?" Tate asked.

"Does tripping down memory lane count?"

He crossed his arms and tilted his head, his brow furrowed as if he was giving it serious thought. "It counts that you showed up." Tate scratched his head. "Been thinking about what you told me the other night. About buying the shop. What's holding you back?"

"I don't want to fuck it up."

41

"Ain't happening. The business is established so you're not starting from scratch. You already manage the shop when Jared's out. You work what ... fifty hours a week?"

"About that." Probably more. I stayed after-hours to clean or do whatever I could to help Jared out. I owed him that, and more. For the past six years, my job had been the only constant in my life, and the only thing I hadn't screwed up. Jared deserved the credit more than I did. Junkies didn't make the most reliable employees, but even after disappearing for months, leaving him in the lurch, he'd taken me back, no questions asked. And I was grateful for that.

"You might need to rack up more hours, do the accounting, and keep on top of all the paperwork. Nobody wants to mess with the IRS. But you've got it covered. You know what you're doing."

"As a tattoo artist, yeah. But the rest of it..." I didn't have a fucking clue.

"If an old dog like me can learn new tricks, a young pup like you should have no problem."

With that, he straddled his bike, strapped on his helmet, and took off down the street.

Ten minutes later, I walked into Killian's gym where his women's self-defense class was in full swing. Back in January, Eden and Ava had taken Killian's co-ed Krav Maga classes, and I was told they'd kicked ass. I smiled at the thought of tiny Ava taking down a guy twice her size.

"Can I get a volunteer?" Killian asked the women standing in front of him. Every hand shot into the air. He beckoned with his hand and Mitch, the weekend bouncer at Trinity Bar and one of Killian's instructors at the gym, trotted over and stood by Killian's side. The women's faces fell when they saw they'd be dealing with Mitch and not Killian. Mitch had a face like a bulldog and was built like a tank.

I chuckled to myself on the way to the locker room.

After putting in two hours in the weight room, I hit the shower. It was the first time I'd worked out since I'd gotten the tattoo, and when I stripped off my clothes, I didn't feel like I needed to hide my chest from any of the guys coming in and out of the locker room. I could shower without shame. Progress.

Showered and dressed, I sat on the bench to put on my boots. My cell phone rang in my backpack and I slid it out, checking the screen before I answered. Jared.

"What's up?" I asked.

"Zeke's here. Says you're supposed to meet."

Fuck no. "Tell him I don't need his help."

"You tell him."

Two seconds later, I heard Zeke's voice on the line. I pinched the bridge of my nose and tried not to lose my shit. "Forget it. I've got this."

"We can talk while you give me a tattoo."

"I'm not giving you a tattoo."

"Yeah, you are. Jared booked me in for twelve-thirty."

"The shop doesn't open until one. I'm fully booked today." Why was I debating this with him? "I'll be there in ten minutes." I cut the call, slung my bag over my shoulder, and stalked out of the locker room. Killian was filling up his water bottle at the cooler and turned to me, screwing on the cap.

"You okay?" he asked.

It was a loaded question. Define okay. "Zeke wants me to give him a tattoo."

Killian's brows rose. "Really?"

I laughed under my breath. "Yeah. Really."

"Huh. You talked to him?"

"Briefly," I said, leaving it at that.

While I was working out, I'd made my decision. I was going to buy the shop and I was going to make a success of it. As for Ava, I needed to find a way to let go and move on just like she had. Unfortunately, I had no idea how to do that.

～✽～

"I DON'T DO YOLO TATTOOS," I informed Zeke as I walked in the door and saw him sitting on the black leather sofa in the waiting area. Jared chuckled, sharing my disdain for YOLO tattoos, and turned on the sound system. Fall Out Boy's "Sugar, We're Goin' Down" blasted from the speakers. Nothing like a little emo to start the workday.

"Then it's a good thing I don't want a YOLO tattoo," Zeke said. "I want a nautical star compass. Right here." He placed his hand on the middle of his chest.

"I don't have that kind of time."

"Yeah, you do," he said with a big smile. I was tempted to punch his teeth in. Instead, I pinched the bridge of my nose, took deep breaths, and counted to ten, a relaxation trick I'd learned in rehab.

I checked the appointment schedule on the computer for verification—my one o'clock had been deleted. Goddammit.

"I'll take care of that one," Jared said. What kind of voodoo had Zeke performed to get his way? In the past, Zeke and I had been casual acquaintances and I'd never had a problem with him. Now I did. And I sure as hell didn't want to spend up-close and personal time with the guy screwing my ex-girlfriend. "He filled out his paperwork," Jared said.

"I thought you were taking the day off," I said.

Jared shrugged. "Change of plan. I told him you were the best."

"Now you're blowing smoke up my ass? What's the world coming to?"

"San Diego here I come."

I shook my head. Wherever you go, there you are. If he thought new scenery and good weather could change everything, he was setting himself up for disappointment. "You should give this more thought."

"And you should get the hell out of my face and get to work," Jared said. "I've made my decision. I'm still waiting for yours."

"Let's get this over with," I said, motioning for Zeke to follow me to my station. Zeke laughed like I'd just told him a good joke.

Per my instructions, Zeke stripped off his T-shirt, and I stared at his smooth chest. Fuck, it was perfect, unmarred by scars. I hated him for it. Hated the thought of Ava running her hands over it, resting her head on it. Fuck, fuck, fuck. I needed to lock it down and stop thinking.

I snapped photos, took measurements, and prepared the transfer—flash art. Normally, I prided myself on my original designs, but this time I didn't give a shit.

Jared taught me the art of tattooing when I was eighteen. The summer I graduated from high school, I came in with the portfolio that had gotten me into Pratt Institute. Jared took me on as an apprentice, and I never ended up going to art school. The scholarship they'd offered me wouldn't even put a dent in the tuition, and I didn't want to be saddled with student loans or let Killian pay my way like he'd offered. Lack of funds wasn't the only reason I'd ditched art school though. I loved bringing my art to life on a human canvas. And, for the most part, I enjoyed interacting with the customers. Listening to their stories. Watching their faces when they looked at their new tattoo for the first time. And knowing that my design would be inked on their skin forever.

After I prepped Zeke's skin and applied the transfer, I warned him that it hurt, and ink was permanent, something I told all my clients. Since homicide wasn't an option, I opted for a professional approach. The sooner he got in and out, the better. "You still want it?" I asked, hoping he'd change his mind and scurry the hell out the door.

He settled back in the reclined chair. "I wouldn't be here if I didn't." Despite his words, his whole body tensed, and I could tell he was holding his breath.

"Take a slow, deep breath and relax."

I waited until he did as I told him, but he still looked nervous as hell. Why should I care? "The first minute is the worst. You'll get used to it."

He nodded. "Thanks."

I started the linework. He winced, but he stayed still so I continued.

I'd hoped we could do this in silence, so I could block out everything and concentrate on the tattoo, not the person sitting in the chair. Or everything this person had come to represent—a fresh start for Ava. She'd been with other guys since me, just like I'd been with other girls, but I'd never met any of the guys she'd hooked up with, and none of them had lasted long. It had been the same for me over the years, and I sometimes wondered why I bothered when I knew that nobody would ever come close to her.

"Ava and I ended it," Zeke said.

I didn't react, but I wanted to know if Ava ended it or Zeke ended it. Why should it matter? Just because she wasn't with Zeke didn't mean she wanted to be with me.

"She's still in love with you," he said.

I finished outlining the design and lifted the tattoo needle from his chest. "Another word about Ava and you'll need to find a different tattoo artist."

"Just putting it out there."

I switched needles and got back to work, shading and coloring. He kept his mouth shut, but the silence didn't last.

"My older brother Alex taught me how to sail," he said. "That's why I went for the compass. It's symbolic, you know? Trying to find direction in your life ... some people have a harder time than others. I don't know. Maybe it's just that everyone's wired differently. Alex had everything. My family is loaded, my parents are good people. We grew up wanting for nothing. He went to Harvard, and maybe the pressure got to him or something. Nobody noticed that he'd developed an opiate addiction. Until he overdosed and ended up in the ER."

"Why are you telling me this?"

"Just making conversation."

Bullshit. "What did Ava tell you?"

"Nothing. She never talked about you." I believed him. Ava had always kept my dirty secrets to herself. Zeke lowered his voice, so he wasn't overheard over the buzzing needles and music. "Last year, I found your prescription in the desk drawer. I saw you after you'd been beaten up and I knew that had to hurt like hell. And yet, Ava was keeping your meds under lock and key. It didn't take a rocket scientist to figure out why."

Anger and shame burned inside me. I hated that Zeke could be so smug, so superior, armed with the knowledge that I needed my ex-girlfriend to monitor my pain medication. "Congratulations. You're a fucking genius."

"Hey, I'm not judging you. I get how hard it is. I watched Alex go through hell. He relapsed twice. But he's in a good place now."

A good place. That's what we all strive for, isn't it?

"So, listen, about the business..." he said a few minutes later. "I talked to Jared earlier..."

"Forget it."

"I'm on your side. I want to help if I can. Why do you and Killian make it so difficult?"

"Must be the way we're wired."

"He came around. Eventually."

If Zeke had gone for Eden, hell would have frozen over before Killian came around. Of all the girls Zeke could have had, why did he need to go for Ava? Why did *she* go for him?

I needed to win her back. I would show her that my life was on track and that I'd changed. I wasn't hell-bent on self-destruction, and I wasn't running from anything. I was standing my ground and weathering the storm.

This time, I wouldn't be careless with Ava. Everything could be different. I would find a way to make her fall in love with me all over again.

5

CONNOR

EIGHT YEARS AGO

*A*va raised her arms in the air and did a victory dance before she jumped into my arms and cinched her legs around my waist, the arcade lights flashing behind her. "You're my hero."

She took my Yankees cap off my head and put it backward on her own head before she cupped my face in her hands and pressed her lips against mine. I ran my tongue along the seam of her lips, tasting the salt from the ocean. Her lips parted, and our tongues swirled together. She tasted like the cherry Italian ice she'd eaten earlier. Her arms circled my neck and my hands cupped her perfect ass in tiny denim cut-offs. Her tits pressed against my chest as her legs tightened around me. Jesus.

"Yo. You two. Enough with the PDA. Pick your prize and get outta here."

I released Ava and we both laughed as I set her on her feet and tried to catch my breath. Her cheeks were pink from the sun we'd caught earlier, her white-blonde hair tangled from the seawater. We'd come unprepared, winging it without a brush or towels, instead letting the sun dry our skin. Her gaze dipped to my board shorts that did nothing to hide my hard-on. She turned her back to me and leaned against my chest, her ass pressed against my dick which didn't help matters. I watched her fingers, the nails painted

48

indigo blue, adjust the strap of her red bikini top that had slipped down her shoulder. Red was my new favorite color, I'd decided earlier when she'd tossed her skull-print tank top and shorts onto the sand then raced me to the water, my longer legs easily overtaking her. I'd scooped her up, thrown her over my shoulder and waded into the water with her laughing and pounding my back with her fists.

I wrapped my arms around her as she surveyed the prizes on offer before finally choosing a stuffed Hello Kitty.

Next to us, a little girl with blonde pigtails watched us with interest. "I love Hello Kitty," she said, her mouth forming a pout. She crossed her arms and glared at the man next to her. "Daddy, can't you just try again?" She held up her index finger. "One more. Pretty please."

"It's already cost me an arm and a leg. This place is rigged."

Ava turned in my arms and gave me a little smile, her eyes asking a question I understood without her having to say the words. "Go for it."

Ava knelt in front of the girl and held out the Hello Kitty. "You know what? I think Hello Kitty would rather go home with you."

The girl's eyes widened. "You do?"

"Yeah, I do," Ava said. "Just promise me one thing."

"Okay."

"Give her lots of cuddles and make her feel special."

The girl nodded, her pigtails bouncing up and down.

"We can't accept that," the man said, shooting me a look.

"Sure you can," I said. "My girlfriend wants your daughter to have it. And I want whatever makes my girlfriend happy." Damn, I was whipped, but I didn't give a shit. I was crazy about this girl and I'd do just about anything to make her happy.

Ava smiled up at me and I wrapped an arm around her shoulder as we walked down the boardwalk, scented with hot dogs and French fries. The air was hot and muggy, heavy, like it was holding its breath and waiting for something. Or maybe that was just me. "You never called me your girlfriend before."

"You okay with that title?" I asked.

She leaned into my side and wrapped her arm around my waist. I'd take that as a yes. "This is the best first date I've ever been on."

I laughed. "Compared to what? All your other first dates?"

Ava laughed. "Good point. But even if I'd been on hundreds, this would still be the best."

"We haven't gotten to the main event yet," I said, guiding her toward the Comet. Ava loved roller coasters which was why I'd brought her to Coney Island today. That and the chance to see her in a bikini.

"You're the main event," she said.

"You're really laying it on thick tonight," I teased. But I loved it. I loved that she thought I was someone special. Someone worthy. I loved the way we could talk for hours about everything and nothing and never get bored with each other. I loved the way we could be silent. Our silence was never empty or awkward and neither of us felt the need to rush in and fill it up. With Ava, I felt like I was enough.

"How many hours of stocking shelves did that Hello Kitty cost you?" she asked as we lined up for the ride.

Five hours. But I didn't give a shit about the money. I was just happy to spend some time with her. We'd only crossed the line of friendship into something more a month ago, on her sixteenth birthday when we'd kissed for the first time. Since then, it had been difficult finding time alone together. Her mother didn't approve of me.

"She quit her dance classes because of you," she'd accused me.

"Ava quit because it didn't make her happy anymore," I'd countered. What I'd left out was that her mother's constant pushing had taken the joy right out of it for Ava.

"Ever since she met you, she's changed. Ava used to be reasonable. She used to...talk to me." Her mom flapped her hands in the air. "Now she thinks she can do whatever she wants. And I know it's your influence."

I grabbed Ava's hand and gave it a squeeze as the line moved forward. We got lucky and were the last two to make the cut. We climbed into our seats, the safety bar came down and soon we were off and picking up speed. Ava raised her arms in the air and screamed bloody murder throughout the entire ride. I watched her face and saw the joy she used to get from dancing. As soon as the roller coaster ground to a halt, the safety bar rising, she grabbed the back of my head and tugged me closer, planting a kiss on my lips.

We rode the coaster three more times, our kisses growing more frantic, our laughter and her screams getting louder before we took the subway back to Bay Ridge. On the train, we shared earbuds, one for her and one for me. We listened to the British playlist on my iPod. The Rolling Stones, The Smiths, Led Zeppelin, The Verve, Oasis.

"Let's go to your place," she said, checking the time on her phone. "I still have time before my curfew."

"You sure?" I asked as the train screeched to a halt at my station.

"Positive," she said, grabbing my hand. "We just need to hurry."

As we exited the station, thunder rumbled, and lightning flashed across the sky. "I love summer storms," she said, her face lit up.

So did I. "The wrath of Zeus."

"You're so smart."

I snorted. I wasn't all that smart. But I'd gotten onto a Greek mythology kick last year. My favorite story was Odysseus, and I'd told it to Ava a few months ago, about how he'd come up with a cunning plan to get the Greek army inside the walls of Troy by hollowing out a wooden horse to hide the Greek warriors. After winning the war, Odysseus set sail for home. It took him ten long years to reach his home in Ithaca. Along the way, he passed through dangers and temptations, fought with gods and monsters, the sea, and magicians and men. No matter what difficulty was thrown at him, Odysseus battled through it all and never gave up.

The first drop of rain landed on my nose. We'd only walked half a block when the skies opened and unleashed the rain. Ava spread her arms and turned in a circle, her face tipped up to the sky.

"Come on, crazy girl. I'll give you a ride." I crouched, and she hopped onto my back, holding her flip-flops in her hand. She nuzzled my neck as I jogged the three blocks to the apartment I shared with Killian above a deli.

By the time we got inside, our clothes were stuck to our bodies and Ava's hair was dripping onto the uneven parquet floor. I kicked off my Nikes and retreated into the bathroom. I peeled off my wet T-shirt and hung it on the shower rail then grabbed a dry towel for Ava. When I returned to the living room, Ava had stripped down to her bikini. The tiny pieces of fabric left something to the imagination but not much. I swallowed hard as I handed her the towel. She thanked me and wrapped it around her shoulders as I picked up her wet clothes and hung them on the wooden chairs at the kitchen table to dry.

"I'm just...I'm going to change into dry shorts," I said. Now that we were up here, alone in the apartment, I didn't know what to do with myself. She'd been here before, a few times after school, but we'd just hung out on the sofa and watched TV or did homework together. But she hadn't been here since our first kiss and she certainly hadn't been in a tiny bikini.

Fuck.

I went into my bedroom, a box room barely big enough to fit my double bed, just a mattress and box spring, and a beat-up dresser Killian and I had bought at the Goodwill. I changed into basketball shorts and hung my board shorts on the radiator. A flash of lightning illuminated my room and I heard her footsteps behind me, the floor creaking under her weight.

"Can I borrow a T-shirt? Just until my stuff dries."

"Yeah. Sure." I handed her a Rolling Stones T-shirt from my drawer and she slipped it over her head. It reached mid-thigh.

She ran her tongue over her lower lip, her eyes trained on my bare chest. Then she lifted her eyes to mine and took a step closer. I cradled her face in my hands and her arms wrapped around my neck. I closed my eyes and kissed her and while the summer storm raged on outside, I felt at peace in a way I only felt when I was with Ava. Our hands explored each other's bodies, her skin so soft and her kisses so sweet, my Rolling Stones T-shirt tossed to the floor as we fell onto my bed. She hooked a leg around my waist, pulling me closer and I rolled onto my back, bringing her down on top of me. Ava put her palms on my chest and sat up, her legs straddling me as she ground her body against me. I gripped her hips and guided her movements. I'd never been harder in my life.

"Oh," she said, her eyes closing and her lips parting. "Oh God."

Jesus Christ. This was the sweetest form of torture, watching Ava get off. Her legs trembled and she rode me harder, grinding her body against my erection, her short fingernails digging into my shoulders. "Connor," she cried as the orgasm ripped through her, her lips parted on a gasp, her eyes closed as she rode it out. She collapsed on top of me, boneless, her head resting on my shoulder, her soft breath on my neck. I wrapped my arms around her and tangled my hand in her wet hair, my dick so hard it was painful. She lifted her head and kissed me.

"Show me what to do," she whispered.

Something about the way she said it and the way she looked... like she was nervous, made me hesitate. "You don't need to do anything."

"I want to make you feel as good as you made me feel."

I chuckled. "I didn't do anything. I was just laying here."

"Then show me what you do to yourself. I want to watch."

"You want to watch me jerk off?"

"Yes," she said without hesitation. She rolled off me and lay on her side, her head propped on her hand, her eyes trained on the bulge in my shorts.

It wouldn't take long. I pushed down my shorts and wrapped my hand around my dick.

I woke with a start and blinked into the darkness. Ava's warm body was curled up against mine, her breathing deep and even. Instinctively, my arm around her tightened as the pounding on the door grew louder and more insistent. "Open the door," Seamus growled from the other side.

Fuck. I leaped out of bed and grabbed Ava's clothes from the chairs, still damp, but they'd have to do. She sat up in bed, rubbing her eyes.

"What's going on?"

My father was outside our door, pounding on it, and there would be hell to pay. "I need you to get dressed and stay in the bedroom. Understand? I'll get rid of him and then I'll take you home, okay?"

"But why—"

Her eyes widened as she checked the time on her phone. "Oh my God, Connor. It's two in the morning. My mom is going to kill me. Five missed calls." She fiddled with her phone. "The ringtone was on mute. Oh my God. I'm dead."

"I'll take care of everything. Promise. Just stay here," I said, closing the bedroom door behind me.

I didn't have time to explain. For all the talking we did and all my honesty, I'd kept Seamus' dirty secrets. And for some reason, Ava had never questioned why I was living with Killian and not at home.

I opened the door and faced the man who had raised me. Solid muscle with wide shoulders and slicked-back dark hair. His face was an alarming shade of red, jaw clenched, the muscle in his cheek jumping. It took me all of two seconds to assess the situation. His sweat smelled like a distillery. He'd been drinking, and this wouldn't have a pretty ending.

"What do you think you're doing, boy?" he asked, his voice low and steely, cutting right through me. Seamus Vincent never shouted when he was angry. "Marie Christensen called me. She says her daughter's with you. Was meant to be home hours ago. That right?"

There was no point in lying. The outcome would be the same no matter what I said. "I'm taking her home now."

"She's coming with me. I said I'd drive her home."

"You're not driving her anywhere. You reek of whiskey."

"What did you say?"

"You're. Not. Driving. Ava. Anywhere."

He stared at me and I stood my ground, steeling myself for the impact of his punches. "Your job is the only thing you've got left. You want to jeopardize that? Fine. But you're not putting my girlfriend's life in danger."

Seamus' fist slammed into my face. My head snapped back, and I heard Ava scream.

"Watch your mouth, boy. Remember who you're talking to."

"I don't give a shit if you're the Pope. My girlfriend's not getting in a car with you, old man."

Seamus slammed me against the wall, pinned me down with his arm pressed against my throat and punched me in the stomach, knocking all the air out of my lungs. Little black dots floated in front of my eyes and I couldn't breathe. I barely felt the next punch.

"Leave him alone," Ava screamed, grabbing Seamus' arm and yanking on it. He looked down at her, confused, and loosened his hold on me. It was enough to give me an advantage. I shoved him as hard as I could, catching him off guard and he stumbled backward, crashing into the side of the sofa.

"You little shit," he said, his eyes narrowed as he came at me again.

"What the fuck are you doing?" Killian roared as he came in the door. He grabbed Seamus by the shoulders and pinned him to the wall, getting right into his face.

"Get your hands off me," Seamus said, shoving him away. It was over. For now.

"I need to get Ava home. He's too drunk to drive." I stuffed my feet in my Nikes, grabbed my keys from the coffee table and took Ava's hand, leading her out of the apartment and down the stairs.

"Connor." Her eyes filled with tears and her whole body was shaking.

"It'll be okay," I said, leading her down the sidewalk toward the subway station. Two stops on the R train and a four-block walk from the station to her house. We'd be there in twenty minutes. "Everything is okay."

"Hold up," Killian called after us.

I looked over my shoulder at Killian who held up a set of keys. "I'll drive you. It's faster."

Ava and I climbed into the backseat of Seamus' SUV. He was in the passenger seat and I didn't need to look at his face to know he was furious. Or that we'd pay for this little stunt. He'd humiliated himself, and there would be a price to pay. Seamus usually managed to control himself in public and mete out the punishment behind closed doors. This time he'd crossed over a line by allowing someone to witness his outburst. Not just someone. Ava.

"Text your mom," I said in a low voice. "Let her know you're on your way."

She took her phone out of her pocket with shaky hands and texted, exhaling as she hit send.

None of us spoke as Killian drove through the streets of Bay Ridge.

"I'll drop off your car tomorrow," Killian said as he pulled up in front of the two-story house we'd grown up in. Seamus grunted, knowing he'd been beaten, and slammed the door behind him as he left.

Five minutes later, Killian pulled up in front of Ava's house. The porch light was on and Ava stared out the window, making no move to leave. "Come on, babe. Everything will be okay."

"It's not me I'm worried about," she said quietly, resting her palm on my cheekbone. "Connor..." Her eyes filled with tears again. I couldn't bear to see her cry.

"Don't worry about me." I reached over her and pushed the car door open. She climbed out of the SUV, turning to close the door but I wasn't about to let her face this on her own.

"Be right back," I told Killian.

"You should go," Ava said, her voice hushed as I walked next to her. "I don't want you to get in more trouble. I can handle this. It's no big deal."

I gave her hand a little squeeze as the front door opened and Ava's parents stood in the doorway. Her mother stepped onto the front stoop and planted her hands on her hips.

"Where have you been, young lady? Do you know what time it is? You didn't even answer your phone."

"I just...lost track of time..."

"I had to call Seamus." She shot me a look. "Like your poor father doesn't have enough to deal with. His job is stressful enough without you—"

Ava's hands clenched into fists at her sides. "Seamus—"

"Drove us over here," I said. A quick glance over my shoulder confirmed that the tinted windows and darkness hid the identity of who was behind the wheel of my father's SUV. "It was my fault. All of it. I dragged Ava to a party. She was ready to leave but I wasn't." I shrugged like I didn't give a shit. Her mom's eyes narrowed into slits.

"Have you been drinking?"

"I had a few too many. Ava didn't touch a drop of alcohol."

"Connor doesn't drink," Ava said.

"Babe, you don't have to cover for me." I rubbed the back of my neck. "So yeah...my father insisted I own up and apologize because it's the right thing to do."

"Connor, why are you—"

"It's all on me," I told her mother. "Go easy on her. She tried to do the right thing, but I got carried away." I gave her mom a mock salute and walked away.

"Connor. Wait," Ava called after me. I kept walking without turning around.

"Get in this house right now, young lady," her mom said as I yanked open the passenger door.

"Connor. Wait." Ava put her hand on my arm and I turned to look at her.

"I love you, Connor. I...it feels like I've loved you forever. I don't know. Maybe I have. In another life or something..." She shook her head and laughed a little. "That sounded crazy. But I just wanted you to know. You are loved."

With a little smile, Ava turned and walked away while I stood by the SUV, dumbfounded.

I climbed into the passenger seat and fastened my seatbelt,

watching Ava's house through the window as Killian pulled away from the curb, her words echoing in my head. *You are loved.*

Killian didn't say a word until we'd gotten back to the apartment. "You should have put some ice on it earlier," he said, emptying an ice tray into a kitchen towel.

"Thanks," I said, collapsing on the sofa, pressing the ice against my cheekbone.

"You okay?"

"Yeah," I said, even though my head was throbbing and every breath I took made my ribs scream in protest.

He leaned against the wall, arms crossed. "If you want to keep living with me, you need to be more responsible."

"I know. I will. We fell asleep," I said, leaving out the part that came before it. "Her mom called Seamus. She thinks I still live there."

Killian let out a weary sigh. "Fuck. And Ava saw him hit you."

"Yeah."

"I can't be here to watch over you. I'm not home enough—"

"I don't need a babysitter. It's cool. I'm good."

"You're on your own too much," he said, and I could hear the guilt in his voice. "I'll try and be home more."

Killian spent six hours a day training and nights bartending to chase his dreams and keep a roof over our heads, and I was so damned grateful to have him in my corner that I would have walked over hot coals for him. The last thing I wanted was to jeopardize his dreams. "You don't need to worry about me. You need to go for your dreams. It's going to happen for you. The UFC...the money... all of it. You'll get everything you're working for and it'll be worth it. You're going to be a champion of the Octagon. Someday they'll be chanting your name."

He opened his mouth as if to say something then he shut it and rubbed the back of his neck, uncomfortable with the praise I was heaping on him. "You're so full of shit." He shook his head and chuckled.

"I'm speaking the truth." I wasn't bullshitting him. Killian had the discipline, the talent, and the drive to become a champion.

Not to mention that MMA was his passion. I had no doubt he'd go all the way. I dumped the ice in the sink and returned to the living room. Killian was sorting through a stack of utility bills on the coffee table. We were strapped for cash and the memory of the money I'd blown today made me wince. Not to mention that I'd bought myself a new sketchbook and pencils a few days ago.

"I'll ask for some extra hours...help you out with the bills."

Killian shook his head. "You need to save your money for the future. When you're a famous artist, you can pay me back." I laughed at that one. "You need to cool it with Ava."

"She loves me," I said, still marveling at those words. I'd never heard them before. Not from anyone.

"Yeah, I heard," Killian said. I waited for him to say more but he pointed the remote at the TV and flicked through the channels. Most likely, he'd fall asleep on the sofa to the white noise of the TV like he did most nights.

I shut the bedroom door behind me, stripped down to my boxer briefs and lay on my bed, the scent of Ava lingering on my pillow. I buried my nose in it and inhaled deeply. It smelled like flowers and rain and the sea. It smelled like heaven.

6

AVA

I jogged down the stairs of my fourth-floor walk-up and emerged from my building into a crisp fall morning and a cloudless blue sky. Perfect Brooklyn weather. As I strolled down Bedford Avenue, I pushed all thoughts of Connor out of my head. By the time I'd reached Brickwood Coffee, I'd almost convinced myself that letting him go was the best thing I'd ever done.

The bell above the door chimed as I entered the rustic wood coffee shop and inhaled the nutty aroma of freshly brewed coffee. I loved the smell of coffee but had never acquired a taste for it. I scanned the shop for Eden—since it was small, it only took a few seconds to realize she wasn't here yet. My gaze settled on the guy at the counter and my heart stuttered as his eyes locked on mine, his steps carrying him closer. Turning to go, I gripped the door handle. His hand wrapped around my upper arm to stop me.

"Wait. Don't go," he said in his husky voice. Raspy. Sexy. The kind of voice you wanted to listen to in the dark. My knees still went weak at the sound of it.

He released my arm as I stepped away from the door to let a customer out. "Connor—"

"I ordered you a chai latte."

"Eden's not coming, is she?"

"No."

Even though it wasn't funny, I laughed. I'd done the same thing to Eden over a year ago, attempting to get her and Killian together. It had worked, but they didn't have a complicated history.

"Hey, I'm Connor Vincent," he said.

I turned and lifted my eyes to his, my brow furrowed. "What?"

"Let's pretend this is the first time we met."

I shook my head. "Life doesn't work that way."

"I know. But we can try. Get to know each other with no past ... no bad memories."

Memories couldn't be erased, not the bad or the good. Unfortunately, I remembered them all. Did Connor? I doubted it. He was too busy chasing his next high. "How does that work?"

"We'll start over. I do it every day. One minute, one hour, one day at a time. Baby steps, Ava."

His tone was deceptively light. I knew it couldn't be easy, not for him, and not for us. "I hate you, remember?" But even as I said it, I could hear that my voice lacked conviction.

"We just met, and you already hate me?" he teased.

I rolled my eyes. He gave me a smile that melted the ice around my heart. I loved that dimple in his right cheek and the twinkle in his blue eyes. "Hey, I'm Ava Christensen." *And I'm a fool for going along with this plan.*

His smile grew wider. "Nice to meet you, Ava. Can I buy you a drink?"

I laughed under my breath. This was ridiculous. "I'll have a chai latte."

"I'll bring it to the table."

I nodded, and somehow my feet carried me to a table. I sat with my back to the window and watched Connor walk toward me with two cardboard cups in his hands. Clean-shaven, wearing a blue T-shirt, faded jeans slung low on his narrow hips, and black biker boots, he looked so good he was almost edible.

How could this possibly work? Over the past ten years, he had been so many different things to me—best friend, worst enemy, love of my life, heartbreaker, asshole with a capital A. We'd soared to the greatest heights and crashed to the lowest depths together.

Starting over wasn't possible.

He set my tea in front of me and I thanked him, sounding so prim and proper that I barely recognized myself. Connor flipped his chair around and straddled it. Inwardly, I groaned. I hated when he sat like that. I loved when he sat like that. I was *not* thinking about straddling him on a chair.

"When are you going to learn how to sit in a chair?" I asked, white-knuckling my cardboard cup.

He gave me a slow, easy grin, and drummed his fingers on the back of the chair, tapping out a beat to whatever song was in his head. I wanted to know which song it was, what the soundtrack of our life sounded like to him now, but I didn't ask.

We sipped our drinks and snuck glances at each other like we really were on a first date. Curious, attracted to each other, but not sure how to proceed. *With caution, Ava, that's how you should proceed.*

A black leather braided cord around his neck disappeared inside his T-shirt collar, the silver St. Jude medal he always wore hidden from sight. The patron saint of lost causes—perfect for Connor.

My gaze lowered to the tattoos on Connor's arms. I was well-acquainted with the blue and black inked fish and birds that fit together like a puzzle on his left arm. But his right sleeve was still a mystery. He'd had it inked over the past year, and I took the opportunity to study it now. All the designs were intricate and interwoven and although there wasn't one central theme, they fit together seamlessly. The bare branches of a tree with a skull buried in the trunk, vines wrapped around it like they'd choked the life out of the tree. Stars. Bird's wings. Was that Odysseus? Oh Connor. The closer I looked, the more I saw. The word FREE written in script on his forearm...

Connor caught me staring. Under the guise of scratching his back, he exposed the underside of his bicep. A gray eye framed by long, dark lashes stared back at me. One perfect teardrop fell from the corner.

Oh God. I lifted my eyes to his.

His eyes closed briefly, and that simple gesture nearly killed me. Just like the eye tattooed on his arm—*my eye*. I averted my gaze and tried to steady my breathing.

The silence stretched out between us as his eyes flitted over my face, trying to figure out how I felt about the tattoo. I wasn't sure what I thought about it. I wasn't sure about anything right now.

We used to be able to communicate without words. Now I had no idea what he was thinking. *What's going on in that twisted, beautiful mind of yours, Connor?*

Eden had told me he'd gotten a new tattoo on his chest to cover the scars, but if we were playing this we-just-met game, I wasn't supposed to know that. I cleared my throat. "Do you have more tattoos, besides your arms?"

He gave me a little smile. "I have a falcon on my back. Falcons represent hope and freedom. And a Japanese dragon on my chest."

I nodded, neither of us commenting on the symbolism of the dragon. I was dying to see it though. Connor's designs were always amazing. Special. Unique. Artistic. He was so talented, and it had always amazed me that his big, strong hands could create such detailed, intricate artwork. "Tattoos are cool."

"Glad you think so. I'm a tattoo artist." He took a sip of his coffee and eyed me over the rim. "Actually, I'm buying the shop where I work."

My eyes widened. "You're buying it?"

"The current owner is moving to California."

Whoa. That was kind of huge. Connor would be taking on a big responsibility. Maybe he really was done running. "I always wanted to live in California."

"What stopped you?"

I shrugged. *I didn't care where I lived if you were there.* "Brooklyn's not so bad. I have good friends and a cool job."

"What do you do?"

"I work at a bar just a few blocks from here. I do the social media, book the entertainment, paperwork..."

"I bet you're good at what you do. Irreplaceable."

"I'd like to think so."

"I'm sure it's true," Connor said.

I thought maybe he was talking about something other than my job. *Am I irreplaceable in your life, Connor?* If that was true, why had you thrown it all away? Why had drugs given you something I couldn't? Why had you given drugs so much power over your life? They'd ruined you, us, and everything that was good and real.

"Connor, this isn't going to—" *Work.*

"Ava. Have you ever gotten the feeling that you're on the brink of something really good ... and you're excited and hopeful, but you're nervous because you don't want to fuck it up?"

"Is that how you feel now?" I asked.

"Yeah, that's exactly how I feel. Like I'm on a roller coaster and it's climbing, and I know that soon I'll be at the top, and then it'll pick up speed and I'll be flying. But in the back of my head, I'm thinking ... what if this thing jumps the tracks? It's like that."

I knew that feeling so well, the way your stomach flips with anticipation, fear, and excitement. The giddy high as you plunge over the edge and plummet at breakneck speed. "I love riding roller coasters."

Connor smiled. "I know you do. What else do you love doing?"

"I love dancing in my living room until I get all hot and sweaty and collapse on the floor." He laughed, and I knew he could picture it. "I love belting out an Adele song or singing along with Lana Del Rey. I love her lyrics and her sultry voice. She's my girl crush. And I love rummaging through all the crap at the flea markets and vintage shops. Because I know, just know, that I'm going to find something unique and weird and wonderful. It's like a treasure hunt, you know?" He nodded, and his smile grew wider, like hearing everything he already knew about me was unique and weird and wonderful. I left out my newfound joy, the aerial silks class I'd started taking eight months ago. That was my thing, and I didn't share it with anyone. "What do you love doing?"

"Sketching and drawing. Graffiti. Tattooing. Riding my Harley to the mountains or the beach or anywhere, really. I love reading books that make me see the world differently. Or just make me wonder what the hell was going through that person's head when they wrote that. I've been reading Bukowski. His stories are raw and gritty and dirty. The other day I read one of his poems that reminded me of..."

"Reminded you of what?" I prompted.

He shook his head. "Just a girl I used to know."

"Was she raw and gritty and dirty?"

"Our relationship was."

"Not always." Once the words were out, I wished I could reel them back in.

"True. For a while it was amazing. The best thing I'd ever known. *She* was the best thing I'd ever known."

My eyes darted around the shop, seeking refuge. I couldn't do this with him. "I need to go."

He let out a breath. "Yeah. Okay."

We stood, and he ushered me out of the coffee shop. He was so close that I smelled the faint scent of cigarette smoke mingled with his own scent—pheromones and masculinity. I hated the way cigarettes smelled. It should have been a huge turn-off. Somehow, it wasn't. When it came to Connor, I'd always bent the rules.

By the time we exited the coffee shop, I felt like I'd been sucked back into Connor's world, a dangerous, intoxicating, heady place to live. Sometimes, I felt so tiny next to him, probably because he was a foot taller than me. But other times, he made me feel like I was ten feet tall. Like I was ... amazing. He had the ability to make me feel like I was his whole world. Until that world had crashed and burned all around us.

"You need a ride?"

I shook my head. I needed to walk so I could clear my head. Riding on the back of his Harley, my arms wrapped around him, wouldn't help me do that.

"Can I take you to dinner?"

"No. I—"

"Lunch then. Lunch is safe."

Nothing is safe with you. How many times could I let him break my heart? At nineteen, he destroyed me. At twenty-four, I was still picking up the pieces. I made the mistake of looking at his face. In the sunlight, his eyes were almost translucent, framed by a tangle of thick, dark lashes. My gaze dipped to his mouth, his full, sensuous lips. I knew what that mouth was capable of, what his lips and his tongue could do to my body. He could make my body sing, make me writhe in pleasure and pain. Nobody gave such good pain like Connor did.

Stay strong, Ava. It's one thing to get tricked into seeing him, but only a fool would go into it knowingly. "I can't have lunch with you. Or dinner. Or anything else."

"All I'm asking for is another chance to make things right."

"You're asking too much."

"My tragic flaw. But I'm asking anyway. One more chance to get it right." He moved closer and dipped his head, his warm breath on my neck sending shivers down my spine as he whispered in my ear. "'Wild Horses.' That was the song playing in my head."

I took a few steps back to put distance between us and shook my head, trying to clear it, but he'd put the song in my head. Now it would be stuck there, playing on repeat. Why was I still standing on the sidewalk in front of him? A sane girl would have left as soon as she'd entered the coffee shop.

"Lunch," he said. "You, me, food, conversation. Perfectly harmless. I'll text you."

Without giving me a chance to respond, he strode away. It had been so much easier when he'd honored my wishes and hadn't texted, called, or tried to see me. Maybe he'd be too busy running the shop to make time for me. Maybe he'd forget to text like he used to before everything fell apart. But no, he wanted to show me that he'd changed. He wanted to show me the possibility of us. I just needed to decide if I was emotionally prepared to go along for the ride.

Little did I know at sixteen that the roller coaster was going to be our life together.

"You're evil," I told Eden after she unlocked the door of the boutique to let me in. Even covered in paint splatters with her blonde hair in a messy topknot, Eden was gorgeous. The wicked witch cackle she emitted was not so pretty.

"Payback is a bitch," she said, returning to her painting. She was painting a mural on the wall of a boutique on Bedford Avenue that would be selling funky clothes and jewelry and was set to open next month. Normally, I'd gush over Eden's artwork, but my brain was too scrambled to appreciate it. I wrung my hands and paced up and down the shop floor.

"So ... how did it go?" she asked.

"Terrible. You can't meddle in our lives because ... it's not the same as you and Killian. We're ... Connor and I..." Good Lord, I couldn't even form a coherent sentence. I planted my hands on my hips and glared at her back. A complete waste of energy. "Was this your idea?"

"It was Connor's idea. But I thought it was the perfect way to get you two together."

"Congratulations. Mission accomplished." I flopped down on the drop cloth protecting the hardwood floor and lay there, staring at the funky crystal chandelier above me, and the midnight blue ceiling with metallic gold stars. "Did you paint the ceiling?"

"Yep."

"It's cool," I said grudgingly.

"This shop is going to be cool. You'll love it." I turned my head to look at the wall she was painting. A celestial scene. It was cool. I loved it.

"So ... tell me about your coffee date," Eden said.

"It wasn't a date," I snapped. "You and Connor conspired to ... destroy me, I think."

She glanced at me over her shoulder. "You don't look destroyed."

"I'm lying on the freaking floor like a ragdoll!" I yelled.

"Your lungs still work."

I sighed. I was acting like a six-year-old, reduced to throwing a tantrum. It must be a rebellion for all those years of striving for perfection and trying to live up to my mother's expectations. How horrible for her that I'd derailed all her carefully-laid plans. How horrible that Connor still had this kind of power over me. "You don't know what he does to me."

"Tell Dr. Madley. I'll talk you down from the ledge."

"You're on his side."

"I love you both. I'm not taking sides. In fact, I was hoping you'd be my maid of honor."

"Really?" I asked, brightening up at the prospect. I loved weddings, and even though I'd never gotten through one dry-eyed, I still loved them. And I loved Eden and Killian, separately, but even more as a couple. They were perfect for each other.

"Will you?" she asked.

"I'd love to. But you'd better not make me wear an ugly dress."

She scowled at me over her shoulder. "I should be offended by your lack of faith in me."

"Sorry. I know you wouldn't do that. You're not Lana. She made me wear a dress that looked like a hot pink toilet brush. I swear to God, it was the ugliest dress in the history of bridesmaid dresses."

Eden laughed. "We'll pick it out together."

"Will Connor be the best man?" How sad that I even needed to question that.

"I don't know," Eden said quietly. "It should be a given, but Killian ... well, you know..."

I did know. My heart hurt, just like it did every time I thought about the night those four men came seeking revenge.

Connor's face ... I'd barely recognized him. Those men had beat it to a pulp. Carved letters in his chest with a switchblade. They would have shot him, and maybe Eden too, if Killian and his father hadn't shown up on a rescue mission. I'd sat by Connor's bedside in the hospital because Killian couldn't ... or wouldn't. I'd held his hand and sang to him, because I didn't know what else to do. I'd sat next to him in the limo on the way to his father's funeral, hung onto his arm during the service and the burial. I'd shed enough tears to fill an ocean.

All I'd cared about was that Connor was alive. But as the days turned into weeks, and his body began to heal, my anger had taken over. He'd gotten himself into that mess and dragged everyone else into it.

I knew I needed to get him out of my life and eliminate all contact with him. I needed to find a way to forgive him for all the pain and hurt he'd caused. All those years of worrying that he'd end up dead from an overdose, or a drug-fueled accident on his Harley, or any number of crazy things that *could* happen to a junkie. His five-month disappearing act when he'd taken off for Miami and we didn't know if he was dead or alive...

And yet, I'd just hung out with him at the coffee shop. *You really need to get your head examined, Ava.*

"We still have plenty of time to make it work," Eden said. "We're not getting married until June. Tell me how the coffee date went."

"Connor suggested a do-over. We pretend we just met and we get to know each other all over again. I can't see how that's going to work."

"It sounds like the perfect plan. Why not start fresh and give it a fighting chance?"

Why not, indeed. I could think of a million reasons.

"Hey," Eden said. "Remember that art exhibit we went to last year? *Destruction and Renewal?*"

"Yeah." I remembered it perfectly. It had been the day I'd set up Eden and Killian on that coffee date, and afterward, she'd met me at the gallery. I had told Eden that one of the sculptures, a pile of recycled junk all glued together, looked like my life.

"That's your relationship. The destruction is behind you, and now you can work on the renewal. Pick up the pieces and put them back together. Sometimes you end up with something that's a lot better and stronger than what you had before."

"Sometimes you end up with a twisted scrap heap posing as art," I muttered.

"You might be surprised. In a good way," she added. "I have faith in Connor. He's trying so hard to put his past behind him and he's doing everything he can to make things right. I know I wasn't

there for all the bad stuff but ... I don't know ... just have a little
faith in him."

"Why didn't you ever blame him for what happened to you
that night?"

"Because I'm fine. And because he blames himself. He carries
so much guilt. That's more than enough punishment for anyone. I
understand why you needed a break from him, and I think it was
good for both of you. He's really gotten his act together. And
you're so strong, Ava. You stood by him when he needed you most
... and now..."

"And now?" I asked, hoping she had the magic words to turn
this tragedy into a fairy tale.

"You can build a newer and better version of what you had
before."

I valued her friendship and advice, and I wanted to believe her.
She was one of those people who built you up instead of tearing
you down. I'd learned the hard way how rare that was in female
friendships.

But I couldn't go down that road. I needed to keep him at a
safe distance. That was the smart thing to do.

My mind made up, I jumped to my feet, ready to take on the
challenge of keeping Connor out of my life. "Thanks for the chat.
I'll see you at work tomorrow. And your mural looks great."

I arrived at the bar just as a delivery van pulled up in front. A
guy hopped out of the driver's seat, disappeared into the back of
the van, and came out with an enormous bouquet of flowers.

"Can you sign for this delivery?" the guy asked as I unlocked
the front door.

"Sure." I scrawled my name on the little screen with the stylus.
It always ended up looking like a kindergartener's scribble on these
machines. "Who are they for?"

"Ava Christensen."

Holy crap. Connor Vincent sent me flowers. Blue delphiniums,
blush pink and white roses, white stock. I carried them inside,
ignoring Louis's raised brows as I passed the bar, and set them on

70

the desk. Sitting on the swivel chair, I opened the small envelope with my name on it and read the card inside.

Ava, I love your smile. Hope to see it again. Connor

I fired off a quick text.

AVA: Thank you for the flowers, but you shouldn't have sent them. I can't do this. I need to protect my heart. It's never been safe with you.

Ugh, why had I said that? I should have deleted the last two sentences before hitting send.

7

CONNOR

"*A*va Blue," I said as she walked out the front door of the warehouse in Bushwick, her backpack slung over her shoulder.

She planted her hands on her hips and glared at me. My texts had gone unanswered, so I'd opted for the surprise element. Judging by the look on her face, it wasn't a good surprise. "Are you stalking me now?"

"Just offering you a ride home."

"I'm taking the subway."

"You can ride on the back of my bike."

"Hey, Ava. Are you coming?" a guy asked.

"No," I said. "She's riding home with me."

The guy looked from me to Ava. "Just give me a sec," Ava told the guy.

"You can go," I said, waving him off. Come on, the dude had a man bun. What did she need him for?

He crossed his arms over his chest. The guy looked squirrelly. I disliked him on sight. "I'll wait for Ava."

My eyes narrowed on him. "Who are you?"

"Orlando. I'm training Ava for Cirque de Soleil. We're running away together," he said, winking at her. I wanted to wrap my hands around his throat and throttle him. Instead, my hands curled into fists and I glared at him.

"I need to talk to Ava," I said.

"Does Ava need to talk to you?" Orlando asked.

Douchebag. I ignored him and focused on Ava. "I want to show you something. It's important." She chewed on her lower lip, and I could tell she was considering it. I still knew her so well. I flashed her a smile and threw in a please for good measure.

"It's fine," Ava told Orlando. "See you next week."

He pulled her into a hug and whispered something in her ear. When he released her, Ava gave him a big smile that lit up her whole goddamn face. I wanted to be the one to put that smile on her face. With a final look at me, Orlando turned and walked away.

I crossed my arms over my chest and narrowed my eyes. "Did you sleep with him?"

"That's none of your business."

Fuck. Was that a yes? How many guys has she been with since me? I took deep, calming breaths. I needed to control my jealousy. It wouldn't help my cause. "What kind of class is this?"

"Why are you here?"

"Get on the back of my bike and I'll show you." I unhooked the bungee net from the passenger seat and retrieved the spare helmet. Her helmet. I had bought if for her when I'd gotten my first Harley six years ago. No other girl had ever worn it or ridden on the back of my bike. She took a few steps closer. "After that, I'm taking you for empanadas."

"Great. A blast from the past," she grumbled.

Back in high school, she used to come with me when I graffitied walls in Bushwick. Afterward, we always stopped at the twenty-four-hour diner for empanadas. She loved them as much as she loved Jimmy's tacos, and that was saying something.

"How can you turn down an offer like that? You know you're dying for an empanada. The spicy chorizo one ... mmm." I licked my lips and let out a low moan.

"Stop talking about empanadas," she said. "How did you know where to find me?"

I tilted my head and studied her face. Her hair was pulled back in a ponytail and her face was makeup-free. Natural. Unadorned. In a hoodie, leggings, and Nikes, she looked younger, unjaded. Ava had always been stunning, with an ethereal beauty that had always felt just out of reach. "Was it a secret?"

"It's my thing. Something I do just for me. I don't advertise it. Which means you *have* been stalking me," she accused.

Stalking made me sound like a creep. I'd made it my business to know where she was and what she was doing in her free time. But finding out about her Thursday evening class in Bushwick had been purely accidental. "A few weeks ago, I came over to Bushwick to buy art supplies. I saw you coming out of the subway station."

"And you followed me?"

"I noticed where you were headed," I said, correcting her. I hadn't stalked her or waited outside the building until her class was over like I'd wanted to. I'd forced myself to keep driving, honoring her wish to keep me out of her life. But I'd taken note of the Aerial Arts Studio sign on the warehouse and Googled it when I'd gotten home. "So, what do you do? Trapeze?"

"Aerial dance. With silks. You climb the silk ropes and then you do modern dance, acrobatics..." She waved her hand in the air to indicate it was all that and so much more.

That sounded so fucking cool. I'd love to see her do that.

"You can't just turn up, Connor. Like I said, it's my thing and if I wanted you to watch... which I don't ... you'd need an invitation. And you're not getting one."

That hurt. I rubbed my chest and her gaze dipped down to my hand. "You always did that," she said softly.

"Did what?"

She shook her head a little and diverted her gaze.

"Come with me. I'll make it worth your while."

She looked over my shoulder, debating. Ava had an expressive face and watching it was like reading a story. I could see the moment she conceded. She pulled the elastic out of her hair and shook it loose, lavender hair tumbling down her back. Before she could change her mind, I pulled the helmet over her head and adjusted the strap under her chin, my fingers brushing against her silky soft skin. God, I wanted to touch her everywhere.

It had been a while since she'd ridden on the back of my bike, but she climbed on behind me like an old pro and placed her feet on the foot pegs. I waited for her to wrap her arms around me. When it didn't happen, I looked over my shoulder. "Ava. Come on. Play nice."

"I'll hang onto the seat."

Like hell she would. I reached behind me, clasped her hands in mine and wrapped her arms around my middle. "Hang on tight," I said, revving the engine.

I pulled away from the curb with enough speed that she had no choice but to hang on. Too bad. I loved her arms around me, her chest pressed against my back. She was right where I wanted her. Well, not exactly, but I'd settle for it. For now.

The wall I'd bombed late last night was only three blocks away and minutes later, I pulled up in front of it and cut the engine. She unwrapped her arms and dismounted. Removing her helmet, she set it on the seat and moved closer to the wall to inspect my graffiti. I hung my helmet on the handlebar and joined her on the sidewalk, watching her face as she took it in. There was no doubt it was mine. But, if there had been any doubt, I'd signed it with my tag name: TRISTE. We'd come up with the name when we were sixteen and had thought we were so clever. Triste was French for blue, like sad.

She studied my graffiti, and I wondered what she thought of it. It was her face in profile, her long lavender hair blowing behind her like it was being swept up by the wind. In her hands, she held an anatomical heart. *My* fucking heart.

Ava crossed her arms over her chest for protection. "Why do you do this to me?" She turned her back to the wall and faced me, her eyes flashing with anger. "Why do you do this to me?" she repeated.

"Baby..." I said, taking a step closer.

"No." She held up her hands to ward me off. "You don't get to call me *baby* or *babe* or *Ava Blue*. You don't get to play with my emotions and manipulate my heart..." I took another step closer. She planted her hands on my chest and shoved me. I didn't budge. It pissed her off. She pounded my chest with the sides of her fists. It was almost comical, like Tweety Bird taking on the Incredible Hulk. I didn't feel a goddamn thing. I wrapped my hands around her wrists and backed her up against the wall.

"Show me some of your self-defense moves," I said, pinning her hands to the wall. "Hurt me."

"Fuck you, Connor."

I pressed my body against hers, trapping her. "Break free of my hold, Ava."

She stared at me, her chest heaving, her gray eyes wide.

I dipped my head and found the shell of her ear, "Defend yourself," I whispered, feeling a tremor go through her body. My mouth moved down to her neck just below her ear, and I pressed my lips against her racing pulse. She smelled like vanilla and something that was just her. Sweet and warm with a touch of spice. She smelled like heaven. She smelled like the only home I'd ever known. "Do. It."

She rotated her body, breaking my hold with her shoulder. She was fast, and she was strong. An elbow jammed into my ribs followed by a swift kick to my groin.

Fuck. I doubled over, blinded by pain.

"You asked for it."

I did. But I hadn't expected her attack to be so brutal.

"I didn't kick you as hard as I could," she added, her voice tinged with regret.

Thank fuck for that. I took deep breaths, trying to fight the nausea until it passed, and I could see again. She stroked my back, although I wasn't sure how that could help my bruised balls.

It was official. We were crazy. A train wreck waiting to happen.

I gritted my teeth and straightened. Fuck, that hurt.

"I'm sorry," she said, chewing on her lower lip, her brows drawn together.

"As you've just demonstrated, the power is all yours. You can defend yourself against me."

"Physically ... but that's not the kind of pain you give."

True. I've never laid a hand on her or any woman, and I never would. At least Ava could trust me with her body. After that little display, I wasn't so sure I could say the same about her. "My heart needs as much protection from you as yours does from me."

"I didn't break your heart," she whispered.

"Yes. You did. Or maybe I broke my own heart." After Ava's ultimatum to choose her or drugs, I'd gotten clean with Killian's help, a detox clinic, and methadone. I'd been a wreck, my emotions all over the place. Amidst my personal hell, Ava's mother had paid me a visit. She'd told me if I'd ever loved Ava, I needed to let her go. She'd said I wasn't good enough for her daughter. I didn't deserve her, and I never would. She'd been right. After I pushed Ava out of my life, I returned to my mistress—heroin. But I never stopped loving Ava. Not even in my darkest days.

She opened her mouth as if to say something. Then she clamped it shut and strode away, right past my bike. She sped up, jogging down the cracked sidewalk like she couldn't get away fast enough. I caught up to her and wrapped my arms around her waist, pulling her back against my chest. "Don't go. Don't run away from me."

She hung her head. "Why, Connor? Every. Single. Time. You're like quicksand."

"I thought I was like an onion," I joked.

"Don't you get it? You and I are no good together. We're toxic."

I turned her around to face me. "Look me in the eye and tell me you don't love me."

Her eyes didn't reach mine. "Love requires trust. I don't trust you. My heart has been broken by you so many times ... so many times, Connor."

I pulled her into my arms and held her. She leaned into me, her cheek pressed against my chest. "Baby, please ... I'll do whatever it takes to make this work. *Anything.*"

"Anything?" she asked, her voice muffled.

"Anything that doesn't require letting you go. Because I don't know how to do that. I've never found a way." I closed my eyes and breathed in her scent. I could feel her trembling, her resolve weakening.

I released her and took a few steps back. "Let's find our way back to being friends," I said.

She bit down on her lower lip, considering it. Did I deserve another chance? Probably not. I was asking her to take a leap of faith. I knew why our relationship had broken down, and I knew what I needed to do to fix it. I dropped down on one knee and held my hands together as if in prayer. "You hold my beating heart in your hands. Don't squeeze the life out of me."

Ava rolled her eyes, trying to suppress a smile. "You're ridiculous."

I chuckled and got to my feet. "I know. But that's why you love me."

She shook her head but didn't bother denying it. Small victory. "Are you still offering empanadas?"

"All the empanadas you can eat."

"Good. I'm starving." She poked me in the chest. "And you're buying."

8

CONNOR

*A*va ordered enough food to feed a small country. Like China. "I'll have what she's having," I told the waitress.

When she left our booth, I fed coins into the table jukebox and flipped through the music, punching the buttons to make my selections. I loved this thing. It still took quarters and the music hadn't been updated in decades, a lot like this old diner. A Formica-topped table separated me from Ava and silver duct tape patched the tear in my red vinyl seat, but the food made up for the shabby decor.

My first selection started playing—Johnny Cash's "I Walk the Line" and Ava groaned like it was truly painful.

"You're really going for it, aren't you?" she asked.

"Go big or go home, sweetcakes."

She held out her hand and wiggled her fingers. "Hand over the quarters, beefcake."

I held up my empty hands. She shot me a look that sent me right up to the register for change. What a chump, I thought, as I came back to our booth with a handful of quarters for my little princess. She rewarded me with a smug smile, and I wondered if she'd choose the same songs she used to. There was always some

Elvis, "California Dreaming," the Beach Boys, "Wouldn't It Be Nice," and a Tammy Wynette number, "Stand by Your Man."

"The usual?" I asked when she leaned back in her seat, satisfied with her choices.

"I mixed it up. No Tammy."

I gave her a little smile. "Maybe next time."

"You'd need to earn that."

"Tell me how."

"We need to set some ground rules," she said, all business now. "Shoot."

"No sex. If I get drunk and call you, don't cave, even if I beg you to have sex with me. I won't know what I'm talking about and I'll regret it the next morning."

I smirked as the waitress served our papaya juice.

When the waitress left, Ava said, "Wipe that smirk off your face. No sex. I mean it."

"Oh, I'm sure you do." The fact that she felt the need to bring up sex meant she was tempted. She should have known better than to set herself up like that. "Even if you beg me for sex when you're stone-cold sober, I'll say no. I'm not that kind of guy." I pointed to myself and then her. "What we've got here is a friends-without-benefits arrangement. If you choose to honor that, then we're good to go." I puffed out my chest. "You can't use me for my body. In fact, I'm offended that you would insinuate such a thing."

"You're annoying."

"You're adorable." I stared at her plump pink lips, her delicate nose, and those wide gray eyes that could turn from icy to stormy in a heartbeat. God, I loved her face. I loved her everything.

She huffed out a breath. "At least we got that straight."

"Absolutely. No sex. Not even if you beg me." I leaned back in my seat and spread my arms along the top of the booth. "Anything else?"

"If you say you're going to be somewhere, you need to be there. You'll get a fifteen-minute grace period, but if you're late, or if you haven't called with a valid excuse, I won't be hanging around waiting for you. I need to know I can rely on you."

"Done."

She drummed her fingers on the table. "No lying. No empty promises."

"I only made empty promises when I was using." *But I'm still a liar.*

"I know." She leaned in, resting her folded arms on the table. My gaze wandered down the column of her neck to the scoop of her black sports tank, exposing her creamy skin and a hint of cleavage. She snapped her fingers to draw my attention back to her face. "If I ever find out you're doing drugs, I'll never speak to you again. There won't be any more chances. Not as friends or anything else. I just ... I can't go back there."

I couldn't go back there. I had too much at stake to lose the fight now. "I know. And I'd never expect you to."

Ava's face crumpled. "I feel like I lost the boy I loved. There were so many times I was scared for your life. And I never ever want to feel like that again."

I reached for her hands and clasped them in mine, my thumbs tracing lazy circles over the thin skin of her inner wrists. "I'm done with that life. It's over. I worked too hard to get out to fall back into it. I never want to go through that again, and I never want the people I care about to suffer because of it."

She looked down at our joined hands but didn't try to pull hers away. "We'll try this. As friends though ... nothing more."

I released her hands as the waitress transferred the plates of food from her tray to our table. "Thank you," I told the waitress.

"Uh huh," she said, tucking the tray under her arm. She was middle-aged with pasty skin and thinning brown hair pulled back in a tight ponytail, her lips pressed in a flat line. I wondered when she'd last smiled or lit up with joy. As she walked away, I saw defeat in the slump of her shoulders, like life hadn't gone easy on her. She looked as worn down and battered as this old diner, frayed around the edges, patched together with duct tape.

"I don't think she's found job satisfaction," Ava said.

"When you have six kids and an unemployed husband to

support, it can't be easy," I said, falling into one of our old story-telling games, wondering if Ava would play along like she used to.

Ava picked up an empanada and took an enormous bite. Chorizo juice dripped down her chin. I reached across the table and wiped it away with my thumb. She didn't seem to notice or take offense. It probably felt familiar. "The man never leaves his La-Z-Boy," Ava said, continuing our story. "Remote in one hand. Beer in the other."

"He's a champion bowler though. His team won the cup last year."

In between shoveling food into our mouths, Ava and I filled in more details about our waitress and her fictional husband and kids.

I watched in amusement as Ava devoured her empanadas then dug into the rice and beans like she was still starving. For such a tiny girl, it had always amazed me that she could put away so much food. I loved her huge appetite. Not only for food but for life. Back when this girl was mine, she loved me with her whole heart and didn't hold anything back. That was what I strived for now, to somehow get back to that magical place where she could love me like that again.

When we finished eating, she leaned back in her seat and rubbed her flat stomach, groaning like she always did after she ate enough food to feed a football team.

"You good?" I asked.

"I'm about to go into a food coma. Other than that, it's all good."

I chuckled.

"One more rule..."

I raised my brows. She looked at the jukebox in accusation as Elvis's "Don't Be Cruel" started playing. Another one of my choices.

"This thing is rigged. It didn't even play my songs."

I laughed and shook my head. "We can stay longer." I settled back in my seat in no hurry to leave. Hell, I'd stay here all night if I could, just to hang out with her and keep talking about everything and nothing. No girl had ever intrigued me like Ava did. On any given day, she was a mixed bag. I liked it that she always kept me guessing.

"I have a rule, too," I said. "No more kicking me in the balls."

"That was a one-off." She pointed her finger at me. "You provoked me."

"You could have punched me in the nose."

She shrugged one shoulder. "Hindsight is twenty/twenty. Don't try to convince me to watch a horror movie with you," she said. "I'll have creepy dreams for weeks, and I'll be convinced that slashers and zombies lurk around every corner. Trust me, you don't want to go there."

I didn't want to go there. I had to hear about it for weeks. "That's funny ... I seem to remember one Halloween when *someone* thought it would be a great idea to watch back-to-back slasher and zombie flicks. And who suggested that midnight visit to the cemetery afterward?"

"I think that was you."

"That was all you. I was the poor schmuck who went along with it."

"Poor schmuck? You grabbed me in the dark and scared the shit out of me."

That was funny as hell. Until she nearly split my eardrums. "Your screams were loud enough to wake the dead."

"I got them dancing on their graves."

"It was the monster mash."

"We're such weirdos." She gave me a big, happy smile she hadn't shown me in a long time. She was remembering us at seventeen. But the smile faded all too quickly as if she'd caught herself doing something she shouldn't.

"We should go," she said, zipping up her hoodie.

I flagged down our waitress and asked for the check. She fished it out of the pocket of her apron and set it on the table. "Can I borrow your pen?" I asked.

She set it on top of the check and walked away. I flipped the check over and drew a peacock, then threw down enough money to cover the bill and a generous tip. Ava gave me a soft smile as we slid out of the booth, the first notes of Johnny Cash's "Ring of Fire" coming out of the jukebox. Ava's choice.

"That's harsh," I said, rubbing my chest.

She arched her brows. "I should have known better than to play with fire."

"You were the arsonist, baby. You set my world on fire."

"You left me with the ashes," she said, her voice low but loud enough for me to hear it.

I wanted to tell her that she was the phoenix that rose from the ashes, but I didn't know if it was true or not. Ava could be tough, but she said I made her vulnerable and fragile. Five years ago, we went to Brooklyn Glass to watch the glass-blowers. Such a cool thing to watch. On the way home, Ava told me her heart was made of glass, that someday I'd shatter it in my hands and she wouldn't know how to pick up all the pieces. She wanted to protect her heart, but she gave it to me anyway and trusted me to keep it safe. I didn't.

I held the door open for her and followed her out of the diner. Tonight, those summerlike days felt like a thing of the past. The air was cool and damp, the kind of weather that settled in your bones. Ava hugged herself for warmth, and I wanted to warm her up with my body heat. Instead, I took off my hoodie and handed it to her.

"Won't you need it?"

I shook my head.

She thanked me and threaded her arms through the sleeves, zipping it up. "I look ridiculous," she said, rolling up the sleeves. She was drowning in my hoodie, but she didn't look ridiculous. I smiled to myself when she burrowed her nose in the collar, closing her eyes as she inhaled my scent.

"Your tattoo..." she said when I handed over her helmet. "Is that the only way you remember me? Crying?"

I took a deep breath and let it out. My right arm was a tapestry of my life over the past few years, a reminder of where I'd been and the journey I'd taken to reach this point. Drug-free. Hanging on to life by the skin of my teeth. Choked by the vines but still surviving. My skull buried in the tree. Ava's tears. Hope. Despair. The death of my old life and a rebirth. I'd sketched the designs during late nights when sleep wouldn't come, and over the past year, Jared had inked it on my skin piece-by-piece until I had a full sleeve.

When you hit rock bottom, you're led to believe there's nowhere to go but up. What nobody tells you is how long it takes or how hard it is to dig and crawl your way out of that hellhole.

"No," I said. "That's not the only way I remember you. It's more like a reminder ... I'm trying to bring good things into my life now. And you ... are the very best thing. I won't ruin us. Not again."

"Can you make that kind of promise?"

I wasn't sure. "I can promise that I'll try my best."

She studied my face, and I felt like she could see straight into my soul and read all the things I wasn't saying. "That's a good start."

"Am I redeemable, Ava?" I teased.

"Time will tell, Connor." Her gaze dipped to the vintage silver Harley skull and crossbones belt buckle she'd given me for my nineteenth birthday. "That's a jazzy belt buckle. The person who gave it to you has good taste."

I swung a leg over my bike and kicked up the stand. "Watch yourself, girl. You shouldn't be looking at my belt buckle. And don't even think of what's below it."

"I wasn't. It never crossed my mind," she said primly.

"I know it's *hard* not to think about something so *big* but put it out of your mind."

Ava groaned. "Oh God, you haven't changed a bit."

I grinned. "Some things haven't changed." I grabbed my crotch, and her gaze lingered there. It was too much fun not to push for more of a reaction. I stroked myself through the fabric of my jeans. I was still tender, but as if by magic, my dick hardened under my touch. "Barbells aren't just for lifting in the gym," I said, reminding her of the piercing she used to love. I'd gotten the apadravya for her when we were eighteen, having accepted her dare.

Her tongue swept over her bottom lip. Jesus. I wanted that tongue where my hand was. We used to be daring. Ava had a thing for having sex and giving blow jobs in places where we might get caught. I stifled a groan. God, that was fantastic.

I stopped touching myself. If I kept going, I'd explode in my jeans.

I winked at her. "Get on the back of my bike, baby. I'll take you for a ride you'll never forget."

"Cocky asshole," she muttered. I chuckled under my breath as she pulled on her helmet and climbed on, her arms circling my waist without my having to prompt her. She once told me that she loved having the power of the Harley between her legs. It always got her wet. I tried not to think about that as I drove her home, knowing damn well she wouldn't invite me up to her apartment.

9

AVA

*I*t was just Sunday brunch. Nothing to get worked up about, I thought, as I stepped outside my apartment building into a cloudy, gray October day. Connor was leaning against the pillar of my red brick pre-war apartment building, watching the world go by on Bedford Avenue. He was one of those guys who was born to lean. Like a James Dean character. A rebel without a cause. The bad boy girls wanted to fix.

Connor's gaze swept over me, taking in every detail from the top of my head to the baggy gray sweater, tartan pleated mini skirt, thigh-high ribbed socks and Doc Marten boots. Harajuku girl meets bag lady. My eyes skimmed over his fitted black Henley under a black leather motorcycle jacket and back to his face. I was tempted to run my fingers over the stubble on his chiseled jaw. Drag my hand down his hard chest and feel the warmth of his skin under the fabric of his shirt. Lick the hollow at the base of his neck. Instead, I pressed my lips together and clasped my hands behind my back.

"Your mom got hold of you," he guessed, looking at my hair.

I shrugged. "It was time for a change."

After my mom's constant nagging and non-stop texts, I'd gone to her salon yesterday. It had been a mistake, not because of my hair color, but because of the conversation.

Connor wrapped a lock of my white-blonde hair around his fingers, his gaze fixated on my mouth. "I love those cherry-red lips." My tongue darted out, and I swept it across my lower lip, watching his eyes darken. "You look like someone I used to know."

"Was she raw and gritty and dirty?"

"Sometimes. But in the very best way," he said, his gaze lingering on my mouth.

My cheeks flushed with heat. I glanced over my shoulder at the front door, entertaining the notion of returning to the safety of my apartment. He grabbed my hand and guided me to his parked Harley, my stomach doing somersaults.

Helmet on, I climbed onto the back of the bike behind Connor. Closing my eyes, I let out a breath as I wrapped my arms around his waist. It felt good, just like it had three nights ago. And dangerous. And familiar. I could feel his muscles flexing against my arms, the tautness of his stomach. As he took off down the street, the power surged between my legs, and I felt wild and free.

Part of me wanted him to head out of Brooklyn, onto the open road and just keep driving, up the road hugging the Hudson River or to the end of the world. That was what we used to call Montauk, the easternmost tip of the Hamptons. The other part of me was scared he would take me away and I'd lose my bearings. Conflicted, as always, when it came to us.

Yesterday, while my mom was performing her magic on my hair, I'd gotten a text from Connor. She saw it. My mom didn't miss a trick.

"Ava Christensen, don't you dare let that boy back into your life. You're well and truly rid of him."

I tossed my phone in my bag, safe from her prying eyes. "We're just friends."

"You can't be friends with someone like him."

"What do you mean ... someone like him?" I asked, my hackles rising. How weird that I fought him, yet I defended him to my mother. I always had.

"No mother wants to see their daughter with a drug addict," she hissed, keeping her voice low so the other customers and stylists wouldn't overhear those dirty words coming out of her mouth. *Drug addict.* "I warned him to stay away from you. He promised me he would. Broke up with you and everything ... but I should have known better than to trust that boy. He just can't leave well enough alone, can he?"

"That was you? He broke up with me because of you?" Four and a half years ago. He'd been trying to get clean. He *had* gotten clean. Then he broke up with me and went right back to the drugs. And my mother had been behind that?

"What did you say to him?" I asked.

"That he didn't deserve you. That he wasn't good enough for you and he never would be." There was no hint of guilt or remorse in her voice.

"All his life he'd been told he wasn't good enough." I pictured his graffiti, my hands holding his heart. "How could you have said those things to him? He was trying to get clean, but you—"

"Oh no, missy. Don't you dare blame his weakness on me. I did what any good mother would do. Your father and I were worried sick about you. Because of him, you couldn't even enjoy your college experience."

"It wasn't your decision to make."

"He knew he never deserved you. He admitted it."

"All his life he was told he wasn't good enough. You know what Seamus did to—"

"I never believed that for a minute. Seamus Vincent was a good cop. God rest his soul. And because of Connor, he's dead."

"Good. He got what he deserved."

My mom sighed loudly. "Sometimes I don't know where you come from, Ava. I tried to raise you right. With good morals and values. Just like Seamus did with his boys." I bit down on the inside of my cheek so hard I drew blood. "It couldn't have been easy for that man. Left on his own like that ... and those boys had trouble written all over them. It didn't surprise me when Killian killed that man in a fight either. He'd always been violent ... getting into all those street fights like he did..."

"He's not violent. And Johnny's death wasn't his fault," I said through gritted teeth.

My mom sniffed. I was wasting my breath. In my mom's book, the Vincent brothers would always be bad news. She'd made up her mind a long time ago and nothing they did now would ever change it.

It was useless trying to argue with her. She saw the world as black and white, right and wrong. She saw what she wanted to see, and even when she was wrong, she refused to listen to reason. My father was a saint for putting up with her for thirty years.

Before I left, my mother hugged me and told me I looked beautiful. "I love you. I only want what's best for you."

I knew she loved me and wanted the best for me. But she wanted what *she* thought was best for me, regardless of what I wanted.

As I rode on the back of Connor's bike, my arms wrapped around him, I thought about the peacock Connor had sketched for our waitress. A reminder that she could walk tall and proud and find her inner beauty. I'd nearly cried when I saw it. That was what Connor did though. He tried to make people's day just a little bit brighter.

Connor had always been sensitive, attuned to people's feelings. He felt their pain and suffering so deeply. When we were in high school, he used to do sketches of homeless people. He would bring them coffee and sandwiches. Hang out for a while and talk with them. In the winter, he bought them blankets, hats, and gloves. He used the money from his job stocking shelves at the supermarket to fund it. Most people would have kept walking, turned a blind eye, but not Connor. He couldn't bear to see anyone suffer.

Maybe that was why he'd started doing drugs. The real world was too much for him sometimes.

Connor didn't take me out of Brooklyn, but he took me back to a place I rarely ventured now. Park Slope. As we passed the brownstone with turrets where Killian and Connor lived for four years, I looked up at the windows of the second-floor apartment they used to rent, and I imagined us at eighteen ... so impossibly young. Invincible.

The drive-by had been on purpose, a blast from the past that wasn't on our way. The restaurant he took me to was in Crown Heights, a short walk from Brooklyn Botanical Gardens, one of my favorite places. After a ten-minute wait, the waiter showed us to a two-top and handed us menus. I sat with my back to the exposed brick wall and studied the menu. It was a toss-up. Pancakes topped with fresh fruit or eggs benedict.

Connor saw my struggle. "Should I pick a hand?"

"Why would you do that?" I asked coyly. That was our thing. When I couldn't decide between two menu items, Connor helped me.

"You look undecided."

Pancakes. Left. Eggs benedict. Right. "Okay."

He squinted at my hands on the table and tapped the right one. "What is it? Pancakes or eggs benedict?"

I laughed. I couldn't help it. He knew every stupid, little thing about me, right down to the two items I would choose on the menu. "The eggs."

Connor wasn't as predictable as me. "Shredded kale salad and a smoked salmon omelet?" I asked when the waiter left our table. Killian had always been the health nut, not Connor. "They have burgers with bacon and cheese and French fries..."

His mouth quirked with amusement. "Yeah, I read the menu."

"Oh. Right. Okay." I looked around the restaurant, admiring the art deco light fixtures and the glossy wood bar across from me. It was a hipster haven filled with pretty people, more subdued and fancier than the restaurants we used to frequent in the past.

A family of four was sitting next to us, the parents speaking in modulated tones. The two little boys were identical twins, dressed in matching Polo sweaters over white button-down shirts, their hair slicked back so perfectly I could see the comb marks. The mother reminded me of Lana, with styled hair, perfect makeup, and a black wrap dress that was probably designer. Her smile was tight and looked forced to me. Her husband was non-descript, wearing a blue Oxford shirt and khakis. I got the feeling they weren't Brooklynites. They looked too uptight for city dwellers.

When one of the boys talked with his mouth full, his mother reprimanded him. I tuned her out while she coached her sons on proper restaurant etiquette.

The waiter delivered Connor's Virgin Mary and my sparkling water and pomegranate juice. Connor handed me his celery stick and I chomped away on it absently. He hated celery. Always had. "This is weird," I said, taking a sip of my drink to wash down the celery. "Does it feel weird to you?"

He nudged the toe of my boot with his under the table. "Just go with it. Weird isn't bad. You're a weirdo, but I still like you."

I laughed. "Tell me about this shop you're buying."

"Jared and I are meeting with the lawyer on Tuesday to sign the papers."

"Wow. That's a big deal."

"I know." He pushed up the sleeves of his Henley and rested his folded arms on the table, putting him too close to me. Instinctively, I leaned back in my seat and crossed my arms then uncrossed them, trying not to look like I was on the defensive.

"Are you nervous?"

He shrugged one shoulder. "Jared gave me a crash course in accounting this morning. My head still hurts."

"I can help you out with that stuff ... and the social media ... if you ever need—" Seriously? I needed to bitch-slap myself. Why was I offering my help?

Connor gave me a big smile. "Yeah?"

"Well ... only if you can't figure it out on your own, which I'm sure you will. You're a smart guy."

He didn't comment on that, so I asked him more questions about the business which seemed like a safe topic. "Jared's sticking around until the end of October until I get the hang of it and hire a tattoo artist to replace him. My lease is up in a few weeks, so I won't lose my deposit when I move into his place. It's all working out."

"Jared's place is nice," I said, for lack of something better to say. But it was nice. He'd renovated the interior and put in a new kitchen with granite countertops and stainless-steel appliances, a sleek bathroom with limestone-tiled floors, and dark hardwood floors in the bedroom and living room.

"Yeah, it's a nice place," he said, his eyes clouding over as if he was remembering the month he'd lived there. And maybe the day I walked out of his life.

Our conversation, already stilted and overly polite, came to an abrupt halt. Connor leaned back as the waiter delivered our food. A few minutes later, Connor asked if my food was good. I said yes and asked him the same question. Yes, he answered. After that, we concentrated on our food instead of trying to make conversation. Despite the silence and the tension, I managed to eat every bite of my food. I stared at my empty plate, racking my brain for something to say.

Our silence was interrupted by one of the little boys from the next table who was around five or six. He approached our table, his eyes glued to Connor's left arm.

"Hey buddy," Connor said with a smile. "You good?"

He nodded and held out a blue magic marker. "Can you do that for me?" The boy pushed up the sleeve of his sweater, indicating that he wanted a tattoo on his arm. It made me laugh.

"This isn't magic marker," Connor said. "It's a tattoo. It's permanent."

The boy's eyes widened as he stared at the birds and fish on Connor's arm. "You can't wash it off? Ever?"

"Nope."

"Never?"

"Never."

His brother joined him, curiosity getting the best of him. "How did you do it?"

"With special needles and ink."

The boy shuddered. "I don't like needles. Did it hurt?"

Connor smiled. "A little bit."

The boy cocked his head, his brow furrowed. "What if you change your mind and you don't like birds and fish anymore?"

His brother elbowed him in the ribs. "That's dumb. Everyone likes birds and fish."

The kid shrugged. "I guess. But you can draw some birds and fish on my arm and I can wash it off, right?" he asked, his voice hopeful.

"You'd need to ask your parents for permission," Connor said, surprising me. But most likely, he'd observed the same things I had about the boys' parents and had decided to err on the side of caution for a change.

The kids raced over to their parents and proceeded to beg and plead, all the while pointing at Connor.

Their mother pursed her lips. "Magic markers are toxic. You can't put that on your skin."

"But—"

"No buts. We're leaving," she said, packing the markers and coloring books into their backpacks.

"When I get bigger I'm getting a tattoo," the little boy said.

"Over my dead body," the woman said, handing the boys their backpacks while their dad signed his credit card receipt.

"We don't pay all that money for private school, so you can turn into a hoodlum," the dad said, shooting Connor a look.

"What's a hoodlum?" the kid asked, his brow furrowed.

"It's a kid from the wrong side of the tracks," Connor said. "They usually turn into junkies. You don't want to mix with those kinds of people."

The father wrangled his kids out of the restaurant, but the mother stayed behind and stood by our table, hands on her hips, her glare aimed at Connor. "That was not necessary," she hissed.

"I was trying to help your cause. You have a good day now, ma'am." Connor gave her a mock-salute, with an insolent look on his face that I knew so well. It was the same one he'd used at school whenever the teachers had disciplined him. It made him look like trouble and had never done him any favors.

After the woman left, he leaned back in his seat and crossed his arms, holding my gaze. He was waiting to see how I'd react. "How do you feel about hanging out with a ... *hoodlum?*"

I decided to go with my first instinct. "They obviously don't appreciate good art. They were pompous asses."

He gave me a soft smile. "I like it when you're on my side."

"I used to always be on your side."

"I know. I remember."

A minor tussle ensued when the waiter delivered our check. "Let me pay half," I insisted. "That's what friends do."

"Let the hoodlum pay." Connor threw down enough cash to cover the check and a tip and dragged me out of the restaurant.

"But you're starting a new business and—"

"Brunch won't bankrupt me."

"Thank you."

"How about a guided tour of the Botanical Gardens?" he said, looking up the street.

"Who's the guide?"

"Me."

I probably knew the gardens better than he did, but I went along with it. He led me to the Japanese Hill-and-Pond Garden, my favorite part.

"Mr. Santos taught me how to look at a tree," Connor said.

Mr. Santos was the only teacher Connor had respected. He helped Connor put together the portfolio that got him into Pratt Institute. Mr. Santos saw Connor's potential. He encouraged him and built him up instead of trying to knock him down like the other teachers who treated Connor like a troublemaker in need of a firm hand and discipline.

"What do you mean ... he taught you how to look at a tree?" I asked.

"A tree doesn't float in space. It has roots and it's firmly planted in the ground, so you need to show that when you sketch a tree. You want to feel the texture of the bark. Show the way the branches are attached to the trunk and the leaves to the branches. He told me to study the negative space between the branches. Branches are never straight. To give a tree life, you need to show the kinks and knots. The gnarled trunk. The shadows and the heavier weighted lines. Trees are so complex. They're perfectly imperfect."

I tried to look at the tree through the eyes of an artist like Connor did. When I'd first looked at this tree, I hadn't seen its imperfections. All I'd seen was the tree's beauty and elegance, the red-russet leaves in stark contrast with the dull gray sky. I hadn't noticed the gnarled, twisted branches, the slightly-bent trunk or the roots pushing up from the ground.

Perfectly imperfect. Like Connor. Like me. Like us.

I glanced at Connor. He was watching my face, not the tree. He was putting down roots. He was shadows and light. Complex. Beautiful and damaged, but maybe ... not beyond repair.

When he reached for my hand, I let him take it. As we walked around the gardens, talking and laughing, I pretended that we'd just met, and we were still in the getting-to-know-you phase. If that had been true, I would have said yes to another date because this guy ... he was someone I wanted to know better.

10

CONNOR

"How did it go with Ava yesterday?" Tate asked as we walked out of our Monday morning meeting and up the street to our Harleys. Somehow, we managed to snag the same parking space every week, in front of a scraggly tree outside a weathered blue house, the paint chipped and peeling. An old couple sat on webbed lawn chairs next to the moss-covered bird-bath in their tiny front yard fenced-off from the sidewalk by white latticed wrought-iron. The woman was wearing curlers in her hair, a housedress, and slippers. The man was dressed in a ratty white T-shirt and dress pants. They sat, staring into the distance, not talking. I turned my back to the house and Tate and I stood on the edge of the sidewalk, facing the street.

"It had its ups and downs," I said, thinking about the silent brunch and our stilted conversation. But then she'd taken my side. And our walk through the Botanical Gardens had been... nice. We'd talked and laughed, and she'd let me hold her hand. "Mostly good though." I shook a cigarette out of the pack and lit up.

"You sure this is a good idea?" he asked. "You've got a lot on your plate right now."

I took a long drag and exhaled, looking up at the sky where the sun was trying to break through the clouds. "Are you saying *you* don't think it's a good idea?"

"It's not my call. But I do know she's one of your triggers," he said, eyeing the Winston clamped between my lips. I usually waited until after I'd hit the gym to smoke. "You were a wreck when she left you."

"I was a wreck because of all the shit that went down. That was my rock bottom."

"I know that. But that girl gets you all twisted and tied up in knots."

I couldn't deny that. Yesterday had been hard. One step forward, three steps back. She was still trying to protect herself from me. "You ever been in love?"

"Yep. Been there, done that, got the T-shirt."

"What happened?" I asked.

"I fucked up. Got sent to prison. Told her I didn't want her anywhere near me. She wanted to visit me in the state pen. A woman like her should never set foot in a place like that. If she'd been smart, she would have stayed a mile away from me. She should never have had anything to do with the likes of me."

"Love isn't logical. The heart wants what the heart wants."

He shook his head. "Yeah, I know. Makes people do some crazy shit."

Tell me about it. Wishing and hoping. Trying to toe the line for one more shot at something that might never be again. But Ava couldn't deny that she still loved me. That had to count for something.

"Whatever happened to the woman?" I asked, tipping back my head as the sun made an appearance.

"Married. Two kids. Nice house. She got the life she was meant to have."

"Is she happy?"

He narrowed his eyes, looking off into the distance, maybe shuffling through his memories of the woman he loved. "She's better off."

I took a drag of my cigarette, mulling that over. "You still love her?"

"No point in dwelling on it. I did what was best for her."

I'd take that as a yes. Love doesn't go away. It lives on in our fragile hearts. When you love a woman, she gets under your skin, haunts your dreams and your waking hours. Lovesickness, I'd decided, is a real thing. "You're saying love is about self-sacrifice?"

"Sometimes it is. Sometimes it ain't."

I chuckled. "Thanks for clearing that up."

"Never claimed to be an expert. Just trying to look out for you, that's all. The road to recovery ain't paved in gold. It's hard work. And if the people in your life aren't supportive, that just makes it a hell of a lot harder."

"She's supportive," I said, jumping to her defense. "I put her through a lot. It's hard for her."

He clapped me on the shoulder. "Take care of yourself first. Keep doing the work and don't let your ship get tossed around by every storm."

"That was deep. Did you read that in a fortune cookie?"

He chuckled and shook his head. "You know what I'm saying, smartass."

"CONNOR. HANG ON," Killian called after me as I was leaving the gym.

I released my hold on the front door and turned to him, raising my brows as he came to stand in front of me.

He rubbed the back of his neck, his eyes not meeting mine. "I should have been more supportive. About buying the shop. It's a good idea."

It looked like it had pained him to say those words. "Did Eden put you up to this?"

He shrugged. "She made me see the error of my ways. But I'm serious. I'm proud of you. You're doing good."

I'd waited a long time to hear those words, and now I wasn't sure how to handle his praise. I rubbed my hand over my chest. "Thanks."

He nodded and fixated on a spot over my shoulder. We sucked at this warm and fuzzy shit and now neither of us knew what to say or do next.

"Do me a favor?" I asked.

Killian's eyes narrowed. He crossed his arms over his chest, widening his stance. I smothered a laugh. Good old Killian. Always on the defensive.

"Cash that check I gave you."

He rolled his shoulders and relaxed his stance. "I don't need the money. Put it into your business."

"If you don't need it for yourself, put it into your program. It's not just about the money. It's about taking responsibility for my actions." The check I'd given him covered the amount he paid for my rehab and the cash I'd stolen from him over the years to fund my addiction. To say that I wasn't proud of stooping so low was the understatement of the century, and I needed him to understand that. All the rest of it... what had happened last year, I couldn't do a damned thing about it. But this was something I could make good on. "It's important to me."

Killian studied my face for a few seconds before he nodded. "Okay."

I let out a breath of relief. One more item to tick off the long list of amends I needed to make. "Thanks."

His phone buzzed, and he checked the screen. "I'm supposed to invite you to dinner tomorrow night. You free?"

It sounded like no big deal, and maybe it should have been perfectly normal for him to invite me to his home for dinner. But it was a first. I knew this was Eden's idea. But Killian was going along with it. That gave me hope. "Yeah. But I'll be late. The shop closes at nine. Is that okay?"

"I don't get home until then so yeah, it works."

I exited the gym, feeling lighter and better-equipped to handle all the shit going on in my life. Killian was taking tentative steps to be supportive, and that meant more to me than I could ever put into words.

I PARKED my bike in Killian's underground garage and retrieved the box of chocolate truffles, Eden's favorite, from the bungee net. Luckily, the box was still intact. Killian raised his brows. "You brought Eden chocolates?"

"You're not married yet. I've still got a shot with her."

"In your dreams."

"She's always in my dreams," I said, goading him.

He scowled at me. "She'd better not be."

I chuckled. Eden was great, but I loved her like a sister. *A sister.* I pushed thoughts of Keira Shaughnessy out of my head as I followed Killian into the elevator. "You take an elevator to the third floor? You're getting lazy in your old age," I joked. He spent twelve hours a day in his gym, teaching classes and training amateur fighters. Lazy wasn't a word anyone would ever use for Killian.

He gestured with his hand. "You're welcome to take the stairs."

"I'm good," I said as the doors closed. The elevator stopped at the lobby and the doors opened to the girl who really did visit me in my dreams, an enormous bouquet of snapdragons in her hands.

"Fuck," Killian muttered.

"Nice to see you, too," Ava said. "Thanks for the welcome."

"I didn't know you were invited," Killian said. By the look on his face, he wasn't happy about it either. Killian endeavored to keep me and Ava separated. Our screwed-up relationship fucked with his head, as he'd told me on numerous occasions.

"Eden's done it again," Ava said, turning her back to me and Killian.

"Looks that way," I said, silently thanking Eden for meddling. Killian shot me a look. I shrugged. *Not my fault, dude. Take it up with your wife-to-be.*

"Were you in on this?" Ava asked the elevator door.

"Not this time."

I looked down at the top of Ava's blonde head. I had nothing against the lavender hair. It was cool. But now she looked more like the Ava I used to know. When I saw her on Sunday, I couldn't help but wonder if it was symbolic. The cherry-red lips and blonde hair. She knew I'd always had a thing for those red lips. They looked so ripe and kissable. Tempting as a poison apple.

"I'm only going along with this for Eden," Ava told me in a low voice as we walked into the loft.

Two could play this game. "I'm only here for the lasagna," I said as the scent wafted my way.

My eyes raked over Ava, taking in the curves of her body that she'd hidden underneath a baggy sweater on Sunday. She untied the belt of her long black cardigan, revealing a silky black strappy tank top and painted-on jeans. Were they leather? Jesus. She looked like she was going clubbing. My eyes traveled down her legs to ankle boots with a heel. Then back up to those fuckable red lips and white-blonde hair framing her gorgeous face. It was almost too much to handle.

"You look hot," I whispered. "Not that I noticed."

"So do you," she whispered back. "Not that I looked."

I winked at her. "Too bad my body's off-limits to you."

"Right back at you."

She tossed her hair over her shoulder and sashayed into the kitchen. I watched her perfect, tight ass and the sway of her hips, knowing she was putting on a show for me as I followed behind.

Eden thanked us for the chocolates and flowers, pulled us into hugs, and shot down our offer to help. Dinner was ready. The table was set and all we had to do was take our seats.

I was seated next to Ava and across from Eden with a view of the midtown Manhattan skyline from the wall of windows across the expanse of their open-plan living/dining area. The loft was cool with soaring ceilings, exposed brick walls, and distressed hardwood floors covered in faded oriental rugs. A plush sectional and over-stuffed chairs were grouped around a vintage railroad cart coffee table. Eden's abstract paintings hung on the walls and I studied them from afar. She used a lot of drabs and blues with bursts of color to break up the darkness.

"Don't judge my paintings too harshly," she said when she caught me studying them. "Killian insisted on hanging them. If it had been up to me, they'd be living in the closet."

"Tell her they're good," he prompted. I didn't need prompting.

"They're awesome. You should set up your own show in a gallery."

"That's what I told her," Ava said, flashing me a smile like we were on the same team for a change. She returned her attention to Eden. "I'll promote it for you."

"Do it," I told Eden. "You can rent the space. You'd sell enough to cover the cost and end up with a profit."

"You make it sound so easy."

"It is easy." I had no doubt that people would buy her paintings. Painting with oils on canvases had never been my chosen art form, but I could tell from across the room that her abstracts were layered and textured. They had life and form and movement. No two people would see the same thing when they looked at them which was the beauty of good art. It was open to interpretation. It demanded that you sit up and take notice. "What's the worst that could happen?" I asked, spearing a bite of salad.

"Everyone will hate them. They'll call me out for being an amateur. And nobody will buy them."

"Not happening," Killian said. "Your art is amazing."

"You're biased."

"Am I biased?" Killian asked me and Ava.

Ava and I said no in unison, once again in agreement over something. "Do it," I said. "Life's too short to worry about other people's opinions. If someone doesn't like it, fuck them."

"Connor's motto," Ava said. "He never worries what anyone thinks."

I side-eyed her. "I care about some people's opinions."

"I meant it as a compliment."

"In that case, thank you."

She gave me a brilliant smile. "You're welcome."

I took a bite of my lasagna and caught Eden's eye. She grinned. "I've just come up with the best plan." Killian groaned, and she smacked his arm. "Hey. I'm full of great ideas. Look how great this dinner is turning out. It's already a success."

My left hand wandered over to Ava's thigh. She didn't swat it away. Success.

"The night is young," Ava muttered.

I gave her thigh a gentle squeeze, testing it out, and once again she didn't deny me. Ava and Eden took over the conversation, chatting about bridesmaid dresses, color schemes, flowers, and all things wedding-related while Killian and I powered through our dinner. It sounded as if Ava was not only the maid of honor, but she'd assigned herself as the wedding planner. I wasn't sure I'd even get an invitation to the wedding, let alone get asked to be the best man.

"We'll put together a spreadsheet tomorrow," Ava said, warming up to her topic. God help Eden. When Ava took over a project, you could be certain she'd go over the top and throw herself into it one hundred percent.

My hand ventured farther, sliding along her inner thigh. I heard her suck in her breath as my fingers found her sweet spot and rubbed against her clit. Her lips parted, and her breathing shallowed so I applied more pressure. She bucked against my hand.

"Ava?" Eden prompted. I felt like she'd been talking for a while but we'd both missed whatever she had said.

"Hmm?" Ava lifted her glass of wine to her lips and took a sip. "Great wine. Great food... everything is..."

My dick strained against my jeans as I rubbed between her thighs. Oh God. This was the sweetest form of torture. I was so turned on I could barely see straight.

"Great," Ava finished, her voice breathy.

Eden was talking. Ava was nodding in agreement. Maybe she was even answering. Who the hell knew?

Ava lifted her wineglass again and I could tell she was close by the way her legs trembled. I stroked her, my finger pressing against her clit through the leather. Her body spasmed and her glass tipped. Red wine splashed down the front of my shirt.

She set her glass on the table and eyed my blue button-down shirt. "How did that happen?"

I smirked. "No clue, butterfingers."

Eden jumped up from the table and grabbed paper towels from the kitchen. Killian retreated to his bedroom and came back with a clean T-shirt. I blotted the wine with paper towels before I stood, my shirt stuck to my skin. "I'll help you clean up," Ava said, nudging my arm. It sounded like a promise, one I was all too willing to go along with.

When Ava and I got into the guest bathroom, she closed the door behind her, forcing us into a confined space that was too small for both of us. "I can't believe I just let you do that," she said, her voice low. "We're supposed to be friends... not..."

I gave her a wicked grin as I adjusted myself in my jeans. Christ, I was so hard. Her body brushed against me as she tried to get past and I sucked in my breath. "Maybe you should give me a minute on my own."

Her gaze lowered. "Are you going to jerk off in their bathroom?"

"Wanna watch? Or do you want me to finish what I started?"

"Yes. No. Absolutely not," she said, pressing her lips together.

She turned her back to me, ran a washcloth under the water and squirted hand soap on it. She was watching me in the mirror above the sink as I unbuttoned my shirt, waiting for the big reveal, no doubt. I could have stepped aside to give us more space, but I stayed where I was, right behind Ava. I peeled off my wine-stained shirt and tossed it on the tiled floor. She turned around to face me, her eyes studying the dragon on my chest. For a few long moments, she stared silently before her eyes lifted to mine. "It's so beautiful," she said, her voice hushed.

I gave her a little smile. "To hide the ugly."

She lowered her eyes and ran the washcloth over my chest, her movements jerky. I could see that she was struggling for composure, taking deep breaths to calm herself. Her face always gave her away. She was on the brink of tears. I'd never been able to handle her tears and had always wanted to kiss them away, make things better for her. Ironic that I'd made her cry more than anyone ever had.

I took the washcloth out of her hand and finished the job myself then rinsed the washcloth and wrung it out. I pulled on Killian's T-shirt and Ava snatched up my stained shirt from the floor. "I'll wash it for you."

"Don't worry about it." I took the shirt out of her hand. "I can do my own laundry."

Cupping her chin, I tilted her face up to me. Her gray eyes searched mine, her lips slightly parted. I lowered my head and brushed my lips against hers. Gripping her bottom lip between my teeth, I bit it then sucked on it to take away the sting. Her body leaned into mine, soft and yielding and I wanted to take her right here, right now. Lift her onto the vanity and fuck her until the only word on her lips was my name. But this wasn't the way I wanted her. I wanted all of Ava.

I released her and walked out of the bathroom, wiping her lipstick off my mouth with the back of my hand before I joined Eden and Killian in the kitchen.

I nudged Eden away from the sink. "I'll do that."

"Thanks."

I rinsed and stacked the plates and silverware in the dishwasher while Killian ground fresh beans and brewed coffee in his sleek Italian machine. No doubt the coffee was for me, the only person at this little party who had to abstain from alcohol. He pressed a mug of coffee into my hands and topped off everyone else's wine glasses. Sucks to be me. I added milk and drank my Columbian roast to the tune of Macklemore's "Starting Over." At some point, Ava joined us, and she and Eden powered through the chocolate truffles.

"So… here's my idea. We can do an exhibit together," Eden said, smiling at me like she'd just solved all our problems. "I'll do it if you do it with me."

I shook my head. "Not happening."

"Scared?" she taunted.

"I'm too busy to work on something like that." Christ, I just bought the shop this morning. I couldn't even think about an art exhibition.

"You probably already have tons of stuff you can exhibit," Ava said, popping a chocolate into her mouth.

"I don't," I said, watching her lick the chocolate off her fingers. It was so fucking sexy I almost forgot what we were talking about. God, she loved to torture me. "I'm not a painter."

"Yes, you are. You're a graffiti artist," Ava said. "That's painting. Besides, you're really fast. You can whip up a piece in a few hours."

"Exactly," Eden said. "It takes me days, sometimes weeks, to finish a piece."

"Because you're a perfectionist with your art," Killian said, not masking the pride in his voice.

"There's no such thing as a perfectionist when it comes to art," Eden said.

Eden was confident in every area of her life except for her art. She still didn't believe that she was good enough, but I understood exactly where she was coming from.

"If you won't do it, I'm not doing it," Eden said, crossing her arms.

Killian jerked his chin, indicating that I should follow him. How the fuck had my innocent suggestion come to this? We wandered over to the wall of black steel-framed windows. From the kitchen, I heard Eden and Ava talking, their words drowned out by the music. "I'd owe you one," Killian said.

I wish I'd never suggested this idea. It was meant for Eden, not for me. I wasn't lying when I said I was busy. I already had a shit-load to deal with. Running the shop. Getting up to speed with the accounting and paperwork. I'd be working long hours and I had no time for this. Not to mention, I had zero desire to ever display anything in a gallery. That wasn't my scene. Perfect for Eden, a terrible idea for me. "Eden's art belongs in galleries. Mine doesn't. I'm a tattoo artist."

He stared out the window, lost in contemplation. "You've

always had the same problem Eden does. Thinking your art's never good enough," he said. "Seamus was wrong. You need to stop believing the things he said."

I rolled my shoulders, remembering some of the things he used to say. *You call that art? A kindergartener could do better than that. Stop wasting your time doodling and do something useful. Get your head out of the clouds, you fucking pussy.*

"Have you?" I asked Killian

"I'm working on it."

"Still seeing the shrink?"

"Yeah. I'm singlehandedly funding his exotic vacations."

I chuckled. "That bad, huh?"

"It's not easy, that's for damn sure."

"I know."

"I know you know. We lived it. But we came out the other side. Stronger. More resilient."

Killian never talked like this. Was he putting me in that same category? Stronger? More resilient? His shrink sessions must be paying off. Yesterday he said he was proud of me.

"Why couldn't you display graffiti in a gallery?" Killian asked.

He was asking for a favor and it was in my power to grant it. He didn't remind me that I owed him and Eden for everything I'd put them through last year. Because of my fuck-up, Killian had been shot three times in the chest. Thank God he'd been wearing a bulletproof vest. He'd shot and killed the man who had threatened Eden's life. Eden, who had been punched and kicked, bound at the ankles and wrists, a gun held to her head while I'd been tied to a chair, unable to help her. But it felt like Killian was trying to put that behind us. I didn't want to do this exhibition, but it looked as if I needed to. "No reason I couldn't."

"Good. And next time you want to get your ex-girlfriend off, don't do it at my dinner table."

I chuckled under my breath. "No idea what you're talking about."

11

AVA

"They're going to kill me," I told Killian on the phone after I'd given him all the details of the gallery space—six hundred square feet of exhibition space in Bed-Stuy. Inclusion in a bi-monthly newsletter with two thousand subscribers. Social media exposure on the gallery's website and Facebook page. A gallery technician to oversee the art installation. Music and a PA system. And a picture hanging system. Perfect. Except for one thing. A recent cancellation had freed up the only dates available for a year and it was only two months from now. Every other gallery space I'd called was booked for a year to two years in advance.

"It's better this way," Kilian said. "Less time to get themselves worked up about it. Book it." He gave me his credit card details and assured me it would be fine. When we hung up, I booked the gallery, not so sure it would be fine.

"Great news," I told Eden when she came into the office to pick up her paycheck. A positive attitude was the best approach. "I booked the gallery. For mid-December. That gives you two months to prepare." I gave her two thumbs-up. "Perfect, right?"

Her jaw dropped to the floor and she slammed the door shut behind her. "Are you insane?" she shouted. "I won't be ready in two months. I need more time... I need..." She stopped talking and started hyperventilating, pacing the floor, and saying "Oh my God" on repeat.

I reached into the desk drawer where I kept my emergency supplies and tossed her a pack of Twizzlers. "This is one of those situations where you just need to take the plunge," I said as Eden chewed furiously on the licorice. "Dive right in."

"Easy for you to say. You have no idea how stressful this is."

I propped my feet on the desk and leaned back in my chair with my arms crossed. "Tell Dr. Christensen. I'll talk you down from the ledge."

"This is payback, isn't it? For that coffee date and the dinner set-up. You're trying to punish me for meddling in your relationship," she accused.

"I should be offended you think so little of me." I tossed her the Buddha stress ball. "Give Buddha a few squeezes. You'll feel better. And no, this is not payback. Killian and I are doing this for you. It's a great idea and you can thank us for it later. It's going to be a total success. I believe in you."

She chomped away on her Twizzlers and squeezed the stress ball in her other hand. Eden would be fine. She had Killian's full support and she'd finished painting her mural on the boutique wall, so she'd have time to work on her paintings.

"Was Connor cool with it?"

Connor. I knew he was just doing this for Eden and Killian. He'd never had any desire to exhibit in a gallery. I cleared my throat. "He doesn't know yet. I'm going to tell him in person. Today."

Her eyebrows shot up. "Really? You're going to Forever Ink?"

I shrugged like it was no big deal. I used to hang out there a lot, but it had been a few years since I'd set foot in the tattoo shop. That was Connor's space and I'd steered clear. "I can't text or call him with something like this. I need to tell him in person."

He's going to kill me.

Eden nodded and replaced the Buddha on the shelf but kept the Twizzlers. "Do you think he can handle all of this, Ava? I didn't even think of everything he's dealing with when I railroaded him into this."

"He'll be okay," I said, hoping it was true. "He does his best creative work when he's under the wire. You should have seen him when he was working on his art school portfolio. He'd never planned to apply to art school, but his teacher believed in him and encouraged him to go for it. Connor decided to go for it one month before the deadline. Then he worked his ass off to get the pieces ready. And they were amazing."

"And he not only got in, he got a scholarship."

"Killian told you that?" I asked, surprised. I knew Connor wouldn't have. He never bragged about it. I doubted he ever told anyone other than me, Killian, and Mr. Santos.

"Yeah. He's proud of Connor," Eden said. "He just has a hard time expressing it. But he's getting better."

"They seem like they're doing better." What I'd seen on Tuesday night had given me hope.

"Yeah. I think Killian's ready to move on and put the past behind him."

"That's good. They need each other."

"Yeah, they do," she said thoughtfully. "So, what about you and Connor? Are you ready to put the past behind you?"

"I'm—"

The door swung open and Zeke stepped inside, saving me from having to answer the question. "What are you girls gossiping about?"

"You," Eden and I said in unison and high-fived each other.

Zeke gave us a big wink. "Bet it's juicy."

"See you guys later," Eden said, waving over her shoulder.

I groaned. "I hate the word juicy."

Zeke laughed. "I know. Juicy. Moist. Nibbles."

I shuddered. "Stop torturing me with your word porn." I jumped up from my chair and pulled on my white cardigan, doing up the tiny pearl buttons then shouldered my bag. "I'm out of here."

"Something I said?" Zeke asked, taking my seat and rolling it in front of the desk.

"Somewhere I need to be." I didn't know Connor's schedule. I'd probably catch him in the middle of tattooing. It had been years since I'd watched him work. But I used to love it. Before I left, I filled Zeke in on everything I'd done today. Paid invoices. Updated our social media. Booked a Christmas party for a corporate law firm.

"You're a star," he said.

"I shine bright," I agreed, happy with the way things had turned out with me and Zeke. It was like we'd never hooked up. We'd gone right back to being friends and colleagues with no awkwardness whatsoever. If only the rest of my life could be that simple.

"Love the hair, by the way," he said, his fingers flying over the keyboard as he typed an email.

"They say blondes have more fun. Thought I'd test that theory again."

"How's that working out for you?"

I thought about the near-orgasm Connor gave me at the dinner table two nights ago. And the teasing kiss in the bathroom. He'd left me wanting more. On purpose. We couldn't do that anymore. From now on, I wouldn't allow myself to cross the lines of friendship. "Early days. But so far, so good."

"I'm digging the Granny chic style," he said.

I looked down at my white chiffon midi-skirt, black tights, and Doc Martens, not sure if that was a compliment or not. On my way out, I picked up a taco from Jimmy's truck and asked him to put it in a to-go container. Carnitas was Connor's favorite. Maybe a food donation would soften the blow.

On the fifteen-minute walk to Forever Ink, I made a mental inventory of how I could help Connor. I knew Jared used the same accounting software we used at the bar. I could help him with that and organize the office for him. I could set up an Instagram account for the shop, something I'd encouraged Jared to do ages ago, but he'd never done. The shop was open one to nine, seven days a week. Fifty-six hours a week plus the extra hours for cleaning the shop and sterilizing the equipment. On top of that, he'd have to pay invoices, do the inventory and ordering, and the accounting. It wouldn't be easy, but Connor could do this.

Despite barely scraping by in high school, Connor was smart. When he did study and put his mind to it, he'd easily pull off As on his exams to bring up his average to a passing mark. In our senior year, his English teacher accused him of cheating. She insisted that he'd either plagiarized or gotten someone else to write his essays. She called them brilliant and insightful and didn't believe Connor had it in him to produce that kind of work. He'd flown off the handle, stalked out of her classroom, and slammed the door. The guidance counselor and principal had been called in to deal with it. Fortunately, the guidance counselor wasn't a total tool and suggested that Connor write an essay in his office. The teacher grudgingly admitted that it was up to the same standard as the others, but Connor never got an apology which pissed him off. As a result, he handed in mediocre work for the rest of the year and ended up with a C instead of an A.

By the time I entered the shop, I felt good about my decision to support Connor. Maybe it would lessen the blow when I told him he only had two months to prepare for the exhibit. A girl with long dark hair, a lip ring and multiple ear piercings, peered at me over the counter. "Do you have an appointment?"

"No. I'm here to see Connor."

My gaze wandered over to his station. He was tattooing a guy's arm and laughing at whatever the guy said. Connor looked like he was in his element, like he was somewhere he belonged. Happy. Confident. Relaxed. In complete control of the machine in his hand. My gaze lingered on his face. He was in the zone, and nothing around him existed except for the guy and the tattoo he was working on. He got like that when he was working on his art, the same way I did with my aerial silks class.

"Connor's busy," the girl behind the counter said, drawing my attention back to her.

"I can wait."

"He might be a while. And he doesn't like to be interrupted when he's working."

"I'll just sit on the sofa and wait for him to finish."

"Suit yourself."

Fine, I'll suit myself.

I sank down into the black leather sofa, set the taco container on the coffee table, and crossed my legs to wait. While I waited, I watched Connor. He looked so good in his faded jeans and fitted white T-shirt, the muscles in his arm flexing as he inked his design.

God, I missed his body. I missed his everything.

I'd tried so hard to forget him. But he had been there in every song, in every memory, in every teardrop.

"Hey Ava," Jared said, coming to stand in front of me. "Long time, no see."

I stood and hugged Jared. After we chatted for a few minutes, he introduced me to Claudia, the girl behind the desk. "You should show Ava the jewelry," he told Claudia. "She doesn't mind a piercing, do you, girl?"

I already had three piercings in each ear and a belly button piercing, all of which I'd gotten at this shop when I was eighteen and had gone on a piercing spree. "I have a few, but I think I'm good."

"How do you all know each other?" Claudia asked, trying to sound casual but she was obviously fishing for information and her eyes were narrowed on me.

"We go way back," Jared said. "I met Connor and Ava six years ago. They were inseparable."

"Once upon a time," I said.

Claudia arched her brows. "The fairy tale ended?"

I looked her straight in the eye and saw it written all over her face. She wanted Connor. That's why she'd given me attitude. She viewed me as the competition.

"The fairy tale isn't over yet," Connor said, coming out of nowhere. He slung an arm across my shoulder and tucked me close to his side like he was trying to prove something. "Ava is still my princess. I'm working on being her white knight."

I lifted my eyes to his. "Sounds like a good story."

"Guaranteed to have a happy ending."

"You're making guarantees now?"

He lowered his head and whispered in my ear. "Are you here to take advantage of me? That can be arranged."

Without giving me a chance to respond, Connor guided me away from the desk and to the private room in the back. When we got inside, he closed the door behind me and caged me in his arms. "Miss me?"

Every. Single. Day.

His lips brushed across my jaw. My eyes closed, and I leaned back against the door for support. "Connor," I whispered.

"Tell me what you want, Ava."

He pressed his body against mine and I could feel his erection pressing against my hip. Oh God. How easy it would be to give myself to him. To let him take me on the tattoo table. Against the wall. Anywhere. He worked his kisses down my neck. They were just whispers of a kiss, so soft and gentle they almost hurt. I wanted to grind my body against his, release the ache between my thighs. Instead, I stayed perfectly still, the palms of my hands flat against the door, my legs trembling underneath me, my breathing ragged.

I need you. Now.

"Connor..." I panted.

"Tell me to stop." The back of his fingers brushed over my nipple. My bra and T-shirt offered no protection. My nipples hardened under his touch and I was dizzy with need and want.

"Stop," I whispered, knowing that he would do as I asked.

He dropped his arms to his side and took a few steps back. My body betraying my words, I leaned against the door for support.

"Your wish is my command."

I hadn't really meant it. But I wanted to mean it. "Did you sleep with Claudia?"

He tilted his head, studying my face. "Would it bother you if I said yes?"

I shrugged like it didn't matter to me one way or the other. But it mattered. I couldn't bear to think of him with her or anyone who wasn't me. "Just curious."

He grinned at me. "Give me an honest answer and I'll tell you."

"Whatever. It's none of my business. We're just friends."

"That's right. So why are you here, *friend?*"

Why was I here? Crap. I needed to tell him about the exhibit. "When's your next customer?"

"Fifteen minutes. You looking for a quickie?"

"Get your mind out of the gutter."

He escorted me out of the room and outside behind the shop. "I need some fresh air," he said, lighting a cigarette.

"Doesn't smoking defeat the purpose?"

"You know me. I'm a walking contradiction." He took a drag on his cigarette and exhaled out the side of his mouth, the smoke drifting in the opposite direction of me. "So, what's up, besides my dick?"

It was almost an invitation to look. Anyone would. The bulge in his jeans was hard to miss. Connor was... well-endowed. Yep, he had a big dick and he knew how to use it. Oh, did he ever.

"Are you checking me out?" he asked.

"No." I leaned against the wall and crossed my arms, ignoring his chuckle. I side-eyed him. Smoking wasn't supposed to be sexy. But when Connor smoked, it was sexy. When he inhaled, his eyes narrowed, the little lines around his eyes crinkling.

"Okay, listen, I've got something to tell you. Don't freak out. I'm going to help you."

"Help me do what?" he teased. "Are you going to get me off? My hand could use a rest."

I stifled a groan. I didn't want to think about him using his hand. Stay focused.

"I've booked the gallery for mid-December—"

"*What the fuck?*" He glared at me. I squared my shoulders and held my ground.

"It will be okay," I said, trying to reassure him.

"Okay?" he asked incredulously. "I've got a shitload of things to deal with. I can't—"

"You can. You're an amazing artist, Connor. And like I said, you're fast. You can do graffiti on canvases or... would you use canvases?" He was still glaring at me. I waved my hand in the air. "Anyway, it'll be just like throwing something up on a wall. Except you won't need to worry about getting caught."

He took a drag of his cigarette and blew the smoke in my direction.

"Rude," I said, waving it away.

"Do you want me to fail, Ava?" he asked, his voice low and angry. But I heard the hurt in his voice, too. "Is that why you did this?"

"No. I don't want you to fail. How could you think that?"

He snorted. "No idea. Maybe because you booked a fucking gallery, two months from now. Thanks for having my back, *friend*."

"You're not going to fail. I know you can do this. I watched you tattooing that guy and—"

"I'm not worried about the tattooing," he said through gritted teeth. "Do you know how hard I need to work to stay away from drugs? I ran into Danny—" He stopped himself before giving the full name, but I knew exactly who he was talking about. Danny Vargas, scum of the earth. "He said he could hook me up. The people I used to know... the ones who are still using... they don't want me to be clean. It pisses them off."

"But you said no, right?"

He shook his head. "You still feel the need to ask. I guess that says it all."

He tossed his cigarette on the ground and lit another one as he crushed the first one under the sole of his boot. I bit my lip to stop myself from calling him out on it. Smoking wasn't great, but it was better than what he did before.

"I just... I worry about you, okay? Danny Vargas is a horrible human being. I blame him for getting you hooked—"

"Nobody forced me to do drugs. It was my choice. But now... I am trying so damn hard to make sure I don't slip. And until just recently, I didn't have Killian's support. I didn't have yours... hell, I still don't know if I do. I don't know where I stand with you on any given day. You love me. You hate me. Maybe you don't even like me. What's the point of being friends or anything else if you can't even trust me?"

I want to trust you. "I'll do whatever I can to support you. I'll help you with the paperwork and the accounting... I can do an hour a day and I can take care of your social—"

"Thanks, but no thanks. I need to do this on my own."

"No, you don't. I want to help you. Don't let your stubborn pride get in the way."

He clenched his jaw. I sighed. I still knew him so well. Which meant I also knew how to get through to him.

"Remember Jake Masters?"

"Fucking douchebag. How could I forget Jake Masters?" He took an angry drag on his cigarette, his eyes narrowed into slits.

For some reason, out of thousands of students, he'd targeted me. "In the beginning, he used to flirt with me. Like I should feel honored he chose me. But I told him I wasn't interested, to stop bothering me. It started with just words..." Connor knew all this, but I felt the need to remind him. "He called me ice princess. He asked me why I acted like I was better than him."

"Because you were better than him. And you didn't let him take something you weren't willing to give."

"Jake came into the bar about a year and a half ago." He hadn't changed much since high school. He still had a permanent smirk on his face and tousled brown hair he probably spent a lot of time styling. As proof that life wasn't fair, he'd landed a trading job on Wall Street and had bought a waterfront apartment in one of the glass and steel monstrosities in Williamsburg, something he'd been quick to brag about. "I was in the front talking to Killian when he came in."

Connor ground out his cigarette under his boot and waited for me to go on. His jaw was clenched, the little muscle in his cheek jumping.

"It had been so long, but as soon as I saw him, I was four-teen again. He made me feel... helpless, like he still had all the power." Memories washed over me, but there was still one that I always blocked out. "I got that sick feeling in my stomach, you know?"

"Yeah, I know," he said, his voice soft, his eyes filled with concern. "What happened?"

"Killian wanted to kick him out, but I told him I needed to confront Jake. So, I did. And after I went off on him, he said, 'Why are all the hot chicks so fucked up?'"

"Fucking asshole," Connor ground out and then in a softer voice he said, "I'm sorry, baby. I'm so sorry."

"It's okay. I'm glad I confronted him. But afterward, all I wanted to do was call you and talk about it. Because you used to be my best friend. And you're the only one who would have understood how it made me feel."

He lowered his head and rubbed the back of his neck. "But I was in Miami."

"Yeah. But I'm not telling you this to make you feel bad. I'm telling you this because you were my white knight, Connor."

"Killian was your white knight. He beat up Jake, not me."

That still bothered Connor, but he hadn't even been there when it had happened. By chance, Killian had come outside and caught the tail end of it. "I know and that was great. I appreciated what Killian did. But you were the one who picked me up and helped me put the pieces back together. You made me believe it wasn't my fault. You were always there for me. You made me feel beautiful and special and cherished. I felt like Jake broke something inside of me—"

"He didn't," he said, sounding angry that I would even suggest that. "You were too strong to break."

It was nice that he believed that but, at the time, I did feel broken. And ashamed. Scared. Angry. Victimized. And so alone. Until Connor had befriended me. "Because it only lasted a few months. But you... what you lived through... I never would have been strong enough to live through that. It would have broken me. It didn't break you, Connor. You're so much stronger than you know. And I always used to be on your side because you were always on mine. Remember when we were on the same team?"

Connor squinted into the distance. "I remember."

"When I lost you, I not only lost a boyfriend, I lost my best friend."

He closed his eyes. "Ava..."

"I've missed you," I said, being more honest than I'd been in a long time. "So much."

"Missed you too. I've been gone a while, but I'm back now."

"I want to believe in you again." It wasn't the same as saying that I did believe in him, but it was a start.

"What were you thinking, Ava? *Two months?*"

"It was the only date available for a year. But you can do it. I know you can."

He exhaled sharply. Claudia poked her head out the back door. "Connor. Your next client is here."

"Be right in."

I looked over my shoulder as the door closed behind Claudia. "I didn't sleep with her."

"I didn't sleep with Orlando." He smiled, happy that I'd admitted it. Orlando was just a friend, and he was a good instructor. Not to mention that he was more likely to go for Connor than me. "So..." I clapped my hands together and rocked back on my heels. "You'll accept my help, right?"

He gave me a wicked grin I didn't trust. "Since you're offering... there's something I need."

"Dinner? I brought you a taco."

He shook his head. "Not what I had in mind."

"What do you need?" I asked warily. If he was talking about sex, the answer was no. Absolutely not. No sex with the ex.

"An invitation."

12

CONNOR

*T*here were four women in the class, but I had no interest in watching the others. I was only here for Ava. I leaned against the wall, out of the way. Multi-colored silk ropes hung from the rafters of a double-height ceiling. Ava was wearing Lycra leggings and a sports bra, her toned stomach on full display. She was all lean muscle, she'd always been in good shape, but this was the fittest I'd ever seen her. Christ, she was strong and so flexible it got me thinking about things I shouldn't.

She was trying to forget I was here, so she could get in her zone. But every now and then she glanced over at me then shook her head a little like she needed to stop doing that. I didn't want to mess up her class or ruin her concentration, so I fiddled with my phone for a while and Googled random things—glass blowing, the graffiti on the Berlin Wall, and Rio de Janeiro. I scrolled through photos of Christ the Redeemer, arms open wide above a sprawling city. Sandy beaches and rolling green hills, colonial architecture, the carnival. The vibrant street art in a city riddled by crime, inhabited by the wealthy and the wretchedly poor. It seemed like my kind of place, a city with a heartbeat, heat, color, and contradictions.

When the first notes of Muse's "Undisclosed Desires" started playing, I pocketed my phone and tipped back my head, looking up. Ava had climbed to the top, a turquoise silk wrapped around her ankle, her hands holding the silk tie taut, back arched and her body suspended upside down and high above. I could tell by the look on her face that she was fully in the moment. Everything around her had ceased to exist. I couldn't say what she was doing. I didn't have the names for her moves. All I knew was that it was brave and daring and so fucking beautiful. Flying and dropping down in a free-fall. She made it look effortless, her flexible body bending to her will. Fluid and graceful. Her moves synchronized to the music.

Ava, my muse, my inspiration. She would be my art.

She didn't notice when I snapped photos on my phone. Or the way I stared at her, in shock and awe. Fragile, my ass. This girl wasn't made of glass. She was forged of malleable steel.

If Ava were a tree, she'd be a willow. They bend, but they don't break.

When the class ended, I waited for her to come to me. She dressed in her hoodie and Nikes, said goodbye to the others, and walked toward me with a smile that was just for me. I recognized that smile like a song I hadn't heard in a long time but still remembered all the lyrics.

"You amaze me."

"It's not easy to amaze you," she said. "With your short attention span."

True. I had a low threshold for boredom, but Ava had never bored me. I found her endlessly fascinating. "You always manage to keep me entertained."

"Empanadas?"

I laughed and took her backpack off her shoulder and slung it over mine.

"I brought my iPad," she said, following me out to my bike. "We can make a plan. I also have a roll of quarters and a huge appetite."

"You should have been a Girl Scout. Always prepared."

"I wouldn't have lasted a day. I don't play well with others, remember?"

I laughed. Her second-grade teacher had written that on her report card and it still bothered her. "That's because you were still playing your perfect princess role. You left that girl in the dust years ago."

"Right about the time I met you."

"I ruined you for all others," I said.

"You did."

"What about Zeke?" I asked.

"What about him?"

I was about to put her helmet on for her, but she took it out of my hand and did it herself. "Let's go," she said. "I'm hungry."

On the short drive to the diner, I tortured myself with thoughts of her and Zeke together. What could they possibly have in common? Besides working together. And sleeping together. Fuck. I needed to let it go, but it was hard.

When we were seated in a booth with menus in front of us, she smashed the roll of quarters against the table edge and spilled them onto the table. "We can play quarters with our papaya juice."

"Fun times."

"Don't do that," she said, feeding quarters into the machine.

"Do what?"

"That thing you do when you're pissed off. You get all cranky and disagreeable."

I am peaceful. I am strong. Blah, blah, fucking blah.

I leaned back against the seat and crossed my arms. "How many guys have you been with?"

She jabbed at the keys on the jukebox, ignoring my question, then gathered up the extra quarters and tossed them in her bag. Ava smirked when "I Heard It Through the Grapevine" started playing.

"Funny."

"Does it really matter how many guys there were? If none of them—"

"If none of them... what?"

Our conversation was cut short by the waitress stopping by our booth to take our order, a different waitress from last time. I did the ordering for both of us. Stupid, really. Like I had something to prove. Like I needed to be in control of something in my life.

After the waitress left our booth, Ava leaned her folded arms on the table. "It doesn't matter if I've been with two guys or twenty."

Twenty. What the fuck? It mattered to me.

"It's not like you haven't been with other girls."

"I haven't been with anyone since that night with you." Eighteen... nineteen months ago. It was a few days before Killian had hauled my ass off to rehab. Ava had called me when she was feeling low and I was flying high. The sad part was that I barely remembered that night with her.

"Not even... just for a night?" she asked.

I shook my head. Her gaze dropped to my chest then she pulled out her iPad and a keyboard and set it up on the table. "Let's get organized," she said, pulling up a spreadsheet. Little Miss Efficient.

"You think a spreadsheet will solve all our problems?" I asked, watching her type something into one of the boxes. She kept right on typing, her brow furrowed, like this spreadsheet was the most important thing in the world.

"If you're sexually frustrated, then maybe you should do something about it," she said, still typing.

"And what do you suggest? Should I take Claudia up on her offer?"

Her mouth dropped open and she lifted her head from the screen. "She offered to have sex with you?"

"Don't look so horrified. Some women think I'm hot."

"*Most* women think you're hot." She lifted her eyes to my face then lowered them again. "It's just... Claudia doesn't look like your type."

"And Zeke was yours?"

She shrugged. "It was fun for a while."

"Fun," I said like it was a dirty word.

"It was easy, okay? Don't judge me for that. I was trying to get over you. I've been trying to get over you for years."

"And how did that work out?"

"You tell me. I'm sitting across the table from you in a diner we used to go to when we were madly in love. And I don't want you to be with Claudia or anyone else. But all I can offer you right now is friendship and my organizational skills. Don't force my hand, Connor. Don't tempt me to give you something I'm not ready to give you." Her bottom lip trembled, and she gripped it between her teeth.

For a few long moments, neither of us spoke. I knew she wasn't just talking about sex. She wasn't ready to trust me with her heart. "I'll wait for you," I said, finally.

"I don't know how long it will take...or even if—"

"I'll wait."

"Connor..."

She sat back as the waitress served our food. For a few seconds, she just stared at it spread out in front of us. Then she lifted her gaze to me and we both laughed as Tammy Wynette started singing about standing by your man. "Such a lame song," she said, picking up an empanada. "Tammy wasn't much of a feminist."

"After all, he's just a man," I quoted.

"Exactly. What can you expect?" she asked, taking a big bite of her empanada. "Sounds like the woman has to do all the heavy lifting."

I jerked my chin at her iPad. "You should be taking notes. Tammy's giving you some good advice."

"How to build up the weaker sex. How to accept everything he does even when you don't understand it. How to forgive him for every shitty thing he did... over and over. I should have earned a badge for that."

I narrowed my eyes at her. She diverted her gaze and I could tell she regretted saying the words, but she'd said them anyway. When you love someone, you give them the power to destroy you. With a careless word. A look. A gesture. You know how to hurt them more deeply than anyone else ever could. Love makes you vulnerable, exposed, your soul bared to them.

"I'm sorry," she said quietly. "I didn't mean that."

"You did. But it's okay. You earned the badge."

She didn't respond. While she ate, she devoted her attention to building a spreadsheet. An extensive to-do list of all the things *we* needed to accomplish over the next two months, all designed to get me ready for this fucking exhibition while I also ran the shop and did everything else I needed to keep myself on the straight and narrow. Gym time. Healthy eating schedule. My weekly meetings. It sucked. All of it. I'd always considered myself a free spirit, a law unto myself, but that hadn't worked out so well. As much as I hated following a schedule, following all the rules, it was now one of life's necessities.

Ava and I had changed. Life had changed us. Turned us into people I sometimes didn't recognize. But sometimes I still caught fleeting glimpses of who she used to be. Back when Ava was more trusting, more open, more willing to believe that I could be someone good. Someone worthy. Someone she wanted to build up instead of tear down. Maybe I was still clinging to the past, holding on to fragments of a dream that had vanished.

"Does working at the bar make you happy?" I asked her when I dropped her off in front of her apartment.

"I love my job."

"Good."

She tilted her head, reading the skeptical look on my face. "Why the doubt?"

I shrugged. "I always thought you'd do something creative. Dance or choreography... I never pictured you working in an office."

"I studied business in college."

"I know." That had surprised me, too. I had always thought Ava belonged in a spotlight, not hiding behind textbooks and computer screens.

"Who knows? I might run off to the Cirque de Soleil someday."

"You'd be the star of the show."

Her smile faded. "I hate it when I hurt your feelings." I shrugged one shoulder like it was no big deal. I wished the words would just slide off my back, but they never did. Words had always hurt me more than fists. I'd learned to roll with the punches years ago, and had developed a tough exterior, but words... they still got under my skin and echoed in my head long after they were said.

"I'll try to refrain from bitchy comments."

"Say whatever you need to." I pounded my fist against my heart. "I'm wearing my suit of armour."

"You can handle the slings and arrows from my sharp tongue?"

"Even the poisonous ones. Let 'em fly."

"My knight in shining armour," she teased.

I winked at her and watched her walk away. When she reached her front door, she turned and blew me a kiss before going inside. I held my hand against my heart.

Ah, Ava, you slay me.

13

AVA

It had been three weeks since the night Connor came to watch my aerial silks class. Last week, Killian helped Connor move into Jared's place. It didn't take them long. Connor didn't have a lot of stuff and most of what he had ended up at Goodwill because Connor bought Jared's furniture. Jared wanted to make a fresh start in San Diego when or if he ended up settling down there. First, he was going traveling and had no plans beyond the next few months.

"You again," Claudia grouched, standing on the other side of the partition of Forever Ink's office. You couldn't really call it an office. Just a space in the back partitioned off from the rest of the shop.

I lifted my mug of green tea to my lips and eyed her over the rim as I took a sip. "You should get used to me. I'm going to be hanging around a lot."

She rolled her eyes and rested her folded arms on the partition. "What's the deal with you and Connor?"

I arched a brow. "Are we friends now?"

"I know when to cut my losses. Besides, he never paid me the slightest interest."

I smiled at her admission. It shouldn't matter. Unfortunately, it did.

"Don't gloat. It's annoying."

"Ugh. I know. You're right," I said, wiping the smile off my face. "Where is he?"

She looked over her shoulder. "Consulting with a client. Up front." She returned her attention to me and raised her eyebrows, waiting for an answer.

"We're just friends."

She snorted. "That never works."

"It's working." I'd been refraining from bitchy comments and Connor had been treating me as a friend. Sort of.

"Take it from me, it will end in one of two ways. You'll either get back together and it will all work out because you're older and wiser and you've forgiven each other for past mistakes. Or you'll be reminded of all the reasons you couldn't be with each other and you'll realize that people don't change that much."

"Are you speaking from experience?"

"I have a degree in psychology. It's useless for everything except giving advice. I'm great at dishing it out. Taking it is a different story."

"Well, thanks for the chat."

"Anytime. And for the record, I'd still do him."

"For the record, if you go after him, I'll scratch your eyes out." *What was my problem?* I didn't want him, but I didn't want anyone else to have him either? Who was I kidding? I still wanted him. I just didn't *want* to want him. I squeezed the stapler a few times in frustration, the staples forming a heap on the desktop.

She made a meow sound. "The kitten has claws."

I brushed the staples into the wastepaper basket, hiding the evidence. "And wicked Krav Maga skills. Watch your back."

"Damn girl, I love it when you get all Kill Bill."

I looked over my shoulder at Connor, eyeing the Led Zeppelin T-shirt he'd had since high school. It never used to fit him so... snugly. He needed to stay away from the gym or start wearing looser T-shirts. This was far too distracting. "Where did you come from?"

He grinned. "Watch your back. I was right behind it."

I swung my gaze to Claudia, my eyes narrowed. She shrugged. "I thought he was up front."

"He moves like a ninja," I muttered.

Claudia disappeared to the front of the shop, leaving me alone with Connor. He tossed his electronic cigarette on the newly-installed shelf behind me. A few days ago, I'd gotten Connor to hang shelves on the wall to store the color-coded binders I'd set up for him. It was easier than digging through the cardboard filing boxes Jared had used for the paperwork. "That thing sucks."

"Vaping won't blacken your lungs like nicotine, tar—"

"Yeah, yeah. I heard your lecture already."

"So, buy a pack of cigarettes and stop blaming me for caring about your health and well-being. Your choice, Rocket Man."

"Rocket Man? Oh no." His mouth quirked with amusement. "Don't tell me you still listen to that song."

"It's a great song."

Connor snickered. "Does it still make you cry?"

I shrugged. "Maybe."

"What makes you cry?" Lee asked, stopping on his way outside, a pack of Camels and a lighter in his hand. His dark hair stuck up all over, defying gravity, with the help of a liberal amount of gel.

"Electronic cigarettes make me cry," Connor said, eyeing Lee's cigarettes.

"No shit, dude," Lee rubbed his middle finger over the silver barbell piercing in his right eyebrow, like he was flipping the bird to electronic cigarettes. "They're not satisfying."

"They also won't cause lung cancer," I pointed out.

"Everyone's gotta go someday. Might as well enjoy life while you can. If you need a smoke, I'm outside," Lee said, pushing through the back door.

"I'm leaving now," I said. "Do whatever you want. Smoke. Don't smoke. It's your life."

Connor put his hands on either side of the armed swivel chair, his face so close to mine I could smell his cinnamon gum and his clean manly scent. It gave me a head rush. My gaze swept over his face, to the tangle of dark lashes framing his blue eyes and down to his mouth. He ran his tongue over his bottom lip and I swallowed hard. My pulse was racing, thrumming in my ears. He knew what he was doing to me. He knew his nearness messed with my head.

His mouth curved into a smile, showing off his straight white teeth and the dimple in his right cheek. "Get out of my space," I said. *I can't breathe.*

He chewed on his gum, a lazy grin still on his face. I was tempted to smack it off. God, he made me violent. I still couldn't believe I'd kicked him in the balls. That was an all-time low. He'd been in so much pain it had made *me* nauseous.

"Would you really scratch out Claudia's eyes?" he asked, letting go of my chair. I scooted the chair back before I stood so I wouldn't be in his personal space.

"I was just joking," I said, putting on my army jacket and shouldering my bag.

He tilted his head, a smile tugging at his lips. "You sounded pretty serious."

"I need to go back to work." I tried to walk around him, but he blocked my exit with a wall of muscle. I flapped my hand in the air. "Get out of my way."

His smile grew wider. I planted my hands on my hips and glared at him.

"I'll pick you up after class tonight," he said, still not budging.

"You need to be here. I checked your appointment schedule. You're fully booked until the end of the night."

"Shit," he muttered.

"It's a good thing. And I'm okay getting home on my own. You know I can defend myself. I'm a badass."

He chuckled as I drew myself up to my full five feet, three inches.

"A badass in a fun-sized package."

"Fun-sized," I scoffed. "Get out of my way before I make you."

Connor stepped aside to let me pass and fell into step with me.

"Don't forget to take pictures of awesome tattoos," I said, glancing over at the tattoo stations where Gavin and AJ, the new tattoo artist, were working. AJ's red hair snaked over one shoulder, her tank top showing off her colorful tattoo sleeves. She used to work at a shop in the city with Gavin, so she had no trouble making the transition to this shop. Tattoo artists were like free agents who brought in their own customers and paid a percentage of their earnings to the shop, so Connor didn't really need to manage them. He just had to keep track of their days off and put in orders for their supplies. "Your followers on Instagram are loving it."

Connor was too busy humming "Rocket Man" to care about his followers. Not that he'd care anyway. I didn't know what he had against social media, but he'd always been weird about it. He'd never had personal Facebook, Instagram, or Twitter accounts. I've been keeping the Forever Ink accounts updated, although he specifically told me not to include photos of him.

"Stop it with the 'Rocket Man,'" I said as he sang a few verses, holding the front door open for me. He had a good singing voice, but I refrained from mentioning it. No need to encourage him.

He stopped on the sidewalk in front of me and squinted in the afternoon sunlight. I slipped on a pair of oversized tortoiseshell sunglasses to cut the glare. "Why does that song make you sad?" he asked, his gaze settling on my face.

Because *you're* the rocket man and you were gone for such a long, long time. High as a kite. Maybe the song wasn't about drug abuse at all, but that's how I'd always interpreted it. "It just sounds so lonely," I said, because to me, it did.

"I'm back on earth," he said, and I guess he understood all the words I hadn't said. Maybe he could still read my mind the way he used to. What a scary thought.

"See you tomorrow," I said, walking away. "Same bad time, same bad place."

"Best part of my day," he called after me.

Mine too. I waved goodbye over my shoulder. Connor probably didn't need my help, but I enjoyed the hour I spent at the shop each day. I loved seeing him in his element. I loved seeing him clean and sober, and happy in a way he hadn't been in a long, long time. As I walked to the bar in the mellow sunshine, the air crisp and cool, smelling like freshly-sharpened pencils and wood smoke, I thought about what Claudia had said. The reason Connor and I had broken up wasn't an issue anymore. He was drug-free and working hard to stay that way. Like he'd said at the diner, his lies and empty promises had stemmed from his drug use. He'd always tried to cover it up, justify it, hide it from me.

Should I continue to blame him for all the wrongs of the past, hold a grudge, refuse to forgive him for the hurt he'd caused? I wanted so much to let it all go, to trust him and believe in him again. My life didn't feel complete without him in it.

14

CONNOR

I blew smoke out my open window and watched it curl into the night air. My new plan was to stick to vaping during the day and reward myself with the real thing at night after the shop was closed, and I was home, alone. Pathetic. But smoking was the last vice left to me and I wasn't ready to give it up.

My TV was playing in the background, a nature program, and I watched from my spot at the window as a lioness chased a gazelle across the African plains. The gazelle was beautiful. Swift and graceful. And about to become the lion's next meal. Against all odds, I was rooting for the gazelle to win. Nature was cruel. Survival of the fittest. The gazelle didn't stand a chance against a hungry lion. I turned my head. I couldn't bear to watch it.

My phone rang in my pocket and I slid it out, checking the screen. Why was Ava calling me at midnight? "Are you okay?" I asked.

"Yeah. I couldn't sleep."

"You need me to sing a lullaby? Some Elton John?" I took another drag of my cigarette and exhaled out the side of my mouth.

"Are you smoking?"

"Yep."

She was silent for a few seconds and I waited for her to curse me out or deliver another lecture. "That's really good."

I laughed. "Yesterday you went off on me like the Attorney General issuing health warnings. And now it's really good?"

"Not the smoking. Your honesty."

There was a time when everything I told her was the truth. But that was a long time ago. "How was class? Were you flying high?"

"Yeah. It was a total rush." She talked about the way it made her feel and I was listening to her words, but mostly to her voice. Her speaking voice was sexy. Breathy. But when she sang, it was different. She could sing low and sultry, with a smoky, jazzy quality to her voice and she could hit the high notes when she sang those Adele songs she talked about belting out. When I was in the hospital and she sat by my bed, singing softly, or talking to me, it was her voice that had soothed my troubled soul. Her voice that had dragged me back from the edge and gave me hope that the world couldn't be so fucked-up if she was in it.

I heard a rustling sound like she was settling into bed.

"Are you in bed?"

"Yeah."

"What are you wearing?" I pictured her in one of her sexy, matching sets. Her lingerie was the stuff of my wet dreams. Underneath her flea market clothes, she always wore lacy numbers. Or silky ones. At night, she wore those little silky camisole and panty ensembles. Feminine. Sexy as hell.

"We're not playing this game," she said.

I let my imagination fill in the blanks. Her outfit was silky and red, the same shade as her lipstick. The camisole was trimmed in lace, showing off her cleavage. I tossed my cigarette out the window, making a mental note to clean up the butts tomorrow, and sank into the sofa I bought from Jared. Midnight blue velvet and comfortable as shit. I propped my feet on the coffee table and leaned my head back against the cushion. Across from the sofa sat two distressed leather chairs. My flat screen TV, sound system, and books fit into the modern shelving unit on the opposite wall. It was the perfect set-up. I pointed the remote at the

TV and flicked it off, plunging the room into silence and darkness.

"Why can't you sleep?" I asked.

"Just thinking about you."

I wanted to ask if she was thinking good things or bad things, but I didn't. "That keeps you up nights?"

"I like listening to your voice in the dark. It's been a while."

"Yeah, it has."

Back in high school, we used to talk late into the night. When she still lived under her parents' roof and finding time together was a challenge, often thwarted by her mother who tried to keep us apart.

"Did you do any interesting tattoos today?"

I flexed my right hand, still cramped after today's six-hour session. "I finished tattooing a guy's sleeve. He wanted a Japanese theme. I did koi fish, cherry blossoms, a Shinto temple... a samurai warrior... a mountain with the Kanji symbols for the quote: Fall down seven times, stand up eight."

"That sounds amazing," she said, and I heard the excitement in her voice. Ava had always been fascinated with Japanese culture, fashion, food, and design. I wondered if she still had the Japanese tea set I gave her for her eighteenth birthday. "I hope you got photos."

I did, but they were going in my portfolio, not on social media.

"Ugh. You didn't," she said. "You need to show off your work."

"Lee, Gavin, and AJ were uploading photos all day. Perfect for your little Instagrammer heart."

"I want *you* to be on there."

"My customers find me by word of mouth." I was booked months in advance. That was good enough for me. "That's the best advertising."

"Maybe," she muttered. "But it would still be nice if you showcased your talent."

I didn't want my name on social media, and I didn't want photos showcasing my talent or anything else about my life. All I wanted to do was fly under the radar, run a successful business, and do my tattooing. End of story. The last thing I needed was for Keira Shaughnessy to track me down. Or, worse, Ronan. He knew where I was, but I didn't want to draw attention to myself. A year later and I was still looking over my shoulder, wondering if anyone was out to get me. For the first time in my life, I owned a gun, a Glock I kept in my bedside table. I hoped I would never need to use it.

"Listen, Ava, do me a favor. Don't put me on your social media or Forever Ink's social media. I don't want photos of myself out there, I don't want anyone to have easy access to every little thing I do in a day. I want no part of it, understand?" My voice sounded harsher than I'd intended but I wanted her to know I was serious.

"Why do you have an issue with social media?"

"I want to keep my personal life private."

"Sometimes you're so much like Killian."

When it came to social media, we shared the same view. Back when Killian was a UFC superstar, Ava had built his brand through social media. She had done such a good job that he'd had half a million followers who knew what he ate for all his meals, how many hours a day he trained, his favorite music... they conjectured on the meaning of every tattoo on his body and virtually invaded his privacy. No, thank you.

"You guys are doing okay though, right?"

"Yeah, it's all good." Killian had offered to help me move, and Eden said it hadn't come from her. That was a huge step in the right direction, and I wanted it to continue that way.

I lit another cigarette and wandered over to the window, looking up at the orange-tinged moon. "Do you think the man in the moon is lonely?"

"Sometimes," she said. "But when he looks down on earth, he sees all the problems people have created and he feels safer where he is."

"Or maybe he sees the rolling green hills and the ocean and the desert and he's jealous. Like, 'what the hell, I've got a load of moon dust and craters and they get mountains, cities, and beaches.'"

"The grass is always greener from afar."

Her words made me sad and angry in equal measure. Ava used to be an optimist. Had I done this to her? "When did you become a pessimist?"

She didn't answer the question. "Would I choose safety if it meant I had to give up all my beautiful memories?"

"Would you?" *Please say no.*

"Would you?" she countered.

"No. You're in every one of my beautiful memories. That would be like cutting out a piece of my heart."

"You've always been so brave."

"In what way?" Some would call me a coward. Escaping into a world of drugs. Brave? Not so much.

"You've never been afraid to say how you feel. That's what made me fall in love with you. You have the soul of a poet."

That would be some shit poetry. "I'm only like this with you."

"I know," she said quietly. After a beat, she asked, "Why did you choose me?"

"Because you're hot and I'm superficial."

She laughed. "Besides that."

I took a drag on my cigarette, thinking about it. Ava had always been my Achilles heel. I didn't know why she made me so vulnerable. Why she touched a place inside me that nobody ever had. Or why I'd always told her things I never told anyone else. "Maybe it's because you believed in me when nobody else did. Maybe it's because of the way you loved me."

"How did I love you?"

"With the power of a thousand suns."

"I don't even know what that means."

I chuckled. Neither did I. "It was blazing hot... and so strong it scorched the earth."

"Great. I'm responsible for global warming. My love was bad for the environment."

I laughed. Sometimes she cracked me up. "Maybe you're safer on the moon."

"Now you know why I don't venture down to earth very often."

"Because I'm living here full-time now?" My tone was light and teasing, but my heart was heavy.

Ava sighed. "What am I going to do with you, Rocket Man?"

"I can think of a few things you can do with me. If my hand falls off, I won't be much of a tattoo artist."

"How many times a day do you jerk off?"

"Today? Three. I might knock out another one before I go to sleep."

"Seriously?"

I smothered a laugh. "Too much? Not enough? What's the recommended daily allowance?"

"I'm sure there's no limit—"

"To my imagination."

"What do you imagine?"

You. "I don't need to use my imagination. I let the porn stars do all the work."

I envisioned her rolling her eyes at that one. "You watch porn now?"

No. "You have a dirty mind. You shouldn't be thinking about my dick or what I do with it."

She was silent for a few seconds, probably thinking about exactly what I told her not to. I smiled into the darkness. What game were we playing?

Ava changed the game again. She was good at turning the tables. "I blamed you... for everything. For the drugs and for disappearing without a word. And then those men... they were going to kill you after they beat you up and carved your chest..."

Eden must have told her that because I never had. I'd tried to tell Ava as little as possible about what had happened that night. Eden thought I'd been unconscious when that guy had carved my chest. I let her think that, even though it wasn't true. I'd felt every dig of the blade as it cut into my skin, branding me with a word that would forever scar me no matter how much ink covered the letters. "But they didn't kill me."

"I never want to imagine a world without you in it. It would be such a sad and lonely place. But I'm still trying to get over..."

I let out a breath and flicked ash out the window. "Get over what?"

"The way you left. I didn't know if you were dead or alive."

Not alive. Surviving but wishing I was dead. I was tempted to tell her everything. About rehab and how I felt like I was crawling out of my skin. The intense cravings. The way it exhausted me, left me wishing I was dead. Those long days riding a Greyhound down to Miami, deluding myself into thinking that I was on my way to something good, that I could somehow make things right.

I wanted to tell her how the reality had kicked me in the ass, leaving me disillusioned and feeling hopeless. I wanted to tell her about Ronan and Keira, about the mother I didn't remember who had spent the past twenty years pretending Killian and I had never existed. And about the night I walked into the ocean, thinking it would be so much easier to sink into oblivion and let the water cover me. Steal all the breath from my lungs. But I'd imagined her face. Heard her voice in my head. I'd swam back to the shore and lay on the beach. Watched the stars reel in the sky and prayed to God for strength and the serenity to accept all the shitty things I couldn't change.

I wanted to dump all my excess baggage at her feet and lighten my load. But I couldn't do that to her, so I kept my mouth shut about all of it.

Silence stretched out between us, but I heard Ava's soft breathing on the other end of the line, so I knew she was still there.

"I'm sorry," I said. What else could I say? "I can't do a damn thing to change what happened in the past."

"I know. I'm trying to let go of the past. I'm working on it. Just... it's hard, you know?"

"Preaching to the choir, babe."

"Did you blame me for leaving you?" she asked.

"Why are you going down this road?"

"It's important to get it all out there."

She left me when I needed her most. Twice. The first time I pushed her away because I was no good for her. Part of her must have been relieved to be free of me. Otherwise, she would have fought to stay. She didn't. She went on with her life, without me. Occasionally, she'd call to see how I was doing. Those calls were hard, our conversation stilted. What do you say to your ex-girl-friend who was living the college life, so far removed from my world she might as well have been living on another planet?

The second time she left me because she couldn't handle what I'd done to put my life and other peoples' lives in jeopardy. She couldn't handle that I'd disappeared without contacting her. Before I left for Miami, we hadn't been lovers *or* friends. We'd been two people with a history, who had kept tabs on each other. Sometimes she'd get drunk or lonely and call me for sex only to regret it the next morning. So yeah, I understood all about trying to let go of the past. But did I blame her? I wasn't sure. She did the best thing she could do for herself.

"I understand why you did it," I said.

"Don't chicken out. Be honest. Did you hate me for it? Because there have been plenty of times I've hated you."

"A part of me blamed you. A part of me hated you for giving up on me. You'd always been a fighter... fearless. But what girl in their right mind could love a junkie? I didn't want to drag you down with me." If it hadn't been for her mother, I probably would have. Addicts are selfish. They take, and they take, and they take, and they give very little of themselves in return. She'd been left with the dregs of me and she'd deserved so much more.

"I never really got over you though. I tried... so hard. But something always held me back."

"What was that something?" I asked.

"My beautiful memories. I want to make more with you. Some-day. Maybe."

Someday. Maybe.

Tate was right. Trying to win back Ava was fucking with my head. Would there ever come a day when we could get through a conversation without playing the blame game? Without dredging up the past?

"I didn't know, Connor. I didn't know that my mom was

involved in our break-up. When you pushed me away, I thought it was because you chose drugs over me. That's why I walked away. But I always felt...so ashamed. Like I'd given up on you."

I squeezed my eyes shut as if that would block out the pain of that memory.

"It's easier to be honest in the dark," she said. "Over the phone."

"Guess so."

"Connor?"

"Hmm?"

"Maybe I'm bad for you. Maybe that's why you... turned to drugs."

I pinched the bridge of my nose and took deep breaths. "You didn't do anything wrong. It was all on me."

"Why? Why did you need them so much?"

God, how could I make a non-addict understand what it's like? There was a hole inside me I couldn't seem to fill no matter what I did. Drugs had filled that hole, made me feel less empty. When I did heroin, it felt like I was injecting sunshine into my bloodstream. After the initial rush, the whole world took on a soft, warm glow. And I kept chasing that sunshine... chasing the light and the warmth...

"Connor?" she prompted.

"I don't know what to tell you. Except that it was never your fault. Don't ever think it was. You gave me everything and I gave you what was left of the broken pieces of myself."

"Are you still broken?"

Probably. Maybe I always would be. Just like I'd always be an addict, no matter how long I went without doing drugs. But I was getting my life together and every morning, I tried to remind myself to be grateful for the good things in my life. "I'm gluing the pieces back together. With superglue."

After a beat, she said, "My boyfriend gave me a tattoo when I was eighteen... bluebirds... but I messed it up with barbed wire. I regret that now."

"Regrets are hard to live with."

"Yeah, they are. I thought maybe you could help me out. I booked an appointment with you tomorrow night. Maybe you can work your magic."

I WOKE up in a cold sweat, my heart racing. Deep breaths. In. Out. In. Out.

"I expected better of you," Marco said. "You let me down, Dylan Connelly... or whoever you are... and this kind of betrayal... it will haunt you, just like my ghost."

Those were his final words. It had been him or me, and I'd chosen me. They shot him three times as I stood in front of him, my arms tied behind my back, a gun pressed to my head. I had watched him die, his words echoing in my head as the life drained out of him. He'd been right.

It haunted me, just like his ghost.

15

AVA

"Surprise me," I said when Connor tried to show me the sketch he'd done last night after we hung up.

"You sure about that?"

"I trust you," I said, walking over to his tattoo station.

"Ink is for life," he reminded me.

I stripped down to my black tank top and set my army jacket and purse on the shelf behind the chair. "Unless you find an awesome tattoo artist who can cover up a bad decision."

"I'm awesome and you trust me now?" he asked, trying to figure out if there was a catch.

"I'm taking a leap of faith."

I climbed into the black leather chair and offered him my right arm. He grimaced at my current tattoo. He'd already told me, on numerous occasions, that barbed wire was so 1990s and every time he looked at my tattoo, it made him nauseous.

"If you don't like it," he said, prepping my skin. "will I get kicked in the balls again?"

"She kicked you in the balls?" Gavin asked, aghast. He looked over from his station, his tattoo needle poised above a guy's shoulder. Strands of blond hair escaped the elastic holding his hair back.

"Maybe he deserved it," AJ chimed in from her station.

Which started a debate with the customers in Gavin and AJ's chairs, both of which happened to be guys. Unfortunately, half-walls divided the four stations, so everyone could chime in with their opinions and be heard.

You kick a guy in the balls once and you never live it down. While they talked, Connor applied the transfer, and I studiously avoided looking at my arm.

"Dude, I hope you're wearing a cup," Gavin said.

"I'm taking a leap of faith," Connor said, winking at me. "Ready?" he asked, the machine buzzing in his hand.

I took a few deep breaths and nodded. "Go for it." I grimaced before the needles even touched my skin.

"Babe."

"Ignore my facial expressions."

He chuckled as I attempted to smooth out my features without success. "It's kind of hard."

"I'm ready. Just do it." I closed my eyes and took deep, calming breaths as the needles dug into my skin. It would be over before I knew it. This wouldn't take long. After a few minutes, I got used to it. Sort of.

Enough to open my eyes, at least. I focused on the opposite wall—moody grey with a concrete paint effect. Connor had painted it for Jared last year, or so I'd heard from Eden, my font of information when Connor and I hadn't been speaking. My gaze wandered to the windows facing the street, lit up with neon Forever Ink signs. I couldn't believe Connor owned this place now. I remember the first time we came in here. After visiting a dozen other shops all over Brooklyn, Connor said this was the one as soon as we'd walked in the door. He loved that it was artist-run and that the designs were original. He loved the feel of the place. Cool, but not sterile, with plenty of character. It wasn't gritty or seedy like some of the other places we'd visited.

"Is it turning out okay?" I asked.

"We'll see."

"That doesn't sound very promising."

He grunted. Again, not very promising.

"I have inker's remorse."

"It happens."

"I was too hasty. I mean, why punish those beautiful birds?"

No answer. It was a rhetorical question anyway.

"Will you be able to cover the barbed wire without ruining the bird design?"

"Nope."

Maybe I'd suspected that, and it was why I'd chosen not to look at the new design. I tapped out the beat of Led Zeppelin's "Going to California" with my free hand. Such a wistful ballad. "You used to love Led Zeppelin."

"Still do."

"I could picture you in a rock band," I said. "You'd be the drummer."

"Sex, drugs and rock 'n roll. Perfect lifestyle for me."

"I would have been one of your groupies."

"You would have been the lead singer."

We fell silent again. "This seems to be taking a long time."

"I'm using more real estate."

"You're making my tattoo bigger? Ugh. No wonder."

"Maybe you should have looked at the design."

"That's women for you," Gavin chimed in. "Always bitching about something." I glanced over at him. All the customers were gone now, the shop was closed, and Gavin and AJ were cleaning their stations.

"And you wonder why you don't have a girlfriend," AJ said.

"When you gonna invite me and Connor over to check out the girl on girl action with you and your girlfriend?" Gavin asked.

I raised my brows. Connor snorted.

"Never," AJ said.

"Is that the kind of porn you watch?" I asked Connor in a low voice.

"I don't watch porn," he said.

"Last night you said you did."

"I was just winding you up."

"Your favorite pastime."

He gave me a wicked grin. "Not my favorite."

I didn't ask him to expand on that. I kept venturing into forbidden territory. No matter how many times I told myself I shouldn't say certain things, it seemed I couldn't catch the words before they flew out of my mouth. Really, I should think before I speak. I should think before I do a lot of things. The barbed wire tattoo was the perfect example of that.

"Invite Ava," Gavin said. "Three chicks, two guys. How hot would that be?"

"Sizzling," I said sarcastically.

AJ laughed as she and Gavin came over to check out my tattoo, still a work in progress.

"Nice work, Con," AJ said with approval. "I like the way you—"

I held up my left hand. "Don't say it. It's a surprise."

Her brows arched. "Brave girl."

"You just said it was nice."

Gavin removed the elastic from his hair and ran a hand through it. "Bold choice, Vincent. I wouldn't have pegged Ava for a snake lover."

My eyes widened. Snake? I cleared my throat. "You tattooed a snake on my arm?"

"That's what you get for trusting me," Connor said, his head bent over my arm.

AJ shook her head no. We smiled at each other in solidarity. Gavin did a double-take and waggled his eyebrows. "Something going on with you two?"

She shrugged, and I caught the teasing gleam in her eye. "Why not? Ava's hot."

"Right back at you," I said.

"You'd do each other?" Gavin asked, intrigued.

AJ winked at me.

"The most I ever did was kiss a girl," I said. "But with AJ, I might be tempted to try more." It was total bullshit, but we were just having fun with it, and AJ knew that.

"Connor, did you know about your ex-girlfriend's bi-curious ways?" Gavin asked.

He shook his head a little. "Ava never fails to surprise me."

"Keeps it fresh," AJ said.

"Absolutely," I said.

Gavin gave me a sly look. "Are you two exes with benefits or—"

"You done here?" Connor asked, lifting his head, and shooting Gavin a look. Gavin was obviously fishing for information, but if he thought he'd get it from Connor, he was mistaken. When it came to his personal life, Connor was a vault.

Gavin held up his hands and backed away. "Out of here. See you tomorrow."

We said our goodbyes and the door closed behind AJ and Gavin, leaving me alone with Connor in an empty shop. Even though the music was still piping from the sound system and the machine in Connor's hand was buzzing, a hush settled over us.

"You kissed a girl?" he asked a little while later.

"Once."

"Tongue?"

"Yeah."

"When was this?"

I leaned my head against the back of the seat and closed my eyes, remembering. "Valentine's Day. I was supposed to spend it with my boyfriend, but he forgot. It was his twentieth birthday." I wasn't sure why I was referring to Connor as if he'd been someone else. Maybe that made it easier. "I kept calling him and texting, but he never answered his phone. So, I ended up going to a party. It was at Scott's apartment. I smoked a joint with him and Megan." Megan had been my roommate and Scott had been her boyfriend at the time. Now, Megan lived in Boston and worked for a consulting company. She worked sixty to seventy hours a week, wore suits to work, and aspired to climb the corporate ladder.

"You smoked a joint?" Connor asked, surprised.

First and last time. It made me nauseous and paranoid, proving that drugs and I were not a good match. As if I needed proof. "I didn't really like it."

I thought about that night. House music was shaking the walls, and it felt like everything was going on around me in slow motion, like I wasn't part of it. I was dancing, the bass thrumming through my body, my head in a hazy funk, and all I'd wanted was to forget. Just like Connor had done. The girl had raven hair and big brown eyes and I never even caught her name. "When she started kissing me, I went along with it just to see how it would feel."

"And how did it feel?" he asked quietly.

"Strange. Interesting. Not bad but not good either. I just felt... like I was someone else. Maybe that's how I wanted to feel."

Connor lifted the tattoo needle and sat back on his stool. "I need to lock up." I nodded, and he gave my shoulder a gentle squeeze. "Almost there. You're doing great."

I watched him stride across the black-and-white tiled floor, his shoulders squared, the lines of his torso forming a perfect V-shape. I didn't notice how good his ass looked in those faded Levi's. Nope, didn't notice.

Connor changed the music and Lana Del Rey's "Pretty When You Cry" piped over the speakers. Connor didn't play fair. He knew how to break down my defenses and he was using it to his advantage.

"Connor," I whispered when he sat down again.

A ghost of a smile flitted across his face before he bent his head and got back to work.

I closed my eyes and listened to the music. Lana's sultry voice, and lyrics that could have been written for us, made my heart ache. Made me long for something I'd lost but wasn't sure what it was or how to find it again.

When the song ended, another Lana Del Rey song came on. I wondered if he made this playlist just for me. I thought maybe he had. As the tattoo machine buzzed, and the music swirled around us, I remembered so many of the things I loved about Connor. The way he listened when I talked, like everything I said was important to him. The way he'd taken care of me when I got the flu in my freshman year of college. He'd ladled soup into my mouth. Warmed me with his body heat when I had the chills. Bathed me with a washcloth when the fever broke. He'd read to me because my head had hurt too much to watch movies. Jack

Kerouac's *On the Road*. In my foggy brain, I had recognized Connor in that story. That mad quest to live, to burn bright, to seek out adventure.

We used to talk about hitting the open road, crisscrossing the country on Connor's Harley. Staying at cheap motels. Eating at diners and dives. Being wild and free. On desert highways where we wouldn't see another car for miles and miles. We would feel like the only two people in the world. We'd watch the sun rise over the Pacific Ocean. Make love under the stars. Dance in the light of a moon that was hung just for us.

I opened my eyes as Connor lifted his head. I looked into his blue eyes and saw the boy I once loved so fiercely that I believed nothing, and nobody, could ever keep us apart. "Were you dreaming about California?" he asked.

"How did you know?"

"Sometimes, I can still read your mind."

"I was thinking about our road trip. It was never about the destination, was it?"

"No. It was about the journey."

"I thought you would have taken it on your own..."

He let out a breath and shook his head. "It wouldn't have been the same." He leaned back on his stool and peeled off his gloves, rolling out his shoulders. "All done."

I squeezed my eyes shut. He chuckled. "Might be easier to see with your eyes open."

The moment of truth. Cracking one eye open and then the other, I looked down at my upper arm and my breath caught. It was the most beautiful thing I'd ever seen. Connor pulled me out of the chair and led me over to the wall mirror for a better view.

A dark pink lotus flower and a multi-colored dragonfly—turquoise, green, cobalt blue—covered my upper arm. "No bluebirds," I said.

"Disappointed?"

"No. It's gorgeous. How did you do this?"

"Magic."

I smiled. He had magic in his hands. I already knew that. The colors were so saturated, so vibrant, that I couldn't see any remnants of the bluebirds and barbed wire. "I can't even see the old design."

"It's still there," Connor said, catching my eye in the mirror. He bandaged my arm and refused to take the money I offered. I'd come back and pay Claudia tomorrow, I decided.

"Thank you. It's perfect."

He gave me a soft smile, his eyes flitting over my face. The air between us was charged with electricity. In a bold move, I ran my hands up his chest and looped my arms around his neck.

His hands caressed my sides, sending tremors throughout my body and I closed my eyes. Right now, in this moment, we were the only two people in the world. He slid a hand through my hair and his other arm wrapped around my waist, pulling me closer. Our bodies melded together, slotting into place like two pieces of a jigsaw puzzle. It felt like forever since he'd touched me like this. Held me close enough to breathe him in.

My hands explored his hard planes and the ridges of his muscles under his T-shirt like it was uncharted territory. I used to know his body as well as I knew my own, but now it felt different. More filled-out. Harder. Like I was holding onto something solid. Something that wouldn't disappear in a puff of smoke if I held on too tightly.

I lifted my face to his and he lowered his head, his lips soft and warm, the stubble on his jaw rough against my skin. He tasted like the cinnamon gum he'd been chewing earlier. Our tongues swirled together, caught up in a crazy dance and I ground my body against his feeling his erection pressing against my pelvis. We kept kissing, our hands groping, wanting to touch everywhere at once.

My hands ventured down his chest and over his flat stomach. He sucked in his breath as I fumbled with his belt buckle and undid the top button of his jeans. He captured my hands in his to stop me.

"If we do this, are you going to regret it?"

"I don't want to live in the past anymore. I won't regret it."

His eyes flitted over my face, trying to gauge my mood. Trying to figure out if I meant what I said. "Promise?"

"Promise. I want you. Right here. Right now."

"Tonight, you're staying with me. In my bed," he said, crossing the room to switch off the lights while I undressed quickly, tossing boots and clothes in a heap on the floor.

I'd already made up my mind, so he didn't need to worry that I'd run away or regret it tomorrow morning. I knew I wouldn't.

"Are you sure?" he asked one more time as I stood in front of him stark naked, his eyes darkening as he stared at my breasts then lifted to my eyes, the neon glow of the sign bathing the room in red.

"I'm sure," I said confidently, meeting his eyes as my fingers fumbled with the buttons of his jeans and I took him in my hand - oh god, he was so hard - and circled the barbell piercing with the pad of my thumb. "Commando, huh?"

He grinned and pulled his shirt over his head, tossing it on the floor. His hands cupped my breasts and he stared at them a moment before he lowered his head and lifted my breast into the heat of his mouth, his hand sliding between my thighs, rubbing between the slick folds. My grip tightened on him and I squeezed his dick, feeling it twitch in my hand.

"What do you want?" he asked, his voice husky.

"Fuck me. Hard," I said brazenly. We had all night for foreplay. I was ready for him now.

His hands slid down my ass and to the backs of my thighs and I was in the air, my legs cinched around his waist, my back pressed against the wall.

"Condom?"

He wasn't asking if I was still on the pill. He was asking if I'd ever slept with anyone else without a condom. I'd sworn that I never would. "Nobody but you."

"Same." His mouth crashed against mine and he drove his tongue into my mouth as he used his hand to position himself at my entrance. My fingernails dug into his shoulders, clawed his bare back as he fucked me. Hard. Our sex was raw, wild, and relentless.

We left our marks on each other, his fingers digging into my ass, my teeth marks on his neck. When I came, I screamed his name. I'd always been loud with him during sex, just like when I rode the roller coaster. The orgasm ripped through my body, my muscles clenching around him, my body shaking as I rode it out. It was almost too much to handle. It was too much of everything. I felt it when he came, his mouth seeking mine, his body shuddering in my arms, a gasp escaping his lips.

He pulled away to look at my face before he set me down and I let him see that this had not been a mistake. My lips curved into a smile and he gave me a soft kiss on the lips. "Missed you. So much," he said as my bare feet touched the floor.

I darted into the restroom to clean up, thinking that it was probably the first time in years that Connor had had sex when he was sober. When I turned from the sink, he was standing in the doorway, my clothes in his arms. "Hi," I said, giving him a little wave.

Connor laughed. "Hi. Hungry?"

"Starving."

"Sushi?"

My smile grew wide. "We can go to our little place." It was a tiny hole in the wall, but the sushi was amazing. When Connor first started working here, we used to go all the time and sit at the counter, watching the sushi chefs prepare our food. I got dressed while Connor cleaned his station.

Connor slung an arm around my shoulder as we walked to the sushi place, only three blocks from here. I couldn't wipe the stupid-ass grin off my face. I felt like a kid on Christmas morning. My phone was ringing, and I dug it out of my bag, checking the screen. I groaned when I saw it was my mother. "It's like she knows I'm with you," I said without thinking. "I mean..." Shit.

He squeezed my shoulder. "It's okay. Just answer."

I tossed my phone back in my bag. I was still pissed off at her after her confession at the hair salon. How dare she?

By the time we'd reached the sushi place, my mom had called twice already, and my phone rang again. I sighed and pressed the answer button, holding up one finger to Connor to indicate that I only needed a minute. He nodded, and we stopped outside the restaurant before going in. "Hey Mom, I'm busy right now. I'll call you back tom—"

"Honey...it's your father."

16

CONNOR

*L*ars Christensen was a decent man. Humble. Quiet. Hardworking. He works as a plasterer. The summer I was eighteen, apprenticing for Jared, he gave me a few painting jobs to help me earn extra cash. I thought it would earn me some points with Ava's mother. Turned out Lars had never told her about it. One day he forgot his lunch and she turned up on the job. I was working for him that day and he never called me for another job again. I didn't bother asking why. I knew Ava's mom called the shots in their relationship. I also knew she hated me. She'd never made a secret of it. She hated me for "corrupting" her daughter. She hated me for "disrespecting" my father. She didn't like my tattoos or my surly attitude, my bad manners, my motorcycle, my prospects for the future which in her eyes, were a big fat zero. In short, she didn't like anything about me, and she didn't want me anywhere near her daughter.

Yet, here I was, escorting Ava into the hospital, my arm around her shoulder, her arm around my waist. She needed my support and I needed to be here for her. I needed to make up for all the times I hadn't been there for her in the past. The night Jake Masters came into Trinity Bar and made her feel like she was fourteen again. Helpless and vulnerable. My twentieth birth-

155

day. She'd baked cupcakes for me. Wrapped the presents she bought for me and wrote me a card. When I showed up at her dorm the next day, she threw the cupcakes and presents out the window.

"Sometimes I wish I'd never met you," she said.

I promised her up and down that it would never happen again. I promised her I'd give up drugs. Promises, promises, promises, all of them empty. She slammed the door in my face, and I rescued the presents, unwrapping them later when I got home—Copic markers and a new St. Jude medal to replace the one I'd lost. When you lose a medal of the patron saint of lost causes, you know you're screwed.

Her mom was sitting in the waiting area, her handbag on her lap, her head in her hands. She looked small and fragile, nothing like the powerhouse who had screamed at me and threatened me to stay away from Ava.

"Mom?" Ava said.

I released Ava and she knelt in front of her mom, taking her hands in hers. "Mom..."

Her mom raised her head and caressed Ava's face with her hand. She loved her daughter, I didn't doubt that for a minute, but her love wasn't unconditional. "If anything happens to him, I don't know how I'd go on," her mom said.

Her words hit me in the gut. They'd been married longer than I'd been on this Earth, and even though they were very different, and they shouldn't work, they had built a life together, raised two children together. Supported each other through good times and bad. Would Ava and I ever have a love like that?

"Is he ... how is he?" Ava asked. "What happened?"

Her mom let out a ragged breath. "He was complaining of muscle aches. And you know your father ... he's so stoic. He never complains. I told him he was working too hard and to stretch out on the sofa and relax. A little while later, I went to check on him and he was ... clutching his chest. I could tell he was in pain. I called 911. The paramedics got there just in time. They hooked him up to all the machines and the IV and..." She stopped and took a deep breath. "They rushed him in for an angioplasty ... and now we have to wait—"

"Mom," Lana called. I looked over my shoulder. Lana's eyes were streaming with tears as she rushed to her mom's side. Her mom let go of Ava and leaned into Lana. "I'm here now. Everything is going to be okay."

"Such a good girl," her mom said, patting Lana's hand. "You've never given me a day of trouble."

Ava stood, her shoulders sagging. It was always like this. Lana was manipulative and cunning. She had always fought for her mother's affections like it was a contest to be won. When Ava stopped being the perfect daughter, Lana was quick to judge and point the finger. And Ava's mom, even in a crisis, felt the need to remind Ava just how much she'd failed as a daughter.

I moved closer to Ava and took her hand in mine, giving it a little squeeze. She looked up at me with her big gray eyes and I wished I could take away the hurt. Make everything better for her. The best I could do was be here for her, let her know I was on her side.

Her mom looked up, noticing me for the first time. Her eyes narrowed into slits before her gaze swung to Ava. "What is he doing here?" she asked, her voice cold and hard.

"He drove me to the hospital."

Her mom pressed her lips in a flat line and crossed her arms, her chin held high. "Ask him to leave."

"Mom," Ava said, horrified. "No. I want him to stay—"

"You need to be with your family at a time like this. He has no right to be here. That boy is trouble. I don't know why you would even speak to him, let alone bring him to the hospital when your father..." She stopped and shook her head.

"But Mom..."

I gave Ava's hand another squeeze to let her know it was okay. "I hope Lars gets better soon," I said.

Her mom nodded curtly but didn't respond or even look at me.

Lana lifted her chin, mimicking her mom's pose. If it had been any other time, I would tell her to go to hell. But this wasn't the time or the place. Ava walked me to the door and stepped outside with me.

"I'm sorry," she said.

"It's not your fault."

"I want you to stay, but..."

I cupped her chin in my hand and tilted her face up to mine. "It's better for you if I go. You don't need any extra stress."

She wrapped her arms around me, and I held onto her, wishing I could. I wanted to be the one to give her strength, to sit by her side and hold her hand. To help her through this. Ava let out a shuddered breath and released me, taking a step back.

"He'll be okay," I said, hoping like hell it was true.

"I know."

"Call if you need me. For anything."

"Thank you. For the tattoo. And for..." She took a deep breath and let it out. "When you were holding me just now, it made me feel like everything will be okay. It reminded me of how I used to feel. Like you could fix things. Like you could hold me together when everything was falling apart."

I stroked her hair and pressed a soft kiss on the top of her head. How it used to be, not how it was now. That hurt, but I gave her a little smile. "Go be with your family."

She gave me a final look before she turned and walked back into the waiting room.

I FINISHED STAPLING the canvas to the plywood and hung it on the bolts I'd drilled into the wall. Floodlights were trained on the empty canvas, my cans of spray paint lined up in a row. I pulled on Latex gloves, strapped on my mask, and plugged myself into my music. Eminem rapped in my ears, the volume so high the music reverberated in my body.

Ava's mother had looked at me like I was trash. No wonder she liked my father so much. They had a lot in common.

Bomb a wall. Make your peace.

My arm and wrist moved across the canvas, the spray paint seeping into the fabric. I willed my hand to paint what I envisioned—Ava's pale hair glowing in the spotlights, the multi-colored silk ties suspending her in the air. She was a blur of motion, her face hidden behind a black mask trimmed in purple feathers. I moved in close for the fine lines, the bars of music swirling across the canvas. On cue, "Undisclosed Desires" pumped into my ears. If this piece had a name, that would be it.

I stepped back and studied my work. Was it any good? Hell, if I knew. If I'd just bombed a wall, I'd pack up my shit and leave before the cops caught me defacing public property. I wouldn't have time to wonder if it was my best work. That was the beauty of graffiti. Under the cover of darkness and anonymity, I got in and I got out. My pieces rarely got covered by other artists, a sign of respect for my work, and that had always been enough for me. With my tattoos, I worked with the clients and when they were happy with my designs, they gave me the okay to ink their skin.

But to have people in a gallery studying my work up close and personal ... I would be judged on my technique, my use of color, my lines and command of a spray paint can. *I would be judged.* Fuck.

My phone rang, interrupting the music and my thoughts. I pressed the answer button on the screen and Ava's voice filled my ears.

"He's going to be okay. He needs to stay in the hospital a couple days, but the doctor said ... he'll be okay." She let out a breath of relief.

"That's good news."

"Yeah, it is." She paused a moment, and in the background, I heard a siren wailing. "Connor, I'm sorry. I don't know why she acts like that with you. I thought it would be different ... with my dad in the hospital."

We both knew why her mom acted that way with me, and in some ways, she had every right to think the worst of me. But she had hated me from the start before I'd ever touched drugs. I tipped my head back and looked up at the inky blue sky. No stars. No moon. "Where are you?"

"I'm standing outside the hospital. I needed some air. Where are you?"

"Outside. Behind the shop."

"Smoking?"

"Painting."

"Painting? Really?" she asked, excitement in her voice. "That's great. I can't wait to see it."

"You'll see it in the gallery." What a terrifying thought. I didn't want to see any of my work displayed in a gallery. I cast a critical eye on my work. It wasn't good enough.

"Wait a minute. You're not going to show it to me?"

"You love surprises."

"Well, yeah, but ... you won't let me see it?" she asked incredulously.

I chuckled. "Nope."

"Oh," she said, somewhat deflated. "I'm staying in Bay Ridge for a few days. Until my dad gets out of the hospital. Hopefully, I'll survive all that time with my mom and Lana. Joe just got here ... Lana treats him the same way my mom treats my dad. But he still loves her."

"Love makes people do crazy things."

"Yeah, I guess it does. Well ... I'll let you get back to your painting." We hung on the line, neither of us making a move to hang up. But I didn't really have anything to say. The darkness was closing in on me. I felt that old familiar emptiness gnawing at me.

"I'm glad your dad's okay. I'll talk to you later."

She let out a breath. "Okay. Bye."

I cut the call and lit a cigarette. It would be easier for Ava if we cut our losses and she moved on with someone new. Even if Ava decided she was ready to be in a relationship with me again, her mother would never accept me into the family. What kind of future could we possibly have together?

Fuck. I smoked my cigarette and lit another one. Three cigarettes later, and I couldn't fill that hole inside me. I ripped the canvas off the plywood and stuffed it in the garbage can.

Grabbing my hoodie, I walked out the front door and locked it behind me. I needed something to take off the edge. Whiskey, maybe. Alcohol had never been my problem. I'd spent a lifetime trying to be everything my father wasn't. Funny how that didn't quite turn out. As I walked the streets, I justified it in my head. Whiskey was the lesser of evils. What harm could it do to throw a few back? I was a drug addict, not an alcoholic, I reasoned, even though I knew damn well it was a slippery slope.

I lit another cigarette, hoping it would take away that itch for something stronger. The devil on my shoulder urged me to give in. Just a little taste. Think how good it would feel. The burn of the whiskey when it hit your throat, heat spreading throughout your body, numbing the pain.

The bouncer at the door asked to see some ID. I showed him my license and he peered at my face then back at the license before he collected my cover charge and stamped my hand.

I descended the stairs to the basement club, subconsciously looking for Danny Vargas. I hadn't been to The Candy Store in two years, but this had always been one of his hangouts. I weaved through the crowd, scoring a spot at the bar next to two women in tiny dresses. The blonde smiled at me, her eyes roving over my face and down my body. "Hey." She leaned in close and dragged a finger down my chest. "Just when I thought this night was a bust, you walked in..."

"Sorry, babe. I've got a girlfriend."

She pouted. "Why are all the good ones taken?"

I wasn't good. Far from it. But my line did the trick, and she and her friend disappeared into the crowd in search of something better. "What do ya need?" the bartender asked.

"Jameson. A double."

He grabbed the bottle from the shelf and poured a double, setting the glass in front of me. I handed him a twenty and stared at the amber liquid before I wrapped my hand around the glass and lifted it to my lips.

My phone vibrated in my pocket, and I read the text from Ava.

AVA: I don't care what my mom says. She doesn't know you like I do. I'm not sure anyone does.

Two seconds later another message came through.

AVA: I love this tattoo. The dragonfly is my new spirit animal. It symbolizes change and transformation.

What in the hell was I doing in this club?
I texted her back.

CONNOR: And beauty and magic and light.
AVA: That, too. I just thought you should know... I believe in you. Goodnight, Connor
CONNOR: Goodnight, Ava Blue

I stepped away from the bar, leaving my drink untouched, and walked down a dimly lit hallway that smelled like jock straps and stale beer. I sidestepped a couple making out against the wall and ducked into the men's room to take a piss before my walk home.

While I washed my hands, I studied my face in the mirror. *You almost fucked up.* Alcohol inevitably led me to make stupid decisions. Like trying to find someone in this club who could give me what I really wanted.

I exited the men's room as a drunk guy stumbled in.

"Jake," a girl purred. "We should go back to my place."

I glanced at the couple who'd been making out earlier. The guy's arms caged a petite blonde who was looking up at him with big doe eyes. He turned his head, and I caught a glimpse of his face in profile.

No fucking way. I froze in my tracks. "Jake Masters."

He looked at me over his shoulder, his eyes squinted, trying to figure out how he knew me. Recognition dawned on him. "If it isn't 'The Kill's' little brother."

"Not so little anymore," the girl said with a giggle.

"If it isn't the asshole who messed with my girl," I widened my stance, my hands curling into fists.

He smirked at me. "Ava was fun."

"*Fun*," I ground out. I grabbed him by the collar and slammed him against the wall. My fist connected with his face. The girl screamed, her shrill voice in my ear. I ignored it and rammed my fist into his face again.

He spit on the ground and headbutted me, driving me against the opposite wall.

"She was gagging for it. My cock was so deep down her throat—"

I lunged for him, bringing him down to the ground.

"She wouldn't get anywhere near you."

"Ask her what happened behind the school."

I roared and locked his legs under me, my fists pummelling his face and chest. He got me in a chokehold and flipped me over. We wrestled and grappled, rolling on the ground, taking punches at each other. A bottle hit the back of my head. *Fuck.* I turned my head and looked over my shoulder at the blonde. Jake's fist slammed into my face and my head snapped back.

"Break it up," a male voice yelled as my fist smashed into Jake's face.

Beefy hands fisted my hoodie and hauled me to my feet. Jake scrambled into a sitting position, holding his hands over his face and moaning.

"The cops are on the way. You're going to pay for this," the petite blonde said, her eyes narrowed on me.

"You called the cops?" the bouncer asked. "We don't need to involve them."

That was for damn sure.

The blonde knelt next to Jake. "Baby, are you okay?"

"He broke my fucking nose."

I laughed harshly. "That's nothing compared to what you did to Ava, you fucking douchebag."

The bouncer shoved me up the stairs and pushed me out the front door on to the sidewalk. He shoved me against the outside wall and held me in place with his arm. It wasn't necessary. My fight wasn't with him. Jake and the blonde exited the club, escorted by another bouncer.

"Look what you did to him," she said, giving me a sucker punch in the arm.

She cradled her injured hand and glared at me through her tears.

"Here's a tip," I said. "If you're gonna punch someone, keep your wrist straight and tuck in your thumb. And here's another tip." I looked over at Jake, slumped over, holding a bar towel to his bloody nose. "Dump that douchebag. You can do better."

"Shut the fuck up, Vincent." He spits blood on the sidewalk. "I'm pressing charges. Daddy isn't around to rescue you anymore."

I laughed. He had no idea how funny that was. The blonde hadn't heeded my warning. She was fussing over him, cooing soft words that agitated him rather than calming him down. I waited for him to turn on her. It didn't take long. "Get the fuck off me," he said, pushing her away.

Those big doe eyes of hers filled up with tears again. "Jake... I'm trying to help..."

Seconds later a police car and ambulance arrived. Fucking perfect.

"Do you require medical assistance?" a paramedic asked me.

"No."

"Let me take a look. You might need stitches—"

I shook my head. "I'm good."

A female officer questioned me. I remained mute. I knew her. Officer Healey. Early thirties, attractive. She'd questioned me a year ago in the hospital and had made it clear how she felt about Seamus Vincent. She thought the sun rose and set on him. I checked her left hand. The gold wedding band wasn't there anymore. I was tempted to ask her why her marriage fell apart. If Seamus Vincent had ruined that, too. I wondered if Officer Healey had any idea that she bore an uncanny physical resemblance to the woman who had abandoned us over two decades ago.

Jake was talking shit from the back of the ambulance, telling the police officer he wanted to press charges for assault. "I was minding my own business when that lunatic attacked me."

If he was still talking, I didn't do a good enough job.

"I need to take you into the station," Officer Healey said with a weary sigh when it became clear I'd stonewalled her. "Will the cuffs be necessary?"

I shook my head and ducked into the back seat of the police car. On the ride to the station, I watched the neon lights blur past the window, Jake Masters' words echoing in my head.

My cock was so deep down her throat...

Ask her what happened behind the school.

All these years and she'd kept that to herself? Did she block it out? Pretend it had never happened?

17

CONNOR

"*D*etective Ramsey will be with you in a minute," Officer Healey said.

"To what do I owe the honor?" I asked.

"He asked to handle this himself." She shut the door behind her and left me alone in a small room with a metal table and a few chairs.

Handle this. Unfortunately, we had some history and I doubted it would help my case.

Five minutes later, the door opened. Ramsey set a cup of coffee in front of me and took a seat across from me.

"Detective," I said, eyeing his suit jacket and tie. He loosened the tie and undid the first button of his shirt. If I had to name the coolest guy I'd ever met, it would probably be Deacon Ramsey. The guy was never ruffled, never fazed. Back in high school, Ramsey had been more interested in partying and bending the law than upholding it, so it had always surprised me that he'd become a cop. "Moving up in the world."

He grinned. "Got the shiny gold badge and everything."

"Good for you." I leaned back in my chair and crossed my arms. He eyed me over the rim of the Styrofoam cup as he took a sip of coffee. "Don't you have something better to do?"

"Slow night. You want to tell me what happened?" he asked.

I had nothing to lose by telling the truth. "I was settling an old score. That douchebag bullied Ava."

"Didn't Killian already beat him up for that?"

"It was my turn."

"He probably got what he had coming to him. He's always been an asshole."

"Are you booking me for assault or am I free to go?"

"You're free to go."

I didn't leave like I wanted to, sensing there was a catch and he wasn't finished with me yet. Tonight would make three times that Deacon had saved my ass.

Just over a year and a half ago, he was the first on the scene of my traffic accident. I hadn't caused the accident and I wasn't high on drugs when it happened. I was on my way home to get high. A white van jumped a light and hit me, knocking me off my bike, before it took off. Instead of busting me for possession, Ramsey called Killian who had hauled my ass to rehab. Even bigger than that, Ramsey had saved Killian's life the night those four men came seeking retribution. And now he was letting me off the hook again.

"You owe me a favor," he said. I should have known he'd want to cash in on his debts, and I couldn't really blame him. Killian had given him a free gym membership for life, but I'd given him jack shit, except a thank you which he'd brushed off.

"You want a tattoo?" I asked. "I can do that for you."

"I might take you up on that one of these days. But what I'd really like is the truth. What happened in Miami?"

"I got busted for weed and ecstasy. Cut a deal with the cops. It's all in the reports." I looked him in the eye. I was telling the truth. But I'd left out a few details.

"I know what you said in your statement." Ramsey ran his hand through his dirty-blond hair. "Why did you lie?" I rubbed my chest and his eyes followed my hand. "Has it healed?"

"It's all good," I said, pushing back my chair and standing. "If we're done here, I need my beauty rest."

He stood and rounded the table, holding out his card to me. "Call me if you feel like talking. You can trust me. I'm not a dirty cop like your father." It shouldn't surprise me to hear that Seamus had been a dirty cop, but it still disappointed me, and it also surprised me that Ramsey would voice it.

"Why are you always saving my ass?" I asked, curiosity getting the best of me. He had no reason to help me. We'd been acquaintances, but never friends.

His cool façade dropped for a split second, long enough for me to see his vulnerability. "I was one of the lucky ones," he said. "My foster family adopted me when I was eight and raised me as their own son. Before that, I'd been passed around to different foster homes. Everyone wanted a cute, cuddly baby, not a troublemaker."

"And what does that have to do with me?"

"Some kids get a lucky break. You and Killian weren't so lucky. But Seamus Vincent got what he deserved. Karma's a bitch, isn't it?"

"Yeah, I guess it is. Thanks. For tonight."

He nodded, still hoping for more, but I pocketed the card and walked out of the room. I had nothing left to say.

Pulling up my hood, I lowered my head as I strode past the desk and out the front door. Outside, I took deep breaths to clear my head.

"What the fuck happened?"

Killian was leaning against his Range Rover, arms crossed, waiting for an explanation.

"What are you doing here?" I asked.

"I got a call from Officer Healey." I let out a humorless laugh. "Get in the car. I'll drive you home."

I looked down Union Avenue, debating, then climbed into the passenger seat. The night played out in my head as we drove in silence, the bass from Killian's music thumping in my head. I massaged my temples, hoping it would ease the pain. I felt like my head might crack in two.

When we got upstairs to my apartment, I flicked on the floor lamp and collapsed on the sofa, my head throbbing. Killian disappeared into the kitchen and I heard the ice dispenser spitting out cubes, the sound of water running. He was playing nurse.

Killian sat on the coffee table across from me and inspected my face. I closed my eyes and leaned my head against the sofa cushion, weariness settling into my bones even as my mind raced. Ava. Her mother. Jake Masters. Ronan. Marco. Miami. All my shitty memories vied for attention as Killian cleaned off the blood with a damp towel. I grabbed his wrist and pulled his hand away. "I'm good."

He scowled and pressed the ice wrapped in a kitchen towel against my cheekbone. "Keep it iced." Killian sat across from me in one of the leather chairs. "What happened?"

I told him the story and by the time I finished talking, my face was numb, and a sick feeling had settled in my stomach. Beating up Jake Masters hadn't solved anything. It couldn't undo what he'd done. I dumped the ice in the sink and returned to the sofa.

"Fucking asshole," Killian said.

I grunted and flexed my hands, looking at the cuts and bruises on my knuckles. They were nothing compared to what he'd done to Ava. I remembered her at fourteen. Tiny and delicate-looking, her eyes almost too big for her face. After the day Killian had beaten up Jake Masters, Ava had chopped off all her hair. She wore baggy clothes to school. Hoodies and oversized sweatpants. Beanies to cover her cut hair. She'd wanted to hide, to disappear, camouflage her body.

"You'll ruin your delicate artist hands," Killian teased.

I snorted. "Does NYPD have a hotline to you? Every time shit goes down, you get a call."

He shifted in his chair, not meeting my eyes. "After everything that went down..."

"Right," I said, filling in the blanks. If I make one wrong move, Killian will be kept informed.

"Good to know you've got my back," I said sarcastically.

"What were you doing in a club?"

"I wasn't looking to score."

He gave me a skeptical look. It was justified. In the back of my head, hadn't that been what I'd really wanted?

"I went in for a drink. But I changed my mind."

He exhaled a breath of relief. "Is it hard...not drinking?"

"Staying away from drugs is hard. Not drinking is..." I was going to say easy. But it wasn't. "Yeah, sometimes it's hard. It's a social thing. Gavin and Lee invite me to parties sometimes or ask me to grab a few beers after work to unwind, but I always say no. I've never learned my limits."

"Sucks to be you."

I laughed under my breath and we were silent for a while, lost in our own thoughts. "Did you ever confide in Deacon Ramsey? About Seamus?" I asked, already knowing the answer before the questions were out of my mouth.

"No. Why?"

I shrugged. "No reason." I had another question, one I'd been dodging for over a year, my guilt and shame preventing me from asking. But I thought about it all the time, and tonight seemed as good as any to get it all out there. "Do you ever think about that guy you shot?"

He was silent for a few seconds, squinting at something in the distance like he did before he answered tough questions. "Yeah, I do. My shrink loves me. I've got more baggage than the cargo container on a jumbo jet."

I burst out laughing and he laughed with me. I didn't know why but it was one of the funniest things I'd ever heard. My humor faded when I thought about the baggage he carried, and the part I'd played in adding to his load. "I'm sorry," I said, hoping he knew I meant it. Sometimes words were so damn inadequate.

"Yeah. I know." He stood and rubbed the back of his neck. "You need me to stay on the couch tonight?"

"It's late. Go home. I don't need a babysitter."

TATE HANDED me a mug of coffee and I added milk, but the color didn't change.

"You brewing tar in that pot?" I asked, glancing at the pot

on the burner in his garage. It was seven-thirty in the morning and I was operating on no sleep. After Killian left, I'd gone to bed and stared at the ceiling with too many thoughts racing through my head. Until finally, I'd hauled my ass into the shower. Then I stopped by to confess my sins to my sobriety companion.

"It'll put hair on your chest," he said.

I took a sip, confirming that it probably would. If it didn't eat a hole through my stomach lining first. But I needed the high-octane caffeine today, so I drank it. A jackhammer was working on my head and every muscle in my body ached.

"You need some aspirin for that headache?" Tate asked, eying my aviators, still firmly in place even though I was inside his dimly lit garage.

I shook my head.

"Don't be a stubborn fool. Take the goddamn pills." He shook two out of the bottle and I popped them into my mouth and washed them down with liquid tar.

We wandered out to the bay and I stopped in front of the '69 Mustang Shelby convertible that Tate's been working on for months. "Sweet ride," I said, running my hand over the custom cherry-black paint job.

"Yeah. I was gonna sell her, but I haven't found the right buyer."

"You love her, and you can't let her go."

"I guess you'd know something about that." He shook his head, looking at my face. Not so pretty in the light of day.

I worked my jaw. "My battle wounds."

"Hurt?"

"Nah. I've had worse." I followed him outside and leaned against the wall I'd painted a few months ago—a titan carrying the world on his shoulders with the name of Tate's garage Atlas Motors. I puffed away on my electronic cigarette, the vapor disappearing almost as soon as it hit the air, and watched the traffic go by.

"You should try meditating," Tate said.

I scoffed. "Meditating? Don't tell me you've taken up yoga, too. Next you'll be telling me you booked us a spa weekend."

"Says the guy sucking on a pen."

I took another unsatisfying drag of my fake cigarette and waited for a rush that never came. But still, I persevered. The definition of stupidity.

"Ava's text stopped me from drinking that whiskey last night," I said.

"You made the decision for yourself. Own it. And next time you get a craving, call me."

"Will you talk me through some phone meditation?"

He snorted. We continued watching the traffic while I vaped and drank my strong coffee. I tipped my head back to catch the early morning sun on my face and tried to convince myself that everything would be okay.

18

AVA

*M*y dad was going to be okay. That was the main thing.

"Stop fussing over me," he grumbled as my mom hovered. She wouldn't let him move a muscle and lying around on the sofa, being waited on hand and foot, was not his idea of a good time. He was desperate to get out of the house, back to work and back to a normal life. If it was up to my mom, he'd be retired by now. She kept leaving stacks of glossy travel brochures on the coffee table, within easy reach, but he barely glanced at them.

Tuesday morning, and I couldn't get out of this house fast enough. I hadn't intended to stay so long, but my mom had guilted me into it. *"Your father could have died. The least you can do is spend quality time with him."*

Quality time had consisted of my dad reading the newspaper and watching TV while I updated the bar's social media, texted back and forth with Eden, the guys at work, and Connor. When my mom hadn't been hovering around my dad, she'd taken me aside for plenty of heart-to-hearts about Connor. Lana, as usual, had sided with my mom.

"Dad just had a heart attack," I told my mom. *"Can you drop this,*

already? What I do with my life is my business. Who I choose to spend my time with is my choice."

My mom pursed her lips. *"That boy will only break your heart again, Ava. Mark my words. But if that's what you want, then be my guest."* She *jutted out her chin. "Go ahead and choose him. See where that gets you."*

I checked my phone as a text came through from Connor.

CONNOR: I'm here

I didn't need to ask where 'here' was. We'd met on the same street corner all through high school. How sad that we were twenty-four and still sneaking around. I jumped up from the faded floral chair in the living room and shouldered by purse, texting a reply as I crossed the room to the sofa.

AVA: Be right out

I hugged my dad goodbye. "Love you, Dad. You'll be up and around in no time."

"Not if your mother has anything to say about it," he grumbled.

I patted him on the shoulder in commiseration. Sometimes I wished he'd fight back, instead of going along to keep the peace. My dad hated confrontation, of any kind, and avoided it whenever possible. Maybe holding all that frustration and bottled feelings inside was what had caused his heart attack. "Love you too," he said gruffly, safely hidden behind his newspaper.

I found my mom and Lana at the kitchen table. Lana was in front of her laptop. She had a sales and marketing job she'd never bothered to explain, but apparently, she had flexible hours and worked from home a lot. Why was she wearing a silk blouse, skinny jeans, and stilettos to sit around in our kitchen?

"Bye Mom. Lana."

Lana didn't even lift her head from the laptop. My mom stood and hugged me, her arms squeezing me tight. She smelled like Coco Chanel, the perfume she'd been wearing for as long as I could remember. When she released me, I set Lana's folded cashmere sweater on the table. It had been an oversight to turn up at the hospital in a tank top and jacket without any clothes to change into. When my mom had seen my new tattoo, I thought we'd have to rush *her* to the hospital for a heart attack.

"Do you need a ride to the subway?" Lana asked, surprising me.

"No. I'm good. But thanks."

She nodded and ducked behind her laptop again, her fingers clicking on the keyboard.

"We'll see you for Thanksgiving," my mom said.

Ugh. Thanksgiving. Too soon for another visit with my family. I shouldn't be so ungracious. My dad had a heart attack, for God's sake. A reminder that my parents wouldn't be here forever. I forced a smile I didn't feel. "Yep."

I exited my house and gulped in the cool, damp air as I walked to the corner. As I got closer, I slowed my steps, taking in the bruises on Connor's face.

"What happened?" I asked.

"Why didn't you tell me?"

"Tell you what?" I asked, confused.

"What did Jake Masters do to you?"

I averted my gaze. "I told you all about it."

He took my hands in his and tugged me closer, looking into my eyes. I stared at the bruises on his face. "Connor..."

"Baby. Tell me what happened."

"Did you get in a fight? Did Jake—"

Connor pressed his finger against my lips. "Tell me what he did."

"We need to go. I have tons to do at work..."

His hands gripped my hips. My feet were off the ground and somehow, I was straddling the bike, facing him. "What are you doing?" I tried to get off the bike, but his hold on my hips tightened, keeping me in place, his eyes never leaving my face.

I fixated on a spot over his shoulder. His hand cupped my chin and he tipped my face up, forcing me to look at him. "What did he do?"

"I'm okay, Connor," I whispered. "I put it behind me."

"Did you tell anyone?"

I swallowed. "No."

"Did you think it was your fault? Did you believe you did something to deserve that?"

I looked into his eyes. "Did you? Is that what you believed, growing up?"

"We're not talking about me."

"It's kind of the same though, isn't it? You never did anything to deserve that treatment. It's so much easier to believe the bad things people say than the good things. He called me a slut. And everyone believed it."

"I didn't. Killian didn't."

"I know. Because you guys... you understood how bullies operate. Better than anyone. Remember Holly?" He nodded. "We'd been friends since grade school. We used to play Barbies together, have sleepovers, share popcorn and a tray of brownies..." They all sounded like such stupid, inconsequential things but in grade school and junior high, those things had been important. "But when we got to high school and Jake started paying attention to me, everything changed. Holly and my other friends shut me out. They believed the rumors... and they talked about me behind my back. They said I'd always acted like I was better than them..." I stopped and took a deep breath, surprised that even after all these years, their words still had the power to hurt. "And I never tried to defend myself. If they wanted to believe the worst, then they weren't really my friends. It hurt, and I felt so alone. Until you. You were the only friend I needed. You were there for me... always."

He wrapped his arms around me and pulled me close, his hand stroking my hair. "Baby... tell me."

"It was a long time ago."

"Tell me."

I'd been holding it inside for so long. Now, when I envisioned it, I felt like it had happened to someone else, not me. "He dragged me around to the back of the school by the dumpsters. And he... pushed me on my knees and unzipped his jeans and..." I swallowed hard, watching it all play out like a movie. Connor's arms around me tightened and I pressed my cheek against his chest, closing my eyes and breathing in the scent of leather and spice. I felt safe in his arms, like the bad stuff couldn't catch up to me if he was holding me close. "He grabbed the back of my head and guided himself into my mouth. I tried to sink my teeth into him... he smacked me across the face and yanked my head up by the hair." I could still feel the tears stinging my eyes, the gravel digging into my knees as I knelt in front of him. "He said if I tried that again, he'd punch me hard. I didn't know what I was doing... he kept pushing my head down and it was gagging me. When he came inside my mouth, I got to my feet and spit it in his face. I tried to run, but he grabbed me and said I needed to be taught a lesson. He tossed me in the dumpster and Killian... that's when he turned up."

Connor didn't say anything. He just kept me wrapped in his arms, stroking my hair.

"It's okay. It was a long time—"

"It's not okay," he said, his voice shaking with anger. "You were fourteen. *Nothing* about that is okay."

I knew that. I was trying to console him. "What made it okay was you. Being with you... the sex and everything... I felt like I was taking back some of my power. Because I was doing something I wanted to do, and you would never force me to do anything I didn't want to. And all those times...when I was daring, and we did it in all kinds of crazy places, I felt empowered. It was like a big fuck you to Jake Masters, which probably sounds stupid but... I didn't feel like a victim anymore."

Someone cleared their throat. I pulled away from Connor and looked over at Lana. She held out the pearl grey cashmere sweater. "I thought you might need it. It's chilly."

I climbed off the bike and faced her, wondering how long she'd been standing there and how much she'd heard. "But it's yours."

She forced it into my hand. "Keep it. It looks good on you. It matches your eyes."

"Do you think a sweater will make up for what you did to Ava?" Connor asked, his voice low and angry.

"Connor... just let it go."

"You're her older sister," he said. "It was your responsibility to protect her and stand up for her. Instead, you stabbed her in the back and you've been doing it for years."

Lana narrowed her eyes and planted her hands on her hips. "And what have you done for her? Besides mess up her life?"

"He was there for me—"

"Seriously, Ava? How was he there for you? How many times did you get in trouble because of him? The *only* thing he ever brought into your life was trouble. You should have stayed with Zeke. The whole family loved him." She turned on her heel and walked away. I was tempted to toss her sweater on the sidewalk and stomp on it, but I tied it around my waist, buying time before I faced Connor. Lana had always been vindictive, and it seemed that time hadn't changed her.

"Zeke met your family," Connor said, his voice flat.

I turned to face him but couldn't quite look him in the eye. It didn't matter. He wasn't looking at me anyway. He was staring down the street, his jaw working to contain his emotions. "Yeah, it was... my dad's birthday lunch. I just... I shouldn't have brought him."

He handed me my helmet and put on his own.

"Connor..."

The Harley rumbled to life and he revved the engine. "Get on the bike. I need to get to work."

I climbed off the back of the bike and took off my helmet. Connor looked straight ahead, his jaw clenched, and I suspected it had been that way for the whole ride. When I'd wrapped my arms around him, hanging on tight as he drove too fast from Bay Ridge to Williamsburg, I'd felt the rigid tension in his body. I looked down the street at the waterfront, trying to find the words. "How about a Chinese takeout and movie night? You can come over after—"

"Ava. Connor. What's up?" Zeke stopped next to me and glanced from me to Connor. Inwardly, I groaned. Talk about shitty timing. "Whoa, dude. What happened to your face?"

Connor locked his jaw and remained mute, his gaze focused straight ahead.

"Hey, Zeke. Give us a minute. I'll see you inside."

"Yeah. Sure."

I watched him walk away and waited until he was inside the bar before I returned my attention to Connor. "Don't listen to Lana. I don't care what my family thinks."

"But I do. I'll always be the guy who fucked up your life."

"Kiss me."

"What?"

"Kiss me. Take me back to a better place."

"Life doesn't work that way, remember?"

He removed his helmet and I leaned in and wrapped my arms around his neck. "It's only ever been you, Connor."

He pressed his forehead against mine, his hands cradling my face. I pulled back to look at his face. After what I'd just told him, I hadn't expected him to look sad. "Did you hear what I said?"

He gave me a little nod and opened his mouth as if to speak, but no words came out. I searched his face. The yellowish-green bruises reminded me of how his face had been battered a year ago. And his eyes... there was no light in them. I took a few steps back, realization dawning on me. "Where did you see Jake?"

"The Candy Store."

The Candy Store? What the hell had he been doing there? At a club he used to frequent... a club I knew damn well Danny Vargas hung out at. All my self-preservation instincts kicked into overdrive. "Why were you there?" I watched his face, waiting to catch him in a lie.

He let out a breath and carved his hand through his hair. "I didn't score. I ordered a drink, but I left it on the bar." Connor held my gaze and I saw that he was telling the truth. When he used to lie to me, he could never look me in the eye. For someone who used to lie often, he'd never been very good at it.

He pulled on his helmet and the Harley rumbled to life. "See you tonight."

19

CONNOR

*A*va's living room glowed pink from the Good Vibes neon sign above her gray sofa. We were eating Chinese food with chopsticks, passing the containers back and forth, not bothering with plates and watching *The Avengers*, although for me it was just background noise.

Listening to her story this morning, about what Jake had done to her had made me nauseous. Furious. Hurt. Angry. Sad. I couldn't help wondering why she'd never trusted me enough to tell me the truth. I would have understood her so much better if she had. I'd tried to be there for her, but at fourteen, what the hell did I know about girls and the way they operated? Not a damn thing. I just remember thinking that she was fragile and that I needed to tread lightly. I'd always wanted to protect her, to show her that not every guy was a scumbag like Jake, but I hadn't known the half of it.

"Are you done?" I asked, jerking my chin at the food containers.

She nodded and stood up from the sofa, reaching for the containers. "I've got it," I said. Ava sat down and tucked her legs underneath her. I cleared the containers and dumped the empties in the trash, stowing the leftover Lo Mein in the fridge. Fucking Jake Masters. I slammed the fridge door shut and pinched the bridge of my nose, taking deep breaths to try and calm the fuck down. It didn't work. I kicked the cupboard below her sink. Once. Twice. Three times for good measure.

Fuck. Fuck. Fuck. How could anyone do that shit to a four-teen-year-old girl?

I felt her hands on my back and then her arms wrapped around my waist, her cheek pressed against my back. I scrubbed both hands over my face.

"Why the fuck didn't you tell me?" I asked, dropping all pretense of being calm.

"I just wanted to forget."

Yeah, I understood that. I'd tried to do the same thing so many times in my life. But the truth always had a way of coming out. I unclasped her hands and pulled her around to face me. "You wouldn't have had to go through it alone. If you'd told me—"

"We were *fourteen*. I couldn't even bring myself to say the words. And you're a guy. I was too embarrassed."

"You've had ten years to tell me. Instead, I had to find out from that scumbag."

"You wouldn't let me give you a blowjob tonight."

As soon as I'd walked in the door, she'd unbuttoned my jeans and knelt in front of me. Like she had something to prove. It had felt so wrong. "I don't want you on your knees for me."

She shook her head in frustration like I wasn't getting it. "It's my choice. I wanted to do it. If you give a bully the power, they've won. You, of all people, should understand that."

Ava was right. After a lifetime of being bullied, I should have grasped that concept sooner. I watched her pull off her sweatshirt, exposing a sheer white tank top, her red bra visible underneath. She pushed down her black leggings, stepping out of one leg and then the other before kicking them aside. Her tank top joined the other clothes on the floor and now she was standing in front of me in nothing but a lacy red bra and matching underwear. She'd worn them for me.

"In the diner," she said. "What I wanted to tell you is that none of the other guys ever mattered. Nobody ever came close to you. And Jake doesn't matter either. I've put it behind me."

I wrapped my arms around her and felt her soft, warm skin under my hands. The rise and fall of her chest against mine. I was conscious that I was holding something precious in my arms. Something irreplaceable. And I was reminded, once again, how tiny Ava was. But she was fierce and strong and brave, too.

I'd been through enough shit in my life to know that when you were being offered a second shot at something, you took it. And you did everything in your power to make sure you didn't fuck it up.

I took her hand in mine and led her to the bedroom. She lay on the bed, her head propped on her hand and watched me undress.

"Come here, lover," she said, her voice low and sultry, teasing. I chuckled as she crawled to the edge of the bed and knelt in front of me. She wrapped her hand around the base of my cock, her eyes on mine as she wet her lips and lowered her head, guiding me inside her warm mouth. Jesus. Her mouth was like heaven. Her other hand grabbed my ass, her short nails digging into my skin. I wrapped my hands in her silky soft hair, holding the back of her head as she sucked and teased, rolling the barbell with her tongue. My balls were drawn up so tight and the suction of her mouth as she deep-throated me was so fucking hot I forgot about everything else and just went with it. But I didn't want to come in her mouth.

I pulled out and she looked up at me, ready to fight me on it. "I want to be inside you."

She shimmied out of her underwear, eager for the same thing. "How do you want to fuck me?" she asked, still using her bedroom voice. It was another side to Ava. The dirty talk, the loud moans and screams. She never held back on any of it.

I pushed her back against the mattress, bent her legs at the knees and spread her legs, putting my head between her thighs. Her fingers tugged my hair and she screamed yes, yes, yes when I bit her clit then flattened my tongue against the tight bundle of nerves, teasing the orgasm out of her before I fucked her with my tongue. Her body spasmed and her thighs clamped around my head like a vice before she went boneless, her legs shaking and her body limp. I kissed my way up to her mouth, my tongue parting her lips to give her a taste of the sweetest thing I'd ever tasted. She wrapped her arms around my neck and arched her back, her tits flat against my chest, my cock jumping as she kissed me long and hard.

I pulled away and sat back on my knees, flipping her onto her stomach. She got on her elbows and knees, ready for me, and knowing what I wanted without having to ask. I fisted my length, dragging the tip through her wetness before I finally entered her. I rolled my hips, thrusting inside her and she pushed her ass against me, taking me in deeper. Sweet Jesus. If I could stay here forever, I would. I reached around and fingered her clit as I moved inside her.

"Oh God," she moaned. "Connor..." She sank onto the mattress, her ass in the air, her arms wrapped around her pillow, face pressed into it.

My grip tightened on her hips, her muscles contracting around me, and her soft moans sent me over the edge, bringing me to an orgasm that was so intense I was temporarily blinded.

20

AVA

I woke up to the scent of bacon and checked my phone for the time, surprised that I'd slept until ten. Connor was not only awake but cooking breakfast? I'd always been a morning person, but Connor used to sleep until noon. I dressed in a tank top and sweats, not bothering with underwear or a bra then darted into the bathroom to brush my teeth.

Go, Ava. You're rocking that bedhead. And check out the rosy afterglow. It wasn't really an afterglow. It was beard burn from Connor's stubble. But I couldn't wipe the stupid-ass grin off my face as I wrangled my hair into a messy ponytail. Multiple orgasms would do that to a girl.

Grabbing my phone from the nightstand, I padded across the hardwood floors, the scent of bacon making my mouth water, and found Connor in the kitchen, his jeans riding low on his hips, the sleeves of his gray thermal pushed up to his elbows, exposing the ink on his forearms. Oh God, he was sexy. I leaned my hip against the doorframe, watching him. Reveling at the sight of him in my kitchen, filling up the space that had been so empty without him. He turned from the stove, a lazy grin on his face, the bruises barely noticeable now. I watched his eyes darken as his gaze settled on my sheer tank top. "Morning, babe."

185

"Good morning. You went shopping?" I asked, noticing the plate of fruit—sliced nectarines, strawberries, and blueberries. Not to mention the bacon which I knew hadn't been in my refrigerator.

"Yep."

I wandered over to my kitchen table by the window and stared at the wildflowers Connor had put in a cobalt blue earthenware jug. *Flowers.* At a table already set for two, the cutlery resting on paper napkins folded into triangles. I knew which one was mine, the one with a bluebird drawn on it. My hand flew to my chest and I held it against my hammering heart that threatened to burst free and fly right across the room and into his magic hands.

Take my heart, I'd say. It's yours and it always has been. Keep it safe.

I lowered myself onto the cane-backed chair and drew my knees to my chest. The radiator under my window hissed and clanged, warming up my kitchen. Pale sunlight filtered through the window. The scent of basil, thyme, and mint from the potted herbs on my windowsill mingled with the scent of melted butter and coffee and bacon. My kitchen felt cozy and warm and my life felt so much fuller. I watched Connor pour pancake batter into the sizzling pan. He flipped on the electric kettle, the spatula in his other hand and I watched his every move in fascination, my chin propped on my knees.

"I love pancakes." I sounded like an idiot. As if he didn't already know I loved pancakes and crispy bacon.

"I know. That's why I'm making them."

I didn't know what to think about any of this, so I just sat there, staring at his back, at his broad shoulders, at the flex of his arms. My gaze ventured lower. Connor had a great ass.

He turned from the stove and I lifted my gaze to his eyes, catching the gleam in them. His lips curved into a smile. "You were checking out my ass."

I snorted like the very idea was ridiculous. "No, I wasn't."

In a few steps, he was standing in front of me. He swiped his thumb over the corner of my mouth. "Drool," he said.

I rolled my eyes. "I'm starving. If I'm drooling, it's because of the food." Liar. I flapped my hand at him. "Your pancakes are burning." He chuckled and returned to the stove. I scrolled through my playlists, opting for a happy, chilled compilation. The Beatles' "Here Comes the Sun" played from my speakers in the living room and I cranked up the volume, letting the music fill our souls. Brighten up an already perfect morning.

"Pour me some coffee, wench."

I laughed and wandered over to the coffee maker, brand new and obviously purchased by Connor this morning on his shopping spree. "How presumptuous of you," I said, grabbing two mugs from the cupboard. "Why would I need a coffee maker?"

"To keep your man happy."

"You're my man now? That was quick."

"Baby, ten years is a marathon, not a sprint."

True. I smiled as I poured his coffee, got milk from the fridge and added it until it turned the color he liked it. Grabbed the bag of sugar on the counter and a spoon from the drawer.

"No sugar," he said.

My hand stilled, the spoonful of sugar poised over his cup of coffee. "You don't put three sugars in your coffee anymore?"

"Nope. Lean proteins, vegetables, Greek yogurt, fruit..."

I groaned and poured the sugar back in the bag. "You're on the Killian diet." I set the mug on the counter next to him. "You used to be a sugar junkie."

"I'm not a junkie anymore, babe. But I still got junk," he said, grabbing his crotch.

I snorted laughter while I fixed myself a cup of green tea.

"I didn't hear any complaints about my body last night." There was nothing to complain about. His body was amazing, the best it's ever been. The last time we'd been together, at the tail end of his addiction, he'd been too thin and when he'd been with me, naked in my bed, it had felt like I'd been holding on to someone else. A shadow of his former self. Nothing is more heart-breaking than watching the person you love destroy themselves. His body. His mind. His personality. Changed by the poison he injected into his veins.

But I didn't want to mention that now or do anything to spoil our day. I'd leave that memory in the past where it belonged. We were making new memories. Good ones.

"Your body is fucking fantastic, by the way," he said, giving me a playful swat on the butt.

I accepted the compliment with a smile and carried my tea to the table as Connor served our food—a stack of pancakes topped with fruit, three strips of bacon next to it. I laid the bacon on top of my pancakes and poured syrup over it, laughing when I noticed Connor had done the same thing.

Eating breakfast together felt so right and so good. It had been so long since we'd slept in the same bed together all night. So long since we'd done any of the typical couple things. I wanted to bottle up this happiness and store it for rainy days. Over breakfast, we laughed and talked about nothing important and it felt as if we'd laid to rest everything that had happened with Jake and Lana and Zeke.

"So... what are you doing before work?" I asked after we'd cleared the dishes and stacked the dishwasher.

"Not sure. I need to check my spreadsheet."

I laughed. Connor hooked an arm around my waist and pulled me against him. "We need a shower," he said.

"We?"

"Mhm. You're a dirty girl."

Connor lifted me off the ground, threw me over his shoulder and jogged toward my bedroom. I pounded my fists against his back, laughing. "What are you doing?"

He tossed me on the bed and stripped naked then helped me out of my clothes and led me into the bathroom. Turning on the shower, he checked the water temperature with his hand before we stepped into the tub and slid the glass door shut. Connor guided me under the spray and I tipped back my head, letting the water run over my hair while his hands soaped my body. I took the shower gel out of his hand and squeezed some into my palm, soaping his body the way he'd done to mine. A very thorough job. My hand wrapped around his hard dick and I slid it up and down. He groaned as he squeezed shampoo into his hand.

"I'll have the cleanest dick in Brooklyn," he said.

"All the better for me to suck on it," I said with a wink.

"Close your eyes, wench." I laughed as he lathered my hair with shampoo and massaged my scalp with his magic hands. I was purring with delight. Putty in his hands.

Connor tipped back my head, rinsing away the shampoo then repeated the process with conditioner. I wrapped my arms around his neck and kissed him under the spray of the water, my hip pressed against his erection. He lifted me up and my legs wrapped around his waist as he pushed me up against the tiled wall and slid inside me, his hands squeezing my ass, our kisses wet and frantic.

My muscles clenched around him as the orgasm rocked my body. Connor came inside me, placing his palm on the wall for support. I opened my eyes and blinked as the world rushed back and Connor's face came into focus. He gave me a big smile that reached his eyes and lit up his whole face and then we were laughing for no reason.

I've missed you, Connor. It's so good to have you back.

21

CONNOR

*O*ver the past two weeks with Ava, I was starting to believe that I could be her everything. I could be the guy she'd always deserved. The shop was successful, my cravings were under control, and my girl was happy. I knew it by the way she smiled every time she saw me. By the way she called me when she was at work and left adorable messages to let me know she was thinking about me. We hadn't said those three words yet, but I tried to show her that I loved her so that when I did say them again, she'd know they weren't empty. She needed to know that I was someone she could rely on. Someone she could trust. Someone who wasn't lying to her or keeping secrets.

I knew I needed to tell her the truth about Miami, but everything was so good right now that I didn't want to ruin it by bringing up more bad memories. Some days it felt like Miami had just been a bad dream and as my life got better, the dream got hazier. I'd tell her. But not tonight.

She wrapped her arms around me from behind and I pulled down my mask, looking at her over my shoulder.

"Are you bored yet?" I asked, setting down the spray paint can.

"Never. I love watching you paint. They're amazing, babe."

She hadn't called me babe in years. I loved that she'd said it now, the word rolling off her tongue as if it was natural. "Because the subject is amazing," I said.

She came to stand next to me as she studied the art. She'd been hanging out here with me every night while I painted. After the shop closed. After we ate a late dinner together. After we fucked in the kitchen, her bare ass on the counter. Or she straddled me in a chair like last night. Tonight, I'd taken her to our sushi place and she'd fed me salmon sashimi slathered with wasabi then we'd fucked in the unisex restroom. Instead of her usual screams and moans, she'd sunk her teeth into my shoulder, biting down so hard she'd drawn blood that seeped through my T-shirt. I could still feel the sting from her teeth marks. We were crazy, Ava and me. I always thought we'd loved each other to the point of madness. Insanity, really. But I didn't know any other way to love her except madly.

"It's me but not really me," she said, referring to the paintings.

These two pieces were loosely inspired by last week's aerial silks class that she'd invited me to. I'd painted two Avas. Fire and Ice. She was right. They weren't really her, but they were the essence of her. Ava on fire. A blur of movement and bursts of color. Flaming hair, billowing red silk, her face aglow, sparks shooting from her fingertips. Ava the ice queen. Silks suspended from a snow globe, silver hair and swirling snow, a bluebird perched on her shoulder.

"They're the best pieces you've ever done," she said, her voice hushed as if she was in church, her breath coming out in white puffs.

She shivered, and I wrapped my arms around her, thinking it was from the cold. "All done here. Go inside and get warm. I'll be right in. I just need to clean up."

"I'm not cold," she said, tipping her head back to look at me, her face lit up in the glow of the floodlights, her cheeks rosy from the cold. And those goddamn eyes. I swear I could get lost in those eyes. "Just happy." Ava gave me a smile that could light up the night sky. And I knew exactly what I'd paint next.

"You're so fucking gorgeous," I said.

"Kiss me like you mean it," she said, her eyes at half-mast, her body leaning into mine.

I held her face in my hands and tipped it up to mine before I lowered my mouth to hers.

MY PHONE RANG, and Ava picked it up from the counter, checking the screen before she answered it. "Hey, Killian. What's up?"

She rolled her eyes and I chuckled as she sighed. "We've been back together for weeks now. Get with the program." Her brows drew together as she listened to whatever Killian was dishing out. "I'm not. Things are good. Doesn't Eden talk to you? I thought she told you everything."

Ava listened for a moment then winced. "Oops. Um, tell her I'm sorry. It's just...oh hey, Eden. You know I love you. When you get back, we'll work on our fabulous Pinterest board and we'll iron out all the details. And we'll go shopping for dresses and..." Ava stopped and nibbled on her fingernail. "I'm not going to say it."

She rolled her eyes again. "Fine. You were right. Happy now? If you're looking for a smackdown, I'm pretty sure I can take you."

I snorted laughter and Ava stuck her tongue out at me. "Real mature, babe."

"You're just saying that because you're the teacher's pet," Ava told Eden. "But I've got mad skills. Ask Connor." She smirked at me and I smacked her ass as she said goodbye and handed me the phone.

"What's up?" I asked, not sure if I'd be getting Killian or Eden. Killian, as it turned out.

"You okay?"

"It's all good. Are you on the road?" Killian was going to spend Thanksgiving in Pennsylvania with Eden's family, just like he'd done last year.

"Yeah."

"Have a good trip and Happy Thanksgiving."

"So you and Ava..."

"Yep."

"Huh."

"I think it's great," Eden yelled in the background. "Even though my best friend and maid of honor has been MIA for two weeks. I still love you both."

"We love you too," I said. "That was meant for Eden."

"Yeah, I figured," Killian said with a snort. "You sure you're okay?"

Funny, he didn't give a shit how I was last Thanksgiving. "It's cool. I've got plans."

"The soup kitchen."

I worked it last year with Tate and I was doing it again this year. After we'd left the soup kitchen last year, I hadn't been in a good place. Tate had walked with me for miles. Not talking. Just being there for me so I didn't do anything I'd regret. "It's a good thing to do."

"Yeah." He was silent for a few seconds and I had no idea what the purpose of this phone call was. "We'll be back Saturday night. If you need me, call me."

If I needed him, which I wouldn't, I doubted that he'd be able to help me from three hundred miles away. Not to mention that Killian wasn't much of a conversationalist. What I didn't tell him was that Tate was my first phone call these days. Not Killian. I didn't want to burden him with any more of my shit. "I'm good. Enjoy your weekend. Catch you later."

He said goodbye, with Eden echoing it in the background and I tossed my phone on the counter, taking a seat at the island next to Ava who was chewing on her lip.

"I wish—"

I placed my fingers over her lips, already knowing what she was going to say. "Shh. It doesn't matter. It's just one day."

"It's not. It's Thanksgiving."

"I'll pick you up in Bay Ridge on Friday morning."

"I know, but it's not right that you—"

I pulled her into a kiss to stop the rest of the words. We'd already been over this. Her family didn't accept me and turning up at their family Thanksgiving would ruin it for her. "Do you want to be with me, Ava? I'm not just talking about tomorrow."

She lifted her eyes to mine. "Yes."

"Do I make you happy?"

"Yes."

"That's all that matters to me. Okay?"

She gave me a little smile. "Okay." But her gray eyes had clouded over and that brilliant smile from earlier was gone.

"Let's go to bed," I said as she stifled a yawn. She nodded and followed me into the bedroom. After we took turns in the bathroom, we undressed and climbed into bed. I pulled the comforter over her shoulder and wrapped an arm around her as she fit her body into the curve of mine. She fell asleep instantly, her fingers entwined with mine, and despite not being able to spend Thanksgiving with her, I was happy. I was at peace. There were no monsters lurking in the dark for me tonight. Just Ava, her pale hair spread across the pillow, her skin soft and warm, her smile from earlier imprinted on my brain.

22

AVA

"He's a nice boy. And so handsome. His mother showed me photos. And he's a lawyer," my mom said. "I gave his mother your number. You can bet he'll be calling you."

Happy Thanksgiving. The table was laden with food, the wine was flowing, and my mom hadn't stopped harping on me since I'd walked in the door. "If he does, he'll be wasting his time," I said. "I'm not interested."

My mom sighed and looked down the table at my father. "Lars, talk to your daughter. Tell her how important it is to find a nice man. Someone who's a good provider."

"Pass the cranberry sauce," my dad said. My mom passed it down the table and it changed hands until it reached me. I set it next to the brussels sprouts in front of him. Did anyone like brussels sprouts? My dad helped himself to the cranberry sauce, ignoring my mother's pointed look.

"What happened to that other young man... the blond one?" my grandma asked.

"He looked like a pansy," my grandpa said, earning him a sharp elbow from my grandma.

"He's just a friend," I told my grandma. "And you can't call a guy a pansy," I told my grandpa. He grunted and shoveled food into his mouth.

"She dumped him for no good reason," my mom said, throwing up her hands. "Can you believe that? Such a good catch."

I sighed and pushed the food around on my plate, thinking about Connor. It seemed so wrong that I couldn't even invite him to my family's Thanksgiving dinner. But I'd probably done him a favor.

I glanced at Lana, sitting next to me, as she sniped at Joe. "I told you I wanted one piece of turkey and a bite of stuffing. I can't eat all this." Joe accommodated her by transferring a slice of turkey and a heaping serving of stuffing to his own plate. The poor man waited on her hand and foot but got nothing but criticism for his efforts.

"Ava. What's wrong with the food?" my mom asked, pointing her fork at me. I wouldn't put it past her to skewer me with it. "I've been cooking for three days. I woke up at six in the morning to get the turkey in the oven and you've barely touched your food."

I stuffed a bite of sweet potato casserole into my mouth and ate a few bites of turkey to keep her happy. Then I guzzled my wine. Before I knew it, the glass was empty. I refilled it, thinking that holidays with my family would turn anyone into an alcoholic. I'd lost count of how many glasses of wine I'd already drunk. Enough to make everything fuzzy around the edges. But not enough to drown out my mom's voice.

"Ava... his name is Nathan," she yelled down the table. "When he calls you, I want you to be sweet and nice. Ask him questions about himself and tell him about—"

"Mom. Stop. Please don't fix me up with any of your friends' sons. Or anyone else. I'm not interested."

"Why not? You've got a better offer?" my grandma asked.

I took another gulp of wine for liquid courage before I dropped the bomb. "Connor and I have gotten back together."

My mother's fork clattered to her plate. "Lars," she said, waving her hands in the air. "Do something."

"What do you want me to do?" my dad asked, his eyes glued to his plate of food.

"Tell her she's making a big mistake. Tell her that boy is bad news."

My dad cut a piece of turkey, topped it with stuffing and a dollop of cranberry sauce, put it in his mouth and chewed in silence.

"He worked for you that one summer, Dad. Was he bad news? I bet he did a good job. Worked hard. Turned up on time. Didn't he?" I knew Connor had done all those things. He'd been grateful that my dad had given him work, and he'd thought it would bring him closer to my family.

My dad shrugged and muttered something unintelligible.

Stand up for him. Stand up for me, I silently screamed.

But he wouldn't. Or he couldn't. He was too much of a coward. It made me so sad because I loved my dad. I really did. But I'd lost respect for him so many years ago, and he'd done nothing to win it back.

I guzzled the rest of my wine and set down my empty glass. Then I pushed back my chair and stood, feeling lightheaded from the wine. Whoa. Headrush. "I love Connor," I announced to the table.

"Who the hell is Connor?" my grandpa asked.

"Exactly," I said. "You don't even know him, and he's been a huge part of my life for ten years."

"He's been nothing but trouble for ten years," my mom said.

"I've always loved Connor. And I always will. I can't imagine my life without him and I don't want to. And I'm sorry that you hate him so much, but you know what? He believed in me when nobody else did. He loves me exactly as I am. And I want to spend my Thanksgiving with him because my family... they won't welcome him into their home and that makes me sad and angry and hurt. So yeah, I'm going."

I stumbled away from the table, somewhat deflated after my grand speech. A scene like that played out better in a movie. "Ava

Christensen," my mom called after me. "You get back here right now. You can't walk out on Thanksgiving dinner with your family."

I paused in the doorway, my back to her. If I looked at my mom's face, I'd lose my nerve. "Watch me."

I grabbed my parka from the hook in the entryway and pulled it on, my hands trembling as I tried to do up the zipper. I shouldered my overnight bag and walked out the front door, taking deep breaths of cold air as I walked toward the subway station. Someone needed to stand up for Connor. I was his person and he was mine. The person you called at three in the morning because you'd had a bad dream and you needed someone to reassure you that everything was okay. The first person you wanted to call when you got good news. Or bad news. Or when you just wanted to talk about everything and nothing and you knew they were the only person who would truly *get* it. Connor *got* me. He'd never tried to change me. Or turn me into an ideal of what he thought I should be.

I pulled my phone out of my coat pocket, all set to call Connor and tell him I was on my way to him. Unfortunately, my phone was dead. *What?* I never let my battery run out like that. I stuffed it back in my pocket. I'd just have to surprise him.

"Ava!"

I stopped and turned as Lana caught up to me. "Hey. Do you need a ride?"

I looked down the street, not sure what to say. "Um... I can take the train."

"I'll drive you. Wherever you want to go."

"Why?" I asked, suspecting an ulterior motive.

"Just... let me drive you. I haven't been drinking."

I followed her to her silver SUV, not sure if I should trust her. But it was cold out here and I was a little bit drunk and a lot weary, so I climbed into the passenger seat and fastened my seatbelt. The inside of her car smelled like new car and fake pine tree from the air freshener hanging on her rear-view mirror. "Are you going home?" she asked, starting up the car and turning the heat on full-blast.

"No. I'm going to a church in Bed-Stuy."

She turned on her GPS and asked me to enter the information, so I did. Then she pulled away from the curb and we drove in silence for a while.

"I didn't know Jake did that to you. I mean... I thought he was just flirting with you and saying things..."

I guess she'd heard everything that day, but I had no idea why she was bringing it up now. "It doesn't matter. Ancient history," I mumbled, staring out the windshield.

She didn't respond, and I was tempted to turn on the music, but I couldn't be bothered so I let the silence stretch out between us. "Jake Masters was my first. I thought I loved him."

My eyes widened, and I tried to process this information, but I couldn't. Maybe I'd heard her wrong. I hadn't even been aware that she'd known Jake Masters. "*What?*"

"I had a crush on him. And the end of our junior year, I found out about a party he was throwing. So, I went. And I got really drunk. I pretty much threw myself at him. After that, we did it a few more times."

Did it? My sister had sex with Jake Masters? Willingly?

My stomach churned. To think that someone would actually want that... not just someone, but Lana, made me feel sick inside. "He came to our house a few times over the summer when Mom and Dad were at work. You were at that performing arts camp. And he..." I heard her take a deep breath and exhale like whatever she was about to tell me was hard to say. "... Jake saw photos of you in my room. And he said things like, 'Your sister's a hottie. Better watch out for that one. She'll have guys crawling all over her.' He wanted to know all about you."

I opened my window, needing the fresh air while Lana just kept on talking, all her secrets spilling out after all these years. "He dumped me and moved on and when we went back to school, he completely ignored me like I'd never existed. Like we'd never had sex or... even knew each other. And then I saw the way he looked at you and I swear I didn't know what was really going on. I thought... you were having sex with him."

Bile rose up in my throat. "Pull over," I said, my voice strained as I rolled down the window all the way.

"What?"

"I'm going to be..." I hung my head out the window and vomited red wine and Thanksgiving dinner. Fucking brussels sprouts. The car screeched to a halt and I yanked off my seatbelt and shoved the door open, stumbling out of the car. I threw up everything that was left inside me, my legs shaky, my stomach hurting.

"Why?" I asked, my back turned to her. "Because you read it on the bathroom walls? I never had sex with him. I was still a virgin."

"Ava. Get back in the car."

I took a few deep breaths and considered striking out on my own, but I was miles from where I needed to be, and I didn't have the energy, so I returned to her car and shut the door. Lana, who had been the perfect Girl Scout, handed me a bottle of water, sugarless gum, and Tic Tacs. I indulged in all three, trying to get rid of the bad taste in my mouth.

"I guess I was jealous," she said, minutes later. "I mean, he never paid me that much attention."

"The wrong kind of attention, Lana. You think I *wanted* that?"

"No. I just wanted you to know... I'm sorry."

I didn't respond. Her sorry was years too late and I would have preferred that she'd been on my side when I'd needed her. I wasn't sure we could ever repair the damage. I didn't even know Lana anymore. I didn't know what she liked to do in her free time, what music she listened to, what her favorite TV shows or movies were. I'd been to her condo a few times, but it had told me nothing about the person who lived there. Everything in her house was brand-new, from a big box store, beige and boring.

Lana pulled up in front of the church and I gripped the door handle. "Thanks for the ride."

"Sure."

I opened the door and climbed out. Before I shut it, I popped my head in and asked, "Are you happy with Joe? I mean... do you love him with the power of a thousand suns?"

She shook her head. "Ava... nobody loves like that."

"I do." I closed the door and walked toward the church. How sad for Lana that she'd never had that kind of love. How sad that she'd ever believed she could be in love with a guy like Jake Masters. I'd rather burn for my love than be indifferent.

23

AVA

*O*lunteers were cleaning the tables, and it looked as if the dinner was over, but I didn't see Connor. I walked through the room and poked my head in the kitchen. I recognized the guy with a ponytail, although I hadn't seen him in a year. "Hey, Tate."

He turned from the sink and I gave him a little smile. "Ava. What's up?"

"I was just... is Connor here?"

"Left about five minutes ago."

"Okay... well, it was good seeing you."

"Hang on," he said, drying his hands on a dish towel. "I'll give you a lift."

"It's okay. You don't have to—"

"I know I don't have to, but I'm gonna." He pointed a finger at me. "Don't go anywhere."

I nodded and waited for Tate, staying out of the way of the volunteers cleaning up the kitchen.

Two minutes later, Tate was back with his coat. I followed him outside and down the block to a black pick-up truck that said Atlas Motors on the side, with an address and phone number advertising his business. "Good thing I brought the truck today," he said, unlocking the doors. "I don't have a spare helmet."

I climbed into the truck and belted up, huddling into my seat as he pulled away, classic rock music playing on his stereo.

"Connor's doing really well, isn't he?" I asked Tate, trying to fill up the silence even though Tate didn't seem bothered by it.

"Yep. Proud of him."

We settled into silence again and I resigned myself to a quiet trip.

"You love him?" Tate asked a few minutes later, catching me by surprise.

"Yes, I do."

"You're willing to stand by him? Not go running off when things get tough?"

I considered his questions and tried not to get offended by them. It was obvious that Tate really cared about Connor and he had his back. He'd been there for Connor when nobody else had been. "I just walked out on my family's Thanksgiving because they don't support my relationship with Connor. They never liked him, and they never wanted us to be together."

"Huh. You don't say. But you didn't answer the questions."

"No. I guess I didn't." I mulled it over for a minute. Tate felt the need to protect Connor from me. That hurt. But maybe it was justified. I'd always thought that Connor was the one who ran away when things got tough but maybe, all along, it had been me. "We're on our way to something good and I don't want to lose him again."

Tate nodded, pleased with my answer, maybe. I didn't know him well enough to decipher his gestures. He pulled up in front of Connor's place and put the truck in park. "Thanks for the ride," I said, hopping out of the truck.

"You got it."

I pounded on Connor's door with the side of my fist, hoping he could hear me upstairs. A doorbell would be handy. I waited, my ear pressed against the door, listening for sounds on the other side. Then I heard his footsteps on the stairs. "Who is it?" he asked, his voice low and steely, and not sounding like him.

"It's me. Ava."

He undid the locks and opened the door, dressed in jeans, shirtless and barefoot. "Hey," I said. "Surprise."

"What are you doing here?" he asked, looking over my shoulder. Tate gave a thumbs-up before he pulled away, and I returned my attention to Connor.

"Are you going to let me in?"

He opened the door wide and if I didn't know better, I'd think I caught him with another girl. I slipped past him and he closed the door, doing up the locks, his back turned to me. I stared at the gun tucked in his back waistband. *A gun.*

"Connor..."

He gestured with his hand that I should go ahead of him. I walked up the stairs and took off my coat, setting it on a chair with my overnight bag. Connor disappeared into his bedroom and I heard a drawer opening and closing. He returned to the living room, running a hand through his hair. "I was about to take a shower..."

"Why did you answer the door with a gun?"

"You need to text me or call me if you're coming over."

He'd been scared. I thought about the night we'd ordered Chinese food. When I'd tried to buzz the delivery guy up, Connor had stopped me and said he'd go down and pick it up. "My phone was dead. I couldn't call or text."

"Let me grab a quick shower, okay?"

I nodded. "Sure."

It wasn't the welcome I'd hoped for. I collapsed on his sofa to wait. My head felt heavy, but inside, I felt hollowed-out and empty. I'd walked out on my family. And Lana had been having sex with Jake Masters. Jealousy, of all things, had prevented her from taking my side. I'd chosen Connor over my family, but I didn't even know if he wanted me here.

I grabbed my toothbrush and toothpaste from my overnight bag and brushed my teeth in the kitchen sink. Three times. Connor walked in as I spit a stream of water and toothpaste into the sink. I lifted my head and wiped my mouth with the back of my hand. Classy, Ava.

He ran a hand over his damp hair and my gaze traveled down his bare torso, the Japanese dragon tattooed on his chest, the tail disappearing over his shoulder. And lower to the sweatpants hanging low on his narrow waist. He grabbed two bottles of water from the fridge and handed me one. "Sorry about that. Let's have a do-over."

"A do-over?"

"Hey babe, I'm glad you're here. I've missed you and I've been thinking about you all day."

"Happy Thanksgiving."

He wrapped an arm around my waist and pulled me close. "What happened? Why are you brushing your teeth in my kitchen sink? And why are you here tonight?"

"Because I missed you. And I'd rather spend Thanksgiving with you than with my family." I told him what happened, and he listened to the whole story, his arm around me tensing. But he didn't interrupt me. When I finished talking, I took a deep breath and exhaled, releasing all the tension I'd felt earlier.

He cradled my face in his hands, his eyes locking on mine. "I'm sorry," he said. "I'm sorry I caused you trouble with your family. I'm sorry Lana's such a bitch."

"Stop apologizing for things that aren't your fault. I got the feeling you didn't want me here."

"I do." He pressed his forehead against mine. "I'm an asshole."

"You are," I said. "You really are."

"I know. But you love me anyway," he teased.

"My tragic flaw."

He pulled back to look at my face, his hands moving to the sides of my neck, his eyes locking on mine. "You love me, Ava?"

Connor had always needed to hear the words, had needed the reassurance that I would always love him, that I would always stand by his side and fight his corner. "I've never stopped loving you."

His face lit up with a brilliant smile that made me feel like everything would be okay, after all, and I knew I'd made the right choice. Because Connor...he needed to know that he was loved. Despite everything we'd gone through over the years, through all the pain and heartache, I had never stopped loving him and I knew I never would.

"I CAN'T BELIEVE you made me watch this again."

"Secretly, you love it," I said.

"The first time. Maybe even the second time. But we've watched it dozens of times."

That was an exaggeration but not by much. "Stop complaining," I said, jamming a handful of popcorn into his mouth, my eyes still trained on *The Princess Bride*.

"As you wish," he said, his hand sliding up my leg. "I love you in my shirt."

I loved me in his shirt too. It was soft and faded from too many washings. A blue plaid button-down a lot like the one he had in high school. I wouldn't be surprised if it was the same one. I smirked as his hand ventured farther up my thigh. If he kept going, he'd be in for a surprise.

"Jesus Christ," he said, sliding his hand between my thighs. Next thing I knew, the popcorn bowl was relegated to the coffee table and I was straddling Connor's lap.

"It's hard to see the movie with my back to it."

"Fuck the movie."

"I'd rather fuck you."

He laughed as he stood up, and still holding me, carried me into the bedroom and laid me down on his bed. I pulled off the shirt and tossed it aside then scooted back so my head was on the pillow. Once again, Connor had gone commando. His sweatpants came off and he was naked and ready for me. Good thing because it seemed I was always ready for him. Connor turned me into a lust-addled, sex-crazed maniac and it felt like I could never get enough of him. He nudged my legs apart and I wrapped them around his waist, my fingers sifting through his hair and holding the back of his head as he cupped my breast in his hand and lifted it to his mouth. I rocked my hips against his erection and he groaned, the vibration making my nipples get harder, my sex clenching.

"I need you. Now," I said, not caring that I sounded desperate. I was so wet, I could feel it dripping down my leg.

Connor wasn't looking for fast and dirty tonight, it seemed. He ignored my plea and his mouth moved to my other breast, his tongue teasing my sensitive nipple, pulling more moans from my lips. His hand slid between my legs, a finger slipping inside me, curling, reaching and then it was gone. He dragged his finger over my lips and slipped it inside my mouth. "Suck on my finger," he said, and I did. I tasted myself, knowing he loved that, and I sucked on his finger, my cheeks hollowed until finally, finally he gave me what I wanted. He took his cock in his hand and guided it to my entrance, then thrust inside me, moving in and out in a slow, rhythmic pace.

"Let me hear you say it," he said, his mouth moving up my neck, his kisses soft, making love to me with a gentleness I hadn't known him capable of. That was what this was. Making love.

"I love you," I whispered.

He kissed the corner of my mouth. "Again."

"I love you." I rocked my hips against him, needing more. "I love you. I love you. I love you."

Connor tugged my lower lip between his lips, sucked on it and slowly released it before his mouth covered mine and he thrust deep inside me, so deep I could feel the piercings as the orgasm shattered me. Like that heart made of glass.

"I love you, Ava Blue," he said, coming apart in my arms. And in that moment, I thought that it had all been worth it. All the pain. All the hurt. Because here we were, after all those detours, falling in love all over again.

I woke up, my body tucked into the curve of Connor's, the room pitched in darkness. "Connor?" I whispered, not sure if he was asleep.

"Yeah, babe?"

"I drank too much wine."

"It happens."

"I should go tea-total. Whenever I drink, I either end up in a puddle of tears or I do something crazy. But you know what? I don't regret anything I said to my family."

"I wish it had been me, standing up for you. I hate it that you have to fight my battle."

I turned in his arms to face him. "I think you've got it wrong. We've always fought for each other. When one of us lays down our sword, the other picks it up and goes to battle."

"When does life stop being a battle?" he asked.

"When right wins over might."

24

CONNOR

*A*nother case of inker's remorse. The morning after a drunken bachelor party, the guy in my tattoo chair—Jason —had woken up with a tattoo of a naked redhead wearing a sash beauty queen style with the name Lola written across it. Now it was my job to fix it.

"Next time you get drunk, don't go to a tattoo parlor," I said.

He shook his head. "Damn straight."

It pissed me off that a tattoo artist would even ink a drunk guy. I would have turned him away and told him to go sleep it off.

The bell over the door chimed. I ignored it and concentrated on my linework. Saturday afternoon and the shop was busy. I was booked for the rest of the day and so were AJ, Lee, and Gavin. If it was a walk-in, Claudia knew to turn them away. Jason let out a low whistle. "Holy shit. I wouldn't mind having her face and body inked on my arm. Check her out, man. You've gotta see what just walked in."

I lifted the tattoo needle and turned my head to look, not expecting much, judging by his taste in tattoos, and nearly fell off my fucking stool.

What the hell was *she* doing in my shop?

The willowy brunette was shock and awe. Like a supermodel

who had just stepped off the catwalk. Trouble with a capital T. I took deep breaths through my nose, trying to calm the fuck down, but I was losing my shit.

"Do you have an appointment?" Claudia asked. She was using that voice she reserved for beautiful women, like she automatically hated them on sight. Keira scanned the shop and her gaze settled on me, a brilliant smile lighting up her face. If she was happy to see me, the feeling wasn't mutual.

"I'm here to see Connor."

"He's busy," Claudia said.

Too fucking bad I wasn't invisible. Too fucking bad Jason wasn't a mute. "That chick is here for you. She's coming over," he said, giving me a play-by-play of the train wreck headed my way. As if I wasn't fully aware.

"Connor," she said. "I...wow, it's really you...here you are."

"What are you doing here?" I asked sharply.

"I came to see you. I have so many questions...so much I want to tell you. We need to talk."

"I'm with a client. Go sit in the waiting area."

"Hell no, you stay right here. Pull up a seat," Jason said. "I don't mind."

"I do," I gritted out. "I need you to get out of my space and go sit on the sofa. Or better yet, take a walk." And don't come back, I silently added.

"These artist types are kinda touchy," Jason said, winking at her.

Keira ignored his comment. "I'll wait on the sofa." Her gaze flitted around my space—*my space*—and landed on my leather-bound portfolio on the shelf. Jason watched her every move as she sashayed past him, picked up my portfolio and carried it to the sofa. Shrugging off her coat, she pulled the portfolio into her lap and flipped through the pages. Not only was she in my shop but now she was poring over my artwork. Even though I let clients browse it for ideas, it felt like an invasion of privacy that Keira was doing it. I swiped the sweat off my forehead with my forearm, repeating my mantra in my head but that sinking feeling of dread pooled in the pit of my stomach. The roller coaster was picking up speed and it was about to jump the fucking tracks. My heart raced and sweat beaded my forehead. I needed to get out of here. The walls were closing in on me.

I peeled off my gloves. "Let's take a break. My hand's cramped up," I lied.

"Sure, man. Whatever you need." He hadn't taken his eyes off Keira who was studying the photos in my portfolio as if she wanted to commit them to memory. I slipped away, undetected, and bummed a smoke off Lee who was in the break room sketching before I exited through the back door. Leaning against the wall, I lit the cigarette and took a deep drag, assaulted by memories of Miami. The Shaughnessy's' Spanish-style house in Coral Gables with the security gate, manicured gardens, and pool. My mother's face when she'd opened the door and saw me standing there. Ronan Shaughnessy in his tailored suit and crisp white shirt. Movie star handsome. Feared as much as he was admired. Charming. Charismatic. Dangerous. The devil in disguise.

"I protect what's mine. You shouldn't have stuck your nose in where it didn't belong. Go back to Brooklyn and keep your mouth shut about everything that happened down here. Have I made myself clear?"

I eyed my Harley, tempted to hop on it and drive away. Take Ava on that road trip I'd promised her all those years ago. I paced behind the shop and smoked my cigarette down to the filter, trying to reason with myself.

What was the worst thing that could happen?

They'll call you out as the liar you are.

Shaughnessy will come up here to haul Keira's ass home.

Just when Ava and I had found our way to someplace good, the whole fucking sky had to fall. She'd walked out on her family Thanksgiving. For me. I'd lied to her again and it was too late to make it right.

Asshole. You should have told her. I went back inside to face whatever was headed my way, knowing damn well it wouldn't be pretty. I washed my hands, popped a few pieces of gum into my mouth and returned to Jason. Tattooing usually calmed me and forced me to focus, and I tried to get in my zone and block out everything else around me.

The bell over the door chimed again and Jason let out another low whistle.

As bad luck would have it, Ava had just strolled in, her cheeks flushed from the cold. Dressed in black from head to toe, her pale hair and cherry-red lips in stark contrast, she looked stunning.

"I need to hang out here more often. You get some hot chicks in here."

I was tempted to shove my fist in his face to shut him up.

"Hey babe," Ava said, giving me a little wave and a sweet smile. I forced a smile, but my face felt tight and the most I could manage was a grimace. Like I was in pain. Which I fucking was.

I tried to swallow past the lump in my throat. "Hey babe. What are you doing here?"

She planted her hands on her hips. "I'm unwelcome. Again?"

Fuck. "No. You're always welcome. I thought you had things to do at the bar, that's all."

"It's my Forever Ink time. Keep up with the schedule, Rocket Man," she tossed over her shoulder. I watched her walk over to the desk and chat with Claudia. *Get back to the office area.* Since when had Claudia and Ava become besties? You'd never know that Ava had threatened to scratch Claudia's eyes out. Keira was watching with interest and her eye caught mine. I averted my gaze.

"Who's the other chick?" Gavin asked from his station.

"Nobody," I muttered.

"Did you sleep with her?" he asked, keeping his voice low.

Deep breaths. I had no idea why Gavin persisted in asking me about my sex life when I'd never once confided in him. He, on the other hand, gave me detailed reports of all the women he screwed. Tall tales, if you asked me.

"Not that I mind sharing..."

"She's off-limits," I growled. Then I realized that I was defending and protecting Keira like an older brother would. What the fuck?

Jason barked laughter. "He's keeping them both for himself."

Once again, I had to refrain from planting my fist in his face. I ducked my head and got back to work. Forty minutes later Jason's tattoo was done. I'd managed to keep my mouth shut the whole time and silently conveyed the message that I wasn't up for a friendly chat, so he'd kept himself busy on his phone. Not that he stayed silent. I got to hear all about his Tinder hook-ups.

I walked Jason to the desk and collected his money, reminding him to follow the rules on the after-tattoo care sheet I handed him. "Thanks, man. Good luck with your ladies."

I ignored him and Claudia's raised eyebrows.

"Hey. Connor." I turned to look at Nico. I'd forgotten he was coming in today. He glanced at Keira who flashed him a smile, throwing him off his game. "Oh...uh..." Nico cleared his throat and dragged his gaze back to me, stuffing his hands in the pockets of his jeans. "I'm early. I can wait. I just thought...I wouldn't mind seeing the design."

"Yeah. Of course, man."

I returned to my station and retrieved my sketchbook from the cupboard, flipping through the pages until I got to the design I'd sketched for Nico. A lion with bared teeth and a thick mane. I struggled to keep my face neutral as I returned to the waiting area, not even hazarding a glance in Keira's direction. But I could feel her watching me as I handed Nico the sketch.

"Oh man. Holy shit," he said, staring at the sketch. I could tell by his voice and the look on his face that he liked what I'd done for him and that was a reward in itself. Making Nico happy was important to me. We'd started working out together on Saturday and Sunday mornings. He wasn't a big talker, but he'd let a few things slip, enough for me to know that he was a good kid in a shitty situation. I understood what it felt like to hurt for someone else, to feel useless and guilty about it. I understood his fear and his anger at the injustice of it all. Bad shit happened to good people all the time.

"You good with that design? I can change—"

"No. I'm cool with this."

"Good. I want you to be happy." Killian had asked me to take care of Nico and to make sure he got whatever tattoo he wanted. It was Nico's eighteenth birthday present and Killian told me he'd cover the cost. I had no intention of charging Nico or Killian for this tattoo. "Claudia will give you the paperwork. Fill it out and I'll be back soon, okay?"

"Yeah. Sure. Take your time. I'm cool to wait."

I looked toward the back of the shop at the office area. No Ava.

"She's making tea," Claudia said. My gaze snapped to her and she narrowed her eyes at me in accusation and lowered her voice. "If you fuck her over, it'll be my turn to kick you in the balls."

This goddamn place. Everyone was up in everyone's business. And apparently, Claudia and Ava had bonded. Time to face Keira. She stood and took a few steps closer, opening her mouth to speak. I didn't want her to say a word in front of Nico or Claudia or anyone else. "Let's go outside."

I strode to the door with Keira on my heels, feeling Claudia's eyes on my back. Fuck. Fuck. Fuck.

"Connor... why didn't you tell me?" she asked when we stopped by the side of the building.

"Tell you what?" I asked, playing dumb.

"That you're my brother."

"How did you find out?"

"I was thinking about you. Actually, I thought about you a lot. So I Googled you. You can learn a lot about a person from social media."

Fuck. "And what did you learn?"

"I found photos of you...you must have been like eighteen or nineteen. You were in Vegas with Killian and the blonde in your shop. I found tons of stuff about Killian too. From his UFC days. And the break-in at your house in Greenpoint. When your father was killed? I found out you owned this shop and that you have an art exhibit in three weeks."

Jesus Christ. This was why social media was dangerous.

"So anyway, I did some digging on your father because I had a weird feeling...like I should have seen it. You look so much like my mother. And sure enough, I found out that he was once married to Maggie O'Rourke. I can't believe my parents kept this from me." She shook her head. "What am I saying? I can believe it. My father's a control freak and my mother is..."

"What's your mother?" I asked, still curious despite myself. When would I ever learn?

Keira shrugged. "My dad calls the shots and my mom does whatever he asks because she's too scared of losing him. They're, like, obsessed with each other. And she adores him. No matter what he does, she turns a blind eye." She drew herself up to her full height, just a few inches shy of six feet, and squared her shoulders. "But I'm not my mother."

"Yeah, well, you shouldn't be here. *Why* are you here?"

"I want to get to know you and Killian."

"He doesn't even know you exist."

"Well, you'd better tell him. Because I'm staying."

"Like hell you are. I'm putting you in a taxi and you can go right back to the airport and catch the first flight home."

"I drove."

"You drove," I repeated.

She gestured with her hand and I stared at the silver Porsche 911 with North Carolina plates. *North Carolina?* "I need to unload this thing. Do you know anyone I can sell it to? Preferably someone who's not going to ask for any documents."

"You stole a car."

"I borrowed my dad's keys. He's just not getting them back. So, yeah, technically I stole it. But I changed the plates."

Fucking perfect. A criminal in the making. Like father, like daughter. "Get back in that car and head south. Keep going until you get back to fucking Miami."

"I'm staying here. In Brooklyn. And I'm getting to know my brothers. I was planning to stop at Killian's gym—"

"Killian's away." Thank fuck for small favors. Unfortunately, he'd be back late tonight. "You need to let me talk to him before you stop by for a surprise visit. Understand?"

"Sure. So, you never told him about me or anything that happened in Miami?"

"No."

"Who's the blonde? She's pretty. Is she your girlfriend?"

"Leave her out of this."

"Connor," Ava called.

I turned my head to look at Ava, her arms crossed over her chest, eyes blazing with anger. "I thought you said you weren't with anyone in Miami."

I rubbed the back of my neck. Welcome to the shit storm that was my life. It would be easier if Keira had been a girl I'd hooked up with. "I wasn't with anyone. And she was just leaving."

"I'm Keira. Connor's sister. And I'm not going anywhere."

Fucking hell. Ava gasped, her eyes wide. "You have a *sister?*" she yelled.

Might as well announce it to the whole fucking neighborhood. I blew air out of my cheeks. "It's a long story."

"Well, I'd love to hear it. But right now, I can't even look at you, let alone listen to another *story*." Her gaze swung to Keira. "I'm Ava and I'll be happy to be your tour guide."

"Great," Keira said, giving Ava a dazzling smile. "Do you happen to know where the nearest pawn shop is?"

I stared at Keira. What the fuck? "Why do you need a pawn shop?"

"I have some jewelry to sell," she said like this was perfectly normal.

"I'd be happy to take you," Ava said, smirking at me. "Let's go."

I watched helplessly as Ava climbed into the passenger seat of Keira's Porsche. Two seconds later, engine roaring, Keira shot out of the parking space and rocketed down the street like a Formula One race car driver. The girl was a loose cannon. If Ronan had wanted to keep her on a short leash, he had failed miserably.

Universe, do you hate me? No matter how hard I tried to put the past behind me, it always caught up. And this time, there was no way to outrun it. Trouble was headed my way. Again.

I swiped my phone and called Deacon Ramsey.

25

AVA

I had a million questions I wanted to ask Keira, but I had no idea where to begin. She didn't look anything like Connor and Killian. Her eyes were amber-brown, and her hair was a few shades lighter, cut in long layers and highlighted with caramel and honey. She had perfect bone structure, high cheekbones, a wide, full mouth, and a set of perfect white teeth. She was stunning, not to mention that her Moncler jacket and the Louis Vuitton bag sitting at my feet, probably cost more than everything I owned.

She shifted and floored the accelerator, something you couldn't do in Brooklyn. A car pulled out in front of us and she hit the brakes, screeching to a halt. My head flew back against my seat, and her bumper kissed the car's in front of us. The driver shot her a look in his rear-view mirror and she gave him a little wave and a brilliant smile.

"Who taught you to drive?" I asked.

"Anthony," she said. "He works security for my dad."

"What does your dad do?"

She side-eyed me. "He runs a nightclub."

I had a feeling that running a nightclub was not the only thing he did. She floored the accelerator again only to slam on the brakes at the next traffic light. This ride was giving me whiplash.

"Take it easy, Mario. This is Brooklyn. You need to share the road with others."

She laughed and eased off the accelerator. Slightly. "You need to take the next right," I said, directing her to the pawn shop I'd Googled. According to the reviews, it was the most honest one and paid the fairest prices. Having never stepped foot inside a pawn shop, I had no idea what that meant.

"How long have you known Connor?" she asked, hanging a right and narrowly missing a cyclist. If we got to the pawn shop in one piece, I'd consider it a victory.

"Ten years. We were friends first and started dating when we were sixteen."

"Wow. I didn't even realize he had a girlfriend."

"We broke up for a few years, but we got back together a little while ago." Although, at this point, I was seriously questioning that decision. He'd lied to me. He'd lied to everyone. Why?

"I didn't know I had brothers until a week ago," she said.

I looked at her in surprise. "Connor didn't tell you?"

She shook her head.

"And your parents..."

"Kept it from me. I should have seen it though. Connor looks so much like my mom. If I'd known, it would have made everything so much less... awkward."

"Awkward?" I asked.

"When I met him, I thought he was just a hot guy on vacation in Miami. So, I went for him."

"You went for Connor?"

"Big time. My ego took a bruising. He pushed me away like the very idea of being with me was repulsive. But now I know why."

"Where did you meet him?"

"At a coffee shop near campus. I misread the signs and thought he was flirting with me. We exchanged numbers and met up for lunch. And I loved hanging out with him. Plus, he's hot."

"Yeah, he is. And when he's not being a dickhead, he's great to hang out with." The pawn shop passed by in a blur. "You just drove right past it. Turn down the next street."

We circled the block and got lucky when a spot opened two doors down from the pawn shop. She backed into the space and after one adjustment, her tires brushed the curb and she cut the engine. "That was impressive," I said, handing over her bag.

"Driving is my favorite hobby. I love anything with an engine. Planes, cars, motorcycles... anything that can take me away from it all."

I wasn't sure what to say about that, but she was already out of the car, her Louis Vuitton bag in the crook of her arm. I joined her on the sidewalk. Next to her, I felt like a midget. She had at least six inches on me. "Why are you selling jewelry?" I asked, looking at the blue neon sign in the window that said: DIAMONDS.

"Cash is king. And it doesn't leave a trail." She grabbed my arm to stop me from going inside. Why was she worried about leaving a trail? I was still trying to make sense of that little tidbit she'd dropped in my lap about getting cozy with Connor. Coffee and lunch, exchanging numbers... and she'd had no idea he was her brother? "By the way, my name is Grace Matthews. But you can call me Gracie."

She let go of my arm and placed her hand on the door handle. It was my turn to grab her arm and haul her back. "Why are you using a fake name?" I looked up and down the street. From what I could tell, everyone was going about their business, not the least bit interested in the vertically-challenged blonde and America's Next Top Model. "And who would be following a trail? Are you on the lam?"

"Not exactly."

Not exactly? Maybe she was a jewel thief. I glanced at the Porsche, and the words grand theft auto flashed across my brain. "Is the jewelry yours? Is the Porsche yours?" I hissed.

"Yes. And... kind of."

"Kind of?"

"The jewelry is mine. The Porsche is my dad's."

"Did he lend it to you?"

She dodged that question. "Are you with me, Ava? Or should I do this alone?" There was a challenge in her voice and it took me all of two seconds to make my decision. I was all in. I wanted answers and I wanted to see what this mysterious sister was up to.

"You're not going in there alone, *Gracie*."

She gave me a big smile. Connor had a shitload of explaining to do. If I ever spoke to him again. This was getting crazier by the minute. Blindsided by the appearance of Keira who I knew nothing about. Connor and Killian's sister. I still couldn't wrap my head around that. Which meant that Connor had gone down to Miami with a purpose. To find his mother. But why had he kept it a secret?

We walked into the brightly-lit pawn shop, and I was kind of disappointed that it was so sterile, and nothing like an antique shop which I'd envisioned. According to the sign on the wall, they paid cash for diamonds, gold, silver, and electronics. A long glass case spanned the wall on the left, and I cast my eye at the collection of coins and watches.

"Can I help you, ladies?" asked the middle-aged man with a barrel chest and a combover behind the counter.

Keira pulled a velvet drawstring bag out of her Louis Vuitton and emptied the contents onto the glass countertop. I gasped. A diamond tennis bracelet. Diamond studs that must have been one carat each. And a small mountain of gold.

"What's your best price?" she asked.

The man held a loupe to his eye and inspected the diamonds. I studied the contents of the case, my eye catching on a display of diamond engagement rings and wedding bands. How sad that someone would need to sell an engagement ring. Or worse, they'd gotten divorced and she'd rather have the money than a reminder of a broken promise.

For better or worse. In sickness and health. Until death do us part. People repeated those words every day, making vows and promises to love each other for the rest of their lives. The words were easy to say but hard to put into practice.

I loved Connor. He was the love of my life, and I'd never

doubted that for a minute. But every time we turned around another obstacle was thrown into our path. I'd wanted to believe that our love had been strong enough to weather any storm. To deal with any curveball life threw at us. Ironic, really, that every time I convinced myself that he'd changed, that we were headed somewhere good, another curveball hit me from left field.

Keira nudged my arm and I dragged my eyes away from the display. "You okay?"

"Yeah."

"Victor's going to get me the cash."

"Did he offer you a good price?" I asked, having missed the entire transaction.

"A fraction of what it's worth, but I expected that. Everyone needs to earn a living somehow."

"Do you work?" I asked.

"No. I was in college," she said, running her hand over an acoustic guitar, part of a collection hanging on the wall across from the glass cases. "But I'm not going back to finish my degree. I'm staying in Brooklyn. I'm going to get a job and an apartment." She gave me a bright smile as if that prospect thrilled her.

"How old are you?"

"I'll be twenty-one in January."

I did the mental math. Connor's mom would have already been pregnant with Keira when she'd left them.

"How old were they when she left?" Keira asked, reading my mind.

"It was right after Killian's seventh birthday, in August. Connor was three and a half."

Whatever she thought about that, her face gave nothing away. The bell over the door chimed and a guy with dirty-blond hair entered the shop. Deacon Ramsey. I hadn't seen him since that night at the hospital over a year ago. Instead of wearing NYPD blues, he was dressed in a dark suit and wingtips. He belonged in a glossy magazine advertising cologne and expensive watches, but I had a bad feeling that his appearance wasn't accidental.

"Good afternoon, ladies." He gave us a panty-melting smile,

fully aware of his charms and the effect they had on women. "How've you been, Ava?" he asked as if he genuinely cared.

"It's all good," I said, wondering if that was true. "How are you?"

"Can't complain." His gaze swung to Keira, his eyes doing a full-body scan without bothering to hide it.

"Let me guess," Keira said, leaning her hip against the counter. "Victor called the cops."

"Deacon Ramsey," he said with a slow, easy grin. "What makes you think I'm a cop?"

"Grace Matthews. I have a sixth sense for these things."

His mouth quirked with amusement. "Is that your Porsche, Grace?"

"Yes, Officer. Am I parked illegally?"

"I'll need to see some ID."

Unfazed by his request, Keira whipped a license out of her wallet and handed it to Deacon who studied it. Since I was right next to him, I glanced at it, wondering how her story would hold up. Sure enough, the license said Grace Matthews and the photo was of her. I wasn't an expert, but the license looked like a good fake. "A North Carolina girl," he said, handing back the license.

"Go Tar Heels," Keira said, pumping the air with her fist.

"You went to Duke?" Deacon asked.

"UNC. Duke is the Blue Devils. Watch yourself, Officer. If you ever head south of the Mason Dixon line, talk like that could get you in trouble."

Deacon grinned. "Thanks for the warning. Be right back." He strode to the back of the shop and when he disappeared, I exchanged a look with Keira.

"You swear the jewelry is yours?" I asked, keeping my voice low. There were CCTV cameras all over the shop and I wondered if Deacon Ramsey was back there, studying them right now.

"Yep. It's cool."

"What about the license plates?"

"They're clean." She cleared her throat. "I think."

That didn't put me at ease or answer any of my questions, but I couldn't probe for more information because Deacon and Victor had returned. Victor handed Keira an envelope and she glanced at the bills inside then stuffed it in her bag without bothering to count it. "A pleasure doing business with you," she said, turning to go.

Deacon strode ahead and held the door open for us then followed us onto the sidewalk and to Keira's car. "Just passing through?" he asked. "Or are you planning to stay awhile, Miss Mathers?"

"It's Matthews," Keira said.

Deacon grinned. "So, it is. I have a bad memory for names. But I never forget a face."

"In answer to your question, I'll be staying a while."

"Good. I have a feeling we'll be bumping into each other a lot."

Keira smiled as she rounded the front of her car. "Not if I see you first."

"Game on."

I climbed into the passenger seat, once again completely clueless as to what was going on. Besides Deacon and Keira flirting, I got that. But this was getting old. Fast.

"What do you know about Deacon Ramsey?" Keira asked, watching through her rear-view mirror.

I knew he'd saved Killian's life last year. I knew he'd saved Connor from getting busted for drug possession. But I didn't mention either of those things because I wasn't sure how much to confide in her. I wasn't sure what to think about her or if she could be trusted. The girl was running around town in a Porsche, selling diamonds at a pawn shop, and using a fake name and ID. "Not much. He was three years ahead of me in high school. He was in the same year as Killian."

"Are they friends?"

I shrugged noncommittally. "Acquaintances."

She fired up the engine. "Oh well. Could be worse. If someone's going to tail me, at least he's hot."

Deacon Ramsey was hot, I'd give her that, but she didn't seem surprised that NYPD would be tailing her. "Why would he need to tail you?"

"Are you ready to give me a tour of Brooklyn?" she asked, revving her engine.

"Are you going to tell me what's going on? I hate being left in the dark."

"I know the feeling."

Yeah, I guess she did. If what she said was true, she'd been left in the dark her whole life. I couldn't imagine what it would feel like to find out you had brothers you knew nothing about. "Why didn't your mom tell you? Why did she need to keep Connor and Killian a secret?"

"You'd have to meet my parents to understand. Even then, you probably wouldn't. My dad thinks he owns us. He doesn't like to share."

"And your mom?"

"Is a bird in a gilded cage."

"Are you close?"

"I love my parents. But sometimes I hate the things they do."

That was something I understood so I took her on a guided tour of Brooklyn. We drove around Park Slope and I pointed out the apartment where Connor and Killian had lived. Prospect Park. The Brooklyn Botanical Gardens. We passed the gallery in Bed-Stuy where Connor and Eden's exhibition would be held in two weeks. Then headed over to Bushwick for a graffiti tour. Whenever we passed a wall that Connor had bombed, I pointed it out and she'd pull over and snap photos before moving on. We ended up at the diner and I ordered for both of us—empanadas, chicken and rice and beans.

"I went with him once... to watch him do his graffiti," Keira said after we'd eaten and were waiting for the check. "Actually, I followed him. He didn't know I was watching. He'd disappeared, shut down his cell phone, and I wanted to track him down. We'd talked about graffiti over lunch that day and I'd told him the best place to do it. So, I kind of stalked him and hit it lucky one night."

"What did he paint?" I asked, curious to know what his state of mind had been. I tried to picture him in Miami but since I'd never been there, I couldn't.

"The ocean. With a hand coming out of the water. Just a hand," she said.

A wave of sadness washed over me. Connor had been drowning. But somehow, he'd pulled himself out of it and he hadn't let the water suck him under. Once again, my heart ached for Connor. No matter what he'd done, I still loved him. For better or worse. In sickness and health. But a relationship couldn't be built on lies.

"I need to unload the Porsche," she said when we were back in the car. "Do you know anyone who could help me?"

At this point, nothing she said should surprise me. Of course, she needed to unload the car. I only knew of one person who might be able to help. Twenty minutes later, we were outside Atlas Motors, already closed for the night. I pounded the side of my fist against the door, on the off-chance that Tate might still be inside. After a few more knocks, I turned to go, ready to tell Keira that we'd have to try again tomorrow.

The door swung open and I turned around to look at Tate. He looked at me then at the Porsche and back to me. "We need your help," I said. "She wants to sell her car."

If Tate was surprised, his face gave nothing away. He gestured for me to come inside then unlocked and opened the roller door high enough to accommodate the Porsche. Keira pulled in and hopped out of the car.

"I'm guessing the license and registration won't match," he muttered, sliding the door shut and locking it again.

Keira and I exchanged a look.

"I'll take care of it," he said.

Tate disappeared into the back somewhere and Keira wandered over to a vintage Mustang. "She's a beauty," she said when I joined her. I peered in the side window, at the black leather seats and the wood-grain console. My car knowledge was minimal, and I'd never been particularly interested in them beyond getting me where I needed to go, but I had to agree with her. This car was gorgeous. I could see myself behind the wheel, driving along Route 66. Connor was with me, the music blasting, a summer breeze blowing through our open windows. Sunshine and open roads for as far as the eye could see. We were golden. Wild and free. Invincible.

If only my real life could be like my glorious dreams and visions.

My phone rang, interrupting my thoughts and I checked the screen, expecting it to be Connor. He'd already called me twice, but I'd let it go to voicemail both times. I hadn't been ready to talk to him. But it was my mom, not Connor. We hadn't spoken since Thanksgiving and as much as I didn't want to talk to her, I felt like I should.

"I'll be right back," I told Keira who was under the hood of Tate's Mustang. I wasn't sure how happy Tate would be about that, but I figured she was capable of dealing with him on her own.

I answered the call as I walked up Richardson Street and stopped in front of an apartment building two doors down from the garage. "Hey Mom," I said.

"Don't you 'hey Mom' me," she said. "I've been waiting for a call. I deserve an apology."

Normally, I'd cave and apologize just to keep the peace. But I couldn't bring myself to do that this time. I was angry with Connor and hurt that he'd kept this from me, but my mother didn't deserve an apology. "I'm not going to apologize."

She was silent for a few seconds. "You're choosing *that boy* over your own family?"

"I shouldn't have to choose."

"I don't understand where I went wrong. All your life, I made sacrifices to give you the things I never had. Was I such a horrible mother that you feel the need to punish me for loving you?"

This was what she did. She laid a guilt trip on me. Used her passive-aggressive approach to get me to admit that I'd been wrong. To tell her that she wasn't a horrible mother.

"You ruined Thanksgiving," she said. "After I worked so hard to make everything perfect. The least you could have done was be thankful for all the good things in your life. It's a time to enjoy family, not to argue and stress out your poor father. He almost died. Did you think about that? No, you didn't. You were being selfish, thinking only of yourself."

I took deep breaths of cold air, biting back all the bitter words that threatened to break loose.

"What do you have to say for yourself?" she asked.

"Nothing," I said. "I have nothing to say for myself."

She sniffed. "I'm disappointed in you, Ava."

And I'm disappointed in you. "I'm sorry you're disappointed in me. Goodbye, Mom." I cut the call, took a shaky breath and played back the voicemails Connor had left, his raspy, sexy voice filling my ear.

"Hey, babe. I fucked up. By now, you should be used to it. I was trying to outrun my past. But it always has a way of catching up. I had my reasons for not telling the truth. If you're willing to listen, I'll tell you everything. It's not a pretty story, but my stories never are."

I listened to the next one.

"I just listened to 'Rocket Man.' I get why it makes you feel sad." I heard him take a drag on a cigarette and pictured him standing behind the shop, blowing smoke into the air. "Yeah, I'm smoking. Sorry about that. I'm an addict, babe. No matter how long I go without touching drugs, I'll always be an addict. And I've done so many things in my life that I regret. So many fucked-up things. I'd give anything to rewind time and undo them. But I can't. I just need to find a way to live with my mistakes. I never wanted to drag you into this mess. And I'm so fucking sorry."

I pocketed my phone, wondering what kind of mess he was talking about.

26

AVA

*C*onnor pulled into the lot in front of Atlas Motors and cut the engine. Removing his helmet, he climbed off the bike and entered the garage. I stayed where I was, waiting for him to come to me which I knew he would. Even though he hadn't glanced my way, he had seen me. Minutes later, he walked out of the garage without his helmet and headed my way. He stopped in front of me, his eyes flitting over my face, trying to gauge my mood. Good luck with that. I had no idea how I was feeling. Confused. Hurt. Sad. Angry. My moods had run the gamut today. He was chewing his gum like his life depended on it, the scent of cigarettes mingling with leather and soap and cinnamon. For a few seconds, we just stood there looking at each other, a police siren cutting through our silence.

He looked over my shoulder, his eyes squinted, his upper lip gripped between his teeth. "I'll walk you home."

"What about Keira?" I asked, stuffing my hands in the pockets of my down jacket.

"She's talking cars with Tate. I'll come back and get her."

I didn't question why we were walking instead of riding on his Harley. Connor was better at talking about important things when he was on the move. Always running. We crossed under the BQE,

228

the cars trundling over our heads, the air scented with motor oil and exhaust fumes, my mind racing with so many questions I wasn't sure where to begin.

"You went to Miami to find your mother."

"Yeah."

"Why would you keep that to yourself?"

"It sounds stupid now, but I wanted to do something good for Killian. Didn't go to plan."

I wasn't sure if I wanted to punch him or kiss it better. "How did you know where to find her?"

"Seamus told me. I went to see him after I got out of rehab. I wanted to confront him. I was tired of pretending none of that had ever happened," he said, sounding like he was almost talking to himself. "When I got there, he was drinking. But he didn't get nasty or violent. It was like he was lonely or something. I saw another side of him. I didn't hate him any less, but it made him seem more human. He told me he loved her and when she left, it had destroyed him."

Seamus Vincent had loved a woman. To the point where her leaving him had destroyed him. It was hard to reconcile the man I'd known with the one who could love a woman like that.

"He told me she'd been having an affair," Connor said. "Gave me the man's name and said they live in Miami. I don't know why he told me, after all those years of keeping it to himself. He didn't even remember having told me."

Maybe Seamus hadn't remembered a lot of what he'd done when he was drunk. The same way Connor hadn't remembered things he'd done when he was high. But Connor had never gotten violent or abusive. I'd never been scared of him, only scared *for* him.

"What's your mom like?" I asked as we stopped at the corner and waited for a car to pass before we crossed over.

"Beautiful. Cold. Distant. At least, that's the impression I got. I only had five minutes alone with her." He shrugged like it was no big deal, but I knew better. "I always thought she'd stayed away because of Seamus. And I couldn't blame her for that. But now …

yeah, she made it clear that she's not interested in being part of our lives."

Connor had never blamed his mother for leaving them. He had a greater capacity for forgiveness than Killian did. Than I did, if I had to be completely honest. Sometimes I thought I was more like my mother than I'd care to admit. "I'm sorry," I said. "I'm so sorry, Connor."

"I should have known better."

"So you weren't running away. You were trying to find something." Somehow that made everything better, knowing that he had a reason for leaving, although I still didn't understand the need for secrecy. "But why... I don't understand why you didn't tell me," I said, unable to hide the hurt in my voice.

"I was going to tell you. So many times, I wanted to. It's just a lot of heavy to lay on someone."

"I'm not just someone."

"I know. And I would have told you eventually. But we were trying to find our way back to something better. I didn't want to saddle you with more of the past."

I wasn't sure what that said about our relationship. Was it so fragile we couldn't trust each other with the truth? "So, when you were in Miami, you were upset... and you went out and bought drugs?" I asked, trying to make sense of this and fill in the gaps.

"I didn't buy those drugs. Keira's father told me to stay out of his business and stay away from my mother and Keira, but I didn't listen. He set me up. Two undercover cops busted me for drugs I never bought and forced me to play the role of informant, so I spent a few months getting cozy with a drug dealer." He let out a breath. "He just thought I was a tattoo artist, looking for a fresh start in Miami. I had a fake ID. My name was Dylan and I grew up in Vegas."

"Dylan from Vegas. You were someone else."

"Still me, unfortunately. Only my name and hometown were different."

"What happened to the drug dealer?"

"He's dead," he said, his voice flat. He rubbed his chest with his right hand. He'd always done that, like it would somehow ease the pain in his heart.

"How did he die?"

Connor shook his head. "It doesn't matter. He's dead."

It probably mattered a lot and most likely Connor had been in danger, but I let it go. Once again, I was grateful he'd come out of that alive. Although I was still trying to make sense of this story. "Why would Keira's dad do that to you? None of this makes sense."

He studied my face, noting the skepticism and narrowed his eyes. "What I just told you is the God's honest truth."

"Yeah, well, excuse me for having a hard time wrapping my head around this story. Your sister... Keira... is running around town with a fake ID. Selling jewelry at a pawn shop because cash is king and doesn't leave a trail. Not to mention that she needed to unload the Porsche with license plates she got from God knows where." I threw my hands up in the air. "Explain this to me."

"If I could, I would. Some things in life are just fucked up... I have no explanation. All I know is that it fucking happened," he said, his voice hard.

"Why didn't you tell Killian?"

"Our mother wants no part in our lives. And when I got back from Miami, he was with Eden. He was finally happy, and I didn't want to mess that up for him. If I'd told him the truth about what happened, he would have gone down there and tried to fix it. But he would have set himself up for a shitload of trouble."

Connor was right. Killian wouldn't have let it go. "You were trying to protect Killian."

"I thought it would make a nice change."

Connor had gone down to Miami because he'd wanted to play the hero, but he'd failed. I thought about a conversation we'd had when we were sixteen, a few weeks after the night Seamus had punched Connor.

"Do you think that's why your mom left? Because of your dad?"

He shrugged. "That's what I always thought."

"Do you still think about her?"

231

"Sometimes. Not as much as I used to. When I was a kid, I had this fantasy that I'd rescue her. Sword fight to the death to keep her safe. Like she was the queen and I was her loyal knight." He laughed, but it was only to cover up his hurt. *"Stupid kid."*

"None of this was your fault, Connor. You were a victim—"

"I wasn't a victim," he said, his voice angry. Victim was the wrong word choice. Such a weak word. "It didn't matter how or why it happened. I'm still the guy responsible for bringing those men to our house. I'm still the guy who took off for Miami without telling anyone where I was going. The details...they don't change any of that."

But the details changed something for me. He hadn't been running away and he hadn't bought those drugs. Why hadn't he stood up for himself? Why hadn't he told me that none of it had been his fault? I thought about those engagement rings. Vows and promises. That stupid Tammy Wynette song. Maybe he'd wanted me to stand by him no matter what he'd done. Love him for better or worse. Because his mother hadn't. And God knew his father hadn't. I used to believe that I'd have the strength to stand by him, to be there for him, even when he was at his lowest, but maybe I'd failed him as much as he'd failed me.

"This story makes more sense to me though," I said. "You'd go to jail before you'd snitch." Connor had very little respect for authority figures, so it would have taken a lot of persuading to get him to cooperate with cops, dirty or otherwise. I side-eyed him, wondering what they'd done to coerce him into acting as an informant. If they'd tried to bribe him with money, he would have told them to go to hell. "What did they do to you?"

"Babe ... you don't need those details. It doesn't matter anyway."

I sighed loudly. "Which details do I need? Because it feels like you're leaving out a lot. Stop trying to protect me from the truth. I can handle it a whole lot better than empty promises and lies. I'm just ... don't sugar-coat the truth, okay?"

He worked his jaw then nodded as if he'd made up his mind to

tell me the important parts. "I didn't come straight back to Brooklyn. After I left Miami, I traveled for a few weeks."

"Where did you go?"

"Everywhere and nowhere. I hitched rides."

God, he really was like Kerouac. It sounded reckless and
dangerous, but maybe he hadn't cared about the risks after everything that had gone down in Miami. "Who picked you up?"

"Mostly long-haul truckers. Guess it gets lonely driving all
those hours. I don't know. Some talked. Some didn't. Sometimes I
slept for the whole drive. For the last leg of it, I hopped a Greyhound to Port Authority. And I got out at the station, thinking it
was time to go home but I wasn't ready. My head was in such a bad
place. So, I took the Jitney out to Montauk. I spent a lot of time
thinking about those four days we spent out there."

"Our first vacation." And our last. It was the summer we were
nineteen and we'd stayed at a campsite. I'd still been in denial about
the extent of his addiction. We were supposed to be there for a
week, but Connor had only made it through four days before he'd
needed a fix. He made up some bullshit excuse for needing to return
early, and as soon we'd gotten back to Brooklyn, Danny hooked him
up and he'd disappeared for two days, tarnishing my beautiful
memories of Montauk with the ugly reality of addiction. What had
stuck in my mind was that our four days in Montauk had been idyl-
lic. Amazing. Yet it hadn't been enough to keep the demons at bay.

"I hated myself for what I did to you," he said, his voice
cracking on the words. Instead of rushing in to tell him it was okay,
I stayed silent and listened, knowing he wasn't finished yet.
"Remember that beach we went to? Right in front of that house
on the cliff? It was quiet and we felt like we had it to ourselves?"

I nodded. I remembered. Farther down the beach, it was
crowded with people from the hotels and condos and we wondered
why everyone wanted to be on top of each other. I envisioned our
strip of beach, the sand so soft and white, the sky as blue as
Connor's eyes. We'd stayed on that beach all day, our skin hot, the
sea cold, and the surf wild. At night, after grabbing food in town,

we'd come back and lie on the cool sand, stargazing, the sound of the waves crashing against the shore. Connor knew all about the stars and could trace the constellations with his fingertip.

"When stars die, they collapse and explode, leaving a black hole behind."

"So, we're all made of stardust," I said.

We'd reached my apartment building, but we stayed outside in the November cold and sat on my front steps, side by side, only inches apart but not touching.

"One night I walked into the ocean," he said, and I had the feeling I wouldn't like this story so much. "I swam out past the breakers and the plan was to keep swimming until I got too tired to swim anymore. My arms were tired. I didn't think I could go any farther. And I was ready to just let myself go, sink into the water. Into oblivion. But it's the craziest thing ... I heard your voice. *You are loved*, you said."

The sting of tears pricked my eyes. A hand rising from the ocean. Just one hand. A cry for help.

"I floated on my back for a while and then somehow I made it back to the shore and lay on the sand. I watched the stars ... and I thought how tiny and inconsequential we are compared to the universe. I thought about the last time we'd been in that same spot, watching them together. My girl made of stardust. And I thought about those glow-in-the-dark ones I stuck on the ceiling for Killian and how you could only see them when it got dark."

Tears streamed down my face and oh, my heart, it hurt.

"And I thought maybe...just maybe...I'd be able to find my way home and back to you. I could be your Odysseus."

Oh, Connor. Why did you always have to break my heart? Connor wrapped his arm around me and I buried my head in his chest, my tears falling onto his leather jacket, his hand stroking my hair so gently it made me cry harder. I cried for him and for us and all that we'd lost. I didn't even know what exactly I was crying for except that I couldn't seem to stop.

"Do you believe in soul mates, Connor?"

"How could I not? I met mine when I was fourteen."

Ten years of memories, the good and the bad and the ugly and the beautiful, so many beautiful ones, played out like a movie in my head.

"I'm sorry, Ava. I'm so fucking sorry. About everything." He cradled my face in his hands and swiped away the tears and smeared makeup with his thumbs.

"We both made mistakes, Connor. We lost our way...we took so many detours on our way back to each other. And when you got back from Miami...I wasn't even talking to you. I was too busy convincing myself that I hated you. But it was never you I hated. It was your father and the drugs..."

"I was the one who started doing drugs, Ava. You can't blame that on my shitty childhood. Killian and I grew up in the same house with the same father, but he never turned to drugs."

"You're not Killian. No offense to Killian...I love Killian...but you're a lot deeper and you're more..." I was going to say sensitive which was true, but Connor would probably put that in the same category as victim, even though it was a good quality, one of his best. I cast around for the right word. "Emotionally intelligent."

Connor snorted. "Where did you come up with that one, babe? One of your quizzes?"

I rolled my eyes. I'd taken the quiz only a few days ago, not that I'd admit it now. "Whatever. Just roll with it."

We were silent for a few minutes and I tried to wrap my head around everything he'd told me tonight, and everything I'd learned from Keira today.

"What happens next?" I asked, hoping he'd have some answers, hoping he'd tell me how the rest of our story would play out, but my gut told me I wouldn't like the answer. "Will we ever get our happy ending?"

"I have to believe that we will. Someday. But there are some things I need to do first to make this right."

"What are you saying?"

"Wait for me."

I took deep breaths, trying to fight the tears that threatened to fall again. After all we'd been through, after all the stops and starts,

I had really believed that this was our second chance. That we'd find a way to make it work this time.

"Why are you pushing me away when you need me?"

"I don't want to be the boy hiding in the closet anymore. I don't want to be the guy harboring secrets and lies. I want to be the man you deserve. I want to be worthy of you. I thought I was ready...for you...for us. But I still have a long way to go."

I fished my keys out of my bag and he followed me to my front door as I jammed my key in the lock and pushed the door open. He held it open with his hand and blocked the entrance with his body. "You're an ass. I've always thought you were worthy, even when you didn't believe it yourself. Even when I hated the things you did. Even when I left you. I never once thought you were unworthy. But it doesn't matter how much I believe in you. You need to start believing in yourself. You're enough, Connor. *You are enough*."

I reached up to touch his face and rested my palm on his cheekbone. He wrapped his hand around my wrist and leaned into my hand, his eyes closing briefly as he exhaled. I wasn't stupid. I'd always known he was damaged and more than a little bit broken. I knew there was no quick fix. But I hoped that in time he would realize what I'd known all along. He was worthy. He deserved good things in his life. "I get that you feel you have to do this on your own..." I stopped myself and took a deep breath. "That's a lie. I don't get it. If you feel like you have something to prove, you don't need to do it alone." By the set of his jaw, I knew his mind was made up and there was nothing I could do or say to change it. I crossed my arms over my chest. "Just for the record, I think it's stupid."

His mouth quirked in amusement. "Stupid, huh? I'm working on being your white knight."

"I'm not a damsel in distress and I don't need you to save me."

"I know, babe, but I need to do this. For you. For myself. For us. I need to slay the dragons, or I'll never be free." He was asking me to try and understand. To wait for him to sort out his life.

"When does life stop being a battle?"

"When right wins over might."

I studied his face in the dim hallway light and silently wished him luck before I slipped past him into the foyer. "If you need someone to carry your sword into battle, you know where to find me."

"At the corner of Badass and Fun-Sized," he called after me.

Har har har. I flipped him the middle finger as I climbed the stairs and heard him chuckling, the door closing behind him, the locks clicking into place.

"That smells good," Keira said, coming into the kitchen, freshly showered, her face scrubbed clean, wearing pajama bottoms and a University of Miami sweatshirt. She pulled up a stool at the island, twisted her wet hair into a knot and secured it with the elastic on her wrist. Keira had inherited her father's looks and her mother's cheekbones. So sharp you could cut diamonds with them. It felt strange to have her in my space, her toiletries already cluttering my bathroom, her bags parked in my bedroom. We were strangers who shared some DNA and it hit me all over again that this girl sitting at my island was my sister. "What is it?"

"An omelet with peppers and onions and cheese. You hungry?" I asked. Feeding her, at least, was something I could do. "You can have this one and I'll make another one."

"No. Ava and I went for empanadas."

Keira was rail-thin, built exactly like a model. The time we'd gone out to lunch, she'd ordered a salad and overpriced water. "Did you eat the empanadas?" I asked, not sure why I was concerned with her diet or anything else about her. "Because you look like you don't eat."

"I eat. I was nervous with you." My brows went up a notch. She seemed too ballsy to be nervous about anything. "I thought it was a date, okay? And I'd never...well, I'd never been on a date."

I turned my back to her and tended to my omelet, feeling a twinge of guilt. She'd only been nineteen at the time, but I found it hard to believe she'd never been on a date. Not for lack of offers, I was sure of that.

"What's the deal with you and Ava?"

I slid the omelet onto a plate, grabbed a fork from the drawer and sat at the island across from Keira. I hadn't eaten since breakfast, so I inhaled my food, not answering her question. I was acting like a dick, but Keira's appearance hadn't exactly been a happy surprise and I was still trying to come to terms with it.

"My parents are in the Cayman Islands. They won't be back until Tuesday. They don't know I'm here. I left yesterday right after they did and drove for eighteen hours."

I kept eating, turning over the information she'd given me. If she'd wanted to disappear, stealing her daddy's Porsche hadn't been the smartest plan.

"It's just temporary. I won't stay long."

"Judging by the shitload of bags you brought, looks like you're planning to stay awhile." Tate had to bring Keira's bags over in his pickup truck. How she'd fit all that shit in the trunk of a Porsche was a mystery, but it looked as if she'd packed everything she owned. The logos on her luggage matched the ones on her purse, and I didn't know shit about designer goods, but even I recognized Louis Vuitton.

"I'm staying in Brooklyn. I'm not going back to Miami. I just meant that this living arrangement is temporary. Until I find a job and an apartment."

I shoveled the rest of the eggs into my mouth, set the plate in the sink and grabbed a bottle of water from the fridge. "Water?"

"Yes, thank you."

I grabbed a bottle for her, set it in front of her and leaned against the counter, giving us plenty of space and an island between us.

"So...what do you want to know?" she asked. "Ask me anything."

Her face was open like she had nothing to hide. So different than my mother who was not an open book and Ronan who was a sick, twisted motherfucker. "Tell me about your parents."

She nodded as if she was expecting that question. "My mom hates confrontation. She doesn't ask my dad any questions about his business because she knows she won't like the answers." My brows raised. Maybe Keira knew more than I'd suspected. "She adores him, and he adores her. Growing up, I sometimes felt like the third wheel. Like there wasn't enough room for me." She shrugged and let a curtain of hair fall over her face to mask the hurt. "Not the kind of love I want but that's their deal."

"And she does whatever he says?" For some reason, I still held on to a sliver of hope that my mother...*our* mother...wasn't a cold, heartless woman, all evidence to the contrary.

"Yeah. She's too afraid of losing him. My father isn't very good at sharing. He thinks he owns us."

That didn't surprise me. "What do you think of him?"

"I love my dad. He was always the one I went to first when I was a kid. Out of my two parents, he was the one who made me feel the most loved," she said. "Maybe you find that hard to believe."

Surprisingly, I didn't. It hadn't taken me long to figure out that Maggie and Keira were Shaughnessy's greatest weakness. Or that he loved them, in his own sick and twisted way, and would do anything to protect them.

"When I was a kid, I thought my dad walked on water and my mom was the most beautiful woman in the world," she said. "It sucks growing up and finding out that they're human and flawed. It's like finding out there's no Santa Claus."

I wouldn't know about that. When I was a kid, my dad had always been the bad guy and my mom had always been MIA.

"All my life I've been sheltered. Imagine my surprise when I found out normal kids didn't have a hulking dude shadowing them and reporting on their every move." She shrugged. "It just taught

240

me to be more resourceful," she said, with a wicked gleam in her eye.

I wasn't sure I wanted to know what being more resourceful meant in Keira Shaughnessy's world. Those 'hulking dudes' probably had their hands full, looking after her.

"Your turn. What's your deal? For real?"

I narrowed my eyes and ran my tongue over my lower lip, debating how much to tell her. Fuck it. New and improved Connor. No more secrets. No more lies. "I'm a recovering drug addict. Heroin."

She tilted her head and studied my face for a moment, not overly surprised by my admission. Like Killian, Keira had mastered the art of locking down her emotions and hiding behind a mask. "How long have you been clean?"

"I got clean a month before I met you."

She arched her perfect brows. "So why were you hanging out with drug dealers in Miami?"

"How do you know I was hanging out with drug dealers?"

"I know a lot more than people give me credit for."

"Did you tell those four thugs where to find me?" I asked, watching her face. I doubted she'd give anything away, but even the best liars had tells.

"The ones who broke into your house?"

"They didn't break in. They came after me."

She shook her head. "I never told anyone about you. At first, I was mortified that I'd gotten it so wrong. I'm usually good at reading people. I was intrigued so I might have stalked you a few times." She shrugged. "But I'm my father's daughter so I know when to keep my mouth shut." She held my gaze, and I knew she was telling the truth.

To say I trusted her was a stretch but I believed her.

"Did my father have something to do with that?" she asked.

"He had everything to do with that." What the hell did I have to lose? I told her the story I'd told Ava earlier. After keeping it to myself for so long, I was singing like a canary now.

"I wish I could say I'm surprised," she said when I finished talking. "My father's a prick. You must have gotten too close to something he didn't want you to see."

"I tried to get too close to you and your mother."

She shook her head. "He wouldn't have set you up for that. It had to be something more. My father's moves are calculated. He doesn't let his emotions rule his business and he keeps his life compartmentalized. He never lets his business dealings seep into his family life." She chewed on her bottom lip, her eyes narrowed, thinking. "Miami is a big city. If all you knew was his name, how did you find him?"

I considered her question. When I'd gotten to Miami, it had taken a few days to find Shaughnessy. I was beginning to think it was a wild goose chase and that Seamus had been too drunk to know what he'd been talking about. He had let it slip that he and Ronan had grown up together in Hell's Kitchen so I'd gone there first, trying to find out as much as I could before I headed to Miami. People either didn't remember him or weren't talking, although I did find out that he used to run a nightclub so that's where I started in Miami. Gradually, my quest had changed. Instead of a son looking to reunite with his long-lost mother, I'd felt more like a private investigator trying to dig up dirt on the elusive Ronan Shaughnessy. There had been no public records, not of real estate transactions, his marriage, nothing. When you wanted information, you sought out people with loose lips. Drunks. Addicts. People looking for quick cash to fund their habits. Ironic that I was a recovering addict, fresh out of rehab, yet I got my information from a junkie.

"It's gonna cost ya."

"You haven't told me anything yet." I dangled the hundred-dollar bill in front of him.

"That's not gonna buy jack shit."

I pocketed the money and walked away, knowing he'd chase after me. He did. At the time, I'd taken pride in the fact that I'd never sold information for a fix. Asshole.

"Okay. Okay. He runs a club in South Beach."

"What's the name of the club?"

"I don't know." He scratched his head. "Collins Avenue. Just off Twenty-Second? Twenty-First, maybe. It's a private club. Like a grown-up Disneyworld for rich assholes who can get whatever they want. But that ain't how he makes his money."

"What's he involved in?" I sweetened the offer with another fifty bucks to keep the guy talking. He licked his lips, thinking of what the money could buy him. A grown-up Disneyworld.

"You name it, he's involved in it. But nobody's gonna do nothing about it. He's got important people in his pocket and they're all making a profit off the back of it." He leaned in closer and lowered his voice, his eyes darting around, paranoid we'd be overheard even though I didn't see anyone else on the beach. He was close enough that I could smell the stench of his breath as he talked. "Word on the street is that he got into bed with a drug and arms dealer. Took a cut of the profits in exchange for security. The dealer screwed him out of some money." He held up his hands. "You didn't hear nothing from me."

"What's the dealer's name?"

He shook his head and pressed his lips together. "Can't say. Why you so interested in Shaughnessy? His daughter screw you over or something?" He cackled, baring his yellow teeth.

"He has a daughter?" I asked, stunned. "How old is she? What's her name?"

His eyes shifted to the left. "I'm done talking. Gimme the money."

I handed him the money and a pack of cinnamon gum which he tossed into the sand before he stumbled away in search of his next fix. I took deep breaths, trying to fight off the cravings, and lit a cigarette. My new addiction.

"I asked around," I said. That junkie hadn't been the only one to give me information.

"That's one way to get yourself in trouble," Keira said.

She was right. Word on the street traveled, and even in big cities, the circles were small.

"What are we going to do about it?" she asked.

"*We* are not doing anything."

"But you have a plan, right?"

I tilted my head and studied her face. "Whose side are you on?"

"Mine. And yours. I did the right thing by coming here and I'm not going back to Miami. I'm staying. This is my life to live…not my father's and not my mother's…mine. And I want to live it on my own terms." She sounded defiant, and looked me in the eye, waiting for me to shoot holes in her plan. I wouldn't. Keira and I had a lot more in common than I would have suspected.

I wasn't sure when I'd decided that she deserved a shot at freedom and happiness, or that it had become my mission to help her get that, but I had. "If that's what you want, I'll do whatever I can to help."

"Really?"

The first time we'd met, she'd been a means to an end. I'd been hoping to find out more about my mysterious mother. I'd told her my real name and that I was from Brooklyn, and I'd known from the look on her face, that she had no idea who I was or that we were in any way related. I could also tell that she found me attractive, so I played her. A part of me had hated her, resented her for having my mother in her life when Killian and I had been left by the wayside. But she shouldn't be made to pay for the sins of her father. None of that was her fault. Our mother may have abandoned us, but Keira wanted to be a part of our lives and I wanted her to have that chance. Truth be told, I was warming to the idea of having a younger sister and over the course of this conversation, I had started to like her as a person.

"Really. I understand what it's like to need a fresh start."

"I guess you would," she said, no judgment on her face or in her voice. "How do you know Tate? He only agreed to help me unload the car because of you."

"He's my sponsor."

She nodded. "He seems like a good guy."

I eyed her suspiciously, knowing damn well she had an angle. Tate told me she'd been a nuisance, poking around under the hood of his prized Mustang, peppering him with questions about his business. She'd suggested that he buy muscle cars and restore them to turn a profit. "Sounds like she wants to run the damn place," he'd grumbled. "She asked me for a job. No way in hell am I gonna hire a woman like her."

"Afraid she'll boss you around?" I'd teased.

"Wouldn't put it past her to try."

Keira gave me a dazzling smile and I'd already figured out it was the one she used to get her way. I suspected a lot of men fell for it. "I want to work for him," she said, not beating around the bush.

"Yeah, I got that."

"Maybe you could put in a good word for me."

I chuckled and shook my head, thinking that I'd never hear the end of it if he did end up hiring her. I eyed her manicured hand wrapped around the bottle of water. "I'm not afraid to get my hands dirty," she said, reading my mind.

"You just got here. Let's give it a few days." To see if you'll still be around by then. I noticed that she hadn't checked her phone once, so I assumed she'd left it behind in Miami. Her father probably had tracking devices on it.

She conceded, but I knew it wasn't the end of this discussion. "Now that we're on the same side, what's the deal with you and Ava?"

"You're like a dog with a bone."

"I'm tenacious. And curious. We're bonding."

"Bonding. Right. Ava and I are taking a break. I'm trying to make things right."

"You're a good guy, Connor."

"Not always."

"A little bit of bad is good for a girl. Otherwise, she'd be bored out of her skull."

Her logic was skewed, but I appreciated the effort.

"She loves you. That much was obvious. What's so wrong about that?" she asked like she really wanted to know, and my answer mattered to her.

"It's complicated."

"The best love stories always are." She propped her chin on her hands as if she was waiting for me to tell her the whole story. We didn't have that kind of time.

"Have you ever been in love?" I asked, expecting her to laugh it off or say no if what she said about never going on a date was true.

"I...love someone. But it could never work out."

"Why not?" I suspected it was related to her daddy issues.

She closed one eye as if trying to figure out how much she was willing to tell me. "He works for my dad."

"Anthony," I said, taking a wild guess. Anthony had been Ronan's driver and from what I gathered, the man he trusted most. He was quiet, mid-thirties if I had to guess, and ex-military. A step above Ronan's other foot soldiers. Anthony was a fixer. His job was to get rid of Marco's body, but I didn't mention that.

"Yeah. Anthony."

It was my turn to be intrigued. "Did it go both ways?"

"If love were a contest, he would win. I've loved him since I was like...twelve. Maybe even before that. When I turned eighteen, I thought maybe we'd have a shot. Wishful thinking. We could never be together. Especially now..."

"Because you're in Brooklyn?" I asked, knowing there was more to separate them than geography.

She gave me a sad little smile. "Anthony loves me, but he's not *in love* with me. In his eyes, I'll always be my father's daughter, a person he wants to protect. He would never cross the line into something more, but it never stopped me from hoping for more. Sometimes you have to let someone go. Because you love them enough that you want the best for them. But sometimes... when you find the right person, you have to hold on tight and never let go." She gave me a shrewd look and I knew the last sentence was tacked on for my benefit.

"I don't remember asking for advice."

"You didn't. I'm giving it for free."

"That's big of you."

Keira laughed. "Since we're going down the whole honesty route...it's refreshing, by the way...I was using you too. When we met, I was trying to find a guy closer to my age. Someone who wasn't forbidden. I thought you were the perfect candidate." Her eyes widened. "Wow. That was a fail. I must be a magnet for forbidden love."

We both cracked up over that one. This whole situation was so crazy that all I could do was laugh.

"Are you and Killian a lot alike?" she asked me a little while later as I made up the sofa where I'd be sleeping.

Killian. Tomorrow morning, I had to break the news to him. That should be fun. I considered her question for a minute. "We look a lot alike, but that's where the resemblance ends. We're very different."

After she left me alone in the living room, the bedroom door closing behind her, I wondered how true that was. Killian had a tough exterior and was better at hiding his emotions, but I suspected he felt things as deeply as I did. He just dealt with it in a different way.

Before I fell asleep, I envisioned Ava just like I did every night, in hopes she'd visit me in my dreams. She never did. Maybe I was a fool for asking her to wait for me. Maybe I should have held on tight and never let her go. But I didn't want her to fight my battles for me or put her through more of my shit. I needed to do this on my own and show her that I could be the kind of man she could depend on. I knew why she hadn't told me what Jake Masters did. She'd been trying to protect me from the truth. Ever since that night we were sixteen and Seamus paid a visit, Ava had made it her mission to 'fix me.' She had believed that her love would be enough to save me, and in an ideal world, it would have been. But we didn't live in an ideal world. And her love was no match for my quest to self-destruct. I didn't want to be broken anymore. I didn't want her to be left to pick up the pieces. She deserved better than that.

28

CONNOR

"What did you need to talk to me about?" Killian asked, taking the cardboard cup of black coffee I handed him as we walked to the end of the pier at Transmitter Park. At this early hour, we had it to ourselves. "Do you need relationship advice?"

That was funny. Before Eden, Killian had never had a relationship. It had been one-night stands and casual hook-ups for him. "You're an expert now?"

"Yep." He chuckled, recognizing the humor in that statement. "You and Ava doing okay?"

"We've got some things to work out."

"Huh."

"How was Thanksgiving?" I asked, partly because I didn't want to talk about Ava, but also because I cared.

"Good. You should come with us next year."

"Yeah. Maybe." I stared out at the choppy water of the East River, bracing myself against the cold wind as I wracked my brain for the right words. Fuck it. There were no right words. He'd either support me or walk away and shut me out. "I need to tell you what really happened in Miami."

"Don't pull this shit on me. Not again." He turned to go.

I grabbed his arm to stop him from leaving. "You need to stay, and you need to listen."

He squinted at something in the distance, his jaw clenched, but I released his arm and he stayed. I repeated the story I'd told Ava last night about the night I'd gone to see Seamus.

"...he told me she'd been having an affair, gave me the man's name, and said they lived in Miami."

Killian leveled me with a hard look. "Why didn't you tell me any of this?"

"I wanted to find a way to make things up to you. After all you did for me—"

"You thought that feeding me more lies, keeping secrets, was the way to repay me?" he asked incredulously.

"I thought I'd go down there, find her, and she'd tell me she wanted to be a part of our lives. I thought I'd be able to call you and say, 'Hey, I found our mom. Come on down.'" It sounded ridiculous and so naïve now, but at the time I'd truly believed I was doing something worthy. Making good on a promise I'd made so many years ago.

"Fucking hell, Connor. I would have gone with you. We could have done it together." He sounded more hurt than angry. "Did you see her?"

"Once. Briefly." I envisioned the woman I hadn't even remembered. She was still beautiful, with dark, glossy hair and the same blue eyes Killian and I had inherited from her. "She said it was nice to see me again, but it had been a long time and she had a new life now."

I saw the hurt flash across Killian's face before he locked it down and clenched his jaw. "That's it? That's all she gave you?"

I nodded, wishing I could tell him something kinder but that was all I'd gotten from the woman. That, and her plea not to tell Keira who I was. It was obvious that she was more interested in protecting her daughter than her sons. She'd chosen her second family over her first, but I didn't understand why she needed to keep us a secret. I didn't understand any of it and I'd given up trying to figure it out. Some things weren't worth the effort.

"I always thought Seamus abused her... that she was scared," I said. "Maybe he threatened her and that's why she had to leave us behind."

"I don't know," Killian said, rubbing the back of his neck. "I have no memory of it. But I'd walked in on her with another man once. She'd asked me to keep my mouth shut."

I let out a harsh laugh. So many secrets and lies. When would it end? I took some comfort in the fact that Killian was still standing next to me and hadn't stormed off.

"What's his name?" he asked.

"Ronan Shaughnessy. He owns a nightclub. Among other things," I said. "He set me up. I never bought those drugs. The cops busted my motel room and conveniently found drugs in my bag."

"You didn't buy the drugs," he said, fixing me with a look.

"No." I held his gaze until he saw that I was speaking the truth. I left out the part about how they'd 'coerced' me into cooperating with them.

"Why? Why would he do that?" Killian's brow furrowed, trying to inject logic into a situation that defied it.

"He warned me to stay away from Maggie," I said, using our mother's first name. She didn't deserve the title of mother. "... and his daughter Keira. But I didn't listen." I played with fire and I got burned.

"His daughter..." I could see the wheels in his head spinning, trying to put the pieces of the puzzle together.

"Keira is our sister."

"What the fuck?" he asked, his face registering shock.

I gave Killian a few minutes to process all this information. It was a lot to take in at once. Killian was usually sharp. Not a lot got past him, so it had surprised me that he'd bought my story about getting busted for weed and ecstasy. If I had bought drugs, it wouldn't have been a dime bag and some club drugs. Not to mention that the Miami Vice had bigger fish to fry than busting some noob for marijuana.

"How old is she?"

"Twenty-one in January."

He did the math in his head, coming to the same conclusion I had. Our mother must have been pregnant with Keira when she left us.

"Fuck," he said, and then said it three more times for good measure, reduced to the only word that fit this situation. "Why did Shaughnessy set you up?"

Because he could. "I stuck my nose in his business. The drug dealer I got cozy with had screwed him over. The cops who busted me... they must have been on Ronan's payroll. They busted the warehouse where Marco, the dealer, kept his drugs and weapons and they killed Marco. Ronan's men cleaned up the mess and confiscated a shitload of coke and weapons. And I was granted my freedom." I let out a bitter laugh. The irony of it all. Freedom was a myth. My chest tightened, and I rubbed it, trying to ease the guilt. "Shaughnessy hadn't needed me. He already knew how to get to Marco. He's just a sick, twisted motherfucker who used me as a pawn in his game. And that's what it was to him. A game."

"Fucking hell," Killian muttered.

"Shaughnessy promised me my safety in exchange for returning to Brooklyn and keeping my mouth shut about everything that happened down there."

"You could have told me this when you got back last year," Killian said. "I would have—"

"You would have what?" I asked, knowing exactly how he'd respond.

"I would have gone down to fucking Miami and taken care of it."

I shook my head. "That's *why* I didn't tell you. What would you have done? Beat him up? Round up all the men working for him? The undercover cops? Security? He's a criminal in an expensive suit with enough money and power to get whatever he wants in that town."

Killian considered this for a minute. "Why didn't you go to the cops...honest cops...and report his ass?"

Yeah, that sounded easy. Why didn't I do that? "At the time, I figured it was smarter to keep my mouth shut. Who would have believed the word of a junkie? Shaughnessy has connections in Miami..." I let my voice trail off. Killian got it now. I could see it on his face that he believed me.

Last night, before I'd gone to Tate's garage to see Ava, I'd told Deacon Ramsey the whole story. Every detail I'd left out in my statement. I trusted Ramsey more than I'd ever trusted Seamus. Ramsey had believed my story and hadn't treated me like I was unreliable or a liar because of my past and for that the man had my undying gratitude. Since Miami was out of his jurisdiction, I needed to go to the Feds with my story. Which I planned to do today. I told Killian my plan and he nodded in approval.

"Good. I'll come with you. We'll—"

"No. Listen...I appreciate the support." I wasn't sure how I'd expected Killian to react to my confession, but I hadn't expected this kind of support. Maybe I should have given him more credit. "But I need to do this on my own. It's another thing I have to do to make amends."

He was silent for a few seconds and I waited for him to agree. "Okay."

"Okay."

"Why did Shaughnessy go to so much trouble to keep us away from her?" Killian asked.

I wasn't sure if he was talking about our mother or the sister we never knew about. Either way, the answer was the same. "Why does anyone do what they do? Why did Seamus beat the shit out of you? Why does Nico's stepfather knock his mom around? Maybe guys like that get off on hurting people. Maybe they're so insecure they need to exert their power to make them feel like men." I shook my head. "I couldn't even begin to tell you why people do what they do."

"This past year... I thought the worst of you."

"You had every right."

He shook his head. "You've been through a lot."

"We all have," I said.

"Stop being so fucking reasonable."

I huffed out a laugh. I rarely got accused of being reasonable. "Listen... if I ever thought those guys would have come to the house, I never would have let Eden hang out there with me. I don't think Shaughnessy sent them. I suspect they were low-level street dealers who got cheated out of some money. But I'm so fucking sorry you and Eden got caught up in that. You have no idea how sorry I am."

He nodded, his expression thoughtful. Free of my lies and secrets, I felt some of the burden being lifted off my shoulders. Apologies were just words, but I could tell he knew I meant them. "I know. But you should have—"

"I told Seamus," I said, knowing that was where he was headed with this. Killian had told me once before that if I'd told Seamus, he could have put his best men on the case to protect me. Bullshit. I knew better. "I told him everything three days before those guys turned up at our house."

Killian's face registered shock and for a few stunned moments, he said nothing. "Fucking Seamus. He *knew*... and he did nothing to help."

It was all out there now. The whole ugly truth. For some reason, Killian had always clung to the belief that there was a sliver of decency in Seamus. Maybe because he knew him before the drinking started. Before our mother left and Seamus started knocking him around. He'd always thought Seamus was a good cop, and Killian had been grateful he'd come to our rescue that night. Now I'd shown him the story in a different light and he didn't know what to think. Welcome to the fucking club.

"Do you feel better knowing the truth?" I asked.

"You were the one who showed me how important it is to confront the truth," he said. "You were the one who confronted Seamus about what he'd done."

"As I remember, you weren't too happy about that." Not long after I'd returned from Miami, I'd answered the door to Seamus. He punched me for old time's sake then demanded to know where I'd been for the past five months. I could tell by the look on his face that he had no recollection of having confided in me. Eden and Killian had been upstairs, and Killian had come down, once again trying to protect me, but I'd decided it was time to air our dirty laundry. Killian had been furious with me and even more furious that Eden had overheard it.

"It was the right thing to do," Killian said. "You've always been good at facing up to the truth."

I stared at him like he had three heads. "I was always lying."

"Not about the things that really mattered. We'll get through this," Killian said. "I won't let you down. Not again."

"You never let me down."

"I took away your power. I sent you to the closet. Pushed you away. Belittled you just like Seamus had."

I worked my jaw, not sure what to say about this unexpected confession. I envisioned myself at six, seven, eight... hiding in the closet, my hands covering my ears, trying to block out the sound of Killian taking a beating. With every punch he'd taken, a little piece of me had broken until I had so many cracks and fissures inside that I couldn't patch them up. That gaping hole inside me grew wider, bigger than the fucking Grand Canyon. I remembered that feeling of helplessness. The guilt that crept in at my own uselessness to stop the abuse or help Killian. And Killian's words that I'd blocked out, echoed in my head.

"What the fuck is wrong with you, Connor? You had everything, but you threw it away."

"Everything I did was to protect you and for what? So, you could kill yourself with drugs? Drugs are for fucking losers. You wanna be a loser all your life?"

"Why is everything so much harder for you, Connor? I have my own shit to deal with. I don't need your shit."

And then the day he dropped me off at rehab. *"Get your act together. I'm tired of cleaning up your messes. If you go back to drugs after this, I'm done with you. Understand?"*

"You did the best you could," I told him because it was true. We were just two kids trying to find our way out of a shitty situation the best we could. "You were always there for me. You kicked me in the ass when I needed it. Let's not play the blame game.

Lose the guilt. I'm the captain of my own fucking ship. Master of my soul... and all that bullshit."

He squinted into the distance, trying to come to terms with a past we couldn't fix or change. We'd come a long way though. Five years ago, even a year ago, we never would have been able to have this conversation.

"This sister of ours...Keira," he said, testing the name out. "What's she like?"

I was about to drop the next bomb on him. "Ready to meet her? She's here."

"Here? In Brooklyn? Why the fuck am I just finding this out now?"

"She arrived yesterday. It was a surprise."

"Asshole," he said, giving me a punch on the arm, not hard enough to hurt me. I punched him back and then we both laughed like idiots as we walked to the coffee shop where Keira was waiting for us.

I'd gotten my brother back, and for the first time ever, it felt like we were on a level playing field. All my life, I'd felt like I'd been living in his shadow. Tagging along after him. He'd been bigger than life. The strongest. The bravest. The one Seamus loved best, in his own sick and twisted way. Seamus had respected Killian, had been proud of his MMA career. He'd always reminded me that Killian had made something of his life while I'd been the fuck-up, the sorry excuse for a son. But it was time to let it all go. To shine a light on those bad memories so they no longer had the power to destroy me.

"You look nervous," I said, noting the way Killian kept rubbing the back of his neck.

"Nervous," he scoffed.

I chuckled under my breath. He'd never admit it, thinking it was a weakness. Some things never changed. We entered the coffee shop and I jerked my chin in Keira's direction.

"Jesus Christ. That's her?" I nodded. That was her all right. I'd left her twenty minutes ago and she was already being hit on by a bearded hipster dude. I could tell by the polite expression on Keira's face that this guy didn't have a chance in hell.

"Another woman for me to worry about," Killian muttered.

I laughed. He had some crazy idea that every woman in his life needed his protection. Most of the time, they were more than capable of not only looking after themselves but kicking our asses. I had a feeling Keira would fit right in with Ava and Eden. She was a force to be reckoned with. "You'll have to get her in one of your Krav Maga classes. Teach her how to kick guys in the balls."

Killian chuckled. "I heard about that."

"Glad you're amused," I muttered which only made him laugh harder.

Keira looked up as we stopped by her table. Killian scowled at the guy in the seat across from her and jerked his chin, indicating the guy should scurry the hell out the door. He was such a pain in the ass sometimes. I didn't know how Eden put up with it.

"Thanks for keeping me company," Keira told the guy. "My brothers are here now."

Brothers. Killian's brows went up a notch.

The guy wrote his number on a paper napkin before vacating his seat. "Call me. We'll hang out. I can show you around Brooklyn."

"Sounds good," Keira said, giving him a dazzling smile that I knew was fake. I also knew the guy would never get a call.

"Nice meeting you, Gracie."

Killian gave me a what the fuck look. I shrugged and flipped a chair around, straddling it as Killian sat in the seat across from Keira.

"Wow. Killian. I've been dying to meet you. This is kind of weird, right?"

"Yeah, it is." He looked awkward as fuck and I stifled a laugh as he ran his hand through his hair and gripped his upper lip between his teeth, trying to come up with something to say, but he was at a total loss. His gaze settled on the mug in front of her and he was halfway out of his chair before he asked if she wanted another coffee.

"No, thanks. I'm good." Killian settled back in his seat and Keira gave him a smile I knew was genuine and meant to put him at ease. She rested her elbows on the table and propped her chin in her hands, her face an open book like last night. Which was surprising, considering the way she'd been raised. "So...what do you want to know?"

An hour later, we left the coffee shop, the initial awkwardness a distant memory. It was strange how quickly we'd bonded. How easy it was to talk to Keira. But we'd skated around the elephant in the room and now I was about to snitch on her father. I didn't know if the FBI would be interested in my story, if they'd believe it, or if they'd even bother investigating it. That was how much faith I put in the criminal justice system. Nevertheless, I was going to live up to the word carved on my chest and this time I felt no remorse.

"Hey Connor," Keira said, moving closer to my bike as I straddled it. Killian was standing a few feet away, talking to Eden on his cell, and waiting to walk Keira to his gym.

"About my dad...what's your plan?"

I could lie but I wouldn't. "I'm not looking for revenge, but I'm hoping for justice."

"And what does that mean exactly?"

"You might be forced to choose a side."

"I choose me, just like I told you last night." Her voice rang with conviction and I recognized the stubborn set of her jaw.

"I'm going to the FBI."

"Hold out your hand," she said, digging something out of her jeans pocket. They were so tight it was a wonder she could fit her hand in there.

I held out my hand and she placed a flash drive in my palm. "What's this?"

"A gift."

"What's on here?"

"Extra ammunition. Enough to put him away. It's white collar stuff. There's no treasure map leading to the buried bodies," she whispered, trying to pass it off as a joke.

"Where did you get the information?"

She shook her head, unwilling to tell me. *Anthony. If love were a contest, he would win.* "It doesn't matter. It's not a trick. The information is real."

Killian and I exchanged a glance before my gaze settled on Keira. "You sure about this?" I held the flash drive between my thumb and index finger, giving her a chance to change her mind. The piece of plastic I held in my fingers was featherlight, belying the weight of everything she'd handed me. Even if the FBI didn't believe my story, they'd love to get their hands on this kind of information. I suspected Ronan did his share of money laundering. Who the hell knew? Maybe it was only tax evasion. All the best criminals got taken down for that. But there was a reason Keira wasn't turning this information over, and instead had given it to me. Guilt. "Can you live with this? Will you be able to sleep at night?"

I wanted her to think long and hard before I pulled away from this curb and handed over the information. If she was right and there was enough evidence to put him away, she'd have to accept the responsibility for her actions.

"You said you wanted justice, not revenge. I want to help you get it. And I need to do this for my own reasons. For myself and for my mother. Not that she'll see it that way. But he's been controlling her for over twenty years. I can't keep pretending that my father is one of the good guys. Everything he does is for his own gain. Even his love comes at a price. He demands our unquestioning loyalty and tries to keep us locked in an ivory tower. Too bad for him that I got tired of playing by his rules a long time ago."

She acted tough, but I wondered how much it had cost her to turn over information on her own father, a man she loved despite the things he'd done. My mind made up, I pocketed the flash drive. Time was running out and if Shaughnessy didn't already know that Keira was in Brooklyn, it wouldn't be long before he found out.

29

*O*nce again, I was getting my information from Eden. Keira's dad had been arrested and Connor had been the one to turn over the information to the FBI. She'd told me that privately. It wasn't something we felt comfortable discussing in front of Keira. I tossed my pizza crust in the box and took a swig of beer, staring at the lights on Eden and Killian's big-ass Christmas tree. They'd gone to Pennsylvania last week to chop it down and transported it on the roof of their Range Rover. If possible, it was bigger than last year's tree which was saying something. My eyes caught on the canvases propped against the wall, covered in brown paper, ready and waiting to be hung tomorrow for the exhibit. Connor had come over a few mornings this week and he and Eden had stretched their canvases onto frames, or so I'd been told.

Eden flicked my arm with her index finger. "Ouch," I complained, rubbing my arm. I flicked her back because we were so mature. "What was that for?"

"This is the best part of the movie. I didn't want you to miss it."

I rolled my eyes and Keira laughed. The Christmas movie marathon, the beer and the pizza, had been for Keira who had confided that she'd never had a girls' night. She'd never even had a sleepover and Eden had found that too sad for words so here we were, three movies in, lounging on the sofa, watching the finale of *Love, Actually*.

"It's all about the grand gestures," Eden said as the credits rolled. As if on cue, Killian walked through the door and Eden flew across the room and leapt into his arms as if she hadn't seen him in years. As if their love was still brand new and shiny. I wanted my life with Connor to look like that. I wanted to welcome him home. I wanted to share a home with him, cook dinner with him, kiss him goodnight and wake up to him in the morning.

"Hey, Sunshine," he said before his mouth covered hers. I sighed loudly and turned my head, so I didn't have to witness their public display of affection. I was jealous, and it made me feel small that I'd succumbed to self-pity, an all-time low.

"Connor will come around," Keira reassured me, sensing that I'd been thinking about him.

"You've gotten close," I said, thinking it was wrong of me to feel sorry for myself, considering how fucked up her life was. But Eden had told me that Keira and Connor spent a lot of time together, even though she was staying in Killian and Eden's spare room now. I guess Connor had become a regular visitor here.

She smiled. "Yeah, he's a good guy." Her smile faded.

"Is your mom...have you heard from her?" I asked. Their mother was a touchy subject and it was hard for me to ask about her without letting the resentment creep into my voice.

She shook her head. "No. But I'm not surprised. I doubt she'll ever forgive me."

"Forgive you for what? For leaving?" I felt like there was a part of this puzzle still missing.

"No. For betraying my dad."

"How did you betray your dad?"

"I gave Connor a lot of information on him. Enough to put him away."

My eyes widened. "Oh. I didn't realize...wow. Does he know it was you?"

"Connor didn't tell the FBI where he got it, but I'm sure my dad could figure it out. It was the right thing to do. He's hurt a lot of people and he needed to be stopped."

"It was a brave thing to do. It took a lot of courage," Killian said, joining us, his arm around Eden.

Keira let out a breath and tried to muster a smile. I wondered if she regretted doing it. I hoped she didn't.

"You ready to go home?" Killian asked me, twirling his key chain around his index finger then capturing the keys in his palm. "I'll give you a ride."

"Okay, thanks." I pulled Keira into a hug, feeling like I needed to reassure her. In a weird way, we were all family now— Keira, Killian, Eden, Connor, me. A dysfunctional family but still ... family. "Everything will be okay. We're all in your corner."

"Thanks," she said as I released her. I hugged Eden goodbye, grabbed my coat and bag and followed Killian out the door.

Before Killian sold his share of the bar to Zeke, I used to see him every day, but it had been a while since the two of us had been alone together. Not that Killian had ever been a big talker. But I used to make up for his silence. "You good?" he asked as we pulled out of the underground garage.

"Hanging in there. How about you? Now that you've got a sister? That must have come as a shock."

He shook his head and let out a breath like he couldn't quite believe it himself. "A shock. But a good one." I stared at his face in profile and his lips curved into a smile. He'd changed a lot, for the better, I thought. His edges had gotten softer and I knew a lot of that had to do with Eden, but I also knew that he'd been putting in the work.

"You're not angry with Connor," I said. A statement, not a question. Eden had already told me that Killian wasn't angry.

"No. I'm not. I get why he didn't tell me. Not saying I like it. Just that I get it."

"Did you talk it over with your shrink?" I teased.

Killian chuckled. "When did I get so pathetic?"

"When you fell in love with Eden," I joked. "She ruined you. In the very best way."

"Yeah, she did." We fell silent until he pulled up in front of my apartment building. "I almost walked away from her last year, thinking it was the best thing I could do for her. I thought I didn't deserve her." He looked down at his hands and flexed them, his unspoken words loud in the silence. Killian had killed two men, one was an accident, the other in self-defense. Neither one had been his fault, but that didn't change the fact that he had blood on his hands or that it weighed heavy on him.

"You made the right choice," I said. "If you'd left Eden, it would have broken her heart. And yours."

He let out a heavy sigh. "Yeah. I'm so damn lucky to have her in my life."

"Yeah, you are. But she's pretty lucky too. I think that any girl who wins the heart of a Vincent brother is a lucky girl."

He didn't respond and we sat in silence for a few seconds. "I wanted to talk to you about something. Connor donated the rest of the money he inherited from Seamus to my program."

That didn't surprise me. I'd expected him to do it sooner, truth be told. Connor had never cared about money, but he did care about good causes. "I also got a donation from Zeke's dad. A sizeable donation."

"That's great."

"Yeah, it is. Zeke helped me set it up as a non-profit organization." I nodded, knowing this. "We need someone to run it. You'd be perfect for the job."

"What? Me? I don't know anything about...what would this job entail?"

"Fundraising. Grant writing." He waved his hand in the air. "Zeke's putting together a job description. You meet all the qualifications. There's nobody we'd rather have."

"I have a job. A job I like."

"A job you're bored in. You need a new challenge."

"Who told you this? Connor?"

"Connor. And Zeke."

I opened my mouth to protest but closed it again. I'd gotten comfortable at Trinity Bar, but Killian wasn't wrong. I wasn't challenged anymore. I could do the job in my sleep but this sounded like a big job and I didn't know if I had the skills. "Killian, I'm not corporate. I don't think I could talk to bigwigs, you know. And you see how I dress..."

"It's a non-profit for at-risk youth. Your outfits will fit right in."

I snorted laughter and smacked his arm. "I don't know if I can do it."

"Ava. You were twenty-one when you started working at the bar, fitting it into your college schedule and still getting the work done. You built my UFC career. Because of your social media skills, I got sponsors. I never would have done that on my own."

That was bullshit. His fans loved him, and he was one of the most popular UFC fighters ever. But he knew why I did that for him. It was my way of saying thank you so I didn't dispute what he said.

"Think about it," Killian said, referring to the job.

"Okay."

"I'll see you tomorrow night. If you don't come, Eden will never forgive you."

I laughed a little. "No pressure then."

"He wants you there. He needs you." Killian shook his head. "He's just being..."

"A bonehead? Runs in the family. You've had your moments."

"Yeah, I know." Killian chuckled under his breath then his humor faded and his face grew serious. "Give him some time. Me and Connor...we're trying to learn how to be good men," he said, looking more vulnerable than I'd ever seen him. He rubbed the back of his neck and I knew it made him uncomfortable to expose himself like that.

"You and Connor don't need to learn how. You already are good men. Boneheads. But still...good men. The very best kind of men." I pushed open the door and hopped out of the SUV. "Thanks for the chat," I said before I closed the door.

He held up his hand and watched through the window. I knew

he'd keep watching until I was safely inside. As I climbed my stairs, I thought how lucky I'd been to have the Vincent brothers in my life. They'd both been there for me, in different ways, at different times when I'd needed them. I'd be there tomorrow night. I didn't want to miss the chance of seeing Connor get all the praise he deserved. I knew how good his art was and I knew that everyone who walked into that gallery would see it too.

CONNOR

CHRISTMAS TREE LIGHTS shone through the lace curtains of the bay window, the flicker of the TV in the background. I climbed the steps to the porch and took a few deep breaths before I rang the doorbell, smiling as "Joy to The World" signaled my arrival. Through the frosted glass panes, I saw the hallway light come on.

"Who is it?" Lars asked from the other side of the door. It was only eight o'clock which I'd hoped was a civilized time for a visit, but I'd come unannounced.

"Connor Vincent."

The door opened, and Lars Christensen stood on the other side, his brows going up a notch as he eyed the flowers in my hand. A Christmas bouquet, red and white flowers with sprigs of berries and eucalyptus. I'd deliberated over these flowers for so long the lady at the shop had been concerned for my welfare. "Who are they for, honey?"

"My girlfriend's parents," I'd said, not expanding on that.

"Oh well then...you wanna make a good impression. I have a feeling they're going to love you, with or without the flowers but we'll make sure they're beautiful, just to be on the safe side." She'd winked at me like we were in on this together and I had no doubt that she'd meant well but, unfortunately, she had no idea how wrong she was.

"What does he want?" Marie called out from behind him.

"I'd like to talk to you. Both of you. Is this a good time?"

Lars ran a hand over his hair and let out a sigh as he held the door open wide. "Come on in."

I walked past him and held out the bouquet to Marie. Powdered sugar or flour dusted the green apron she wore over a sweater and jeans. She planted her hands on her hips and narrowed her eyes. "What's this for? Did Ava send you?"

"Ava doesn't know I'm here."

She sniffed and stared at the flowers without making a move to take them out of my hand, but still, I held them out to her, waiting for her to accept them. It was pathetic how much I needed her to acknowledge this small token.

"Someone brings you flowers, you accept them with a thank you," Lars said gruffly, surprising me.

Marie straightened her spine, took the flowers from my hand then turned and walked into the kitchen without saying a word. I followed her, uninvited, into the warmth of her cheerful yellow kitchen, the scent of butter and sugar from freshly baked cookies scenting the air. I watched her snip off the ends of the flower stems with scissors, her back turned to me as I stood awkwardly in the middle of her kitchen, unsure what to do. Lars pulled out a chair at the kitchen table and gestured for me to sit.

"You want a drink?" he asked then cleared his throat. "Water or—"

"No. I'm good. But thank you," I said, remembering my manners. That had been part of the problem. I'd never gotten off to a good start with them, constantly on the defensive as a teen. I'd talked back, acted surly, and flew off the handle more than once in my dealings with her family. Not Lars so much, but Marie who knew how to push all my buttons with just a glance or a sharp word.

Marie filled a glass vase with water, arranged the flowers in it then carried them to the kitchen table and set them down in the middle. "The flowers are pretty," she said grudgingly. "Festive."

"Glad you like them." I waited for her to sit at the table across from me, worried that she wouldn't. That she'd leave the room and refuse to speak to me. Finally, she pulled out a chair and took a seat, her back ramrod straight, arms crossed over her chest.

"If Ava didn't send you, what are you doing here?" she asked.

"We haven't really met yet. I thought I should introduce myself. I'm Connor Vincent."

"Don't be ridiculous," she scoffed. "We know perfectly well who you are." She pressed her lips together in a flat line, but I ignored the judgment on her face and didn't let it dissuade me from continuing.

"No. I don't think you do. We didn't get off to a good start and that was my fault," I said, willingly accepting all the blame for my past behavior. I'd been through enough counseling and had attended enough meetings to know that the first step in trying to make amends was to accept responsibility for your actions and acknowledge it. "I'm sorry for all the hurt I caused you in the past. For all the times I was disrespectful. I'm sorry for a lot of things and I just wanted you to know that. That's why I came over here tonight."

She clasped her hands on the table and for a few long moments, nobody said a word. My apology hung in the air between us, unacknowledged. But she was still sitting at the table so maybe that was a small victory. "I feel like we lost Ava," she said, and I heard the hurt in her voice. "She picked you over us. And like I told you before, you never deserved her. You caused her nothing but heartache and misery. Our girl...she was the perfect daughter until you came along and filled her head with all kinds of ideas. None of them good, mind you."

I took a deep breath and let it out. I'd expected this. I'd prepared for it. But that still didn't make it easier to hear. I tried to choose my words carefully, not wanting to be on the defensive. "I loved her. I still love her. I'll always love her. Ava is her own person, she makes her own choices, and in my eyes, she's always been perfect just as she is. I broke up with her just like you asked me to because I felt like I didn't deserve her. I went back to drugs and I'm so ashamed of that. I'm ashamed of all the bad things I put her through. All the sleepless nights and the empty promises...

all of it. All I can do now is try my best not to fall back into my self-destructive ways. And I work hard every single day to make sure I don't. I'm not asking you to like me. I'm just asking you to give me a chance to prove myself. Not for me but for Ava's sake. If I'm going to be a part of her life again, which I hope I will be, I don't want Ava to feel like she has to choose between me and her family."

"She hasn't even called me. I haven't spoken to my own daughter in almost three weeks."

"I'm sorry."

"You should be. You came prancing back into her life and turned it upside down again. That's what you do. You make it so she can't even think straight. She loses sight of the important things in her life whenever you're in her life. Family comes first. And now you come here with your flowers and apologies and you expect us to forgive you? After everything you've put her through? You're asking a lot." She fixed me with a look that would normally send me right out the door. Pissed off. Feeling like shit. But this time I stayed and once again I dug deep and tried to find the right words.

"I know. But I'm asking anyway. I'm trying to be a better man. I have struggled with right and wrong all my life. When I was a kid, I knew the difference. It was all so clear to me. I wanted to be good. I wanted to change the world. Right the wrongs. Fight the injustice. But somewhere along the way, I lost touch with that boy. I escaped into drugs. I kept secrets. Told lies. I never took respon-sibility for my own actions. And I was delusional enough to believe that the people around me, the people I loved, should just accept me as I was and love me anyway. Because none of it was my fault. It was Seamus' fault. It was society's fault. My mother's fault." I stopped and took a breath, my gaze swinging from Lars whose face was neutral to Marie who refused to meet my eye. "And not so long ago, I barged back into Ava's life and I turned it upside down again. But despite everything I have put her through, Ava still loves me. I don't know how it's possible or how I got so lucky to have her in my life, but I can promise you that if she'll have me, I will do everything in my power to make her happy and to give her the kind of life she deserves." I'd said too much or maybe not enough. Hell, if I knew. Nobody had said a word to interrupt my little speech which had sounded a lot like something I would say at an NA meeting. But it was honest, and I had meant every word of it so that was the best I could give them. I stood to go, grabbed my leather jacket from the back of the chair and placed the art exhibit invitation on the table.

"What's this?" Marie asked, eying he invitation but not making a move to pick it up.

"An invitation to an art exhibit. If you want to see Ava the way I see her, stop by. All my paintings...they're all Ava."

"Will she be there?" Lars asked.

"I don't know, but I hope so," I said honestly. "Sorry to interrupt your evening. Place looks good. Festive."

"Well, it should," Marie said. "We've been decorating for days."

Lars stood and escorted me to the door, turning the handle and holding it open for me. This visit had not been a success, and I was no closer to gaining acceptance than I had been before I walked in this door tonight.

"Wait a minute," Marie called after me. "Let me pack up some of these Christmas cookies. I made enough to feed an army."

"I'm good. I don't—"

"Accept the damn cookies," Lars said quietly enough that Marie wouldn't hear.

Obviously, I hadn't gotten the hang of this yet. She was extending an olive branch and I was rejecting it. I wandered back into the kitchen. "I'd love some Christmas cookies."

"Well, who wouldn't?" She filled up a Christmas tin with an assortment of cookies, separating the layers with sheets of wax paper. I remembered her cookies from years ago when Ava used to bring them into school and share them with me at lunch. "Everyone loves my cookies. I use all butter and all good ingredients. Not like my sister's cookies. You can't use margarine and expect them to taste good." She pulled a face as she fitted the lid on the container and pressed it into my hands.

"Thank you," I said, taking it from her.

She nodded once. "You're welcome."

I turned to go, once again thinking we were done here. "Connor?"

"Yes?"

"Ava told me your father used to hit you and Killian. Is that true?"

I nodded, my back still turned to her. "It's true."

"Well... I guess he did get what he deserved, after all. Now make sure you keep the lid on the tin so the cookies don't get stale. They should last you until Christmas."

"Thank you."

She followed me out to the door. "You don't have a warmer coat?"

"I'll be okay."

"Well, it's freezing out there. And you're still riding that motorcycle," she said, eying the helmet in my hand. "The wind's gonna cut right through that thin leather. Where are your gloves?"

"Stop fussing, Marie. The boy's fine."

I knew this was the kind of thing that drove Ava nuts, the way her mom was constantly nagging her about little things. But me? I loved it that she cared enough to nag me. I'd take this any day of the week over being ignored or treated like I was dirt under her shoe.

As I drove back to Williamsburg, the cold wind cutting through my leather jacket just like she said it would, I had a smile on my face. Maybe there was hope for us yet. Maybe Ava and I had a shot at something real and something good. I'd learned a lot over the past three weeks. I'd learned that telling the truth was easier than hiding behind secrets and lies. As it turned out, Ronan Shaughnessy had been a person of interest. When I turned over that information, the Feds acted like I'd given them an early Christmas present, and I readily agreed to testify against him. The only person I worried about was Keira, but Killian and I agreed that we'd do whatever it took to support her. We'd be the brothers she never had. We were her family now.

30

AVA

I watched Connor through the art gallery window. Was this how he used to feel when he watched my dance classes? On the outside looking in but seeing so much. There he was in a dark blue button-down shirt cuffed at the elbows, exposing the ink on his forearms and dark wash jeans, talking to Mr. Santos. I smiled, happy that my trip to our old high school had been worth it. I'd braved the metal detectors and security guard at the door, the hallway that still smelled like hormones and bleach, and the dingy beige walls to deliver a message to Connor's Art teacher.

They shook hands, Connor nodding in agreement, a genuine smile on his face—God, I loved his smile—before Mr. Santos walked toward the door to leave. Connor's gaze swung to the window and our eyes met through the glass. I lifted my hand, giving him a little wave. For a few moments, we just watched each other, frozen in time, the people milling around the gallery fading away.

I miss you. So much. My stomach swarmed with butterflies and I took deep breaths of menthol-cold air, trying to calm myself. It had only been three weeks. In the past, we'd gone weeks, months, years without being together. This should have been easy, but it wasn't. Connor strode to the door and then he was outside, standing in front of me.

"Are you planning to come in?" he asked.

"I don't know. I kind of like the view from out here."

"I kind of like the view from out here too," he said, his eyes raking over me, down my fishnet stocking-clad legs to the fuck-me stilettos on my feet. Overdressed for the occasion but underdressed for the weather. "What's under this coat?" he asked, fingering the lapel of my black wool dress coat, a gift from my mom that had lived in my closet until tonight's appearance.

"My birthday suit," I said with a smile.

He blew out a breath and carved his hand through his hair before he guided me inside, into the warmth and chatter of the gallery, his hand on my lower back. I cursed the layers of clothing that prevented me from feeling the warmth of his hand on my skin. He led me through the gallery to a small room in the back.

I unbuttoned my coat and he helped me out of it and draped it over his leather jacket hanging on the back of a chair. His eyes darkened as I smoothed my hands over the red off-the-shoulder dress that hugged every curve of my body, the hemline hitting just above the knee.

"Ava..." He stopped and took a breath and let it out. "Fucking hell. This dress..." He scrubbed a hand over his face and stifled a groan. My lips, painted red, curved into a smile. "Did you wear this for me?"

"Maybe." Of course, I wore it for him. I gripped my bottom lip between my teeth. He swallowed hard, his Adam's apple bobbing, and carved a hand through his hair. Too bad. I wasn't playing fair and I had no intention of making it easy on him. "Why don't you show me the art now."

"Nobody will be looking at the art," he muttered, casting sideways glances at me as we walked through the gallery space, to the start of the exhibit. Eden and Killian were deep in conversation with what I guessed was a potential buyer.

"Where's Keira?" I asked, scanning the room but not seeing her.

"You just missed her. She went to hang out at Tate's garage. Wanted to check out a Charger he just bought at the auction."

"That's an interesting way to spend a Saturday night."

"She's an interesting girl," he said with a smile.

"She's pretty great. But I expected nothing less. After all, she is your sister. That automatically makes her cool."

"Really."

"Yup."

"Almost as cool as you. You invited Mr. Santos. For me."

"I thought he should see the success you've made of your life. He told me you were one of his most gifted students. Teacher's pet," I teased.

He huffed out a laugh. "How've you been?"

"Great. Busy. How about you?"

"Yeah. Busy. I...yeah, I've been busy." He took a deep breath and let it out. We were acting like acquaintances, overly polite, right back to the way it was that day in the coffee shop. Except that this time I wanted to be with him and he was the one holding back.

Connor guided me through the exhibit and I stopped in front of each painting, marveling at how amazing they looked, the canvases stretched on frames on the white walls with spotlights trained on each one.

"You're the star of the show," he said as we stopped in front of one I hadn't seen before. It was me, a black mask with purple feathers hiding my face, bars of music swirling across the canvas. "That's the first one I did," he said. "I tossed it in the trash, but the next day I found it in the break room. Claudia rescued it."

"Why would you ever toss this in the trash?"

He shook his head but didn't answer. It must have been the night I was at the hospital after my mom had asked him to leave. Before he'd gone to The Candy Store. He must have thought it wasn't good enough. How wrong he was. I'd have to thank Claudia for rescuing it.

"Come on. There's something I want you to see." He led me

around the corner and we stopped in front of a dividing wall with only one painting on it, bigger than the others.

"Connor...it's so beautiful." And it was.

"Remember when you said we're all made of stardust?"

I nodded. "I remember. I remember everything," I said softly. It was the night sky filled with stars, shimmering above a moonlit ocean. Shades of deep blue and purple and stardust scattered across the sky. Without thinking, I reached for his hand and it clasped around mine. "Look at what you've done, Connor. You took blank canvases and you created beautiful works of art. I'm so in awe of your talent. I can't even...you amaze me."

He squeezed my hand. "You like it then?"

"I love it. And Connor, I know you said that you need time but—"

"Excuse me, are you the artist?" a woman asked.

Connor dragged his gaze away from me and focused on the woman. "Yes, I am."

"Hey. I'll leave you to do your thing," I said, giving him a little smile.

He opened his mouth as if to speak but closed it again and nodded.

"I love this piece," the woman said. "It would be perfect..."

I took a deep breath as I walked away. This art...it was far too personal to belong to anyone but us. Good thing it hadn't been left up to me. I would have put round orange stickers on all of them to let everyone know they'd already been sold.

"Hey, you made it," Eden said, pulling me into a hug then holding me at arm's length. "You look amazing. If that dress doesn't get Connor crawling back to you, then he's an idiot."

"Connor's not an idiot."

Eden's smile grew wide. "Ha! You're defending him."

I shrugged one shoulder and steered the conversation to her art. "Talk me through them," I said, and listened to her description of each piece. We stopped in front of the final one. Two kids with dark hair and blue eyes, one a toddler, the other a few years older with his arm slung around the younger one's shoulder. It was their smiles that captured me. They looked happy, their faces lit up with joy in a way I'd rarely seen from either of them. So young and innocent with no idea what their futures held in store.

Killian wrapped his arms around Eden from behind and studied the painting as if he'd never seen it before, although surely he must have. "I found the photos in a shoebox in Seamus' closet when I cleaned out his house last year," he said, by way of explanation.

"Do you think your mom took them?"

He shrugged. "I don't know. I was surprised he'd kept them."

"You were adorable." He was. They both were. Unlike Connor, Killian had a matching set of dimples and Eden had captured them perfectly.

He snorted, but Eden agreed with me. "It's a great painting," I told her. "I love it." I noticed the round orange sticker that indicated it had been sold. Disappointment punched me in the gut. I was the worst. The whole point of an exhibit was to sell the pieces, yet I didn't want anyone to buy them. "Who bought it?"

"Keira."

I was relieved that this painting would stay in the family. It seemed fitting that Keira bought it, a little piece of her brothers from a childhood she'd missed sharing with them. After listening to Connor's story, I'd decided that I hated their mother. She was no better than their father. In some ways, what she'd done was even worse. But I kept it to myself out of respect for Keira.

"Your paintings look amazing in a gallery," I said.

"Connor's don't look too shabby either," Eden said.

"He did good," Killian said, and I got the feeling he was talking about something more than the art.

"Ava." I turned at the sound of my mother's voice.

"Mom?" I looked past her to my dad, confused. I hadn't spoken to her in three weeks, and I'd never told her about the exhibit. "What are you guys doing here? How did you even..."

She pressed her lips together. "Connor invited us."

My brows shot up. "Connor invited you? You *talked* to Connor?"

"Hello Killian," she said, and my jaw dropped to the floor. What was going on here? I stood back as Killian greeted my parents and introduced them to Eden just as if this was the most natural thing in the world. Like they were old friends, catching up on each other's lives. After the introductions and some small talk between my mom and Eden, Killian guided Eden away, leaving me alone with my parents.

"You look beautiful," she said, taking in the dress and heels, not even commenting on the tattoo peeking out of the sleeve of my dress. She swept my hair over my shoulder. "Did you use the curling tongs I gave you?"

I nodded dumbly. I'd done my hair in soft waves just like she'd showed me. "You look like you belong on the red carpet."

"I wouldn't go that far," I said, giving her a little smile. "You look beautiful, too."

"Oh well, I thought I should make an effort." She smoothed a hand over her updo. It went with the black dress and pearls, a lot classier than my outfit. "It's not every day my daughter is featured in an art exhibit. Although Bedford-Stuyvesant is not exactly..."

"Marie," my dad warned.

She held up her hands in surrender. "Okay, okay. I come in peace. Cut me a break, would ya?"

I laughed. Sometimes my mom could be funny. "So how did this happen?"

"Connor paid us a visit and we talked."

"Really?" I asked, surprised. "You talked? Why would he visit you?"

"Because he loves you," she said simply. "I'm willing to meet you halfway, but I'd like an apology." My mom lifted her chin and gave me that stubborn look I knew so well.

My dad's eyes pleaded with me to comply with my mother's wishes, so I wracked my brain for an apology that would sound sincere. "I'm sorry I ruined Thanksgiving dinner." That part, at least, was true.

"There," she said. "Now was that so hard?"

I laughed a little. "Now it's your turn."

She crossed her arms over her chest. "What do I have to be sorry about?"

"Marie," my dad warned. I gave him a grateful smile. After all these years, he was starting to stand up to my mom. It gave me hope. Maybe people really could change.

"Fine." My mom sighed with resignation, but I suspected it was out of habit, more for show than anything. "I'm sorry I didn't welcome Connor into our home on Thanksgiving."

"Thank you, Mom. That means a lot to me."

She sniffed and averted her gaze and I wondered what Connor could have possibly said to cause this transformation after all these years? I wished I'd been a fly on the wall for that conversation. My heart swelled with pride and gratitude. He'd gone over there for me.

I turned to see Connor walking toward us, his eyes flitting over my face before his gaze swung to my parents. My eyes nearly bugged out of my head when my dad stepped forward and shook Connor's hand. When my mom pulled him into a hug, my jaw dropped to the floor. Had I stepped into an alternate universe?

I was still staring, dumbfounded, when my mom released Connor with a pat on his shoulder and wiped a tear out of her eye. "Now, if you don't mind, I'd like to look at this art."

As Connor led them away, he glanced over his shoulder and winked at me. *Pretty proud of yourself.* And rightly so.

"Ava is my muse," Connor was telling my parents when I joined them. "Not that any painting could do her justice."

"Don't listen to him. He's an amazing artist," I said. This was his night and I wanted him to be in the spotlight, to see him get the praise he deserved. I cast a glance at my mom, not sure what she thought of his paintings. She hadn't said a word which usually meant she disapproved.

We continued in silence until we reached the final painting. I wanted her to say something but only if what she had to say was good. I was torn between wanting her to keep her mouth shut and voicing her opinion.

My dad spoke first. "This is damn fine work," he said, looking to my mom as if to prompt her.

"Well, I'm not a big fan of graffiti..." She lifted her chin and I gritted my teeth. Don't do it, Mom. Do not shoot him down. For the love of God, please say something nice. "But I love it."

I exhaled a breath of relief, so grateful to her that I nearly wept with joy.

"They're beautiful," she said. "Real works of art."

"Thank you," Connor said, his face neutral but I knew his feelings were anything but neutral. He'd needed to hear words of praise and acceptance from my mom for years, but it had always been denied him. I didn't know what he had said or done to change her mind about him but whatever it had been, it had worked.

Not even Zeke's appearance dimmed my joy. He'd brought a date, a leggy blonde who looked like she belonged in his world. And true to form, my mom couldn't resist making a snide comment. "You run circles around that girl."

"Mom, she's beautiful."

"Her face is a bit too horsey for my liking."

I sighed and shook my head, jabbing an elbow in Connor's ribs when his body shook with silent laughter. "Watch yourself, Rocket Man."

"Are you jealous?" he asked quietly.

I looked over at Zeke looking handsome and preppy in his navy pea coat, his skin perpetually golden tan even in the winter and his blond hair reaching the collar of his coat, his arm wrapped around the blonde girl, and I didn't even feel a pang of jealousy. Over the two years I'd known Zeke, I'd seen him with plenty of girls. It had never affected me then and it didn't affect me now. He had been what I needed at the time, maybe, a distraction as he'd pointed out. It had been fun and easy, stress and drama-free, with no emotions at play.

"Not even a little bit." But if I'd come in here tonight and had seen Connor with another girl it would have ripped me to shreds.

My parents stayed a little while longer then left, claiming that snow was forecasted and my mom didn't want my father to drive in it.

"I certainly hope you didn't drive that motorcycle," my mom told Connor as we saw my parents out of the gallery, the first flurries starting to fall.

"I got a ride in my friend's truck. It's hard to transport art on a motorcycle."

"Well, at least you were being sensible for a change," my mom said.

He chuckled, not bothered by her little dig and I bit my tongue to stop the words from coming out. No sense in arguing with her when she was trying so hard. Wow. Look how mature I'd gotten. I laughed under my breath, hugged my parents and went back inside with Connor.

"I should probably call an Uber..."

"Or...you could stay and get a ride home with Killian. Save you some money."

I let out a frustrated breath. I wanted him to tell me that he wanted me to stay with him. He was just trying to save me money. Dammit. Why did everything have to be so difficult for us?

"I'm tired of waiting." I wasn't talking about waiting for a ride, but he didn't try to stop me when I typed the information into my phone and ordered an Uber. "Five minutes," I said, glancing at the people milling around the gallery. A couple approached him, recognizing him as the artist from the photo I'd uploaded onto social media that he'd known nothing about. He'd probably never checked the FB page for this gallery exhibit. It could have been the photo that had helped Keira find him. How long would he have kept that a secret if she hadn't shown up?

"Hey, I need to go. It was great seeing you. Really. And your art..." I swallowed before the tears fell. "It's amazing."

"Thank you for coming. Let me walk you out—"

"No. Stay. Do your thing."

"Ava—"

I retrieved my coat and walked out of the gallery into the cold and the snow flurries. A gray Prius pulled up to the curb and I checked that the plates matched the number on my phone before climbing into the backseat and closing the door behind me. I watched through the window as we pulled away from the gallery, half-expecting Connor to chase after me. He didn't.

MY BUZZER ROUSED me from a half-sleep and I tripped over my discarded shoes in my haste to answer. "Hey," I said into the intercom, without bothering to ask who it was because I knew. I *knew* it was him.

"Hey, babe."

Babe. I buzzed him in and opened my apartment door. Downstairs, I heard the door slam followed by a thud and a few choice curse words from Connor. "Watch it, Tate. This isn't one of your junkers. Handle with care."

Tate grumbled something, but I didn't catch the words.

I leaned over the banister and looked down. "Do you guys need help?" I called down the stairwell, unable to wipe the smile off my face.

"We've got it. Tate's not used to handling delicate objects."

"Fuck you," Tate growled. Connor laughed, and those butterflies were back now, invading my stomach and putting me into a tailspin. I knew what that delicate object was, and I was so happy my body could barely contain all this joy. When I'd come home earlier, I'd collapsed on the sofa, dejected. I'd been sad that he just let me go without a fight. No grand gesture. No chasing after my car in the snow. No proclamation about how he wanted to spend the rest of his life with me. I'd felt deflated and even though he'd asked me to wait for him, I had still expected him to realize that we could do this together.

He appeared on the landing, a tentative smile on his face and I held the door open wide to let them inside. The painting was wrapped in bubble-wrap, but I could see the shades of the blue and purple and I knew it was the stardust painting.

"Where do you want this?" Tate asked.

"The bedroom," Connor and I said in unison. I'd already decided it belonged on the wall across from my bed and obviously, Connor had come to the same conclusion.

"Thanks, Tate," I said when they returned to the living room.

"No problem," Tate said on his way out the door. A part of me was still scared that Connor would follow him. That he'd just come to drop off the painting. But he closed the door and turned to face me.

"I thought you sold that painting."

"I couldn't. It belongs to you." He took a few steps closer. "You're still wearing the dress."

"Maybe I was hoping you'd stop by. Or maybe I fell asleep on the sofa."

He smiled then crossed the room to my Christmas tree in front of the window. It wasn't as grand as Eden's, but I loved the sparkly lights and kitschy decorations I'd collected over the years from flea markets and antique shops. "I remember these," he said, holding a crystal teardrop in his palm and running his thumb over it. We'd seen them in an antique shop the summer we were eighteen. We were told they'd come from a chandelier and Connor had gone back and bought them without my knowing it. One day, I came back to my dorm room and found them strung on fishing wire across my windows which he'd decorated with hundreds of fairy lights, turning my crappy dorm room into an enchanted place. I joined him by the tree. He hadn't taken off his jacket yet.

"You said you're tired of waiting. In the gallery," he clarified.

"It's only been three weeks."

"It feels like a lifetime."

"I started seeing Killian's shrink. I've still got a lot of shit to work out."

I braced myself, waiting for him to tell me he was leaving again, that he needed more time. "If you're not staying, walk yourself right out that door. I can't keep doing this with you. I can't keep losing you, Connor."

"If you'll take me as I am, a work in progress...I'm not going anywhere," he said, his hand sliding up my neck and tangling in my hair as he pulled me closer. My arms wrapped around his neck and he lowered his head, his mouth covering mine. We kissed each other with everything we had and everything we were. Every teardrop and memory, secret and lie, every heartbreak and promise. We poured everything into this kiss. When our lips separated, our breathing was ragged.

"I love you," he said. "So fucking much."

"I love you, too."

Connor had heard me say those words hundreds of times, but tonight it looked like he believed the words.

EPILOGUE

CONNOR

*O*ur life doesn't fit in a box and we can't wrap it up in a neat little bow. All we can do is embrace each day as it comes. Recognize it as a gift and be grateful for each new sunrise and sunset. As we put the miles behind us, we keep our gazes fixed forward, not in the rear-view mirror. Our past doesn't define us, but it helped shape us into who we are today—better, stronger versions of ourselves. It was never about the destination. It's the journey that matters. And I want to take every step, every leap of faith with this girl who stole my heart so many years ago and never gave it back. I pull over onto the shoulder of the road and cut the engine, patting the dash of the '69 Mustang Shelby I bought from Tate a few months ago. Turns out he'd been saving it for me. I handed Ava the keys for her twenty-fifth birthday and she immediately started planning our road trip to California. I'd deleted her spreadsheet and told her we were just going where the road took us. No itinerary, no agenda, just us and the open road. We both needed the vacation. Life has been hectic. Busy, but good. Ava started her new job in January. She threw herself into it a hundred percent, like I knew she would, and she says she's glad we gave her a push. The new job is more difficult and the hours are longer, but she says it's more fulfilling.

A few months ago, I testified against Ronan Shaughnessy. It brought me closure. It gave me peace. He's in a federal prison where he belongs. And my mother? I wish I could say that it all worked out, that removing Shaughnessy from her life would have forced her to realize everything she'd given up for that man. But it hadn't worked out that way. She took off and we don't know where she is. I know it hit Keira hard, but we've all tried to be there for her, to make up for her parents' absence.

"I feel sorry for the man in the moon," Ava says, looking up at the desert sky reeling with stars.

"He must be lonely."

"And jealous."

"They're going to kill us," she says, holding up her left hand to inspect the infinity symbol tattooed on her ring finger, identical to the one on mine. Ink is for life. Rings can be pawned, she'd reasoned, and I'd loved it that she wanted a symbol of forever. "But how fun was that?"

I laugh, envisioning our wedding ceremony at the Elvis chapel in Vegas. I couldn't imagine doing it any other way. "If you want a big white wedding, we can do that when we get back."

"I don't. Eden's wedding was great, but ours was perfect. It was just so... us."

I smile in agreement as she climbs over the gearbox and straddles me, her arms wrapping around my neck, head tipped back, exposing the column of her neck. From the moon, we wouldn't even be specks of dust, but from here we're everything. The sun and the moon and the stars and all the planets.

"I love you to the stars and back," she says, bringing her eyes to meet mine.

"I'll love you until we're old and gray and even long after that when our bodies decay... my soul will find yours... always."

"Topper," she mutters. I laugh, and she joins in, the sound of our joy echoing in the night air.

And in that moment, we are perfect, and we are whole.

The End

ALSO BY EMERY ROSE

THE BEAUTIFUL SERIES

Beneath Your Beautiful

Beautiful Lies

PREVIEW OF BENEATH YOUR BEAUTIFUL

CHAPTER ONE
EDEN

I brushed snow off my down jacket and laughed at the inflatable Santa hanging from the porch rafters as I opened the front door. Trevor, one of Luke's housemates, was sitting on the sofa, feet propped on the coffee table, a slice of pizza in one hand and the remote in the other. "Hey, Trev." I took off my beanie and let my blonde hair tumble down. "Studying hard for finals?" I joked.

He tossed the pizza in the box and vaulted over the back of the sofa.

"Impressive. Do you do that for all the girls?" I teased.

He ran a hand through his mussed-up hair, his eyes darting around the room, looking at everything except me. "What are you doing here? It's Thursday."

I laughed. "I'm not allowed to stop by on Thursdays? Is that a house rule?"

"You usually have class all day."

True. I was playing hooky this afternoon. Luke's text sealed the deal. *Ditch your next class. I need you. Now.* He'd never asked me to ditch class for sex. I was so thrilled he was finally letting out his inner rebel, I practically sprinted here. "Is he in his room?"

"Uh, no...he's out."

I furrowed my brow. "He said he'd be here."

"Let's go for a beer. I'm buying."

"I'm still recovering from last night's birthday celebration."

"Hair of the dog."

Hangover sex would be a better cure, but I kept that to myself. "I'll wait in his room." I breezed past him. "Catch you later."

Trevor's hand wrapped around my arm, and he tugged me back. "You don't want to go up there."

I looked up the stairs, dread gnawing at my stomach. "Why not?" I whispered.

"Just...don't do it."

I shook off his arm and quietly climbed the stairs. As I crept down the hallway, voices came from Luke's bedroom. His door was open a crack, and I stood outside it, straining my ears to hear.

"When are you going to tell her?" After three years of listening to Lexie's voice in the dark while we talked late into the night, I knew it well.

"Soon," Luke said. "I just need more time. I couldn't tell her on her birthday. And with finals coming up..."

"This is making me crazy," Lexie said. "I feel so guilty. Every time I look at her, I feel like she knows."

I didn't know. I had no idea.

This couldn't be happening.

"Don't cry, Lex. I'll talk to her. It's just...hard."

Oh God. When? How? I wracked my brain, trying to figure out how any of this was possible.

"Do you still love her?" she asked, sniffling.

I squeezed my eyes shut, holding my breath as I waited for the answer. "I still care about her."

He still *cared* about me? That was the best he could muster? In our senior year of high school, he'd begged me to come to Penn State with him. Like the fool I was, I had followed him to college, telling myself art was just a hobby. I could do it without the fancy degree. Not that my dad would have paid for art school. Still, I could have at least tried to get in, and I would have figured out a way to pay for it myself. But no, I had tossed the art school brochures into the trash.

All because Luke was my first love.

"Luke...I...there's something I need to tell you."

"What's that?" His voice was muffled. Was his face buried in her hair? Was he holding her? Kissing her? My hands balled into fists, my nails digging into my palms. I struggled to get air into my lungs. My heart hurt so much, I could barely breathe.

"Promise you won't get mad," she pleaded. "It was an accident. I don't even know how it happened. But...I'm pregnant."

I leaned against the wall for support. Pregnant? She didn't know how it happened? Bile rose up in my throat. I swallowed the bitterness and squared my shoulders.

Rage flooded my veins.

I pushed the door open, slamming it against the wall. Planting my hands on my hips, I took in the whole scene. Luke was spooning her, and she was facing the door, a smug smile on her face. She was triumphant, and not the least bit surprised to see me. Lexie must have sent that text from Luke's phone. She was the winner, and she was thrilled at her victory.

Luke's face was frozen in shock, his brown eyes wide, his mouth hanging open as if I'd caught him mid-sentence. The short layers of his golden-brown hair were ruffled like Lexie had been running her fingers through it. I diverted my gaze. I couldn't bear to look at the boy I'd loved for five years. *Five years.*

"Did I interrupt?" I asked, surprised by how calm I sounded.

Luke rolled onto his back and covered his face with his hands. Coward. If their clothes strewn across the floor was any indication, he was naked under those covers. And now it became painfully clear why our sex life had dwindled over the past few months. He was getting it from someone else—my best friend.

"Eden...it's not what you think." He sounded so lame, I laughed harshly. "I can explain."

"Save it for someone who cares."

I loved you. How could you do this to me? And Lexie, that backstabber, had been my roommate since freshman year. I took her home with me for the holidays because she said her parents didn't care about her. I let her borrow my clothes. My friends became her friends, and now, my boyfriend was her boyfriend.

My heart was shattering into so many pieces, I didn't know how I'd put them back together. But I refused to give Lexie the satisfaction of seeing me break down. Time for action, not tears. I flung open Luke's closet and reached inside for a baseball bat. I chose the Combat Maxum, a bat for power hitters, and came out swinging. Lexie cowered, hugging herself for protection.

I laughed. "Don't worry, Lexie. You're not worth an arrest for assault and battery."

I walked out of the room, my head held high. When I got into the hallway, I sprinted down the stairs and barreled out the front door. I flew down the front porch steps and rounded the corner, my feet slipping and sliding on the freshly fallen snow as I skidded to a halt in front of Luke's silver BMW, a high school graduation present from his parents. Everything in Luke Prescott's life had been handed to him on a silver platter. An only child of doting parents who put him on a pedestal, he was spoiled rotten. They should have given their son values instead of material possessions. Who got a BMW for graduating high school?

I swung the bat, and it connected with the hood. *Crunch.* Another mighty swing, and I took out a headlight. My body was coiled tight with rage. I needed to unleash it. Anger beat the alternative—curling up into a ball and crying enough tears to fill an ocean.

"Eden. Stop!" Luke yelled. I ignored him and swung at the other headlight. *Bam! Bam! Bam!* I kept swinging, metal crunching under my bat. Hell hath no fury like Eden Madley scorned. Not that I was a violent person. But I pictured Lexie's triumphant smile, and it fueled my anger.

I raised the bat, ready to inflict more damage.

Luke wrapped his arms around me from behind and dragged

me a safe distance away from the car. "What have you done?" Luke wailed, sounding like a big fat baby.

"The same thing you did to my heart."

I struggled free of his hold and dropped the bat to the ground. Crisis averted, he moved closer to inspect the damage, brushing off the snow with his hands. It wasn't nearly enough. But defeat and heartache had drained the fight right out of me. "I'm sorry," he said, his back to me. He didn't even have the guts to look me in the eye. "I'm really sorry, Eden."

"Fuck you, Luke. Take your sorry and shove it up your ass." I strode away, shoulders squared and head held high, trying to hang on to any shred of dignity I had left. Tears lodged in my throat, but I swallowed them. On the way over here, I'd thought the snow looked pretty. Like being inside a snow globe. Now the snow stung my face, impeding my progress. I burrowed into my jacket and stuffed my hands in my pockets.

"Hey, Eden," Trevor called, jogging to catch up to me. He knew what was going on under their roof. I was the last to find out. Wasn't that always the way? "For what it's worth, I think you deserve a hell of a lot better. If you ever wanna grab a beer, call me."

I nodded and kept walking, choking back the tears. I unclasped the bracelet Luke gave me for my twenty-second birthday yesterday, tossed it on the ground, and crushed it under the sole of my boot. It had come in a blue Tiffany's box—a sterling silver charm bracelet with a heart medallion.

Read *Beneath Your Beautiful* for FREE with Kindle Unlimited here: http://mybook.to/BYBAmazon

ACKNOWLEDGMENTS

Writing is a solitary pursuit but to bring a book baby into the world, it takes a village. I'm lucky to have found my tribe in the indie author community. It makes the journey so much easier and a lot more fun.

First of all, a big thank you to Maddie and Lillie for your unending patience and for putting up with all the hours I spend 'daydreaming.' Call me cheesy (I know you will) but I love you to the stars and back. To my beta readers—Petra Gleason, Eliza Ames, Annie Dyer—thank you for your time, your thoughts, and your encouragement, and for loving Connor and Ava as much as I do. And Annie, thanks for kicking me in the ass when I needed it. I hope I can return the favor one day.

To Ellie McLove, I'm so happy I found you. You're stuck with me now and I'm not letting you go. Thank you for everything.

Sarah at Okay Creations, thank you for creating another gorgeous cover. It's not just a photo, it's a work of art. To Jessica Ames for the interior design, and for all the chats and moral support. Thanks for everything, Little Miss Sunshine. To Ena and Amanda of Enticing Journey for arranging the promotions. To all the book bloggers who took the time to read and review and share. I appreciate you and everything you do for the indie community.

To Emery's Rambling Roses, my reader group, thank you for all your support!

And finally, a huge thank you to all the readers who took a chance on an unknown author. I hope you enjoyed reading Connor and Ava's story as much as I enjoyed writing it. Stay tuned for the next book in the series, Beautiful Rush - Deacon and Keira's story.

CONNECT WITH EMERY

Emery Rose has been known to indulge in good red wine, strong coffee, and a healthy dose of sarcasm. She loves writing about sexy alpha heroes, strong heroines, artists, beautiful souls, and flawed but redeemable characters who need to work for their happily ever after.

When she's not writing, you can find her binge-watching Netflix, trotting the globe in search of sunshine, or immersed in a good book. A former New Yorker, she currently lives in London with her two beautiful daughters and one grumpy but loveable Border Terrier.

You can find out more at www.emeryroseauthor.com

Join her Facebook group at
www.facebook.com/groups/1918754445046550

facebook.com/EmeryRoseAuthor

twitter.com/emeryrosewrites

instagram.com/emeryroseauthor